A Distant Mountain

A Distant Mountain

CRAIG A. GRIMES

Matador
9 Priory Business Park,
Wistow Road, Kibworth Beauchamp,
Leicestershire. LE8 0RX
Tel: 0116 279 2299
Email: books@troubador.co.uk
Web: www.troubador.co.uk/matador
Twitter: @matadorbooks

ISBN 978 1800463 769

British Library Cataloguing in Publication Data.
A catalogue record for this book is available from the British Library.

Typeset in 13pt Adobe Jenson Pro by Troubador Publishing Ltd, Leicester, UK

Matador is an imprint of Troubador Publishing Ltd

Cover, from The Valley of Mexico from the Hill in Tenaya, 1870, oil on canvas, Eugene Landesio.
Museo Nacional de Arte, Ciudad de México, CDMX, Mexico.
Photography: Museo Nacional de Arte/INBAL

To K & K

Preface

A DISTANT MOUNTAIN is a work of fiction set about 1350 in the Valley of Mexico, which encompasses both Mexico City and surrounding regions. The valley, it was then the Nahua Valley, was lake filled, with cities and towns arranging themselves between water and the encircling ring of mountains. The Mexica, or Aztecs as they are now most commonly known, have yet to rise to power; they are just one of the many Nahua city-states making up, as they knew it, the One World.

What we know of these people, crushed in an instant by imported diseases and tempered steel, generally begins and ends with ritual blood sacrifice offered within the context of religious services. Yet at that time they arguably had the most modern society of any in the world with, uniquely, free public education for all children, hospitals, efficiently managed public works, an ethical judicial system, and government supported associations that cared for the needy. The towns and cities were orderly, clean, prosperous and efficient.

Which suggests that their society had both a rational and irrational aspect to it, -like most. A Distant Mountain is a story of transition, about how a society begins in one place and ends up, as they usually do, someplace entirely different.

The religious festivals are as generally described by historical works of which a bibliography is given at the end of this book, as is a convenient list of the various gods and goddesses, a guide for pronunciation of Nahuatl words, and a hastily sketched map of the One World.

First Bundle

I

Azcapotzalco

———

Quinatzin now sits upon the *icpalli*, the royal chair of Azcapotzalco. Which is to say of the many voices within the city his is heard most clearly. Stand by yourself in the marketplace and shout, "I am king!" and safe to say you will be mocked, or worse. Do the same with 100 soldiers at your back and events proceed quite differently. Getting the soldiers on your side is the trick, those who change assertion to certainty, from which point power flows outwards like so many ripples across a pond. It is just a question of pattern, mere mechanics invariant across dimensional scales. "We are not wolves," Quinatzin thinks, "no, nor ants nor squirrels, but there are points of commonality: each to its realm, each to its victories."

And of the moment, Quinatzin reflects upon his stepwise journey to the throne, a journey that has required sacrifices, as do all journeys. Quinatzin remembers how a smile hovered on the lips of his father, Acamapichtli, as he slipped away from life, death erasing his disillusions. A pack leader sires many pups knowing that one will rise up to replace him: it's just a question of when, and who. Acamapichtli did not raise his children, or at least not Quinatzin, to rule over a sorry village lost within trackless wilderness.

"I and my father are one," Quinatzin had told the nobles of Azcapotzalco, the high priests, those surprised he had assumed the *icpalli*. "Obey me as you would have obeyed him."

That, and the soldiers, ceased their mutterings; they had chosen Acamapichtli to lead them, they had not chosen Quinatzin. Yet he loved his father, and so too his older brother Coyotzin; there are so many variations, so many tangential angles to love. No matter. "The Eye with which Tezcatlipoca[1] is seen is the Eye with which Tezcatlipoca sees," so goes the philosophical circle; Quinatzin's eye tears, some grain of dust. He knows that surrounded by enemies Azcapotzalco cannot afford a weak ruler: the city could wake up tomorrow to find themselves vassals of another city, or razed to the ground. The past successes of his father are just that, past.

And as to power, the ability to guide Azcapotzalco through the dangerous shoals of her existence, one's imagination builds upon what one knows. There are risks and prizes; there are hazards and rewards. It is all that simple, yet underlying that simplicity is a great

---

1   The God of Fate, also God of the Night Sky, one of the four gods who created the world.

complexity. Quinatzin recognizes certain things can be ordered, the orders backed by threats of violence, but though simple in concept the process is ultimately inefficient. From here, logical sequence, one comes to appreciate the basic concepts public rituals so effectively convey to the population. The priests present a readily understandable model of the universe to the people and, no little trick, just as herding rabbits is no little trick, ensure the people act in a unified and organized manner for the state. Or those who control the state.

And of serving, there are so many facets to existence that many gods and goddesses are required for its sustenance and hence many priests. However nothing comes from nothing, and so we work our way towards a conclusion which is this: For the priests and the eternal gods they represent, both ethereal and of the state, to embrace Lord Quinatzin's ascension to the throne the gods must soon be offered their due. Which requires certain displays, and a quantity of tribute, all of which require a successful war and Tezcatlipoca, wily God of Fate, coincidence of exquisite timing, has delivered the pretext of war to the council hall of Azcapotzalco.

✦ ✦ ✦

Lord Zamacoya, sovereign of Malzinco, a city vassal to Azcapotzalco, a city of the flat hot-lands to the west of the One World, has come before Lord Quinatzin much grieved. Lord Zamacoya has three sons while Tezozo, ruler of Xilotepec, a realm that neighbors Malzinco, has four. Of the seven young men all are quite proud of their place in life, which is to say that between these young men of the two cities rivalries have arisen, and they have formed bands, and with their lieutenants now find purpose by quarreling with the other. Lord Zamacoya informs Quinatzin that the young men from Xilotepec constantly threaten his people, with King Tezozo making no effort to control the actions of his errant sons. Words have given way to blows, blows to weapons, and weapons to blood.

"We beg your help," Lord Zamacoya pleads. "As your vassal, threats directed at Malzinco are threats directed at you, at Azcapotzalco."

Quinatzin nods, momentarily shifting his focus to a nearby window from which comes the enchanting song of a golden-feathered tzintzcan bird, then gazes at his sandal, then at nothing, and considers the riddle put before him. Quinatzin knows enough of Zamacoya to understand he is a dangerous person to listen to, for Zamacoya is perpetually in error saying one thing when the very opposite is true. And perhaps, likely enough, at the heart of Zamacoya's pleading there lies some unseen danger, for Tezcatlipoca has been superseded as the patron deity of the great city of Azcapotzalco by Xihcutli,[2] the necessary outcome of a shifting of alliances. It was the warrior-priests of Xihcutli who stood at his back when he first informed the realm he was king, who stand at his back now. Quinatzin wonders if this necessary shifting of alliances within the eternal realm might have cast a serpent upon his doorstep, perhaps Tezcatlipoca seeking revenge? Or could this be

---

2 The God of Fire.

a neatly laid trap by a more tangible enemy? So on and so forth the wind blows, and always the potential for disaster. Yet for that his spies say all is calm within the Valley, for a time quiescent. Still, is there any reason to believe the things we see and know are more important than those we do not?

Zamacoya fidgets while Quinatzin, stone calm, carefully thinks through the many possibilities and conditionals. After a time, the sun passing a small distance across the afternoon sky, Quinatzin decides that the arrival of Zamacoya must indeed be a blessing from Xihcutli, and though a word to the troublesome King Tezozo might suffice to resolve the issue, Xilotepec being a city of tenuous allies surrounded by many who covet its fertile lands, Quinatzin knows the trick to power is to give everyone what they want. Well enough then: The state requires purpose by which to justify its existence, and by war the state will find that purpose. The priests of Xihcutli require a suitable offering to sustain Xihcutli, and thus Azcapotzalco, and its king of course, for we are all in this together, and so they will have their offering. Lord Zamacoya, loyal vassal, wants peace, and so he will have it, in exchange for a 10% increase in tribute. The sons of King Tezozo wish to spend their brief lives fighting, and so they can. Soldiers want an opportunity to prove their prowess and enrich themselves, and they will have such an opportunity. And the widows, for there will be widows, well many, though of course not all, statistical average, desire a new husband anyway.

Quinatzin shifts his spider-calm gaze to Zamacoya,

and in a voice free of inflection says, "There is no peace in this world (alas!), only for brief moments an equilibrium. I was informed but two days ago by traders recently returned from Xilotepec that King Tezozo prepares his city for war. And since the surest way to defend from an attack is to attack, that is what we must do. This is where events have led us."

Quinatzin gives Lord Zamacoya handsome gifts, and bids him depart to begin preparations.

♦ ♦ ♦

Quinatzin calls the *Tlacochalcatl* to come before him, the one who, among other important duties, is in charge of Azcapotzalco's arsenals. It is to this position Quinatzin has raised up his younger brother Ueue Zacatzin, and this is a point of concern for Ueue seems more inclined to esoteric considerations, such as why the night sky is filled with starry brilliance, than points of detail regarding needed supplies and weapons. Quinatzin impresses upon Ueue Zacatzin the need for him to attend to his duties, for the realm is now at war.

"There is a time for poetry and song," Quinatzin tells Ueue, "and now is not that time."

♦ ♦ ♦

Quinatzin informs his advisors, the council of the wise, that, "We cannot long hold the allegiance of our vassals, nor the respect of our enemies, if insults and threats go unanswered. Further, if we do not subjugate Xilotepec they may well subjugate us, for should Xilotepec themselves with the armies of the hot-lands their numbers will prove overwhelming."

Royal envoys are sent from Azcapotzalco to King Copiltzin of Texcoco, the two realms recently bound in alliance through Quinatzin's sister Miahuitl, now Queen Miahuitl, the first wife of Copiltzin whose offspring will come to rule the city, to request his presence. So too royal envoys are sent to the leaders of vassal towns and cities to inform them that their presence is required, anon. So it is that matters of importance are discussed among the powerful: the Xilotepec insults, the intent of Xilotepec to invade the Nahua valley,[3] and the many riches of Xilotepec. All are pleased to offer Quinatzin the aid of their towns and cities, and return home to assemble their armies.

Five days later, a day the auguries suggest is excellent for such a purpose, the sun just touching the heights of Mount Popocatepetl, Quinatzin leaves Azcapotzalco with his army.

---

3   The physical location corresponds, approximately, to modern Mexico City.

2

The Army

The army passes to the west of Azcapotzalco, climbing the footway that takes them over the range of mountains separating the Nahua Valley from the hot-lands where all grows in abundance. At a bend of the trail on the eastern escarpment beyond which the lake-filled valley will be lost, a soldier pauses for a last look back upon his home. For a time he gazes upon Lake Texcoco, variously pinched and constrained by the surrounding land to be given the characteristics of several individual lakes: here fresh, there salty, here some sort of unpredictable brackish mix, the whole surrounded by a diadem of gem-like multi-colored mountains.

Upon the southeastern edge of this shimmering valley he sees the twin sentinels, radiant Iztaccihuatl, She Who Wears a White Dress, and luminous Popocatepetl, The Hill That Smokes. To the north, on the far eastern edge of Lake Texcoco he sees the luminous great city of the same name, Texcoco, behind which rises up the mountain of Lord Tlaloc, the all-sustaining God of Rain. A small distance northeast of Texcoco one finds Teotihuacan, astounding city within a fertile valley through which twin-rivers flow. Teotihuacan, realm of giants, yopicatl as they call themselves, they who have tamed the rivers into a maze of gossamer thread canals that irrigate vast fields of food.

North of the lake he sees a sere land of widely spaced low hills that gives way to a realm of thorned bushes and trees, a realm called *Teotlalli,* or Sacred Land, for here by thirst or starvation one soon enough comes before the Lord and Lady of Mictlan, that is to say, Lord and Lady of The Dead. Azcapotzalco, Queen of Nahua cities, anchors the western edge of the great lake behind which rises up malachite and beryl-colored forests of cedar and ahuehuetl trees. This will be the last time the soldier sees Azcapotzalco in his present incarnation.

> Fire-glow in the heavens, and I must start my journey.
> The porters make ready to bird song.
> From the mountain height I see my home, Azcapotzalco,
> Ablaze with the colors of harvest.
> I gaze upon the trail that takes me further away from you,
> And have but sorrow in my heart.

✦ ✦ ✦

For every soldier there is a youth who serves as a porter; upon his back a tall wicker basket for carrying the dense quilted cotton armor worn in battle, food, drink, and the warrior's shield. The load is substantial but the youth, lean and hard-muscled, offers no complaint. The footway takes the army through forests of high-mountain pines in which scarlet-winged quechols flicker within an eternal light, past ramparts of bare rock down which water cascades. Through low-hanging clouds, trees and plants familiar yet somehow different: a mythic landscape so enchanting as to seem a dream of vision.

Among the soldiers there is now a common pulse of being. The army, the adventure, the purpose, has become a vital entity strangely compelling: given a chance to turn back now few would take it.

✦ ✦ ✦

It is not a quick march, for it will ill suit the army to arrive fatigued, hence there is time and breath for the soldiers to talk among themselves; and though Tezcatlipoca may hear all that is said within the world we are able to listen to but a small portion, and this we do.

"I visited Xilotepec once," a soldier tells his friend nicknamed 'The Empty Stomach.' It is not the first time 'The Empty Stomach' has been told this story; he could now, just as well, recite the scenic wonders of Xilotepec.

"A beautiful, rich land, fields of cotton and pineapples. The city is majestic, with walls of fine white stone…"

"There are any number of spring-fed fountains," the

Empty Stomach silently recites, anticipating his friend, "and flowering trees of intoxicating scent."

"There are any number of fountains of the most delicious water," his friend continues, "and flowering trees of intoxicating scent. When I was last there…"

A distance further back upon the trail, here a rolling landscape of grass interspersed with large rocks, the wide footpath bordered by yellow flowers above which violet dragonflies gather, one finds a cluster of older warriors, captains of the field, who overtake a few younger warriors one of whom, in particular, appears so young it is difficult to believe his mother would have let him leave the house. The older soldiers ask his name: It is Tlatli.

"And you, Tlatli," one named Platltzin asks, "what are your plans once we reach the battlefield? Seek out the heart of battle? Capture an enemy general or two?"

Without realizing it Tlatli puffs out his chest, then says in a voice that suggests greater confidence than he feels, "I intend to return from this war with such riches that I can afford three wives."

The older warriors laugh. Platltzin slaps young Tlatli on the back, "Three? Now that would be the death of you."

+ + +

First night: The moon, two sharp horns, rises up from behind the mountains to the southeast. The soldiers sleep to the music of owls and wolves.

+ + +

On the second day of the journey, we hear one say to his companions, "Along the edge of the western sea when one dies they place the body within the branches of a tree, saying it is better that birds eat them than the worms of the earth."

"Why don't they burn them?"

There is a rising of eyebrows, a shrug. "I don't know. Perhaps there isn't any wood."

"If 'they place the body within the branches of a tree,' there must be wood."

"Perhaps it is of a type that does not burn."

"All wood burns," his friend snorts. "And what about the bones? Are the trees then filled with bones? That would be a sight."

"The bones they grind to a powder, which they mix with water and ground maize. This they roll into little balls that they set out for the birds. So all disappears back into the world."

"Yes, well we all do that. Soon or late."

♦ ♦ ♦

Second night: In the crystalline mountain air the soldiers see the red light of *Nehoatl* rise in the northeast, the bright orange-red wandering star.[4]

♦ ♦ ♦

There is one soldier on this journey who is best described as in this world but not of it. He walks along wondering

---

4   The planet Mars.

by what quirk of nature he should find himself within this particular portion of time and space. He listens to the neatly defined conversations of his warrior-brethren, most of whom give forth discourses on the deeds they will do upon the battlefield. He considers how when surrounded by monkeys it is hard not to think like a monkey: 'Mine, mine, mine.' Yet grasp as tightly as you will it is all gone in an instant. One day he held his son in his arms, the next day his son was leaving home a grown man. He notices the Mexica[5] walk encompassed within a bubble of silent intent, grim as Mictlan,[6] they of sharp ideology: war is religion; religion is war. "A rabble destined for top of the ant pile," the man thinks. "Such as it is." He muses on the switch of tutelary gods in Azcapotzalco, Xihcutli now placed above Tezcatlipoca. He thinks, for a moment, a smile upon his lips, yet another great faith on the wane. However he knows that upon your death, when you leave this world for the next you will come before Tezcatlipoca who will hold before you his bright obsidian mirror in which you see the balance of your life, the illumination of its hard truth.

✦ ✦ ✦

Along the footpath the soldiers pass a shrine to *Teyollotl*, The Heart of the Mountain, beside which there are several large rock cairns, and to these almost all add a pebble or stone.

✦ ✦ ✦

---

5   Who were to become more commonly known as the Aztecs.

6   Mictlan, realm of the dead.

Third night. A cascade of falling lights illuminates the darkness of the sky. The *Zac Beh*, The White Path, shines from horizon to horizon.

◆ ◆ ◆

Sunrise; the clouds in the eastern sky are lavender in color. On the 4th day of their march the army arrives outside of Xilotepec at a village called White Stone. Yet for the name there are no white stones to be found, nor any stones at all; rather it is a realm of verdant fields nourished by late afternoon rains. The army makes camp and there enjoys the breads, stews, and fruits the people of Malzinco have prepared.

That night, while Quinatzin and the generals discuss stratagems of the forthcoming day's battle they are interrupted by a handful of Xilotepec envoys who, given safe passage, arrive to stand before Lord Quinatzin. Given leave to talk, they say:

> What brings you here, great lord?
> Has someone summoned you here?
> Perhaps your Malzinco vassals have deceived you.
> Consider carefully what you do, for our strength
>   is great.

Quinatzin thanks the envoys for their message, gives them gifts of finely crafted shields and swords, and before they depart suggests that it is not too late for Xilotepec to surrender and become a vassal of Azcapotzalco.

3

Xilotepec

———

Daybreak. The soldiers gather about the tower Quinatzin has had built during the night. From the height of the tower Quinatzin speaks, and we listen; "You who are brave soldiers, know that you do not fight jaguars that might eat you alive, nor do you fight demons that rise up out of the earth. You fight only men. You are brave soldiers who fight for your homes, for your loved ones. Embrace your sword, with which you will slay your enemy. Embrace your shield, which will protect you. And should you die today you will go to rest amid the glory of the next world, and your valiant name will always be remembered."

The signal fires set ablaze the warriors, clad in bright-colored armor of dense quilted cotton decorated with feathers and jewels, who seem so many glittering flowers, at measured pace walk across the field towards the Xilotepec army that awaits them. Approaching, the warriors of each army shriek and whistle at the other such that the world shakes. A rain of darts falls upon the two armies as they close. Spears that are attached to cords are hurled through the air, and then pulled back to be retrieved and thrown again. The heads of these spears are sharply barbed, and should they enter the flesh and then be pulled out, well, it is a terrible thing. Swords, hard wood edged with obsidian teeth are swung and swung again. Amid the ceaseless, unrelenting din men are parted from their lives.

The battle remains balanced for a time, but then the Xilotepec army gains the field slowly pushing the Azcapotzalco army back, whose center does not hold, and as the center collapses so too the flanks fall away. We see now the warriors of Xilotepec on the cusp of victory, the smell and taste of it upon their tongue. But then this: From a shallow trench that borders the battlefield, overlaid with a cover of greenery, one sees fierce Mexica emerge fresh for battle. So too those of the Azcapotzalco army who had but pretended to be faltering, at the very cusp of collapse now push forward with renewed strength. The progress of the Xilotepec soldiers is brought to a stop; they waver, and then amid the dust, din, and blood spray of battle they retreat. Quinatzin, from the uppermost height of his tower, seeing that his troops are on the cusp of victory sounds a golden horn, emblem of victory, ordering his soldiers to pursue.

Having reversed direction, amid the clash of shield and sword, shouts, whistles, arrows and darts, the armies cross this morning's point of demarcation, passing into what was once the realm of the Xilotepec army. Victory for

Azcapotzalco is at hand. However, now a large number of Xilotepec warriors emerge from concealing grass to enter the fray. The momentum of the battle again shifts, and it is now Azcapotzalco that retreats, a Xilotepec victory largely prevented by the ferocious valor of the *Cuachictin*, those with shaved heads who do not ever retreat, a downpour of rain, and then darkness.

After the sounding of a drum, signal of truce, those who remain upon the battlefield are collected by their respective sides. The wounded of the armies are tended, bruises drained, gashes washed with water obtained from freshly cut maguey branches and then sewn closed; in truth, for such injuries the skill of the healers is remarkable. The war is not over, but of the day it belongs to Xilotepec.

✦ ✦ ✦

That night a man approaches an Azcapotzalco sentry and asks leave to speak with the commanding general, General Petlauh, who at first declines the opportunity for there are many details he must attend to. However, perhaps by the whisper of an idea from Xihcutli, he changes his mind and agrees to hear what the man, but a woodcutter, has to say.

✦ ✦ ✦

The next morning Quinatzin again addresses the Azcapotzalco army. The soldiers, unsmiling, stand vulture silent for many of their companions fell the day before, and gone is the promise of an easy victory. Quinatzin speaks, and we listen: "You have come here to war against a dangerous, cruel, and savage people who threaten our home. You have come here to protect your hearths, where you lived happily with your wives and children, mothers and fathers, beloved kin that you may never see again. You have arrived at a place where you may perish like dry grass set afire.

"Yet I ask, why are you so pale? Is it possible you were more courageous yesterday than today? Do not love your life so much that you shrink from death. Show the gods above that you are brave men. You have come here to defeat the enemy or die. Entrust yourselves to your bow and arrows, your darts, your spear, your shield and sword, for these will gain you victory. Let your hearts be angry against a people who have injured you, against a people who have attacked you. Shut your eyes to the suffering of your flesh and search for vengeance. You fight for Azcapotzalco. You fight for Xihcutli. Let Xihcutli aid you. Let Xihcutli strengthen your heart."

◆ ◆ ◆

As they did the day before the two armies array themselves against the other across a distance. Greatly encouraged by the outcome of the previous day King Tezozo, his four sons, and various Xilotepec lords stand amid their soldiers with light hearts.

Across the distance that separates the two armies, slightly more than the flight of an arrow, a son of Tezozo who pronounces his 'z's not with a whisper of air passing

20

over the tip of the tongue held close to the teeth, but with a slipping of the sound, the tongue falling off to the side, shouts, "What is this Ashcapotshalco? Have you come to give us your lives?"

"Is it your death you seek, soldiers of Azcapotzalco?" A second brother shouts. "For why else have you come here?"

Not to be outdone yet a third brother yells across the intervening distance, "You have been tricked into coming here Azcapotzalco, unaware of our valor and strength. Go home. Go home or you will forever remain here."

The fourth brother remains silent, gripping his spear so fiercely his fingers show white: He has had an unsettling premonition as to the outcome of the day.

One Azcapotzalco captain, a warrior of some repute who has heard well more than enough answers their taunts, shouting back, "Look upon us Xilotepec, and look upon your death. For that is what we bring you."

Having confirmed that all of the army are to their places General Petlauh turns to a staff officer, says, "We waste the day. Signal attack."

Drums sound their echo of death, and a pile of oil-soaked wood is set alight that pours forth black heavy smoke. Amid shouts, whistles, cries, and the waving of banners a battle of furious intensity begins that, having begun, now grinds its way towards an unalterable conclusion with the steady subtraction of soldiers from this world. But this: the woodcutter who had met General Petlauh the night before, repayment for an injustice served him by King Tezozo, has revealed a path that winds through gullies, a marsh, seemingly inpenetratable thickets to arrive at the very edge of the wall that guards Xilotepec; guards it, although the wall here is unguarded and easily climbed. Azcapotzalco warriors enter the city, swiftly capture the temple of their patron deity, *Mayahuel*, God of the Maguey plant, and set fire to it. In the confusion of battle it takes some time for the Xilotepec army to learn that Mayahuel has been overthrown, but when they do, smoke from the burning shrine rising up over the city, realizing that the unimaginable has happened they surrender.

For a time the soldiers of Azcapotzalco plunder the city, since Distant Time the soldiers reward. King Tezozo is unable to beg mercy for Xilotepec, for Tezozo is now dead. Thus it is various Lords and high officials present themselves to the victors with their arms crossed before their chests offering obedience and tribute. Quinatzin orders conch shell horns to sound out the victory, and orders the pillaging of Xilotepec to cease.

◆ ◆ ◆

The Azcapotzalco army stays camped outside Xilotepec for five days in which time, depriving the beetles and ants, crows and vultures their feast, the fallen soldiers are collected in a great pile and burned, their souls sent on to the glorious realm of the God of Fire and the ash used to nourish the local fields. A quantity of tribute that Xilotepec will deliver to Azcapotzalco every 80 days is agreed upon, with the sole surviving son of Tezozo raised up to Speaker of the city and so charged with seeing that the agreed upon tribute arrives on schedule, and maintaining peace, or at least quiet. And the woodcutter, whose service Lord Quinatzin has not forgotten, is given the income from a great swath of Xilotepec farmland and slaves to work it. With that it is time to leave, and those of the army who remain in this world return home.

4
Jaguars and Eagles

―――――

For those whose husband does not return home, Senior General Cuauh Petlauh comes before the widows of each neighborhood and says to them, "Let not your sadness, my daughter, overwhelm you. Though we have brought sorrow to your door take courage, know that your husband died for the honor and glory of Azcapotzalco. So too, know that your husband died fighting as the brave man he was. Your husband has departed, going to our great lord Xihcutli, and is now rejoicing with his comrades within the shining Glory of Fire. Your husband will be remembered forever! Therefore weep now for his memory, then live out your days in happiness."

Music is played, dirges using hoarse, dissonant instruments that include the rubbing together of two old bones, the one notched like a ladder, which makes a sound like death itself: whispering, rasping. The widows, their hair loose and hanging close to their faces, wearing what had been their husband's clothes about their shoulders, clap their hands to the beat of a drum that is the thrum of emptiness. In their hands the widows carry that which was once his, -feathers signifying acclaim, or perhaps his favorite cloak. All bow their heads to the earth and weep. One-by-one high officials greet the widows, consoling them, saying, "Thank-you for the honor you have paid to the Master of the Earth, Creator of All Things, and to his children who have died in war."

Images of the fallen Jaguars and Eagles are then brought out, statues some two feet in height crafted of resinous pine, dressed in breechcloths and cloaks, and adorned with miniature shields, weapons, and small feathers. The images are offered tortillas shaped as butterflies to eat, *papalotlaxcalli* they are called, so too offered tobacco and flowers, songs and sorrow. After a suitable duration the statues are placed together, covered with prayers written out on paper, and the whole is set aflame. As the wood turns to ash the widows stand about the blaze, their cheeks wet with tears. When but ash is left General Petlauh again speaks to the widows, saying:

"Be strong, wives and mothers, sisters and daughters: strengthen and widen your hearts. We have bade farewell to those who have departed to become jaguars and eagles. You need understand that these warriors are gone forever, and that you will not see them again in this world. You must maintain your house with your spinning and weaving, sweeping and watering, and know that you have done a great service to the Lord of All

Created Things, of the Day and the Night, of Wind, and of Fire."

With these ceremonies completed, the widows pass to the neighborhood temple to pray, and to make offerings of paper, incense, and that which might please the gods.

That night, alone in her empty house we find a young widow, weeping; her name is Xoco, a name that means 'youngest sister.' She whispers a poem to herself, and from a distance we listen:

> I see his loincloth, his cloak.
> His things are there, just as before, but not the
>   man they belonged to.
> His spirit has taken flight and left me far behind.
> To whom shall I look? On whom shall I rely?
> My tears flow in an endless stream.

5

The Coronation of King Quinatzin

―――――――

In anticipation of his formal coronation King Quinatzin now walks through the storehouses of Azcapotzalco to account for that within, which is to say ensure the counters have counted correctly. Thinking of how often he did this as a child with his father Quinatzin smiles, and reflects upon the humor inherent to life and the seeming finality of death. Yet for that the gods promise an eternity in paradise. Or rather, those who owe their livelihood to the gods so promise. Lord Quinatzin passes a great many bundles of feathers, 'shadows of the gods' they are called, of all kinds and colors imaginable, among the most treasured items in the storehouses. He passes ceramic dishes holding stones of fire, like those he would gaze into so long ago when he was but a child. Yet, that was only yesterday: his father, King Acamapichtli, checking numbers exactly as Quinatzin now checks numbers, Quinatzin left to himself to wander the storehouses. Yesterday, today: how quickly the years pass. The past, but a present that no longer exists and has, in many ways, become imaginary.

Quinatzin passes bundles of fine cotton mantles bearing designs that are no less than life: a crouched jaguar, muscles tensed waiting for the perfect moment to leap; sunlight glinting from the wings of a sharply banking osprey, its keen eyes having just detected a fish near the surface of a still lake. So too there are cloaks, breechcloths, blouses and skirts of lesser elegance, gradations of rank manifest in the quality of weave and decoration, and for the women who serve in the temples there are plain blouses and skirts of soft cotton.

There are ceramic pots that contain dyes of all imaginable colors; red, orange, and yellow from the worm that burrows within the cochineal cactus, the different colors obtained by how the worms meet their death. There are large quantities of maguey paper for use by the painter-scribes, and so too many pots that hold paints and inks. Quinatzin gazes upon all that can be found in the sea: shells of giant turtles, pearls, ambers, and curious bones of unimaginable size. There is copper, gold, tin and silver transformed into the most fantastical art such as birds and butterflies so delicately balanced that it seems but the faintest breeze will send them aloft into the azure sky.

There appears an endless quantity of fine ceramic pots, jugs, vases, pitchers, cups and plates, great and small, some more ornate and some less, Cholula ceramic blackware, and the famous Xipilco orangeware that is traded as far as man has traveled. There are storehouses filled with the flour of different grains, kernels of maize for puffing, -momochitl as it is known, untold quantities of beans, so too baskets of herbs and spices and dried chilies. There are pots filled with white or yellow honey. There are baskets of seeds of many types, some for planting, and some for eating –such as the roasted pumpkin seeds which are ever a favorite. There is a storehouse that holds charcoal, torches, and the most fragrant of incenses to please the gods. There are different resins, and the bark of the movivipana[7] tree that burns with a most beautiful hot flame without smoke and without leaving ash.

What is held within the storehouses is found sufficient to Quinatzin's purpose, and so an auspicious day is set for his coronation. A day determined with the utmost care by meticulous priests, a matter of complexity to be sure for though all carry the same wraith of time upon their shoulder the priests choose to parse out time not with the sun but with their own calendar, the *tonalpoualli*, years of twenty 13-day weeks, and there are lucky days, unlucky days, days pleasing to one god but not another, days promising for certain professions, and as luck pervades our lives, fate, or Fate, wily-Tezcatlipoca, The Mocker- some call him, well, one does what one can to avoid misfortune.

+ + +

Lord Quinatzin orders carpenters set to work repairing and repainting the old so that it glitters in pristine

---

7   Now extinct.

brilliance, making new chairs, couches, and alcoves where the great can observe Quinatzin's coronation in privacy. The city is of such activity, all to their purposes of providing, repairing, and adorning that it is a wondrous sight to behold.

Invitations to Quinatzin's coronation are sent to the lords and ladies of vassal towns and cities. So too invitations are sent to the high lords of towns and cities that oppose Azcapotzalco. Not without risk the royal envoys of Quinatzin come before the lords of these realms to deliver a message few anticipate: "Powerful lord; Lord Quinatzin bids me to say that though at times one must be an enemy, that the opportunities for friendship should not be lost. Lord Quinatzin asks you to put enmity aside and come to his coronation where he will receive you with all the honor you deserve."

As it is wise not to be too trusting, the rulers of these cities send lower-tiered nobles in their stead who return to Azcapotzalco with the royal envoys. These dignitaries are given the finest of lodgings, and there Quinatzin humbly visits them, presenting the worthy visitors with gifts such as jeweled bracelets, headbands of gold in which eagle feathers are set, and beautifully made cloaks and breechcloths. Quinatzin bestows such gifts that it seems his wealth and generosity are limitless, and as he imparts these gifts he says, "These gifts are to give you pleasure, and so that you will know Quinatzin is the king and lord of the great city of Azcapotzalco."

6

Coronation I:
The Tlachtli Game

We have come to the beginning of Quinatzin's coronation celebration. From Tlacho, a city of lovely climate near the coast of the eastern ocean, where the finest *tlachtli* players in the world are trained, come two teams to play out a contest upon the magnificent central court of Azcapotzalco. While the winning team of six players will receive for the duration of their lives the tribute of Ocullan, a prosperous town recently made vassal to Azcapotzalco, the contest has a significance that goes well beyond the mortal world. About the *tlachtli* court gather diviners, priests, and presagers who pose their questions to the gods and spirits and who, by the outcome of the contest, answer.

The crowd gathered, the air crisp with anticipation, Quinatzin passes through the crowd wearing a dazzling cloak upon which one sees a field of ripe maize for which a battle rages. Warriors of ancient Azcapotzalco slash and hack at a band of Xochimilco raiders who wish to carry off the bounty. The maize stalks are drenched with blood. So vividly is the battle portrayed that one tilts their head closer to the weave to better hear the cries and shouts. Quinatzin gives to the gathered nobles gems, singular feathers, tobacco, rare incense, cloth, ornaments of bright polished metal, and as he bestows these rich gifts he says to each, "This is given for your pleasure, and so that you know Quinatzin is king and lord of the great city of Azcapotzalco."

◆ ◆ ◆

Noon. The players, wearing leather helmets and pads on knees and elbows, each carrying their heavy wood hand-paddle, their *manopla*, arrive upon the I-shaped court, neatly defined right-angled realm of smooth limestone. Along the length of the court rise tiers of stone-seats upon which nobles, having carefully adjusted their finely woven soft mats, sit, and there await the contest. The arbitrators, those who decide whether the *tlachtli* ball, made of *olli*, to be later known as latex, has crossed a line, delineation of space determined by red paint upon white stone, and so a point awarded or lost, take their positions. The foremost arbitrator stands above the line that divides the I-shaped court into two equal sections, $I/2 = \perp$. Another arbitrator stands at each end line, the *chachalco*, at the point where the north-south aligned canyon of stone gives way to that aligned east-west, a catchment wherein a missed ball can come to rest. The players are treated as great lords and the arbitrators treated as high priests, for so they are of their realm.

The spectators to their seats, the players upon the court, the arbitrators to their appointed places, -the wagering, the prognostications, and the contest itself begins with a casting and counting of cacao beans that determines which team will serve to start the game. The chief arbitrator hands Quinatzin the *mecalcatl*, the sacred trumpet by which the beginning and end of the contest is sounded. In turn Quinatzin hands the *mecalcatl* to the Queen of Chalco, a considerable honor, who takes a deep breath and sounds out a reverberation, and with this the *tlachtli* ball is tossed into the air by the server that, descending, outcome of gravity, he strikes with his *manopla*. The ball, traveling so swiftly it is difficult to see bounds off the floor, then a wall, and then a player, in anticipation of a future instant, steps forward striking the ball sending it back to where it began. The ball is here a moment, then there, passing like a thought, -like an idea, with the exhilarating freedom of an opalescent hummingbird. The players dart back and forth, bend low, jump high, leap forward and back, and all the while the crowd murmurs their astonishment and appreciation. One sees the players track the speeding ball and, premonition of the future, anticipating its path, strike it. Yet at times, for all their skill, the ball oddly bouncing this way or that one player after the other will miss it, the ball crossing over the *chachalco* with a point awarded by a whistle-armed arbitrator.

And as for points, the objective of the game is to score eight, a prospect simple enough, but not if the teams are well matched in skill and luck, for there are setbacks, life-like circuitous routes. Once a team has two or three points, or six or seven, should they lose a point they are *urre*, that is, on the cusp, the edge, and to lose the next point is to lose all their points. So too, to win four straight points is to erase all the points of the other team.

So the scores rise, and the scores fall, and all the while wagers are made, and to sustain these wagers there is the invocation of many prayers. The game is played and there are murmurs of delight, or fallen hopes, the possession of so many jewels, feathers, art, land, cloth, and slaves changing hands. Encompassing all this is the shimmering, glittering sounds of the *tlachtli*-ball rattles, hollow baked-clay spheres the size of a *tlachtli* ball in which there rests a small pebble, and that when shook gives off a sound that suggests the whisper of rain.

The two teams are sharply balanced, with point after point traded. The scores rise and fall, as the ball itself does, so finely, with such attending skill that no one notices how the sun slides its way across the sky.

2 – 0
2 *urre* – 1
3 – 1
3 *urre* – 2
0 – 3
1 – 3 *urre*

Of an instant one can see the ball, low angle, traverse just above the stone floor of the court: a man sets the edge of his manopla upon the ground, angled just so, and striking this the ball sails up into the air and, trick of gravity, descends; a teammate coming up behind slams the ball back towards their opponents, -the ball flies fast as imagination, yet for that, a manopla finds it and the ball is returned. That one can see the ball, and react to stop its flight is difficult to imagine.

6 – 0
6 *urre* – 1
0 – 2
1 – 2 *urre*

One sees a volley in which the ball is hit harder and harder, each team retreating back within its court: then one player returns the ball and it strikes at a steep angle where the wall joins the floor near the *antlatlco*, the midline that defines the two halves of the court, and the ball bounces an odd, curving, unexpected spin altering its course, and it comes to a stop before the other team can reach it, by which a point is scored.

4 – 0
4 – 1
4 – 2
4 – 3
0 – 4

With time the speed and precision of the players grows less. Once a ball is sent up into the spectators striking a man senseless, but such are the ways of wily-Tezcatlipoca; it costs the errant team a point.

4 – 4
4 – 5
5 – 5
6 – 5
6 *urre* – 6

The players seem to glow as if illuminated from within; they are at the pinnacle of their lives, holding for so long at the interface of their greatest victory, or most aching defeat, that it seems a harsh injustice that one team should lose.

A horn sounds, demarcation of a moment for the spectators to stretch and refresh themselves, and so too for the players to quench their thirst. To those watching the contest attendants bring water, chocolatl, and juice. It is good to be alive and watch such a trial. To be part of the excitement, to wager sums upon the outcome of such a fine game with the warm sun giving chase to the cool breeze; time and space, for the moment, in pleasant equilibrium.

Players and spectators return. The ball ricochets, skips, caroms in and out of sharp angles. There is an abiding determination to the play that goes well beyond mere victory or loss, something elemental to life itself: an embrace of the moment, a revelation of the now.

2 – 0
2 *urre* – 1
0 – 2
1 – 2 *urre*
1 – 3
2 – 3 *urre*

The scores rise and fall, rise and fall, then that of one side rises, and rises, and of a moment, a final passing of a ball across a line, the chief arbitrator sounds the sacred horn and the game is over. The crowd murmurs their approval, shaking their ceramic *tlachtli* ball rattles to show their appreciation of what they have seen, and continue shaking them, the white noise of rain. The players, exhausted, congratulate each other; hands are clasped, each player in turn embraces the other.

The courtyard fills with priests, some singing, some sprinkling wine upon the stones, some to ill-defined priestly purposes we are at a loss to imagine. One hears a high-priestess say something of *Omexochitl*, the evening star, and *Tlahuizcalpantecuhtli*, the morning star, and Quetzalcoatl,[8] and of course the goddess of the *tlachtli* court herself, Xolotl, Wolf-woman, She who guides the sun at night as it passes through the Underworld.

Amid considerable ceremony and pomp an elegantly crafted and decorated chair is brought upon the court and placed at its very center. Xicama, captain of the winning team sits upon this chair and leans his head back, exposing his throat. Priests carefully attend him, -one sees them lay a sheet of clay upon Xicama's face and quickly, deftly, make an imprint of his countenance. By fire this soft clay will be turned to stone, and his face will join the rack of the victorious, a memorial, though one might call it a monument just as well, where the visages of the greatest *tlachtli* players of all time, or a time, are displayed so that one might always see them, so that they may remain eternal.

---

8   One of the four gods who created the world, Tezcatlipoca's brother, God of Wind, and God of Knowledge.

Xicama stands up from the chair, takes the wet cotton towel that is handed to him and cleans the residual film of clay from his face. Toteo, captain of the losing team stands nearby, and the two captains embrace again for there is much between them, a commonality of experience and shared existence. Toteo sits upon the chair Xicama has just left, and leans his head back exposing his throat that a priest, deftly, slices open. The blood of Toteo, his *teoatl*, sacred water, that by which the goddess Xolotl is sustained cascades down upon the court. No sound is heard save the surresh of the *tlachtli*-ball rattles. Toteo's blood pools about him, whisper of mist.

◆ ◆ ◆

Perhaps, strange confusion, we have not seen events properly. Since in an infinite universe all things are possible perhaps there is a switch of potentialities, a stutter-step where cause and effect appear to go one way then shift quickly to the opposite direction. Listening to the surresh of the *tlachtli*-ball rattles the observer falls into a trance and sees things as they might have been, or yet still could be, or for that truly are.

Here is what we now see: The players congratulate each other; hands are clasped, each player, in turn, embraces the other. The courtyard fills with priests, some singing, some sprinkling wine upon the stones, some to priestly purposes we are at a loss to define. Amid ceremony and pomp an elegantly crafted and decorated chair is placed upon the very center of the court. Upon the chair within the courtyard Xicama, captain of the winning team, sits, leans his head back just so and quickly, deftly, a sheet of clay is laid upon his face to make an imprint of his countenance that, once baked to stone, will join the rack of the victorious, a monument to the greatest *tlachtli* players Azcapotzalco has been fortunate to see, a monument that will last for as long as Nahua which then seems, to those living in The Valley, a quantity of time equal to forever.

Xicama is handed a wet cotton towel with which he carefully cleans the residual film of clay from his face. Then, seeing Toteo within the surrounding crowd, Xicama rises from the chair and the two captains again embrace, for there is a commonality of experience between them, a shared understanding. Then Xicama returns to the chair and leans his head back; he is censed, prayed over, sprinkled with wine, and then a priest deftly slices open his throat and his blood cascades upon the courtyard, sanctifying it, sustaining Xolotl, Goddess of the *Tlachtli* Court, and She who guides the sun at night as it passes through the Underworld. It is the utmost honor for Xicama to die as a supreme champion, at the very pinnacle of his skill and strength, to never suffer the disappointment of sagging muscles and rebellious joints. No sound is heard about the court save the surresh of the *tlachtli*-ball rattles. The blood of Xicama pools about him, whisper of mist; his spirit will enter the highest level of Heaven to there live for all time in eternal bliss, each day playing *tlachtli* with the greatest players time and space cast upon the shores of the One World.

7
Coronation II: The Sky Dancers

———

Midnight, a demarcation of time defined with the lighting of so many torches and lanterns within the royal courtyard it seems to burn with the light of day. Lord Quinatzin appears before the gathered visitors, nobles from cities throughout the One World, wearing a dazzling mantel that shows Tilulca, legendary ancient mother of Azcapotzalco, and her two sons Xoloco and Totonaca, busy laying the foundations of the then small village of Azcapotzalco. Totonaca shoulders a mountain peak, a task he seems to find heavy work. Xoloco walks behind, playing his flute, made of bone inlaid with gold and silver, and a boulder twice as large as that which Totonaca carries comes rolling after him. Lord Quinatzin passes through the crowd handing out gifts, be they sandals, feathers, tobacco, jewels, or bracelets of gold, to his guests while saying, "This is given for your pleasure, and so that you will know Quinatzin is king and lord of the great city of Azcapotzalco."

The many visitors seated, a drum sounds out three reverberating beats and after a moment five men emerge from the shadows of the surrounding buildings into the brilliant illumination of the courtyard; two are dressed as monkeys, two dressed as birds, and the fifth dressed as some sort of trickster god, perhaps, or Quetzalcoatl, manifestation of wind, -difficult to be sure as he hurries to his task. And of his task, he runs to a pole, once tree trunk, set securely within the courtyard that rises up some 150 feet, grabs the knotted rope that hangs down from the height and up this he climbs, squirrel-nimble, to be followed in turn by his four companions.

Climbing up into the cusp of darkness the five become but fragments of scattered light against the night sky. Upon the uppermost height the five array themselves upon a small platform, more aptly described as a ledge, with each monkey and bird aligned to a cardinal direction. The trickster god, for surely that is what he is, dances about first balancing on one foot and then the other, and then stands on his hands, -tricks difficult enough to do upon the ground itself, all the while continuing to flute with no note of music out of place.

The trickster god now leaves off with his dancing and flute, sounds out a sequence of chimes upon a copper bell, then stands as rigid as the pole itself, and of an instant in the encompassing silence the monkeys and birds hurl themselves head-foremost to the four directions to dash themselves upon the courtyard below. Save but the intake of breath not a sound is heard for none have seen such a thing before, a feat of unimaginable daring. But this: The four, equidistant from the other, do not smash to the ground, rather they fly about the pole, spiraling around the axis while slowly descending from the height. Gradually approaching the day-bright courtyard one sees a rope tied about the ankles of each, with the ropes slowly unwinding from about the pole; with each rotation they come closer to Earth and soar further outwards into the encompassing emptiness. The monkeys, the one with a drum the other a trumpet, sound out first a tune of mock-fear, then one of joy. The birds turn their feathered-arms this way and that to catch the wind like great eagles, and release small seeds as they fly above the courtyard, so many it appears a trick of magic, the courtyard flagstones echoing with the gentle shimmer of rain.

Coming to brightly-lit Earth, completing their 13th revolution, 4 by 13 is 52, a sacred number, with one hand each reaches up above their feet and grasps the rope, and with the other hand, a mere tug it seems, undoes the knot that binds their feet, a twist and they come to earth running. They make a few skips and leaps, then the four spiral in to the pole, put their backs against it, slide down to earth, lay their heads upon their neighbors shoulder to the left, close their eyes and fall asleep.

The courtyard fills with shouts of delight, claps, murmurs of appreciation, a cascade of sound that embraces and fills all who have seen this death-teasing performance.

The cheers in time diminishing, as if roused by the gathering silence the monkeys and birds awaken to twitter and gambol about the courtyard looking for their missing trickster-friend who, for all their efforts, they cannot find. Then from atop the great height comes the solitary note of a flute. Aha! The motions of the monkeys and birds suggest their concern as to how the trickster-god friend will return to Earth. The birds pantomime jumping off the pole and flying, the monkeys clambering down the pole with, admittedly, neither option being seen as suitable. The four then discover a very long rope that the trickster god has let down to earth; they grab the end of this rope and pull it away from the pole, pull it far out into the darkness that surrounds the courtyard. The rope pulled taunt, the trickster god throws over it a stout bow of polished wood, grabs ahold of each end, and releases himself to the pull of gravity, hurtling towards Earth as swiftly as an arrow, sweeping down past the courtyard to vanish, of an instant, into the encompassing darkness. The crowd is silent, and this silence is followed by but a silence of longer duration.

What's that? A drum, ever so faint, hardly a whisper but getting louder, louder, and then to a sharp crescendo of trumpets the five flyers emerge from the darkness onto the day-bright courtyard, and the crowd cheers, whistles, and claps, and again cheers, whistles, and claps. The musicians arranged for the following dance sound out their enthusiasm with drums, rattles, trumpets and flutes, the music echoing out over the city, the lake, and the surrounding forests. And then begins a great uplifting of spirit, a wondrous exultation to life, which is to say a dance, a dance that will last into the far reaches of the night, a dance that is a celebration of being alive, being here and now: a celebration of the instant.

8

King Quinatzin

———

There is by necessity a balance in the duration of a story, an integer value of words between one and too many. Our story comes now to the coronation itself. At its height within the sky, the great orb of fire finds the priests, the soldiers, and the people of the city gathered about the temple of Xihcutli, the God of Fire. Each tier of the immense temple is decorated with flowers and green boughs, and amid them censers burn copal- the most aromatic and rare of incense. Atop the temple there is a gong of solid gold, this the width of a man's out-stretched arms, the reverberating, shimmering tone of which is used to sequentially partition moments of time. The sky is such a dark blue in color that it seems almost purple; towards the southeast across Lake Texcoco are sky-reaching cumulous dark with rain. To the visiting nobles Quinatzin bestows gifts of that which is rare and valued, and with this last largesse finally empties the storehouses; but to his guests the wealth and power of Azcapotzalco seem endless. As Quinatzin hands out these final gifts he says, "This is given for your pleasure, and so that you know Quinatzin is king and lord of the great city of Azcapotzalco."

Power is a small world of strong gravitation, and the powers of this world now sit within their private alcoves to watch another demonstration of power, and as they wait for this culminating ceremony to begin they talk, sharing perspectives on that which concerns them, and to this we listen. Miahuitl, returned from Texcoco of which she has recently become Queen, she of keen insight, waist-length raven-dark hair for the moment bound within a single tight braid that rests coiled atop her head, here to see the formal ascension of her brother, from a plate held before her by an attendant takes a strip of grilled fish and says to her husband, "Consider the miracle of the fish, who eat the most atrocious things which they transform into a most delicious meal."

Copiltzin, King of Texcoco, while listening to his wife observes how a shifting beam of light changes the color of Miahuitl's sandals, and answers, "It is a miracle, at that. Though one could say the same of a bird. Or deer certainly, and squirrels; most anything it seems."

"Yes." Miahuitl responds, after a moment. "It seems transformation is intrinsic to life. We are one thing, and then we are another. And this raises a question I've been meaning to ask. In the past, as suggested by that which is recorded in our books, to satisfy the gods after a successful hunt our ancestors merely had to raise into the sky the blood-stained arrow. This same belief, or rite, is still carried out by the scattered tribes one finds in the scrublands to the north. It seems to work well enough sustaining their world, so why not for us?"

After looking about, and for the moment satisfied that no one can overhear their conversation King Copiltzin turns his attention to Miahuitl, and answers, "How did our society arrive at where our society is? Always a good question, and one asked by many, I imagine, across time and space. Rise and fall, parable of empires. It's educational to tour the Olmec ruins. They ruled the world for a time, never an easy task, and now nothing is left but scattered stonework. And as to rise and fall, sorry- I digress. More specifically to your question, as a former priest, though not really a priest, long story I'll tell you sometime, I think it has a great deal to do with a certain small, rust-colored mushroom our priests are so fond of devouring. The conventional logic, if I understand it correctly, local cosmology, appears to be that life is such an ordeal it can only have been crafted by spiteful gods, spiteful gods who we hope to placate, placate or sustain, ultimately the same difference, with gifts. And what is a greater gift than our life, as manifest in our blood? Though I do not many, particularly those fond of rust-colored mushrooms, find this a compelling logic.

"I am of the opinion the mushrooms contain a small bit of poison that damages the mind. I know notable priests, knew them as young men, knew them as children, then and now, and over the years their personalities have changed quite dramatically. In contrast the priests not fond of the mushrooms, or not important enough to receive them, stayed over time the same recognizable person. This suggests, of course, that much of what goes on in this land is determined, or at least strongly influenced, by those who don't think properly, are in fact some way mentally damaged. And that cannot be a good thing, as I'm sure you, and your brother, understand. Not that I'm suggesting we live in a failed state, it is just a question of degree. There is nothing absolute with respect to what we think of as justice or law, they are just manifestations of power." He pauses a moment, tries to interpret the look on Miahuitl's face, asks, "Did I answer your question?"

◆ ◆ ◆

To his coronation King Quinatzin invited King Yacacoatl of Xochimilco, who graciously declined instead sending two trusted counselors, Lord Ecama and Lord Malacatl, who now take their ease in one of the finest alcoves offering an unfettered view of sweeping space. Lord Malacatl is eating strips of grilled venison with thin slices of salted-tomato; Ecama points with the index finger of his right hand into the opened palm of his left, says, "Here we are in the center." He draws his finger along the edge of his palm, "Surrounded by enemies. And beyond these enemies," he draws a circle of larger radius beyond his hand, "are more enemies. If we allied ourselves with our neighbors as long-term unequivocal allies then we would, or rather *wouldn't*, excuse me, have to fight these incessant wars over our borders. Further, if barbarians from the far edges of the world attacked, well, we'd have lots of allies between us and them."

Malacatl considers this a moment, says, "That's a good idea, and that's the trick. There will always be boundaries and hence, by definition, enemies. And what would our soldiers do if there were no enemies? And think of all those who earn their livelihood by making swords, shields, helmets and so on, what would they do? But I understand your logic, what you suggest. A logic that predicates making allies not only among the Nahua, which we can imagine, but so too of the barbarians beyond, those of unintelligible languages and outrageous cultures. And how do we do this? Somehow impose a particular cultural model? Insist we all pray to the same gods? This is almost impossible because people who speak different languages see and evaluate existence differently. Sometimes the difference is inconsequential: 'I have hunger' in contrast to 'Hungry I am.' Sometimes the difference requires enough introspection to stop the conversation, 'What will become of me,' versus 'What will I become?' Sometimes the difference might cost you your life: 'A large fierce Chalco fighting warrior,' as opposed to: 'Fighting a large fierce Chalco warrior.' By which I suggest one is tricked by the structure of the language they speak into a certain way of perceiving reality. My point, to speak more concisely, is that our reality, or our perception of reality, is not necessarily that of other peoples.

"However, assume we can make friends and allies with everyone, and I'm not suggesting it's impossible, just difficult. If you make the world safe for Xochimilco then, my opinion, time will find us dogs fatted for supper. The heart of the matter, again this is just my opinion, is that you can organize the best form of government you can imagine and in time fools will come to run it, with the fools acting for the fools to serve the purpose of the fools, and it will fall to shambles. Then those who survive start over. Repeat as necessary."

"So what do you suggest?"

"I don't know. I don't think anyone else does either, unless they're delusional, *then* they know what to do. Each of us sits at the center of their own fog-shrouded world, but for that all is to the greater glory of Xochimilco."

◆ ◆ ◆

A few Xilotepec warriors judged to be potentially troublesome, so too a handful of captured Tenayuca warriors, flotsam of the last conflict the city of Tenayuca saw fit to provoke, the 'We are descended from Toltecs!' Tenayuca who find peace tedious, are brought before Xihcutli's new temple. For the moment these warriors, ex-warriors, white-dusted with chalk, white the color of death, exist in a here-not-here reality, their life forfeit by their capture on the battlefield, and their death, like all deaths, merely postponed. Each warrior, ex-warrior now messenger, wears a small bag upon their back that contains gifts for The God of Fire such as incense, soot, a small bit of ash, or orange feathers. So too each courier has memorized a message for Xihcutli, many of which remind him how faithfully Azcapotzalco serves his cause. However some messages are more specific: Quinatzin, for example, informs his father of recent events, and asks his advice on certain matters.

Nothing lacks for the dedication of Xihcutli's new temple, and nothing lacks for Quinatzin's coronation. It is exhilarating to see the great crowd, the iridescent feather banners standing out upon the gentle wind, the greenery, and the many flowers. Flanked by guards the couriers once-warriors ascend the eastern steps of the temple to the uppermost height, and as they climb the high priest calls out:

> Lord of Fire! I greet you!
> Please remember your children.
> Protect them! Help them!
> Receive, Lord Fire, these humble presents they send.
> May you be pleased.
> Great lord! Hear our voice!

Each courier in turn throws the small bag he carries into the sacred fire of Xihcutli that soon consumes, or accepts- a question of perspective, the offerings. Then, courier by courier, a well ordered sequential series, five priests arrange themselves about and neatly, swiftly, slit said messenger's throat, tipping them over so that their blood will be caught within a basin that, tricks of hydrology, flows into a canal that runs down the eastern side of the temple parallel the steps. The body of the messenger is then cast down the flight of stairs oriented to the west, suggesting the duality inherent in mortal existence. Falling, the bodies make an uncanny rattling noise.

✦ ✦ ✦

Observing the rites Queen Miahuitl ever so slightly shakes her head, and whispers to herself, "I require not a temple, nor smoke, nor fire. Remove the hand you hold before your eyes, and see that I am here beside you."

✦ ✦ ✦

The blood of the messengers, instructive exemplification of power, pooled upon the courtyard, a great chair gilded in gold is carried to the eastern edge of the temple height, scintillation of brilliant sunlight, and upon this chair Quinatzin sits, and is censed over, and prayed over, and about his neck is placed a band of jewels the likes of which have never been seen in the world and, as The Unfathomable knows, never will be again, that in but a handful of years Quinatzin will offer to Chalchiuhtlicue, Goddess of Springs, Streams, Rivers and Lakes, as an appeasement, throwing them into the whirlpool of Pantitlan then draining the great lake of Texcoco. About Quinatzin's head a golden crown is placed decorated with feathers so rare that, well, they are invaluable as the birds no longer exist, having lived only on an island in the western sea upon which there were no predators and the birds, over time, having grown gentle and trusting to a fault, did not anticipate the arrival of man and his insatiable appetite, but so goes the sly give and take of existence. There are songs, there is music, there is the striking of the gong that makes the light of the world shimmer and Quinatzin is, of that moment, by Xihcutli's blessing formally and unmistakably King of Azcapotzalco.

+ + +

On their departure, King Quinatzin gives each visiting noble an exquisitely crafted white shield that is blank as death. The symbolism is lost on no one.

Second Bundle

"In Teotihuacan they built very large mounds to the Sun and the Moon, ...like mountains. It is unbelievable when they say that these were made by hand but at that time giants still lived there."

Fray Bernardino de Sahagun, *Codice Florentino*
Published circa 1577.

9

Some Moments Held Bound Within The Past

───────

Acamapichtli, King of Azcapotzalco, and the four children of his first wife, those destined to rule, have come to Teotihuacan, great city of the yopicatl. It is a festive occasion for the yopicatl, magnified reflections of their smaller human counterparts, celebrate the alignment of certain wandering stars, a periodic but rarely seen celestial event. The yopicatl have invited many popoloca,[9] as the yopicatl call them, and as it would be remiss of them not to attend the popoloca have put aside for a moment their many realm versus realm animosities. However the Queen of Azcapotzalco, disinclined to converse with glib-talking giants, something intrinsic to her disposition, is not present.

The fires of hunger momentarily sated the guests and

───────

9   Barbarians.

hosts break into small clusters, some to sit and enjoy the music, some to discuss points of detail regarding that which seems noteworthy, while those of power mingling with those of power speak of the concerns of power. Some atop the great stone pyramid turn their conversation to humor, to wit among a small group one says to her companions, "The gods of Tenayuca demand their priests, each day before first prayers, leap through a fire to cleanse them of their impurities. It's quite a sight to see all the priests lined up waiting their turn. Those old Toltec gods are a demanding bunch."

"How big a fire?" One of her audience asks.

She holds out a hand mid-thigh. "It's reasonably high, but narrow."

After consideration of the idea one grins, suggests, "That must be hard on the old priests."

"You'd think so, wouldn't you?" She answers, with a flash of a smile. "Maybe they sprinkle water on their robes before they jump."

There is a flourish of laughter, after which another says, "I've heard King Xicatzin, of Culhuacan, has all those who come before him pass through a fire to ensure they bring no poison, nor evil magic."

"Does this work?"

"Hmm, well. So far."

◆ ◆ ◆

Near a table loaded with freshly baked treats they seem reluctant to step away from, one finds a yopicatl in conversation with a Nahua visitor.

"In the past..." the popoloca begins.

"Which is but an illusion of memory," the yopicatl suggests.

"An illusion? No, I don't think so. Let me put it thus: Back within the record of transpired events..."

"You speak of history? There is the past, and there is history. Who knows what gets written, why and when? Memory is but a length of rope knotted here and there, the knots symbolizing what we clearly hold in the mind forever, and the intervals between the knots are but so much vagueness, which is to say, nothing. No. Thing. Think of what an overwhelmingly large fraction of your life you have no memory of, and *that*, friend, is the landscape of your life."

"Perhaps that which we do not remember is unimportant."

"Perhaps," says the yopicatl. "In which case the vast majority of your life is unimportant."

◆ ◆ ◆

There are also yopicatl who, as they are less than keen on the popoloca, generally regarding them as small prone-to-violence monkeys, choose to view the social gathering from a considerable distance.

Or in fact not view it at all, instead leaving Teotihuacan for the comfort of the surrounding forests, and of these yopicatl we listen to the conversation of two: "A long time ago, Distant Time, I saw two popoloca tribes stumble upon each other across the width of a creek. I sat upon a height, an uplifted finger of rock, and with the curiosity of youth intently watched these two tribes of 'The People' parse out the world between them."

"I know how that goes," her companion observes.

"Yes, but I bring this event to mind as I believe it offers sharp insight into their inner quality. That is to say, who or what we are dealing with. So, for possession of this creek, or rather, for their temporal claim to the bounty of its waters, the two tribes fought. You wonder how long they fought, these 'cousins' of ours. Well, as you know intrinsic to each word is a range of ambiguity, and there is a perceptual field to time just as there is to vision, or for that matter all senses, -well never mind. They chased each other back and forth across the creek most of a morning, leaving behind the occasional body. I could only shake my head, troubled as I was with what I saw, but at the same time nod, for in its way, if you could emotionally separate yourself, it was funny."

"Or not so funny."

"Yes, really it was rather sad. However I think of it as population control."

"Hmmpf. I don't know. Though you might think they would kill each other off, by the way they reproduce I'm worried they will soon overrun the world."

◆ ◆ ◆

There is one conversation that is of particular interest, either as a presentiment within the profound mystery of opaline depth that is life, or as a foreshadowing of the future, trick of wily-Tezcatlipoca, or simply as a signal occurrence within the random chaos that pervades and defines existence. And of this conversation, which takes place upon the uppermost height of the greatest of Teotihuacan's monuments, Acamapichtli, King of Azcapotzalco, who is known by some as *Tlatlacatzin*, He Who Flattens the Earth, looks down upon the arrow-straight boulevard that defines the heart of Teotihuacan, some 40 yards wide and 3 miles long, lined with houses that rest beneath towering ceiba and ahuehuetl trees and ends, to the north, at a pyramidal-monument not quite as large as that which he stands upon, but yet for that is of a proportion unimaginable to him, as if one stood before something not quite of this world. Acamapichtli is talking with a yopicatl named Aztacoatl. Acamapichtli, who is partially deaf and speaks as if everyone else is too, points to the monument anchoring the boulevard and asks in a loud, booming, the-world-is-deaf voice, "What do you call that temple there?"

Aztacoatl, seemingly more intent on the food before him than the conversation, answers, "We don't consider it a temple, necessarily, but rather a tribute, or a lasting reminder. Not a temple, no. I think of a temple as more a place for religious practices, though of course that leads to the question of what might or might-not be considered a religious practice. For example, I have met some who consider eating a religious practice, others sleeping. Now while eating and sleeping are certainly necessary, are they a form of prayer? And off you go, question and answer leading to question and answer."

Unfazed, King Acamapichtli, who has known Aztacoatl for well more than a bundle of years, asks, "So what is the name of the lasting reminder over there?

The pyramidal stepped-terrace monument of shaped stone one finds at the northern end of your remarkable boulevard."

Aztacoatl considers the question a moment while eating some cherries, then answers, "Yes, a reminder. Or a monument, that describes it. You might call it that, some nuances of our culture being difficult to explain to those of a different culture, albeit we largely speak the same language, so understand that this is an approximation: a Monument to The Moment."

"The Moon? A Monument to The Moon?" Acamapichtli asks, victim of his poor hearing, the consequence of a passing illness that was otherwise of no consequence. With his deafness Acamapichtli now feels much of the world passes him by unawares, and of this he is correct.

"The Moment," the yopicatl repeats, more loudly. "It's a bit of humor on our part, to build something so permanent to something effervescently transient."

Acamapichtli nods, perhaps to Aztacoatl, or perhaps to acknowledge the fine vista, the carefully tended fields, the towering trees, and the surrounding hills fading into the purple light of evening. Aztacoatl pauses for a moment offering the opportunity for Acamapichtli to comment, but Acamapichtli remains silent so Aztacoatl continues, elucidating the point he is not sure Acamapichtli heard him make. "Take life, if you will," Aztacoatl continues. (He motions with a hand, as if to suggest: Take it.) "A common question is if there is meaning in this life we are living? However the question can be broken down into ever smaller increments: Is there meaning in a month? A day? Ultimately, one comes to: What is the meaning of now? Or now? Or, wait for it, now? Which is to say, the moment."

✦ ✦ ✦

Ueue Zacatzin, King Acamapichtli's youngest son, is entranced by the whole of Teotihuacan, city of astonishing grandeur that he looks out upon from the unimaginable height, realm of irrigated fields, well-kept orchards, and carefully tended forests of immense nut-bearing trees, all on a scale so astonishing that it beguiles the imagination. Ueue, to his nature, begins to compose a poem. Coyotzin, Acamapichtli's oldest son starts to speak but stops himself, deciding to stay silent as he is forever tripping over his tongue. Coyotzin is an excellent speaker when no one is listening to him, but with an audience he stumbles and flutters over his words. After but a moment, at a convenient pause in the general conversation, Ueue Zacatzin stands up and recites the poem he has just crafted:

> They call it Teotihuacan,
> For here are the guardians of the land,
> Giants who build temples the size of mountains
> Honoring the vastness of life.

Coyotzin and Miahuitl laugh and clap justifiably proud of their brother, while Acamapichtli murmurs approval of his son's poem though he has missed several of the words. Quinatzin also murmurs his approval, though Quinatzin thinks that within this realm of giants, the jape of Tezcatlipoca, his father is acting a fool, which he expects of him, and so too his brothers.

Lord Acamapichtli, inspired by his son's effort, offers his own poem:

> The blue duck, the golden butterflies, the green
>   quechol,
> Guard our blue waters, green forests, and the
>   yellow rushes,
> And the sweet-voiced zacuan rules the world from
>   its perch.

Words praising the skill of the poets follow. Quinatzin, sharp fingernail of mystery, realizes he has been lost in speculation and has missed portions of the conversation that flows on without him.

"Throughout your history," Aztacoatl tells Acamapichtli, "you have alternated between governments of centralized or decentralized structures of power. A duality, if you will, between too much liberty and excessive order."

Acamapichtli laughs and shakes his head, "I can assure you that the people of Azcapotzalco have just as much liberty and order as necessary."

Aztacoatl grins, "Oh, I'm sure of that. I'll consider that as a point of utmost certainty. But the idea I am trying to convey is this: The concept of government means some will have power over others. However power poisons every hand it touches, so it is intrinsic to governments to degenerate. The best you can do, as far as I can see, is to try and prevent this for as long as possible."

"You suggest, my large friend, that I am not a good king?" Acamapichtli asks, a wide smile upon his face.

"I do not suggest that at all, King Acamapichtli. In fact, as far as such things go I believe you are an excellent king. My point regarding governments is that it is all a question of time; there are slow acting poisons, to make a metaphorical allegory, and there are quick ones. We recognize the quick ones, but the slower ones, well, not so much."

Quinatzin sighs, his patience for the blabbering yopicatl, and for that matter his father too, almost at an end. He wonders why Tezcatlipoca has not yet seen fit to strike down the yopicatl. Perhaps, speculation or daydream, Tezcatlipoca will raise him up to be King-of-Kings. Then he will drive the yopicatl north into the waterless Sacred Lands and make Teotihuacan his summer retreat, and at that idea Quinatzin smiles.

✦ ✦ ✦

"Not true," says Miahuitl to Aztacoatl, shaking her head while wagging a finger before him. Her broad smile seems to illuminate her face, and her dark eyes sparkle. Her name means 'turquoise maize flower.'

"Oh yes, true, princess Miahuitl," Aztacoatl answers, laughing. "You simply don't understand the males of your species. Here, let me give you an example." He turns to Coyotzin, drapes a yopicatl-large arm about his shoulders and, gently tapping Coyotzin's head says to him, "What, in your opinion, now don't be bashful in sharing your opinion with us, I know you are a thinker, is the essence of your existence save but a good many sparkly stones, glittering feathers, several popoloca females arranged for your convenience, ummm. (He pretends to be trying to remember a final point). Oh yes! The whimperings and cries of your defeated enemies. (Everyone is laughing at Aztacoatl's vision of Nahua desire.) Have I forgotten anything, friend Coyotzin?"

For the first time in what seems ages Coyotzin speaks fluently, "All that which you say, and a large hunk of grilled meat."

There are whoops of joy from astonished family and friends, for it has been years since Coyotzin last talked in public without tripping over his words. After a moment Acamapichtli wipes his eyes and hugs his eldest son tightly.

◆ ◆ ◆

Quinatzin wonders how, if his brothers and sister have the same parents, and how they are products of the local environment, which has by and large been the same, they can be so different. It can only be due to the Will of Tezcatlipoca. He looks carefully at his father, then Aztacoatl, thinks, "Jabber. Jabber. Jabber." He does not like how the yopicatl are always smiling, always talking, prattling on about one inane tiresome subject after another. Again he realizes that he has missed part of the conversation, or not conversation so much as sermon, Aztacoatl unceasingly giving forth on one illogical concept after another like the most tedious of priests.

"Some think the lights that roam the night skies do so because they are pulled this way and that by various gods or goddesses," says Aztacoatl, "and of course that explanation works, at a certain level, but you must admit the idea requires a particular set of suppositions, such as there are gods who are capable of moving the lights, and who care enough to do so in a precisely defined and periodic manner. Is this a logical basis for understanding our world? Perhaps, yet I don't think so. However I think a bad theory is better than no theory since it may, at least in part, be true and thus, on occasion, helpful. Or, if that is too obtuse an example, then let's consider something closer to home, dearer to your hearts: arrows. Does an arrow strike where it strikes because it is the Will of Tezcatlipoca? Or does tension and pull on the bow, aim, how well the arrow has been made, and wind of course- albeit the realm of Quetzalcoatl, have something to do with it? I submit, and this is an important step in one's logical development, that you have already come to see the conundrum and made your choice by practicing to become good archers, rather than praying to become good archers." He pauses for a moment, winks, "Of course, doing both doesn't hurt."

✦ ✦ ✦

The stars and moon turn slowly about the other in their nightly dance. Aztacoatl, seemingly inexhaustible, a yopicatl that enjoys sharing ideas and insights, continues, "Take, as an example that comes readily to mind, the opinions we hold of one another, which are in no sense permanent, but rather as fluid as Lake Texcoco. Now why opinions are so important is that your cities, your realms, are yourselves but multiplied in scale. I speak here of the emotional sense, with cities and realms as selfish and cunning, as violent or as generous, as you yourselves can be at a given moment. That is to say, as goes the individual, so goes the realm, and individuals are predictably unpredictable. Or even, let us say, chaotic. Now if you choose to control this chaos, rather than embrace it, then how? Is order kept only by force? Can one reign in material interests, or supersede them, so that wars can be avoided? And by war I simply allude to murder on a significant scale that carries with it, of course, considerable symbolism. Or if you will: opinion. Hence your need, and I don't mean you individually, but that of 'the government,' structure of power, within the context of satisfying Tezcatlipoca, or whoever, for the occasional ritual sacrifice, or sacrifices. For the perception that a nation is afraid to fight may well lead to it having a fight on its hands. That is to say, as illogical as certain structures may be at first glance there in an underlying utility."

Quinatzin, yielding to a strange urge to argue with know-it-all Aztacoatl speaks up, saying, "War keeps a nation strong. Just as chasing deer keeps the wolf strong. It is that simple. It's not about 'structure of power.' "

"And yet, friend Quinatzin," Aztacoatl deftly answers, "it is. Just because one sees a particular slice of existence doesn't mean there isn't more. Many of our thoughts and ideas arrive from imperfect knowledge. Misperceptions, if you will. Not to be trite, but, I admit, nevertheless... Nevertheless... Arghh. I've forgotten the point I was trying to make." Aztacoatl makes a fist, one the size of a popoloca head, and gently knocks upon his skull, "Rattle. Rattle."

"Existence," interjects Aztacoatl's son, Kulcan, who sits nearby, and has heard the fine points of his father's theory on existence well more than once. "Intersection of different realities. Lines and points and so on, imperfect perception."

"Yes. Existence. Thank-you. A broader scope, a greater wealth of experience."

"And you can take this broader scope of experience with you into the next world?" Miahuitl asks.

"Exactly my point," says Aztacoatl. "That is precisely what I am driving at."

The conversation lapses for a moment, the Nahua guests trying to parse the meaning, if any, of what Aztacoatl has just said, or what they think Aztacoatl has just said. They are unsure whether they have heard him correctly, and if they did, did the ideas he has sought to convey by the use of words, and a number of hand gestures, mean the same to all of them, or something slightly different to each individual, with each mind, while of course admitting to great similarity, having their own distinct chemistries.

"And wolves, Quinatzin, coming back to your point, which I think you made, for all their love of tasty deer, given the chance wolves are more than happy to sate themselves on nuts, acorns and the like, and this seems not to have tamed them. So too it seems growing a few acres worth of maize and beans, amaranth and chilies haven't irreversibly damaged the Nahua fighting spirit. Yet we must all admit to a certain quantity of uncertainty, in fact we can take uncertainty as a constant, as that seems the underlying Will of The Unfathomable."

Kulcan thinks of adding a salient point to the conversation his father dominates, as he likes to do, but instead digs into a nearby plate of tamales while his sister Koxocuitl, the two seem ever hungry, focuses her attention on a bowl of maize and pumpkin soup.

Quinatzin is not sure he spoke of wolves, and remains silent while trying to parse the conversational thread.

"Wolves eat nuts?" Miahuitl asks. "I thought they just ate meat."

"A common misconception, Miahuitl. One finds the bones wolves so love to chew, but of nuts, -well, not so much. And as for what does and does not make wolves what they are, that is difficult to precisely say as their plane of existence, thank-you Kulcan, intersects our plane of existence only along a line. Understanding requires a more substantial intersection, or intersections, plural. And from that idea it is but a small-step to recognize that there are dimensional scales to power that are commonly orthogonal. Consider the empire of a tree-scurrying squirrel, a colony of ants, or the city of Azcapotzalco: each has its exclusive portion of time and space, no more, and each, within the context of the infinity that surrounds us, are as equally important."

"So what's your point?" Koxocuitl interjects. (Who only now does Quinatzin, his mind always someplace else, realize is Aztacoatl's daughter).

"Koxocuitl," Quinatzin thinks, "a pretty name."

Koxocuitl pauses to let her father speak, although he seems to have forgotten the conversation having turned his attention to eating. No others speak, perhaps having become confused with Aztacoatl's logical thread, illogical thread, and so Koxocuitl continues, "Some time ago there was a famous Nahua general, you must know of him, who strove to be King-of-Kings. For all the conquering he did, at the end he relinquished the power he had spent his life gaining and retired to a small hut within the deep forests south of Mount Tlaloc."

Koxocuitl turns to Quinatzin, who is listening to her while looking at the last light of day glittering off the heaven-rising smoke of Mount Popocatepetl, and asks, "Are you familiar with his poetry?"

Quinatzin, startled by her question, shakes his head "No," although he knows he has heard a poem or two of the one she speaks of. Then, trick of memory, he suddenly remembers, "You speak of Nicuican? Koxocuitl?" And to his surprise he returns her smile.

"Yes," she says, "Nicuican. Exactly."

Then, the impulse of an instant, as if making a classroom recitation Quinatzin rises to his feet, and precisely annunciating sings out a poem he learned years ago as a child:

When I was young I learned swordplay,
And in this surpassed Quetzalcuah, the general
    known to all the world.
My fame resounded beyond the mountains.
My spirit was as high as the rolling clouds as I ran
    to battle.
My flags and banners snapped in the wind,
And nothing was heard but the song of my drums.
Yet, a fierce anger tears my heart,
In thinking how I have wasted my life.

After a polite duration of silence in which, presumably, the listeners consider the intrinsic meanings of the poem, Kulcan, a smile upon his face that he tries, unsuccessfully, to suppress, offers, "The poem suggests pursuit of an unsound philosophy."

A comment to which all laugh, save but Acamapichtli who has not heard Kulcan.

◆ ◆ ◆

Hours pass when one is wrapped in conversation, vanishing to a one-dimensional point. From below, a realm that darkness has long laid claim to, the voice of a friend calls up to Kulcan. After a nod from his father Kulcan politely excuses himself to vanish, yopicatl-quick, down the steep-sided monument. Acamapichtli observes that the monuments of the yopicatl serve quite well as playgrounds, or their playgrounds as monuments. A heartbeat or two later Koxocuitl excuses herself and, following her older brother, likewise disappears down the steeply defined height; from below one hears her whoop with joy at her newfound liberation.

The Nahua youths envy the yopicatl their freedom, but understand certain paths exclude others, and there is a decorum one expects from children of a king. Miahuitl leaves her cushion to pass among the food-laden tables. She is uncertain as to precisely what she wishes to eat but knows she will find something. Perhaps a plum, or an amaranth seed cake overspread with honey. In an obsidian plate she catches sight of a young woman, to whom she smiles.

10

Tetelpan

S ince childhood King Quinatzin has observed a variety of fates played out on multiple dimensional scales: individual, family, clan, town, and city. He has seen the most sacred treaties of peace sworn to under the most august of circumstances, the drinking of each others blood and so on, casually put aside for within the structures of power few are ever content. Lord Quinatzin has seen soldiers vanish into the smoking mirror of battlefields, and seen free Nahua relinquish their lives to games of chance, be it the casts of dice or the course of a bouncing ball. So too the fate of those following the most humble of paths are prone to risk: the farmer who suffers too much or too little rain, or the woman of the hearth who dies in childbirth. All of which suggests the gods are as dependable as a summer wind, if not capricious, which suggests, exactly… What beyond randomness?

The question arises, how can Nahua achieve peace save but with one ruler? Yet for that here is the puzzle, the enigma: There can only be one King-of-Kings who rules over Nahua, the One World, but two lay claim to the title: King Quinatzin of Azcapotzalco, and King Yacacoatl of Xochimilco, each with their realm of armies and allies. Of the pieces to the puzzle, on the eastern shore of Lake Texcoco the might of Texcoco, allied with Azcapotzalco, is balanced against the realm of Culhuacan, allied with Xochimilco. Chalco, on the southeastern edge of the valley, could readily tip the balance of power but the Queen of Chalco does not dream of empire and Chalco is too strong a realm to be forced into taking sides.

> From afar I hear a song, a flute.
> Here is Chalco, realm of jade mountains,
> Domain of turquoise waters, kingdom of golden
>   maize.
> On the edge of the forest, where lives the puma.
> Close to the snow, where lives the white quail.

Xochimilco lies south of Azcapotzalco, on the southwestern edge of Lake Texcoco. Xochimilco's northern border is defined and defended by the fortress-town of Tetelpan, which lies a small distance south of where the rock escarpment of Chapultepec narrows the lake road to but a few feet in width. For Azcapotzalco to bypass the high stonewalls of Tetelpan and attack Xochimilco is to have a Tetelpan army at your back. Conversely, to besiege Tetelpan is to have a Xochimilco army at your back. Quinatzin does not have sufficient forces to simultaneously invest Tetelpan and face the Xochimilco armies. Such is the knot of the puzzle that Quinatzin seeks to unravel.

Lord Quinatzin, Senior General Cuauh Petlauh, King Copiltzin of Texcoco, various allied kings and their generals have met many times to consider how Tetelpan might be taken, but the high stone walls have stood for many years and successfully resisted all attempts at conquest. The crenellated walls are well defended with guards who, on pain of death, are unceasingly alert. The outer walls are too smooth to climb, while ladders that reach the parapet height can be easily pushed away or set afire. Fertile fields surround the town the bounty of which fills its extensive granaries, and within its walls one finds several spring-fed fountains. Behind the walls the roofs of the buildings are stuccoed, making them immune to fire arrows. Some suggest the construction of ramps, or towers, but this would take time, certainly time enough for a Xochimilco army to arrive at your back.

◆ ◆ ◆

One Azcapotzalco general, General Hualatzin, successfully argues for an attack under the cover of darkness using ladders with the vanguard dressed and armed as Chalco warriors. All to the good if the attack succeeds, while if the attack fails Xochimilco will view Chalco as an enemy, to the advantage of Azcapotzalco. A reasonable plan, perhaps, if taken as a plan of desperation, but for that it seems as likely to succeed as any that can be imagined. All that is required is secrecy and a lack of diligence by those who guard the crenelated walls, of which there is neither. A number of Azcapotzalco soldiers are slain, an almost equal number captured, and the remainder shamefully scattered into concealing darkness. General Hualatzin and the captains who led the failed attack, all of whom managed to survive the battle, are called before Quinatzin, who sagely considers both what is said and unsaid.

After due reflection, Lord Quinatzin says, "I would have had you return victorious, or not at all." Lord Quinatzin orders General Hualatzin and his captains strangled, and their bodies thrown into the fields for the birds and coyotes.

◆ ◆ ◆

Quinatzin then calls his wizards and sorcerers before him who arrive bearing that which enhances their powers: one carries a hollow gold sphere inscribed in strange runes that none are able to decipher; one carries the brain pan of his father, who in his day was a most powerful wizard; one carries a gold vessel full of a certain sand that, given a chance, escapes into the air; one carries a long-necked gold vessel full of oil the very tip of which has been set alight and burns with a compelling odor; some carry devices made from unknown metals; some carry strings, others kernels of maize that when cast onto water reveal the future; some carry crystals that cast out scintillating spectrums of light; within a carefully sealed silver vase one carries a type of oil that has been mixed with salt, sulfur, and a powder made by crushing a certain reddish-brown stone that bursts into flame when cast out upon the earth or water; more than one wears bracelets and beads carved from bones each of which is larger than a man. Quinatzin orders these enchanters to cast down the walls of Tetelpan.

Taken as a whole the magicians seem ill at ease with the order. "There are realms and realms," one wizard advises Lord Quinatzin, "the realm in which our powers hold sway and the realm of stone. The two realms are, it might be said, orthogonal. That is, non-intersecting."

"Have no doubt, Lord Quinatzin," another mage interjects, "on your behalf we already contest with Xochimilco. The air, the earth, and the water are filled with spirit contesting spirit. Cihuacoatl, Goddess of Childbirth, protector of Tetelpan and Xochimilco, is a powerful goddess."

"More powerful than Xihcutli?" Quinatzin sharply asks.

"No. No." The mage quickly answers. "But powerful, to be sure."

Quinatzin considers all that has been said and unsaid by the wizards, and says to those gathered before him, "I want the walls of Tetelpan cast down. You have ten days."

The magicians, dismissed, bow their heads and depart.

✦ ✦ ✦

That night the moon, a thin sliver in the western sky, and a myriad of stars set against the encompassing soot-like darkness find one of Lord Quinatzin's string-casters, chest like a bird of prey, bushy eyebrows, large eyes, prominent thin nose, within the courtyard of his house accompanied by his keen-eyed daughter. The girl is lean, strong, and though but twelve years old almost as tall as her father. Father and daughter squat upon their heels and gaze intently upon the smooth surface of a water-filled ceramic basin. The man gently drops a cluster of strings upon the water, which father and daughter watch with rapt attention. The message within the strings is so obvious to them that after a few moments, in an abrupt movement, the father sweeps the strings up from the water, squeezes them dry, and tosses them into the hearth fire.

The two wait until the water within the basin is motionless, and then the daughter gently drops a swirl of strings upon its surface, and the strings, some function of gravity, temperature, surface tension, local air currents, string mass and surface area, float or sink and in so doing turn one direction or another. Again, to father and daughter the message within the strings is so clear that there is no need for discussion between them. The father sweeps up this second cluster of strings, squeezes them dry and drops them in the fire, and then empties the water from the basin onto the roots of the blossoming plum tree within the courtyard. The daughter, some confusing mix of excitement and sadness, gazes about her home that she must now leave. The man quietly awakens the rest of the family who, without a sound, quickly gather up food and prized possessions of little weight. Then silent as wolves the family disappears into the western forests.

II

Sorcerers and Magicians

For the task Quinatzin has assigned his sorcerers and magicians, to cast down the walls of Tetelpan, each wizard and sorcerer journeys to the place that gives them utmost power. Some enter the absolute darkness of caves deep within the mountains and there, seated within the confines of magical symbols drawn upon sand floors offer up their blood and invocations. Some eat certain leaves or mushrooms putting themselves into a realm where they are given the strength of giants and so can reach out and stone by stone tear apart the walls of Tetelpan. Some cast certain powders into sacred fires while reciting enchantments that will cause the walls of Tetelpan to catch flame. Some conjure for winds to fall upon the citadel, and others call upon the very earth to shake the walls to rubble. Some stand upon Chapultepec, which overlooks Tetelpan to the south, and call upon the

Lord of Mictlan to claim those of the town. Others, of a more unsavory nature, enwrap themselves in serpents and call upon their brethren to fall upon the fortress and overwhelm it.

Of the wizards who survive the casting of their spells, and not all have, undone by having to control such tremendous powers, they arrive before Quinatzin to admit defeat. As he listens to their excuses Lord Quinatzin carefully considers the constancy of matter, or at least stone- certainly a stone stays a stone, for the most part, though wood, for example, is transitory, subject to change. Yet there are mysteries, a great many mysteries. At times Popocatepetl is quiescent, and at other times pours forth liquid-rock and shakes the very earth. At times the water of Lake Texcoco, though there be no wind, boils and froths. Then there are rainbows, and sometimes double or even triple rainbows. There are those who cast quite accurate premonitions of death, and of death, those on the very edge speak of seeing loved ones, a realm of flowers and light, and rise up into the sky to see the earth revealed beneath them as they fly to the 13 folds of Heaven. Then there are those who recall previous lives in astonishing detail, small children who recall, for example, the exploits of a warrior chief who lived eighty years ago two hundred miles away, or the life of a humble stone cutter whose beloved wife, for whom he still grieves, died in childbirth. Then too Quinatzin knows of temples that have been struck with lightning under a clear sky, and for that matter once a temple simply burst into flames when the sky did not hold a single cloud. Then of course there is the mystery of light, or sound, or the senses, or childbirth, and so on. One exists surrounded by mysteries, by incomprehensible forces.

"How is it possible that you were all defeated?" Quinatzin asks his conjurers. "How is it possible that each and every one of you were overthrown? Why do I have wizards and enchanters in my kingdom? In what way do you serve me?"

After some moments one of the eldest wizards speaks up, saying, "Lord Quinatzin; Xochimilco has sent dark, unseen forces upon you that are intent upon your destruction. Most of our energies are consumed in protecting you, and Azcapotzalco, from these evils."

Quinatzin reflects on this for a moment, remembering a story told by his Uncle Totomotzin, who once within the marketplace of Azcapotzalco came upon a forest recluse who, visiting the city, wore about his neck a wreath of the night-blossoming flower that gives off the gagging smell of two-week old death.

Totomotzin had stopped the man at a distance and asked him, "Why do you wear such a vile thing?"

"To keep jaguars away," he replied.

Totomotzin laughed, "There are no jaguars here in Azcapotzalco."

"For which you may thank me," the man had promptly answered.

"They are idiots who do nothing while protecting me from nothing," Quinatzin thinks, and orders the wizards and seers thrown into cages.

Quinatzin then calls to purpose his counselors and sage judges, to whom he says, "We have entrusted these sorcerers and wizards to guard and protect us. Yet for that they lie to us, mock us, saying they have powers when they do not, -or if they have such powers they disregard my orders to put them to use. Just as I reward those who fulfill their obligations, those who do not must be held accountable. Hence, I order them to be strangled. However to die is natural and is a fate that awaits us all, and so to order their death is little. For ignoring the demands of their duties they must be erased from the earth in such a way that none will remember they existed. I order the justices to go to their houses and see that their wives and children are sold into perpetual slavery, and their houses emptied and razed to the ground so that no memory of them will remain."

Quinatzin then orders his aides to find new sorcerers and enchanters who will take great care in their duties, their spells, and their prognostications. Yet for that time passes with the riddle of Tetelpan unsolved.

12

A Puzzle Does Not Solve Itself

———

With no viable stratagem for reducing Tetelpan, at a point of desperation Quinatzin decides to speak with Aztacoatl, realizing of course that instead of learning how to take the fortress he will receive some interminable yopicatl lecture on a topic both irrelevant and useless. Nevertheless in a swift *acalli* of some 40 paddlers Quinatzin travels to Texcoco, the next day ranging up and down the hills by which one comes to Teotihuacan. He leaves his guards at the edge of the yopicatl realm, there shouldering the finely woven basket of avocados he has had brought as a gift, for though the yopicatl have no shortage of these it seems the soil of Azcapotzalco gives the avocados a taste that the yopicatl much admire. Quinatzin makes his way into the heart of

Teotihuacan, realm of towering architecture that dwarfs mere man, and arrives at the house of Aztacoatl.

"So, quite a surprise," Aztacoatl says warmly, beaming out a bright smile. "Not that you're too far away for an occasional visit, of course." He pats King Quinatzin on the back. "But I know you have a good many cares and concerns, King Quinatzin."

Though Quinatzin has mixed emotions, being King of Azcapotzalco and but a small step away from being King-of-Kings, he bows most respectfully to Aztacoatl, who he has come to like, in a fashion, over the years since they first met when he was, -young.

"I don't interrupt?" Quinatzin asks.

"Not at all!" Aztacoatl says. "We always have room at the table for an unexpected visitor." Aztacoatl hefts the basket of avocados Quinatzin has brought, "This is a treat! I thank you."

Quinatzin inquires into Aztacoatl's family, and Aztacoatl inquires into Quinatzin's family, and so goes the chitchat. After a time Aztacoatl asks, "Now what motivates your visit, Lord Quinatzin, King Quinatzin, carrying a basket of these extraordinary avocados? Though I'm delighted to see you and have a nice chat, I can't help but thinking that, being king, you have much else to attend to." Aztacoatl pauses for a moment, smiles. "You know King Yacacoatl, the illustrious King of Xochimilco, was here a month or so ago, and he struck me as someone who, my opinion, you have a lot in common with. I think, again just my opinion, hypothesis you might say, the two of you could be good friends."

Quinatzin's mind races through possible consequences

of King Yacacoatl visiting the yopicatl, comes to no clear vision of an idea, or specific threat, yet feels threatened. Then, speaking carefully, with a deliberate cadence, Quinatzin says, "You are shrewd to observe the many conflicts among us. If the Nahua were united under one ruler…"

"You'd war on us," Aztacoatl says, polishing off an avocado.

Quinatzin starts to speak, but before he can Aztacoatl continues, "No need to answer, just making a jest. Or, well, maybe not a jest, never mind. Certainly I understand, for one, that authority will ever enlarge itself. Indefinitely. Or to say it differently, continuously, until it encounters a boundary, something that pushes back with equal force. A rule of nature, force equals counterforce. But you suggest, to your line of thought, that if someone ruled the whole valley, the One World, instead of devoting your time and energy to fighting each other you'd do great things, what with all living in peace. Yes? Or do I misunderstand?"

Quinatzin nods.

"And all that stands in the way of this vision of brotherly love is Xochimilco, or more specifically the fortress of Tetelpan?"

Aztacoatl falls silent, waiting (yopicatl-patient) to see what Quinatzin has to say, which is, "Might you share with me a trick, or clue, as to how Tetelpan can be captured?"

Aztacoatl pauses, sighs, scratches an arm, says, "Not to hurt your feelings, but since you're here, I know of no species save your own so steadily and systematically employed in the destruction of itself. What you call civilization, central government, King-of-Kings and on up the ladder, produce no other effect than to allow you to war, on all things, on an ever increasing scale. But, more to the point of your question we, by which I of course mean we yopicatl, have agreed among us not to teach you anything in the realm of weapons or war for, almost all here are convinced, soon or late everything we taught you would come right back at us. Sharp end first. Consider what happened to Xihcutli, not the god, but *the* Xihcutli, Xihcutli himself, you know the story, of course, though actually you probably don't."

Quinatzin shakes his head; he does not know the story.

"Oh. Well, the original Xihcutli figured out how spinning a hardwood stick upon a softwood base creates enough heat to get a fire going. An invention for which he was well rewarded, as you can imagine I'm sure. Well rewarded."

Aztacoatl looks carefully at his companion, who does not seem to imagine how Xihcutli was rewarded.

"Jewels?" Quinatzin finally suggests. "Land?"

"Really?" Aztacoatl laughs, "The King of Azcapotzalco, Honorary High Priest of This That and The Other, and so on, can't imagine how he was rewarded? No? (Pause.) Well, fire is not all good, you know, there are downsides. Burned fingers, hair, and clothes. Houses catch on fire and turn to ash with the occasional child or grandparent inside. Let's just say Xihcutli's discovery was not universally welcomed. There was pushback. You know how it goes: 'god/goddess so-and-so wants us to

eat our meat raw, or He/She would have given us fire.'
A distrust of change seems intrinsic to your species.
Which is not all bad, of course. Often enough it saves
your society from racing off after the idiotic idea of the
moment. There is a balance, needless to say. A duality!
(He winks.)

"But, things may not have balanced out for Xihcutli,
the Xihcutli, as he would have liked. In the end, or his
end, his friends and neighbors made a good-sized fire
(dramatic pause), and threw him into it. Then not too
long afterwards they decided fire was, after all, a positive
development, that perhaps god so-and-so *did* want them
to grill their meat, and had sent the secret of fire to none
other but Xihcutli, and throwing him into the fire was,
in some sort of nagging sense, wrong, and so before you
know it Xihcutli was stealing fire from the gods, and
Xihcutli was, after all, a god himself, and so now others
get to be thrown in the fire to sustain dear ol' Xihcutli."
Aztacoatl pauses, looks carefully at Quinatzin, then at
his left knee which he scratches carefully, sighs, adds,
"Not that there is anything wrong with that. Not for me
to lecture on the moral ugliness of the world."

Quinatzin rocks his head back, asks, "How do you
know all this?"

"Yes, well, that's a question, isn't it?" Aztacoatl replies,
then pauses for a moment. "A very interesting question.
Though we've known each other for some time we've
never really talked that much, or more correctly talked
seriously, you being ever so busy with becoming King,
then being King. Or now, scheming to be King-of-Kings.
So let me tell you: The Outliers, of course. They visit us,

not infrequently." He pauses, for a moment turns his gaze to a distant cloud then back to Quinatzin; "You have no idea what I am talking about, do you?"

Quinatzin shakes his head: No.

"Yes, no. Well then, how best to explain this without stretching your credulity? First principles: we are born, we live, and we die. A universal truth." Aztacoatl pauses a moment, smiles. "I submit, however, with utmost respect that this is an assumption on your part. You see a lot of deaths, certainly, but often enough people just disappear out of your life, or anyone's lives, so you really don't have any idea what happened to them. And, you judge a person's age by their appearance, no more no less, it's not like you can pull a hair or a tooth and count the rings, can you? No. So. Now consider how as a child your body faithfully refreshes itself. A bruise? A cut? In a day all will be healed. Your muscles are firm, your skin elastic! Then presto! Before you know it your body is in a full-scale rebellion all the while slowly sagging Earthwards. Now keep in mind, I do not speak of external influences such as spears or a sharp dart. But as to internal mechanics, it's simply an issue of probability. One out of a large number of each species is a freak of nature, you might say, or an Outlier, whose body purrs along ever so fine, maturing to an ideal vigor and then staying there indefinitely. Indefinitely, as in more or less forever."

"Forever?" Quinatzin raises his eyebrows, looks carefully at Aztacoatl for the suggestion of a joke. "This is real? Fact?"

"Fact. It's simple statistics. Some of each species live but a day, or a breath, some essentially live forever."

Quinatzin's head bounces back a small bit; he raises his eyebrows and shakes his head. "Difficult to believe. Though it makes sense. Perfect sense. Remarkable."

Aztacoatl smiles. "Yes. Remarkable." He pauses, takes a deep breath. "But, as to these Outliers among us, they have some tales to tell! It would do you well to talk with one, or rather not talk but listen, listen carefully, as they can be very informative."

"Why don't I know of these people?" Quinatzin asks.

"Well, obviously, they can't stay around, all their friends dying while they stay young. You know as well as I that if discovered they would be tied up, imprisoned, emptied of their blood that the powerful would swill down like *chocolatl*. No, after awhile they have to disappear, live here then there, or live as some wise hermit/hermitress in a mountain fastness. But, to answer your question, I know the story of Xihcutli because I heard it from one who knew him personally. And if you remain king long enough, or King-of-Kings (Aztacoatl winks), and don't pose too much of a threat, one of these folks will more than likely knock on your door, and be sure to listen to them, that's my advice, listen carefully."

Quinatzin considers this in silence for a time then, after a moment, suggests, "Under one ruler, the Nahua Valley…"

His yopicatl patience exhausted Aztacoatl rolls his eyes skyward, raises up a hand and interrupts, "How long do you think your 'one ruler' model will last? Never mind, I know the answer, and be that as it may you really don't need any advice from me as to Tetelpan. You are a clever species, clever as spiders, and someone will discover a trick to capture the fortress. It's in the natural order of things. Measure. Counter-measure. Arrows. Shields. Shield-puncturing arrows. Escalation, it's called. I can scarcely imagine what your species will be up to a thousand years from now, and I don't want to imagine."

Aztacoatl leaves off talking, instead whistles the up-up-up, sharp descent, up-up-up, sharp-descent, lilting song of a miaua bird, and then laughs at his own joke, a deep-seated reverberating yopicatl laugh.

13

Lady Xocotzin

———

S eason gives way to season. Quinatzin cannot help but remember the woodcutter who revealed the path that lead to the defeat of Xilotepec, and imagine that Xihcutli will send another such agent of victory. Then he thinks that perhaps he should help Xihcutli help himself. As it is no secret, or at least less than surprising someone might want to capture Tetelpan, just as there are those who would wish to capture Azcapotzalco, if possible, or almost any town or city, at a point of desperation Quinatzin asks his generals to ask their captains if they know how Tetelpan can be taken, and have the captains ask their warriors, and the warriors ask their wives, and their children. Ask everyone: fishermen, porters, silversmiths and feather-weavers, ask those who sell spices or wood within the marketplace, who cast and shape copper, ask those who sweep the streets each morning.

✦ ✦ ✦

Just north of Chapultepec, along the edge of marshes fed by the crystalline waters of the Chapultepec spring, lives a woman we met briefly before, Xoco, with her new husband Aquicatl. For his ill-advised wagers on dice[10] games Aquicatl now serves Lord Ocuilatzin, Speaker of the town of Chapultepec, as a slave during daylight hours, overseeing his gardens and orchard, and so he will for three more years.

> Nimbly they leap upward, then downward they
> fall;
> Though handless, they overpower the man with
> hands.
> Cast on the board like bits of magic,
> They burn the heart to ashes.

Xoco is a fowler, and so supports her family; she weaves nets, sets nets, captures the harvest of the air and, depending upon the bird, sells the meat or feathers. Seeing no small number of people climb upon the height of Chapultepec and there gaze upon Tetelpan, Xoco asks her husband what provokes such behavior.

"I do not know," he says, "but will ask Lord Ocuilatzin."

A few days later Aquicatl is able to tell his wife why so many gaze upon Tetelpan and, considering this, she says, "Oh. I know."

But though she says she knows she will not tell her husband, for she knows many are unable to hold secrets,

---

10 *Patolli.*

particularly those prone to wagering their lives on the outcome of a game. After a time Lord Ocuilatzin, having heard from Aquicatl that Xoco knows, or says she knows, calls upon her, and raises the question, but though Xoco's husband is bound to serve Lord Ocuilatzin she is not. However, she confirms to Lord Ocuilatzin that, "Yes, I do know how Tetelpan might be taken and no, I will not tell you, for a secret revealed is no longer a secret."

◆ ◆ ◆

Some religions suggest you can speak with god directly, while others suggest the need for a hierarchical chain of filters, and so it can be in the earthly realm, so much smoke rising up to heaven, with Lord Ocuilatzin speaking to a friend, who speaks to another, so on until word reaches King Quinatzin of a curious woman, a fowler who plies the Chapultepec marshes who says she knows the tug and pull that will unravel the knot of Tetelpan.

King Quinatzin orders Xoco brought before him, and we now see them in the council hall where Quinatzin sits upon the *icpalli* while Xoco kneels before him upon a finely woven soft mat laid upon the chamber floor of polished stone.

"You are a fowler?" Lord Quinatzin asks.

"Yes, Lord Quinatzin," she answers, bowing her head even lower.

"And you know how I may capture Tetelpan? A feat no general no wizard nor priest has been able to do."

Her head bowed, gazing at the floor, she murmurs, "Yes, Lord Quinatzin, I believe I do."

"And you have told no one this trick, or stratagem, nor will tell anyone save me?"

"No, Lord Quinatzin," she says. "Or rather, yes, Lord Quinatzin. I have told no one. One tells one, who tells another. Soon the secret is no longer a secret."

Quinatzin muses on this, knowing the wisdom of what she says. He considers how if the woman jokes, or suggests the use of ladders, he will have her staked to the ground within the forest, have honey poured over her, or perhaps blood, and left there to be eaten by, -something.

"To solve a puzzle no one else can," Quinatzin observes, "is a rare accomplishment. I am known for rewarding those as they serve me, good or ill. And so, I ask you now to share with me your secret."

"Each morning at sunrise, Lord Quinatzin," Xoco begins, "the many birds that live in Tetelpan leave to drink at the edge of the marshes just south of Chapultepec. They spend the day foraging in the fields, then at dusk return to their nests."

Quinatzin weighs her words, and asks, "And how does this reduce the walls of Tetelpan?"

"My lord, you do not need destroy the walls to capture the fortress. The roofs of Tetelpan are thatch, and though covered with stucco will burn from underneath. The birds nest within the thatch."

His patience at an end, Quinatzin is ready to signal for his guards (in fact he can feel a muscle in his right arm twitch to do just that), but then he understands. He too now knows how to capture the smooth-walled fortress and claps his hands in joy.

"How many birds leave Tetelpan each morning, and how many of these can you catch?"

"Hundreds, many hundreds leave Tetelpan each morning," she answers, "and how many of these we catch depends upon how many nets we set about the marshes."

"A hundred torches," Quinatzin says, a smile shining upon his lips. He slaps his hands upon his thighs in delight, stands up and paces about the room. "Hundreds of torches! You can you do this?"

"My nets, Lord Quinatzin, my fingers are sufficient for perhaps fifty birds in a day. Perhaps forty. My lord will require many nets and nimble hands, the labor of Azcapotzalco's fowlers for a day. So too my Lord will require a few pots of tar, and lengths of string. So too, we will need seed and worms to sustain the captured birds during the day. We will need helpers so that all the birds, their strings lit, are released at the same moment, at twilight. Finally, my lord will require an Azcapotzalco force to wait outside the gates of the town for when they open."

Quinatzin motions to one of the guards who stands against the near wall, commands him; "Bring Cuauh Petlauh."

When the general arrives Quinatzin informs him; "This is Lady Xocotzin.[11] She will tell you what is needed for the attack on Tetelpan. For this purpose, you will obey her orders as you do mine."

Quinatzin then returns his attention to her, says, "Pray this works, Lady Xocotzin, for if it does all the lands of Tetelpan are yours."

---

11 The 'tzin' ending of a name indicates the equivalent of Lord or Lady.

Third Bundle

14

The Return of Kulcan

Kulcan, a yopicatl we have met briefly before, has been on a Wandering, as the yopicatl call their journeys of a decade or more in which they pass across the world, following the endless horizon to admire its many sights, and by so doing give thanks to Tloque Nahuaque, The Eternal, for creation of such beauty. Returning home after so much time, nearing Teotihuacan, Kulcan slowly becomes dazzled by what has become of a once familiar landscape as he passes village after village, town after town, and city after city of popoloca that had not been there when he had left. "Poof!" He thinks. "I leave for a moment and they cover the world."

That the popoloca have so covered the land is as unreal to him as if he had long slept and awoken in a land of talking monkeys. From a distance he observes what can only be popoloca priests, painted foot to forehead in black-oily soot. "Curious," Kulcan thinks. He comes to a realization that while on his Wandering everything about the popoloca has become that much greater, as though multiplied by a large integer, but more than this there is an undeniable underlying feeling of unfamiliarity. (Argue over what is real or vision as you will, this much is true: life is flux.) Ill at ease, Kulcan calms himself by trying to parse out one of the subtle riddles The Unfathomable has put before the world:

$$100 = 1 + 2 + 3 + 4 + 5 + 6 + 7 + 8 \times 9$$
$$100 = 1 \times 2 \times 3 - 4 \times 5 + 6 \times 7 + 8 \times 9$$

In the dusk of twilight Kulcan first sees from a distance, gains upon, and then draws even with two popoloca boys upon the trail, each lost to his purpose of carrying a sack of gourds equal in size to himself, and so engrossed are they in their physical struggle that they are oblivious to the yopicatl until he speaks to them, observing, "That's a lot of gourds."

Catching sight of Kulcan the two boys each stare in open-mouthed silence. Kulcan looks behind him to see if there is some lurking danger but there is simply an orchard and so, logical deduction, it must be him that the boys are surprised by. He waits for the boys to speak, but they don't, so after a time in which his yopicatl patience becomes exhausted Kulcan breaks the silence, says, "I am Kulcan, or when so hailed, answer."

Tired of the boys unwavering stare, Kulcan bugs his eyes out at them and stares back, asking, "You've never seen a Yopicatl before?"

"No," the taller of the two boys says. "They said you were all dead."

"I don't think so. Here, let me help you with your sacks." Eagerly the boys hand over their burdensome loads; Kulcan grasps the two sacks in one massive hand and casually swings them over his shoulder.

"Wait. What do you mean by 'All dead'?"

The shorter boy enthusiastically chirps-up, "There was a war, or a battle. Something. You giants tried to take over Nahua. Though some say differently."

Kulcan tries to parse out the words of the boy, wondering if the lad speaks some unquestionable truth or merely repeats a confused tale, so it is with the young, you get one or the other. He assumes, reasonable likelihood, the later, as the first idea is absurd, but then again he knows that when in doubt always opt for what is absurd as it is probably the truth, and now Kulcan is confused, and believes the children are confused.

"Very interesting," he says. "What's up with your priests? Worshipping the god of soot?"

"It's *Teocualli*,"[12] offers the taller boy. "A special ointment they rub upon themselves."

"You're not a ghost?" Asks the shorter of the two boys.

"No, I don't think so."

"Where do you live?"

"Teotihuacan."

Taller: "Are you the ghost of Teotihuacan?"

"That's an odd question. I've been away for awhile, on a Wandering."

---

12 *Teo* is 'Holy' or 'God,' and *cualli* is food.

"Where have you been wandering?"

"The world. I saw the world, -forests that never end, mountains that defy the very words that one might use to describe them. Ice realms, water realms. It's quite a place, the world. Yet for all that it's good to be home. So what is this special ointment? I know your Holy men love their mushrooms, and how said mushrooms might be considered the balanced apex of duality: To cling to existence eat anything, then strained by existence eat something that allows your mind to escape it."

"The venomous black and pink lizard," Taller informs Kulcan.

"And the shaking serpent, who mixes its poison when needed," Shorter adds. "The lizards and shaking serpents are provoked with a piece of meat, which they bite, filling it with their venom. The meat is then pressed to release the liquid and this, in a large mortar, is mixed with ash from the sacred braziers."

"And-" Kulcan begins.

"Then tobacco water is mixed in, and ground centipedes, certain spiders, and scorpions."

"And this is what they rub on themselves?"

"Yes, but first into this they mix ground *ololiuhqui*[13] seeds," Shorter continues. "Or at least that is what is said. Then black hairy worms."

"And this, this is what they rub on themselves?" Kulcan asks, incredulous.

"And soot, from pine torches."

"It gives them courage and visions."

"I don't doubt it," Kulcan offers, most earnestly.

---

13   Seeds of the Morning Glory, a known hallucinogen.

"So armed," interjects Taller, "they are able to perform certain rites."

"Yeah. Well, you know…"

"They say it was the blackened-priests who convinced the soldiers to kill all of you, or, rather…"

"No," Shorter interrupts. "It was the amulets, they gave the soldiers amulets to wear that protected them."

"Kill all of who?" Kulcan asks, "Or whom?" But in asking he comes to a perceived total, summation from zero to N, which is to say: A revelation. Kulcan stops in the middle of the footpath, swaying as if in the throes of an unseen wind. He kneels down, eye level with the boys, and speaking slowly, carefully, asks, "You're saying the blackened-priests, or soldiers, killed the Yopicatl? That is to say, us 'giants'?"

"That's why we thought you were a ghost," answers Taller. "It's said, now said, that Teotihuacan is haunted by a yopicatl ghost. Or perhaps ghosts, plural, suggesting a number more than one. And there are relics."

"Relics?" Kulcan asks sharply.

The boys fall silent.

"Relics like wine-cups made from gold-plated skulls?"

"It's said King Copiltzin has a garden," offers Shorter, "bordered with, urr. Umm."

"The Temple of Tlaloc,[14] urrr, well." Taller's voice trails off to a startled emptiness, and the two boys take to silently gazing at their feet.

Kulcan suddenly feels as if he is swimming through sand. He asks himself: What has become of the world

---

14 Tlaloc, The God of Rain, Lightning, and Thunder; He Who Makes Things Sprout.

I knew? Where in the three times is this land? He thinks, supposition, that perhaps he has entered some interpenetrating world where a different sun glows and other stars shine over another race of beings. He knows that his life, that which he once knew, is over, and that now a very new life has begun. He returns the boys their sacks, nods farewell, and yopicatl-silent vanishes into the encompassing darkness.

15

In Which We First Meet Tlaloc

Kulcan prowls about Teotihuacan, that which he knows as home, knew as home, and finds it empty of yopicatl, the city transformed into a popoloca Tlaloc-dedicated ecosystem of priestly hierarchy. Yopicatl-silent, Kulcan climbs up the northern moon-shadowed side of what is now Temple Tlaloc, known to Kulcan by another name, but no matter; after all life is change. Upon the height of what is now Temple Tlaloc Kulcan pauses to gaze, to the south, upon Popocatepetl, sending forth a plume of smoke illuminated from above by the radiance of the uncountable stars, from below by the orange-red glow of cauldron-fire, and within the smoke itself the occasional flicker of lightning.

There now stands upon the height of Temple Tlaloc a

sky-reaching shrine, all glory to Tlaloc, of steeply angled roof, timber and thatch, walls of mortared stone, the interior gained by a single entrance. Kulcan looks more closely about him and sees a number of priests each armed with their rank-denoting badge and a weapon of some sort, no matter. There are two who watch the stars turn about and, at the proper moment, sound out the markings of time upon a gong made of silver inlaid with gold bands, and there are two whose duty is to ensure the sacred fire, bound within its fathom-wide earthen saucer raised up upon a tripod of stone, remains eternally burning.

Kulcan slips through the doorway of the shrine and arrives before the simulacrum of Tlaloc, a long-standing god who the popoloca took to worshipping when they first took to cultivating fields, and why not? For without rain there is no life. Yet the effigies of Tlaloc, as Kulcan once recognized him, were carved and shaped as a kindly old popoloca of placid countenance; He who brought gentle night-rains. Now, modern times, the Tlaloc Kulcan stands before is… -different, an idol carved of dark wood, he and the idol are almost of a height, shaped and polished shiny red stones for eyes; a fanged-mouth. Tlaloc's face is no longer painted in gentle greens and blues, but red and orange, a god of tender nourishing rains given over to a punishing, easily angered god. In one upraised hand he holds a sinuous thunderbolt, and in his other hand, held out before him palm-up, a burning censer of copal. Upon his head a tiara of feathers and heat-burst maize kernels. His arms and chest adorned with bands of gold. After a moment's reflection Kulcan realizes the appearance of Tlaloc suggests the horror of drought.

Behind this Tlaloc-sanctum Kulcan finds two smaller rooms. Seeking the one which Shorter and Taller were so reluctant to speak of, parable of choice, he enters the room on the right to find any number of chests holding some feathers, a few gems, and various cotton garments. Tiaras hang from hooks set within the walls, great ornamental creations, so too cloaks of exquisite colors. There are shelves of books. Kulcan leaves the finery behind, passing into the other room. When The Immanent first made the world, Distant Time, the rivers flowed in both directions: upstream on the one side, downstream on the other, but at the border between the two there was a thin membrane of confusion, and so Kulcan feels as he steps into the other room, progression of events, and there finds his beloved friend Chimal, not Chimal, who has been killed, emptied of biological matter, and stuffed- presumably with dried grass or the like, mounted upright upon a wood frame, and who now sports two large emeralds for eyes.

Kulcan carefully examines Chimal, his friend-once-friend during what now seems an illusionary past, and cannot help but be impressed with the skill of the taxidermist. After a moment he softly pats his friend, once-friend, on the arm and leaves the shrine, coming upon the two priests whose purpose is to watch the stars turn and swirl about. Swiftly, yopicatl-silent, he grabs each priest by their neck, pinching just so, intending to gently knock their heads together so as to have them sleep for a bit while he talks with The High Priest[15] of Tlaloc. A small, relatively gentle, benevolent bump, yet

15 *Tlamacazqui.*

for all Kulcan's kind intentions he is much angrier than he recognizes, which is to suggest that their colliding skulls make a void-like cracking clunking sound, perhaps like that of a hollow stone falling from a height; there is a spray of popoloca memories, thoughts, hopes, and aspirations. He had meant the priests no great harm, but so things go.

Kulcan swiftly lopes to the front of the shrine where sit the two priests tasked with tending the sacred fire, each to their purpose of adding more bark, resin, or wood. Yopicatl-swift Kulcan grabs a priest in each hand, holding firm to an arm just below their shoulder. Kulcan, right-handed so, as convenient, primal urge, which is to say we live and die in the midst of marvels, without premeditated thought finds himself throwing said priest in said right hand as far off the temple height as he can into the encompassing darkness. Kulcan listens, and after a moment hears an unusual sound, solid yet hollow, hard and yet soft, -difficult, precisely, to describe.

Kulcan looks closely into the eyes of the priest in his left hand, brings the index finger of his right hand to the tip of the priest's nose, which he gently flattens, whispers, "Difficult to predict the fate that awaits us." He beams out a big, yopicatl-friendly smile, "Sorry for the disturbance. I am late for a meeting with the High Priest of Tlaloc, and my anger got the best of me. If you would please tell me where I might find him. Should you do so, I would be happy to release you. Unharmed."

The priest motions towards the rear of the temple height. Kulcan carries him there, to overlook the hallowed Tlaloc compound below. Away from the light of the sacred fire Kulcan notices, indeed takes a moment to consider, how dazzling and encompassing the stars of the night are, the White Path reaching from horizon to horizon.

The priest points to a house nested within the priestly cloister below. "A fine house," Kulcan observes. "Suitable for The High Priest of Tlaloc." Kulcan pauses for an instant, says, "You have been helpful to me, friend priest, for which I am grateful and, as I said, it is my intention to release you, unharmed." Kulcan then spins about as one does to hurl a discus, gaining speed through the spin, and with the speed energy, and momentum- that is a desire not to come to rest. A yopicatl of his word, Kulcan releases the priest unharmed into the darkness, who becomes but another sine and cosine defined arc passing through moonlight, yet another poor victim of the iron fist of gravity. And so Kulcan finds himself alone upon what was once the great monument of Teotihuacan, which was once home, but is no longer home. Kulcan quickly returns to the sacred fire and heaps upon it a goodly pile of godly wood, not his purpose to insult Tlaloc by letting the fire go out, then hops down from the temple height, clambers over the wall that sets the house of the high priest apart, pushes aside the finely woven cloth that hangs across the entrance, bends his head down to pass through the doorway, and enters. Surprise.

16

In Which We First Meet Night Axe

———

The High Priest of Tlaloc, ensconced under his blankets, sleeps peacefully. A man whose once obsidian-black hair is now decorated with gray, a man who has outlasted many summers. Kulcan sits beside the high priest, notices the softness of the thick reed mats covering the stone floor, reaches over and gently prods him, says, "How strange to awake from a dream into another dream. I once had a dream in which I was a butterfly, fluttering here and there as a butterfly, thinking as a butterfly, desiring as a butterfly. I awoke and there I was, a yopicatl. For a long time I was unsure if I was a butterfly dreaming I was a yopicatl, or the reverse, -in truth, sometimes I still have my doubts."

The High Priest, trying to comprehend his vision,

or surprising reality, gapes and gawks like a turtle suddenly pried from its hole. Kulcan allows the priest a few moments then, with utmost politeness, says, "I'm looking for a friend of mine. Chimal, is his name. You'd know him if you saw him, he is about my height, well no a bit taller, thinner in the chest. Longer arms. It was suggested that I might find him here."

The High Priest stares at Kulcan as if he were Night Axe, Demon of Darkness who prowls the night bringing death.

Kulcan smiles as kindly as he can, offers by way of explanation, "You're wondering, perhaps, if my reality is your reality, a question that cuts to the heart of existence. And in answer to that, first and foremost we should all recognize that we are each victims of imperfect awareness. For all that we might speak some fraction of the whole is inevitably lost. By which I suggest some nuances of meaning always go astray. You and I, for example, are left to understand one another with symbols that, at best, are of limited meaning and, in truth, are greatly diminished from what we would like them to be, a mere hand-wave of vaguely defined concept and meaning."

Tlaloc *Tlamacazqui*, eyes glazed, says nothing.

Kulcan pauses, sighs, and after a moment continues. "Just so. I take your silence as a subtle reminder that I have not introduced myself, for which I apologize, my courtesies for a moment forgotten. I ask your forgiveness! Realizing, of course, that forgiveness is a funny thing, with as many layers to it as a stack of tortillas. I am Kulcan. Named after Kukulcan, my grandfather on my mother's side. And you are?"

"Ecatenpatil," the high priest whispers.

"Ecatenpatil. Good. Now, I confess I am not being entirely honest with you, for I know where Chimal is, or a portion of what was once Chimal. You'll note I use the past tense, referring to something 'back in time.' Past, future, and the ever ephemeral now, and as for the 'past,' apparently you saw fit to kill him, then stuff him, and place him in Tlaloc's shrine as if he were a great treasure. Which he was, when alive. And as for the 'now,' I have now come to talk with you about said events."

"An illness-" Ecatenpatil begins.

"Yes, an illness I'm sure. Each of us has their own perspective, or set of motivations, and thus the flexible nature of truth."

"An illness-" the High Priest again begins.

Deftly, Kulcan reaches over and pinches off one of Ecatenpatil's toes, the skin so neatly pressed together that there is but a small drop of misplaced blood. Ecatenpatil stares at the gap-toed grin across the smile of his foot, and then the pain finds him, and he winces sharply.

"Ouch," Kulcan sympathizes. "I bet that stings." He tosses the toe into the embers of the small fire that warms the room.

Kulcan and Ecatenpatil sit but a small distance from each other, yet for that each is upon their own remote island of thoughts, feelings, and ideas as they look at the toe that, after a moment, begins to smoke then, with snaps and pops catches flame. Kulcan, watching the toe burn, considers certain events as well as their unavoidable consequences. Upon a point of emotional confusion he is unable to express Kulcan gathers up paper and ink from around the room by which he might sketch out for the high priest certain ideas: family, love, friends, the Mind At Large. Kulcan draws, Ecatenpatil observes. Yet after some disastrous attempts at a humble sketch Kulcan realizes his drawings fail to make clear even the simplest of impressions, which is to say there is a failure of communication. Kulcan reaches over to Ecatenpatil and pinches off another toe and throws it into the fire, and then does the same with a third.

From outside comes the thrum of rain, gift of Tlaloc. It is difficult to say, at that time, with any sort of precision what is going through the minds of Kulcan and Ecatenpatil. Kulcan, for his part, for whatever reason (how the mind drifts!), thinks of how he once dated a female yopicatl he found so beautiful that he became absolutely hopeless in her presence, his hands shaking, his tongue tripping over itself; he was, when near her, everyone but himself. In the end he had to stop seeing her, or she had to stop seeing him, either way the same result, no matter, yet for that, -never mind. Ecatenpatil thinks of rescue, thinks too of his missing toes, and so too seeing what lays beyond this life, the endless possibilities that await him in the Paradise of Tlaloc. He also considers the idea that he is simply having a bad dream, and will soon awake, though the pain he feels suggests otherwise.

Kulcan realizes Ecatenpatil is on the point of fainting. To help sustain the high priest he collects some pillows from about the room and props him up, making him as comfortable as he can. On a nearby chest Kulcan sees a small pitcher of chocolatl, ground cacao beans mixed with honey and water, a dash of vanilla, then whipped to an airy-froth. He pours out a large cup of this for Ecatenpatil who, after a moment's hesitation takes the cup and sips.

"Tasty, huh?" Kulcan suggests.

Ecatenpatil looks toward the darkness framed by his window, then down at his foot with its missing toes, then up to Kulcan and, holding his head level, says, "I'm sorry."

"Sorry?" Kulcan echoes, and as he falls silent little is to be heard save the rain. Of an instant, a flash of lightning illuminates the night's darkness.

"We were not at liberty to decline Lord Quinatzin's orders," Ecatenpatil continues. "And had we declined, well, there are ways of getting one to agree. And even if we didn't, there are others with knowledge equal or superior to ours."

"Knowledge of what, precisely?"

"Poisons."

"I see. And Quinatzin is?"

"The King-of-Kings."

"To be found in?"

"Azcapotzalco."

"King Acamapichtli, I know him. Knew him?"

"His son."

"*That* Quinatzin?"

Ecatenpatil nods.

"There was an older son, brother, as I recall."

"Coyotzin."

"That's it. And what, oh, never mind."

"There was a dinner-"

"Never mind," Kulcan says more loudly. "And Acamapichtli?"

"I've heard but rumors."

"Tell me the best one. No, don't bother. And the yopicatl, we got in the way? So Quinatzin called upon you, his priestly mixers of potions and poisons. The king gives his blessings to the priests, the priests give their blessings to the king, and on it goes."

"There was a drought. An endless drought destroying the One World."

"Cause and effect. I understand. You know, the one thing all yopicatl agree upon, though I guess past tense is more appropriate, was that you, as a species, were fundamentally untrustworthy, to be avoided if at all possible. When was this poisoning-fest?"

"Years ago."

"Kulcan stands up and turns about as if looking for an answer. He walks over to a nearby wall and raps his knuckles on the hard stone.

"How many yopicatl survived?"

"There are rumors."

"How many rumors?"

"A few."

Kulcan bends down to look directly into Ecatenpatil's eyes, says, "If you ever want to see the shrine of Tlaloc again, friend Ecatenpatil, you will give me the names of those responsible, those who gave the orders, and you will do so now. All of them."

Ecatenpatil gives Kulcan a list of names, and when he is finished, and Kulcan has made sure he has correctly memorized the list of names, and that there are no other names to memorize, and after having given a moment to careful consideration of the immediate future, conditional event following conditional event, logical sequence, Kulcan whispers, "The night wanes, friend Ecatenpatil. A sacred fire may be burning low. A certain gong may need sounding. If I linger too long I assume a hue and cry will be raised after which, supposition, I might encounter soldiers who, assumption on my part, will be hostile." He sighs.

Kulcan picks Ecatenpatil up, tucks him under his left arm, "Let's go visit Tlaloc."

Kulcan clambers back up to the height of Tlaloc's Temple, carries Ecatenpatil to the shrine and enters the room within which Chimal so patiently waits. Kulcan finds himself growing angry, his yopicatl good nature slipping away, so much so that, perhaps, you might consider him a, or the, manifestation of Night Axe, the demon who prowls the night bringing death. Kulcan, Night Axe, lays the High Priest of Tlaloc down upon a soft bundle of tanned deer hides, turns, pats Chimal on the shoulder, leaves the room, finds a convenient stone and with this knocks free the polished timber that spans the doorway; part of the roof collapses, sealing the room. In a soft voice he says to the High Priest, though he doubts the High Priest can hear him, "*Auh in uncan chicunamictlan uncan ocepopolioa quimilhui ceppa.*"[16]

Night Axe empties a basket of *olli* onto the sacred fire, adds bark and dry wood, the whole quickly churning into a searing blaze. He grabs the ends of two burning

---

16 Nahuatl: And there, in the ninth dwelling-place of the dead, they were completely done away with.

logs from the sacred fire and holds these up to the thatch roof of the shrine setting it aflame. Turning his attention to a priestly cloak he tears it into strips and wraps the cloth about his hands making protective-mittens. He hammers one leg of the tripod supporting the sacred fire till it crumbles, then slides the fire-holding saucer down upon the paved stone patio, pushes it to the top of the temple stairs, and there releases it to the embrace of gravity. The fire-holding saucer speeds down the temple steps up which warriors, called to alarm by the burning shrine, now rush. They hoot and cry as if a falling star had come upon them.

Night Axe walks to the very edge of the temple height overlooking Teotihuacan, his home no-longer home, and there stands. Embracing his anger Night Axe roars, sound and fury given voice, a sound that shatters the night and causes Tloque Nahuaque[17] to turn over in His sleep, Her sleep, and for a moment turns the soft rain that encompasses him, gift of Tlaloc, to snow which, trick of gravity, lands upon the temple steps where, due to the latent heat of the rock, melts. Night Axe falls silent, and the snow empties from the sky. Night Axe disappears into the darkness, and here we close.

---

17 Master/Mistress of the Universe.

17

The Tower Of Light

———

Kulcan finds himself upon the lower slopes of Iztaccihuatl, She Who Wears a White Dress, amid a forest of sycamore, cedar, oak, sentinel-pine, and ahuehuetl trees that have looked over the valley for a thousand years, -species Time weighs lightly on. Against the bole of a towering cedar, upon a fragrant mattress of needles, Kulcan sleeps, dreaming a dream that will remain sharply vivid against the duller-lights of mere existence. Kulcan sees a gigantic figure, yet another obscure unpredictable god, beating a drum made from a hollowed log shaped from a tree that sprouted in the world's first age, the trunk of which is intricately carved in shapes and figures he cannot clearly discern. The drum, the drummer, are at the center of a stone courtyard and dancers, who wear garish costumes that cloak their identity, slowly revolve about this drum as if in response to a gravitational pull. The dancers, the drummer, seem enfolded within some sort of primordial release by which they are able to return to a bygone place, some antediluvian world: a place of peace, a place of fertile fields where food grows in abundance such that there is always plenty for all. Which is to say a place that may well have never existed in the first place, or if it did only for the most fleeting of moments. And wherever the feet of the dancers land there are sparks, swirling flames, and the black greasy smoke of burning cities.

Awakening, Kulcan decides to climb to the uppermost height of Popocatepetl to gaze upon the landscape of home, no longer home, lacustrine world that the Yopicatl lived within since Distant Time. And though friends are absent Popo' is alive, stout companion who is eternally whispering, spitting, cracking, rumbling and spewing. "I return, Popocatepetl, Old Friend," Kulcan says to the wind. There is a loud 'popo' that comes from deep within the earth, the sharp retort of stone bent until it snaps. "And so you speak, and I listen," Kulcan muses, trying to joke himself into a better mood. Yet for that he knows the rumblings of Popocatepetl are meaningless, the mindless shifting of earth and rock, and he is alone.

Kulcan, near the peak of the uppermost Nahua height, shifts his focus from some indeterminate distance, a gaze upon nothing, looking to the south and east from which the popoloca cities of Cholula, Huexotzinco, and Tlaxcala rise, each city immersed within encompassing fertile plains where all seeds sprout and grow. He gazes upon what was once the ruins of the Tower of Light, the stones and brick of which the popoloca of Cholula have shaped to serve as a temple in honor of Quetzalcoatl.

The Tower of Light, an event forever sealed in the unchangeable past. Cholula was then no more than a place where two streams met, and it was there the yopicatl built the Tower of Light, eminence upon eminence, height upon height. Distant Time. Nahua was then a yopicatl realm and Tayatzin, Aztacoatl's father, spoke for the realm, hence his title, Speaker, call him an elected king, his hair then silvery-white with age, who together with the Council of Four helped to see what and how things should be done among the yopicatl.

It began, like so much does, as no more than a curiosity, to know where it was the sun came from each day, and where it went each night. To solve this mystery two bands of volunteers were formed who set off to discover these places. Those who journeyed to the west never returned; those who journeyed to the east returned, after many years, from the west. Returned with a great many tales but none so strange as this: The Sun never came to rest upon the earth, but rather stayed high within its fiery kingdom forever circling.

Having grown enamored by the beauty and light of the Sun the yopicatl decided to build a tower so high that it reached up into its airy realm, that its splendor might be seen close at hand. Hence the yopicatl built their tower, digging out valleys of clay to make bricks that were bound with strong mortar; raising up height upon endless height.

Kulcan's father, Aztacoatl, then a young yopicatl, had had the task of helping to bring bricks from the kilns to the top of the stupefying pinnacle where, strangely enough, though one came ever closer to the sun it became colder. So too consider this: Although the sun burned more brightly as the tower grew ever higher, the yopicatl torches and candles, by which work proceeded at night, burned ever more feebly, and work itself became ever more of a struggle. Aztacoatl spoke of how once, having delivered his bricks to the masons upon the crown of the spire, the air no longer blue but a dark purple, he paused to catch his breath there within the very heights of the sky. Breathing heavily, he gazed within the matrix of the brick before him, and doing so found his mind calmed. Gazing intently into form and pattern of stone and air, -small shapes, whirls, and hollows, pebble bound to pebble to make an absolute whole, he came to see Eternity within the convolutions of granules, and Infinity within the aesthetic form of clay turned to stone. For a brief moment, Aztacoatl recalled, he left the world of selves, time, and practical considerations to arrive at a profound revelation, "Who do we think we are, imposing upon the realm of the gods?" And at the idea, the very 'thisness' of it, laughed.

"Are you alright?" A voice from far away asked him.

Aztacoatl looked up to see friend Quicotl staring at him, one of the masons who carefully, ceaselessly, laid down row after row of mortar and brick, a concerned look upon his rugged face. "Just rest a bit," Quicotl suggested, "catch your breath."

But this: As the tower rose up The Lord of the Heights became angry, saying to those who dwelt with him, "You see that the yopicatl, enamored by the Sun and enchanted by the strength of their arms have built a tower so lofty as to enter upon our realm. It is not right for those of Earth, those made of flesh, to mingle with us. Therefore, let us cast them down."

Swift as thought those who dwelled within the Heavens fell upon the tower, led by a Wind Dragon, a spiral of wind so dense and of such fury it pulled to itself the tower's bricks to leave, in the end, a great hill of rubble upon which, years later, -curious joke, the popoloca built a shrine dedicated to none other but their Wind God, Quetzalcoatl. So each place has its intrinsic memory, its own singularity of purpose.

Kulcan, returning to the moment, turning his gaze to the west out upon the heart of Nahua, sees the shallow, sky-reflecting blue waters of the great lake girded by a ring of mountains, the air so clean, so rarefied that the subjective measure of distance becomes a sleight-of-hand, a magician's-trick, with the mountains appearing so close it seems one can reach out and touch them: Diadem of jewels that encompass the heart of Nahua, the very center of the world.

The great lake of turquoise-colored waters;
Now quiet, now angry, sings among the rocks.
Iridescence of light where the splendid swan,
With rippling feathers, swims to and fro.

Of this fairest of realms devised by The Immanent, within the towering ramparts of protective rock that encompass the valley Kulcan sees what is now a Popoloca domain with innumerable columns of smoke rising up from untold villages, towns, and cities. Nestled between mountains and lake lie a necklace of popoloca cities all encircled by cultivated fields of green and gold. For a time, a moment, Kulcan is content to sit upon the height of Popocatepetl and gaze out upon the multicolored hills, follow the play of light upon the waters, admire Nature's coronal of fine gems. Then, pull of the lodestone, he looks upon the western edge of Lake Texcoco to the fair city of Azcapotzalco, realm of towers and temples. Event inexorably progresses into event, which is to say there is an inevitability of many things: he gazes out a final time, sees a land overpoweringly beautiful, but for that now overrun with popoloca. He sighs deeply, and then descends from the height.

18

Beneath The Common Sky

———

Descending into the valley scattered patches of cultivated land appear and become more frequent with, at first, hamlets seen within the sheltered nooks of the mountains and these, drawing nearer to the great lake, becoming villages, and then towns. Kulcan comes upon the southeastern-most tip of the great lake, realm of Chalco, realm of fresh pure water fed by snowmelt from Iztaccihuatl, realm of carefully cultivated fields, fruit orchards, fences and houses to keep turkeys and quail: field and town bordering field and town.

On the southern edge of the lake he passes Tulyahualco, a town of boatyards, docks, and jetties; realm of net-weavers, rope-braiders, and hook shapers. A town known for the craftsmanship of their swift-racing *acalli*, hollowed out tree-trunks turned into arrow-swift boats. He passes Xochimilco, city of narrow *chinampas* stretching far out into the lake, small island gardens, land reclaimed from the shallow lake waters upon the fertile moist soil of which grow a tapestry of colors, bountiful harvests of flowers, fruits, grains, squash, and beans. In some places the popoloca have followed their chinampas out upon the waters of the lake to build their houses upon stilts, and so stand poised above the water like so many wading cranes.

✦ ✦ ✦

West of Xochimilco Kulcan passes Cuilcuilco, the buildings of which are marvels of wood and stone: their wood panel ceilings, carefully sanded and oiled, upheld by great cedar trunks so polished they seem to glow as if lit from within. Overlooking the shore are any number of houses with awning-covered patios from which one can watch the winds play upon the surface of the lake, watch the *acalli* move about on the waters, flitter of motion, and watch the light shift upon the sparkling world. Yet for that the pride of Cuilcuilco is its public gardens, which suggests a greater vision for the use of power. The Cuilcuilco gardens are laid out in regular squares, the intersecting gravel pathways of which are bordered with trellises that support flowering vines that draw to them untold numbers of those creatures who are the iridescence of imagination, or as they are called, *papalotl*.[18] One finds there any number of delicate shrubs whose sole purpose is to fill the air with sweet perfumes, and an aviary of a thousand birds kept prisoner for their plumage and

---

18 Butterflies.

their song. The crowning jewel of this garden is a spring-fed reservoir, walls of mortared stone perhaps a mile in circumference; the waters of this reservoir feed the canals and fountains of the gardens, diffusing throughout the whole a perpetual mist. The reservoir is surrounded by a wide mortared stone walkway, and from this walkway there are occasional flights of steps that lead down into the water where glide any number of fish that one might feed by hand. In the center of this reservoir is an island covered with ancient cypress trees in one of which, high within its branches, the darkness above Mount Popocatepetl beginning to fade before the first hint of daylight, Kulcan rests, and then, after looking out upon an ethereal multitude of lights whose radiance is doubled in the still dark waters of the lake, as if innumerable jewels lay scattered across a raven-dark cloak, sleeps.

✦ ✦ ✦

At nightfall Kulcan passes north from Cuilcuilco, shadowing the wide stone road that borders the western edge of the lake, arriving at Coyoacan within which lies a spring of fresh water famous for its curative powers. There within the darkness he stops to drink, and then lingers to listen to what passing popoloca have to say. Kulcan learns Atlixcatzin, a wizard given the gift of prophecy, rules Coyoacan, but that he dislikes revealing what he knows, for knowing the past and future results in an almost overwhelming paradigm of complexity. Those who seek the advice of Atlixcatzin can only do so by first surprising him while he sleeps and securely binding him, for when caught he tries to escape by turning into a jaguar, an eagle, a serpent, a gust of wind, a fire. Yet if his captor holds him fast at last the wizard will return to his proper form and answer, if so asked, three questions. Kulcan thinks of awakening Atlixcatzin with a Yopicatl-grip about his neck, squeezing him 'just-so' and thus encouraging him to answer a few questions. But as to this Kulcan does not have the opportunity. Word at the fountain is the wizard is out of town for a daughter's marriage, and so perhaps Atlixcatzin and Kulcan escape their fates, or find them; no matter. He continues north, sees to the east the Culhuacan peninsula draw ever closer to the western shore until, at the city of Churubusco, the finger of land suddenly falls away to reveal the broad expanse of Lake Texcoco.

✦ ✦ ✦

With daylight Kulcan arrives at Chapultepec, Grasshopper Hill, an enormous blade of gray stone that rises up from the surrounding forest of ancient cypress trees to reach down to Lake Texcoco, where in a sheer escarpment it abruptly ends begrudging but the narrowest of space for the lake-road. Chapultepec! The name verily says itself, resounding off the tongue; so named for so the rock looks from the side. Upon this knife-edge of rock Kulcan finds a temple dedicated to Tezcatlipoca balanced out over the lake like an aerie, like the idea of a lunatic, a temple relatively modest in size but one that offers an exalting view. About the temple and its modest, unassuming priestly bailiwick is a low stone wall the purpose of which, one can imagine, is not to keep unwanted visitors out, but to keep valued priests in. That is to say, a wrong step by the inattentive would find them taking wing, for a moment, to land at the foot of the precipice where, between cliff and lake, there is a fine spring of fresh cold water.

So it is then that Kulcan, passing through the concealing forest that crowns Chapultepec sees a great many popoloca about a Tezcatlipoca-dedicated shrine, thinks, "A religious fest," and, intrinsic curiosity, decides to watch and listen and learn of the strange yet familiar world he now finds himself in where complexity has built upon complexity to arrive at something unimaginable.

Kulcan rests within the height of a cedar tree atop Chapultepec looking down, rapt fascination, upon a hillside crowded with popoloca carrying to Tezcatlipoca's temple baskets full of maize, fruit, cacao, so too some bring 4-legged dogs or 2-legged birds, pots of honey, bags of aromatic resins destined for priestly censers, a good many things brought by a good many, some sort of trade or requital. Difficult to be certain, since so much is left open to interpretation. The crowd gathered, offerings placed upon the temple steps, the sun having reached a particular place within the sky, a drum sounds and out from the shrine upon the temple height comes, and this a matter of subtlety, not Tezcatlipoca Himself, but the Divine Likeness of Tezcatlipoca. The divine likeness wears a white loincloth, and a cloak of black-edged white squares that suggests a fishnet, the two colors curiously woven such that with each movement it appears the squares chase each other back and forth. On his left leg an anklet of gold bells, they make a pleasant sound, and on his right an anklet of deer hooves to suggest the swiftness of the God of Fate's will.

Upon his chest the Divine Likeness wears a thin plate of hammered gold of a singular, intricate design; upon his arms gold bracelets interspersed with iridescent green stones. In his left hand the Divine Likeness carries four arrows suggesting the punishment that awaits those who deserve punishment. In his right hand a clay flute, and hanging down from the wrist enclosed within a wreath of green, blue, and yellow feathers is a mirror of polished obsidian in which Tezcatlipoca sees that which takes place within the world. From his lower lip hangs a labret, a shiny blue-green stone into which, some cleverness, a pink feather is stuck. He wears earrings of gold, and his hair is in a single queue. About his head a band of burnished gold, shaped so as to make his ears appear rabbit-like, which is to say large and upright at the tips of which are puffs of cotton to suggest, -it takes a few moments for Kulcan to parse out the riddle, that he hears the prayers of those who call upon him, not that his ears are on fire because of what he hears. Stuck within this head-encircling gold band, rising well up above him, a cascade of feathers containing the world's colors. For a time the Divine Likeness of Tezcatlipoca plays a small clay flute from each corner of the temple height, and as he does this the popoloca faithful place a finger to the ground, then bring this finger to their mouth, then as space allows prostrate themselves before Tezcatlipoca so that he might not forsake them, weeping, praying and begging that their cares be lifted, sighing and moaning as if they were truly sorry for their faults, their shallowness of character.

Kulcan stares in rapt attention. Down the steps of the temple comes (the Divine Likeness of) Tezcatlipoca all the while playing his flute to which a great swirl of this that and the other goes on upon the surrounding plaza. Priests swish their censers infusing the heaven-destined smoke with their prayers. Some popoloca lay flat on their bellies and pray; some walk about the courtyard whipping themselves with hemp ropes; some pass about the courtyard throwing out handfuls of puffed maize while others hand out necklaces of the same. The young males smear themselves with black holy soot, while the freshly washed females wear fine new dresses and feather-tiaras. The crowd grows larger, with new arrivals weaving through the many to arrive at the temple steps and there place their offerings. Then, of a moment, a deep-throated drum sounds, and having exhausted themselves praying, weeping, dancing, whipping, handing out necklaces of puffed maize, first act, there is a momentary pause for the midday meal. Families, friends, and priests picnic within the surrounding cedar forest enjoying the pleasant day.

19
Kulcan Arrives At Azcapotzalco

———

The drum again sounds suggesting all are finished with their noon meal, and the sacred ceremony is to continue. Amid considerable fanfare, through much of which Kulcan naps, the Divine Likeness slowly ascends the temple steps while playing his flute, giving away his adornments of gold, turquoise, jade, feathers, all save his loincloth and flute.

"Now what?" Kulcan wonders, reasonably enough, "Now what indeed?"

Having reached the height of the temple, an elevation that offers a view of astonishing majesty out across Lake Texcoco, the clouds in the eastern sky afire with deep red light, the Divine Likeness sings out in a pleasant voice:

Remember Yoyontzin and Cihuapa, who together
    ruled Cuilcuilco for many years,
who were once united in friendship and love, and
    are now united in death.
They have gone to a fertile valley full of flowers
    that glimmer as a rainbow.
Truly there is, in the hereafter, a fertile land where
    there is no affliction.
I hear the water, chattering as it dashes forth from
    the earth,
    singing as it passes about the rocks,
      to which the tzintzcan bird who lives in the
        laurel woods answers.
I must now depart on my long journey.
I ask the water: Where is my path?
The water answers, ask the iridescent butterfly.
The water answers, ask the emerald hummingbird.
In their sparkling perfection, they know where the
    dew-covered flowers bloom.

His attention wandering, Kulcan admires the grace of
the evening star visible to the west, majestic symbol of
Quetzalcoatl, Precious Twin as they call him; the morning
star shuttling over to become the evening star, and then
back to become the morning star, weaving a cloth of time
by which it suggests how much less of it you have. Kulcan
has to clear his nose and does, inadvertently blowing out
a fine mist upon the attentive audience below, who think
it is but a light rain falling from the sky, gift of Tlaloc.

    The Divine Likeness of Tezcatlipoca flutes a bit
longer, then of an instant breaks his instrument into two

and casts the pieces down the steps. Kulcan imagines, supposition, that the Divine Likeness, having played his role so well, danced some, played a little music, will now be rewarded in some way, perhaps a small plot of fertile land with a comely hard-working female. However, the Divine Likeness of Tezcatlipoca is summarily grabbed by four priests who lay him upon a long blue-black stone placed at the edge of the temple height. Then a fifth priest joins them who places a finely polished U-shaped red stone yoke over the neck of the Divine Likeness, its weight against his windpipe, and now a sixth priest joins the activities who with a large obsidian knife puts a good-sized hole in the chest of the Divine Likeness, just below the rib-cage and then, Kulcan wishes seeing was not believing, but alas no, this same sixth priest reaches into the newly crafted hole and grabs the Divine Heart, yanks it out, and holds it up into the air. Blood spray, and the cheers of the spectators fill the air. Kulcan, who has seen a good bit of this world, and a great many things, shudders. The priest holds the heart for a moment, then tosses the heart towards the idol of Tezcatlipoca who rests within his shrine, motionless, as if but a piece of wood, and without further ceremony the Divine Likeness, who is now no longer the Divine Likeness, is rolled down the temple steps.

Last act. The joy of being alive upon them, for the moment immortal, the crowd, joined by temple dignitaries, start to dance and sing upon the plaza. They dance for several hours, and at sunset small candies, an after-festival treat comprised of amaranth mixed with honey shaped into a skull with crossed bones before it, is passed out to all attending. After this a large drum sounds, at which the crowd disperses. Kulcan, leaning his back against the massive tree trunk, scratches idly, wonders at the chain of logic that would bring one to such a curious performance, and finds his quiver empty. "The show's over folks," Kulcan whispers. "Time to go home."

Darkness fills the world save for the stars above, isolated and so defined from fellow stars by intervening darkness. The popoloca all off to their rest Kulcan, curious urge, decides to visit Tezcatlipoca within his comfy shrine and have a word with the God of Fate. He leaves his concealing tree, comes to stand before the temple, climbs the sharply angled steps, enters the consecrated shrine and, overwhelmed by some odd trick of atavistic chemistry, grabs ahold of Tezcatlipoca and throws him, it, far out into the lake.

◆ ◆ ◆

From Chapultepec, Kulcan passes north, skirting the edge of Tlacopan, a city vassal to Azcapotzalco. It is a lustrous realm of temples and towers, houses and schools bound between water and mountain, of which the buildings are made of *tetzontli*, a porous red stone quarried using cords embedded with obsidian-powder, the cords pulled back and forth to slice the stone into the desired shape. And it is north of Tlacopan that Kulcan, and thus our story, arrive at the fair city of Azcapotzalco.

◆ ◆ ◆

Azcapotzalco shines like a red-winged heron
    rising in flight;
The brightness of a rainbow is there,
A book of poems written and painted in colors;
The drums of the city echo like the glimmer of
    turquoise.

✦ ✦ ✦

Kulcan winds his way about Azcapotzalco, realm of
white stone towers and plazas, houses and apartments
built about garden courtyards, all encompassed beneath
overarching shade trees. The cleanly-swept streets of
Azcapotzalco are laid out upon a grid aligned to the four
corners of space, bordered and intersected by canals that
allow *acalli*, like so many flittering water-striders, to come
within the center of the city bringing or taking as needed.
A great central avenue brings one to the heart of the
city, a center demarcated by an encompassing stone wall
some ten feet high carved and shaped as a wind serpent,
a boulevard so perfectly aligned it allows the eye to range
from near to far over the encompassing clarity of distance
into the surrounding dark purple mountains whose
features stand starkly revealed in the crystalline air. So
one enters the central realm of power, to find great halls
and mansions. Within the central city one finds temples
to the 13 great gods and goddesses, with each temple
carved, painted, shaped, and smoothed to suit its special
purpose, each crowned with their inextinguishable sacred
fire, and each tended by small villages of priests. Since all
is recorded one passes buildings devoted to scribes and

books. There are books of receipts and disbursements, books that record wars and their heroes, books that record what passes in the heavens, books that record the labor each district has contributed to one task or another, and so too record births, deaths, and marriages (the male and female popoloca literally, and figuratively, tying their cloaks together), divorces (the male of the family go one way, the female the other, the punishment of remarriage death), who is responsible for cultivating what plot of land, fishing what section of the lake, and on and on. So too Azcapotzalco is a city of armories, storehouses, meeting halls, and market plazas, and it is to this city Kulcan has travelled to find Lord Quinatzin, King-of-Kings.

✦ ✦ ✦

In the depth of night Kulcan slips past guards, alert to mere assassins, to wander Quinatzin's palace. He admires the now empty halls and rooms, the smooth-polished beams and timbers of aromatic wood imported from the southern Hot Lands. The young male and female servants, cleaners and bringers, have been carefully instructed to keep their eyes on the floor. Which is to say they are not inclined to idle, gawk, and spread false rumors of creatures that no longer exist, if they ever did exist, which is to say none would speak of a large yopicatl wandering the palace halls if their lives depended on it, which in fact they do.

Kulcan passes paintings, tapestries of woven cloth, and tapestries of feathers in imitation of birds, insects, flowers, gods and goddesses, and any number of mesmerizing geometrical patterns in the colors of imagination. Kulcan passes sculptures of wood and stone that, after the reflection of a moment, he realizes once decorated Teotihuacan, but have been re-shaped into a new artistic vision that does not include yopicatl. Strange, Kulcan thinks, to disappear from the world while still being in the world. Kulcan looks into rooms holding woven-reed mattresses upon which are piled any number of soft coverlets so one can readily find their needed degree of warmth. Kulcan discovers within the great banquet hall a number of finely prepared pelts that serve to decorate the walls: those of black and spotted jaguars, ocelots, bears, deer, wolves, and what must be, yes, the skins of two yopicatl. Kulcan stares at these for a time, then turns and leaves the hall.

20

Totomotzin

Kulcan sits upon the edge of Azcapotzalco's magnificent Chalchiuhtlicue Fountain, She of the Jade Skirt, the water welling up from the center of a large, intricately carved stone shaped so as to suggest the goddess herself from which the water cascades down into a large circular pool, neatly defined by a low wall of mortared stone, from which the overflow, pouring through a sluice, wanders off into a string of gardens reaching, Time and Space, the lake.

Kulcan, beneath a cascade of stars, eager quarter-moon in the northern sky, at rest by the singular fountain listening to the water as it shifts, splashes, and echoes considers how some theologies espouse repaying evil with good, of letting accounts be settled in the next world, which is to say across the Far Waters, where those who lose the ability to wake up travel. So too he thinks in terms of numbers: the individual, the collective whole. He realizes that he passes upon uncharted territory without a map, to which there is no single answer, or even a best answer. So goes the whirlwind of thoughts and ideas, few of little consequence, that our friend Kulcan, at that moment, spins about his head, when he first hears and then sees an elderly popoloca upon the square that surrounds the fountain tapping out a path of sound before him with a cane, the black and white cloak he wears identifying him as a priest of Tezcatlipoca. Kulcan, bored by priests, yawns, a great cavernous yawn, and at this the priest stops a distance away, sniffing the air and turning his head back and forth; it is all Kulcan can do not to laugh, for the movements of the priest remind him of a rabbit.

"Here friend." Kulcan says. "Come rest your feet by the fountain."

The priest continues tapping out his universe up to the edge of the fountain, rests his cane against the low stone wall, leans over and, cupping his hands, brings water to his lips.

"You heard me yawn?" Kulcan asks him.

"I smelled you yawn." The old priest says with a grin. He turns about, and with well-practiced agility hops up upon the water-bounding wall. "I find the fountain much nicer at night; sit here during the day and you get knocked about with everyone filling their water jugs. And, after all, to me night and day are the much the same."

Kulcan considers this, says, "I am Kulcan."

"I am Totomotzin. Or at least so called, answer. What is it that brings you here in the middle of the night?"

"A glory of stars beckons me on," Kulcan answers, while thinking of the name, Totomotzin. Totomotzin. Then, flicker of yopicatl-prodigious memory; "*The Totomotzin?* Acamapichtli's brother?"

The priest grunts with surprise. "The same. Yet I but serve Tezcatlipoca now. No more. Your accent suggests you are not from Azcapotzalco."

"No, not from Azcapotzalco. I came here to, uh. Trade. I am a trader.[19] Just in from, well, Chapultepec."

"Chapultepec? Maybe you know about the doings there. Tezcatlipoca was overthrown there this passed night. Past. The nights pass, and in slipping by are past."

"Actually, what I have learned within the marketplace," Kulcan offers, "more correctly, is that the image of Tezcatlipoca was found floating in the lake. He was not 'overthrown,' so much as 'thrown over,' but either way, unfathomable."

"Yes, it's The Will of the Unfathomable. I grant you that. So too the events in Teotihuacan."

"Events in Teotihuacan?" Kulcan slyly asks.

"There was a fire, so too some odd happenings. Priests of Tlaloc taking to flight, the sacred fire pushed down the temple steps by Night Axe, that sort of thing."

"Night Axe?" Kulcan asks, a sly grin breaking out as he bugs out his eyes and feigns terror. "You mean the demon who prowls the night bringing death?"

"The same," answers Totomotzin, and idly scratches his ankle.

Kulcan waits for Totomotzin to finish, and it is a moment before he realizes that Totomotzin has.

---

19 *Pochteca.*

"Perhaps a struggle for power between the Gods," Kulcan suggests. "Perhaps Tlaloc, to pick an example, was offended in some way."

Totomotzin taps out a few beats with his cane upon the stone of the plaza and stands up; "Yes, well, He wouldn't be the first. I should be getting back."

"I'll keep you company," Kulcan offers. "If you like." Then considering the premise inherent to 'Night Axe' he begins to chuckle.

"Something amuses you?"

"Oh, no. An odd bit of humor, and I hate repeating myself."

"Well, you're certainly not repeating yourself."

They walk on together in silence; Totomotzin, as if a bit unsteady, unable to walk a straight line, slowly draws closer to Kulcan. Of a moment he raises his hand as if about to make a scholarly point, but reaches out and, smooth swift motion, puts a hand upon Kulcan's massive arm.

"Yes!" He says, then "No!" Then: "I knew some of you would survive. Are there more of you?"

Emotions surge through Kulcan, first surprise, then sorrow, then slowly seeping up from wherever he had hidden it, rage. Kulcan speaks slowly, carefully annunciating so his anger doesn't rise up to wash everything out into the moonlit-lake. "I've heard rumors, suggestions of a possibility."

"Likewise. Possibilities. So, now you're a trader?"

"To settle accounts, that sort of thing."

"Many of us have accounts we wish to settle, I won't tire you with mine. They are of course small in comparison. Have we met before? I visited Teotihuacan a time or two, though that was many years ago. "

"Not that I recall, though I knew of you. You may have known my father, Aztacoatl."

"Aztacoatl! You're his son. I well remember him. He was a good friend of my brother, Acamapichtli, who like your father viewed things with perspective. Maybe too much perspective."

"So that's what happened, too much perspective?"

"Suffice it to say Quinatzin changed along the way. How and why would make a long story and is ultimately unimportant. Unless you are writing a history book, which I doubt."

"The oldest son, as I recall, had trouble speaking."

"Coyotzin."

"That's him. Is he about?"

"In spirit."

"Ueue Zacatzin. I recall he was a poet."

"Yes, Ueue. Quinatzin saw fit to raise him up to a position of some authority, one of the four members of the senior council. And for that, I cannot think of anyone less suited to the task."

"Didn't work out?"

"Nope. I wasn't there, but heard the tale. The harvest collected, the people of Azcapotzalco gathered to help build a section of our then new outer wall, all to their task. Quinatzin standing upon a rise ensuring that all suited his vision."

"Something didn't?"

"It didn't. Quinatzin heard someone singing, poorly at that, witnesses said. Apparently Ueue had had too much wine. Quinatzin asked, 'Who is that singing?'

" 'It is your brother,' some workers answered.

" 'What will those of Azcapotzalco say?' Quinatzin asked sharply, 'To have come here to work and hear this idler covering us with shame?'"

"Hmm. And that was that?"

"That was that."

"There was a sister, Miahuitl, if I recall correctly. She was quite charming."

"Queen of Texcoco."

"Nice. And you? A sudden urge to join the temple?"

"I think it is fair to say that I am more a cautionary tale. Being blinded and forced to become a priest was never my life's objective."

Kulcan reaches out and rests a hand upon Totomotzin's shoulder. "I'm a cautionary tale too. The courtyard here being empty, perhaps we might speak of mutual purpose. Perhaps, if I may be so bold, to speak of action."

"Yes action. Well to begin there are the guards, and the army, and the many youths that serve within the palace, the sons and daughters of queens and kings, nobles, from throughout the valley. A bit more persuasion that their parents won't rebel."

"So, you have a plan?"

"In broad strokes. If a certain King-of-Kings were to be found dead, and at more or less the same time a certain sacred fire were to go out, I can scarce imagine the confusion-"

"Tasks worthy of Night Axe."

"All to the good if you can arrange for Night Axe. Now, if you will attend carefully to what I say, nine nights hence is the second echo[20] of Xihcutli's annual feast. There will be a number of religious pilgrims in the city that day. Not an overwhelming crowd, mind you, but a good number, which is to say there will perhaps be just the right amount of distraction. Enough so that things might get overlooked, but not enough to warrant a city full of soldiers."

"There will be a coming and going of many *acalli*," Kulcan offers.

"Yes, and imagine that with a certain someone dead, and a certain sacred fire suddenly extinguished, that amid the sacred festivities a fleet of Xochimilco soldier-filled *acalli* suddenly land upon the shores of Azcapotzalco."

"Who round up a certain set of popoloca that I have in mind. Not a bad plan. Why Xochimilco?"

"Well, to start these two cities have a history of not getting along. Xochimilco is now vassal to Azcapotzalco, and so required to send along considerable tribute, and has been forced to place a shrine dedicated to Xihcutli upon the temple next to that of Cihuacoatl,[21] their patron goddess. So too, they are forced to send along a number of young hostages and, of course, there is always the threat of unrelenting retribution if one doesn't do everything just right."

"Sure, I get that. Just like everyone else. Why Xochimilco?"

---

20 Two months, or 40 days.

21 Cihuacoatl helped create the current race of humanity by grinding up bones from the previous ages of man that were then mixed with Quetzalcoatl's blood.

"Because of Tzintzuntzan. (Deep breath.) High Priest of Xochimilco whose brother, Cozcatl, was for a time King of Xochimilco."

"Tzin-tzun-tzan," Kulcan interjects. "A musical, alliterative name. I recall a King Yacacoatl. He's gone?"

"Oh he's gone. Lord Quinatzin made Cozcatl king when Xochimilco was made vassal to Azcapotzalco. Cozcatl was betrothed to Quiauhxochital,[22] a princess from Tetelco. Quinatzin had occasion to visit Xochimilco where Cozcatl, to do Quinatzin more honor, had his fiancé attend him during the evenings banquet."

"An interesting decision."

"Not what I would have done. Quinatzin was quite taken by Quiauhxochital and Cozcatl, who was not a young man, soon found himself ordered to take command of a troop of soldiers within an expedition against the Quenongo. Are you familiar with the Quenongo?"

"No."

"They are a savage bunch, make no mistake."

"And that was that?"

"That was that."

"Clever," offers Kulcan.

"Yes, I suppose so."

"And Quiauhxochital? We'd find her in Azcapotzalco?"

"You would."

"And if I follow the logical thread correctly, might we find Tzintzuntzan, who owes the loss of a brother to Quinatzin, on top of everything else, looking for just the right opportunity to settle accounts?"

---

22 Rain Flower.

"I believe we would."

"Well then. The hostages safely away, a certain King-of-Kings found dead, and a Xochimilco army poised to attack. What of Xihcutli's sacred fire? I doubt there is much water upon the temple height."

"Not water, no. However I'll see that Tezcatlipoca gifts a generous quantity of wine to Xihcutli. Special occasion and so forth."

"And Tzintzuntzan, you'll send a messenger?"

"I'm hoping Night Axe himself will serve as messenger. For make no mistake, the wrong word in the wrong ear, a misplaced crumb of suggestion and we'll die very unpleasantly. On that point you can rest assured."

"I don't doubt it," says Night Axe. "That I don't doubt at all."

21

Kulcan Departs for Xochimilco

Leaving Azcapotzalco Kulcan heads west, towards the encompassing mountains, enters verdant forest and then turns south. At a clearing, Kulcan pauses to gaze upon the relucent sunlight of early morning upon the shallow blue-green waters of the lake. To the southeast shines Iztaccihuatl, adorned in her white dress, and Popocatepetl who is now sending up a thick plume of dark smoke. Kulcan re-enters the realm of oak, cedar, ahuehuetl, sycamore, and chestnut. He passes south, forced ever closer to cultivated fields by rock escarpments.

On the outskirts of Tlacopon he comes to a temple of a 2nd tier god, Xochipilli,[23] sort of an afterthought god,

---

23 Flowery Prince, a deity thought to have brought venereal disease to mankind; patron deity of gamblers.

150

and cloud silent Kulcan enters the priestly apartments, finds the occupants sleeping off the night's prayers, and yopicatl-silent takes the opportunity to relieve them of a few robes and an outlandish headdress made of, well, things: a mountain-shaped latticework of wood adorned with puffs of cotton, feathers, and garlands of burst corn. So too he gathers up a small censer, wild artistic vision given shape in ceramic, suspended at each of its six corners by a thin silver chain. Kulcan retreats to a copse of large cypress and there, using a few thorns, securely pins two robes together to make a passable single whole, places the sacred crest of Xochipilli upon his head, puts a fresh lump of resin within the sacred censer, and starts down the well-worn road towards Xochimilco.

Say what you will of the popoloca, parable of humor and tragedy, this much is certain: They all avoid a Xochipilli priest. No need for Kulcan to skulk and creep through concealing forest; he soon realizes the popoloca who see him draw near (an unusually large priest cloaked in a broad swath of cloth, veiled within a shrouding mist of incense, a heaven-grasping headdress) take flight from the road like startled deer. The road winds its way south passing any number of scattered houses, small hamlets, and the village of Ajotzinco with its fine quarry of blue stone where he sees a streak of children playing some incomprehensible game that involves a small spherical ball and a good bit of running and laughing. His yopicatl-pace is so swift and silent that he passes popoloca without their notice while others, gawk of astonishment, see him only in passing. He comes upon a female talking to her little son, *"Nopiltze, nocuzque, noquetzale,"*[24] who, curiously enough, pronounces the *t* sound with a puff of air against the roof of her mouth. She sees the large priest in passing, grabs up her little *Nopiltze* and scurries off.

Kulcan comes to ponder Space and Time, specifically just how could these quantities, or qualities, be un-finite? How is it both can be, simultaneously, finite, here a little bit of space, here a little bit of time, yet also infinite, no beginning nor end to space, no beginning nor end to time? Kulcan tries to imagine a beginning or end to time or space and, like trying to find the start or end of a circle, fails. Kulcan passes Mixcoac, a town of sublime orchards, -cherries, avocados, guava, and plums. Sees out upon the waters of the lake innumerable *chinampas* splendid with the vision of flowers and food, and the water alive with the small *acalli* of the gardeners tending their long narrow strips of land grasped from the lake.

As Kulcan draws near the Culhuacan peninsula a curious event occurs. Though there is no wind, no storm nor tempest, a plume of heavy black smoke rising almost straight up from Popocatepetl, and no shaking of the ground as it is want to do on occasion, the water of the lake takes to boiling and seething. Columns of water surge up tossing about the *acalli* as so much flotsam, overflowing the chinampas, lakeside homes and plazas, -and throughout the land an encompassing omnidirectional cacophony of popping sounds. Slack-jawed, Kulcan watches all this roiling and heaving of water; hears the popolocas screaming, bemoaning their losses, beseeching the angry gods, and to this he smiles.

---

24 Sweet son, my jewel, my precious feather.

22

Tzintzuntzan,
High Priest of Cihuacoatl

———

K ulcan comes to the edge of Xochimilco at twilight,
climbs up into the height of an ancient cedar, gazes
out for a moment upon the now-still waters of the lake,
and falls asleep. He awakens to trumpets sounding out
the time of night when priests interrupt their sleep to
pray,[25] with the gods and goddesses better able to hear
the offered prayers in the silent, less distracted world. He
climbs down, passes to a nearby stream to drink, raids a
few fruit trees, draws himself up to his fullest extent and
silent as starlight passes into the city to pay Tzintzuntzan
a visit.

No more than a shadow Night Axe passes through
Xochimilco, the great garden city of the valley. He glides

———

25 A little after midnight.

by temples large and small, built for gods and goddesses major and minor, each with its glow of a sacred fire providing, as an integrated whole, a warm luminescence about the center of the city. He comes to a soldier's meeting hall and there pauses, listening to the talk of lineage and greet deeds, of training, and of that by which they might survive the next battle. Night Axe passes finely built houses of stone, a cluster of *tlachtli* courts and there senses, somehow detects, curious thing, -difficult to say, perhaps a wolf scent.

Night Axe comes to the Temple of Cihuacoatl, Sacred Mother, a single extended building of neatly joined large stones raised up nine steps above the white stone plaza with but a single, small, tunnel-like entrance; the building itself is called *Tlillan*, The Place of Darkness, and it is a place of darkness for no light burns within. He enters the compound where the priests who serve Cihuacoatl live, finds, easily enough, the room of High Priest Tzintzuntzan, ducks his head low, pushes aside the thick-cotton tapestry hanging down across the door, and steps through the opening.

Surprise. Within his dimly lit room Tzintzuntzan lies upon his bed resting, pondering the imponderables, breathing the smoke of burning leaves, sipping from a cup of water into which has been mixed powdered jade. His face, square-jawed, creased and worn as a dried plum, is first that of panic, eyes bulging like turkey-eggs, but then, to the astonishment of Night Axe, fast as an angry bear, or yopicatl(!), Tzintzuntzan leaps to his feet, knocking aside pipe and cup, tipping over a shallow-rimmed gaily-colored dish that holds crystals of different colors thus sending a scattering of brilliance across the tile that, strangely enough, holds the attention of Night Axe for a moment, a moment within which Tzintzuntzan reaches a convenient spear standing upright in a near corner of the room and, funny, seems intent on using.

Night Axe steps across the room, whips out a hand, grasps the spear and pulls it from the hands of the high priest, and then smiles; "Funny how spears are, a momentary lapse of attention and next thing you know you're leaking blood."

Night Axe sighs, "We're getting off to a bad start. Please (irritably motioning to a cushion), have a seat. Cihuacoatl sends you a messenger, a messenger with a message, and you want to put a spear in him."

Tzintzuntzan sits; Night Axe sits. Difficult to say what Tzintzuntzan thinks he sees before him, while Night Axe sees before him another unpredictable prone to violence popoloca who, strangely enough, has greased and shaped his hair to look like, a duck? "Such are their amusements," muses Night Axe.

"Cihuacoatl?" Tzintzuntzan whispers.

"Cihuacoatl, yes, Her very self, sends me to talk with you." Night Axe is not as pleasant as he should be, put into an irascible mood by the business of the spear. "And Tloque Nahuaque as well. Everyone. Everyone who's anyone sends me, with their regards of course." (Night Axe, annoyed, pauses to collect his composure.)

"The Mercy of Ehecatl."[26] Tzintzuntzan says, his voice soft but steady.

Night Axe puts his arm out straight before him, hand

---

26   In this context Wind, or defied heroes.

like a blade, which he brings back past his ear while making a soft-whistling sound, murmur of a passing arrow. "Yes? Sorry, I don't follow. That went right by me."

"The name of my spear," Tzintzuntzan says nodding at his finely crafted spear that Night Axe lightly holds across his lap.

"There you are," Night Axe says. "Who'd have guessed? Look, let's start over." He snaps the spear in half, flicks the pieces off to the side. "You are the High Priest of the patron goddess of Xochimilco, right? Or is it Patroness? Ex-patroness, I should correctly say, as she now is subservient to The God of Fire? And brother, now once-brother of Cozcatl, formerly King now ex-King of Xochimilco?"

Tzintzuntzan slowly nods.

"Good, right. Now we're making progress."

Slowly, smoothly, with no sudden moves, Tzintzuntzan raises up a hand to point at Night Axe, raises his eyebrows to suggest…

"Of course! Forgive me. I have not introduced myself. You've heard of Night Axe?"

Tzintzuntzan nods.

"There you go. Now we can turn to the task at hand, the purpose of my visit. You've noticed, I'm sure, how The Unfathomable fills and empties the moon, again and again, and so too shifts the rising and setting of the sun, now over here, now over there, all of which suggest the passing of a fair quantity of time since your brother met his untimely death."

Night Axe waits, unmoving; after a time Tzintzuntzan again slowly nods.

"I hear talk of how is was Lord Quinatzin himself who saw your brother to an early death, and how he now enjoys the charms of your brother's ex-betrothed. I hear of how much tribute he demands from Xochimilco, and how he forces Cihuacoatl to share her sacred platform with Xihcutli. Alas and woe! Poor Xochimilco, up against Azcapotzalco!" (Dramatic pause, sly wink, warm smile.)

Tzintzuntzan, no stranger to the matter, after a moment's reflection replies, "For every Xochimilco warrior Lord Quinatzin has five. Try and fail to throw off the ropes that bind us and Quinatzin will raze Xochimilco to the ground, selling off as slaves those not killed."

Night Axe yawns, then casually looks about the room admiring the art.

"Lord Quinatzin, King-of-Kings, is known for sending agents throughout the valley. Trick by trick he comes to find just excuses for wars, for conquests."

"Nothing like a just excuse," Night Axe offers. "Or justice. 'Just us,' the old adage goes. And there is more truth to that than you know. Much more. But be that as it may, the last I knew Night Axe does not answer to Quinatzin, nor does Quinatzin make the waters of the lake boil as they did yesterday, though Cihuacoatl might. Or does." Night Axe stands up to leave, turns towards the doorway, pauses, turns back to Tzintzuntzan and says, "I had been told the soldiers of Xochimilco were 'The Real People,' but no matter. However, know this for a fact: Cihuacoatl is to cast down Xihcutli in Azcapotzalco. The question that remains unanswered is who will aid Cihuacoatl in her task, and reap the consequent honor and rewards? I had thought Xochimilco, but perhaps it will be the city of Culhuacan." Night Axe turns back to the door when, curiously, Tzintzuntzan speaks in verse:

> Our Mother, Cihuacoatl, is adorned with plumes,
> And Her face painted with the blood of serpents.
> She is the protecting cypress of Xochimilco.
> Our Mother leans on her spear; her hands are
> filled with darts.
> The order of battle is given, and the drums sound.

"Very nice," Night Axe observes, turning back towards Tzintzuntzan. "A poem best understood, perhaps, in terms of euphemism and simile. Poetry requires a careful selection of words for proper sound, rhythm, and imaginative associations, in turn suggesting the use of figuratives, indirections, comparisons, and metaphors to obtain a specific emotional response. Nevertheless, I miss your point."

"I do not fear death," Tzintzuntzan says, "as Cihuacoatl knows." And by his wolf-grin Night Axe knows he speaks the truth. "I would fight Quinatzin in an instant, repay insult for insult, but more than my life is in the balance."

"Well," Night Axe offers. "It seems Cihuacoatl, with my help, plans to send a good number of her enemies to Mictlan, including the King-of-Kings, which offers great opportunities for those who She watches over. And Cihuacoatl does not act alone. No, not at all, keep that in mind. We have The Immanent, The Unfathomable, and no less than Tloque Nahuaque Himself, or Herself, on our side as well. All you have to do is see to it that a Xochimilco army, on a particular night, arrives upon the shores of Azcapotzalco, and there do what soldiers do best."

Tzintzuntzan grins, for he knows what soldiers do best. Yet for that, he still hesitates.

"Keep in mind," Night Axe adds, suggesting some casual afterthought, "to again disappoint Cihuacoatl, well… (Meaningful rise of the eyebrows.) It might freeze the stalactites of her heart."

"Stalactites?" Tzintzuntzan asks. "Those are the cave-stones that point up from the ground?"

"No, other way around. Stalactites: You better hold on *tight*. Stalagmites: Be careful, or you *might* trip."

Tzintzuntzan chuckles.

"Yes, good, so to the task at hand. Imagine if you will a predestined night in which Quinatzin is sent on to Mictlan, and out goes the sacred fire of the God of Fire. These are my responsibilities. And on this night 5,000 Xochimilco soldiers, a mere hundred or so *acalli*, land upon the shores of Azcapotzalco and there is a settling of scores. A vast celestial vision you must admit, with the upshot being Azcapotzalco gets to pay Xochimilco a great deal of tribute, month after month, year after year. But you understand this needs to be coordinated: think of the stars that whirl about through the night sky, each turning on their silent axes, save when they don't, then colliding and falling out of the sky. An important insight Tezcatlipoca offers us all."

"Right." Tzintzuntzan says after careful consideration: "Right." His eyes lost to a burning vision of the future.

Night Axe puts his face close to Tzintzuntzan's, says in what sounds less a voice and more a growl, "With Night Axe at their side, the warriors of Xochimilco could overthrow Lord Mictlan himself."

Strangely enough then, though in truth difficult to say what is and isn't strange, Tzintzuntzan suddenly asks, "You, you are a yopicatl?"

Night Axe considers this, adeptly shifts the momentum of logic to a new course, "Each of us are many things, friend Tzintzuntzan, many selves. In the past, yes, a yopicatl would be a sufficient description, perhaps, though some would call me son, or brother, or friend. Who we are changes with time, with the events we experience. Which is to say we, by which I mean you and I, are dynamic, complex creatures that begin in one place and end up in another. You'll have noticed, I'm sure, that there are many aspects to your gods. Your gods are complex creatures because you're complex creatures. Which is to say, if you follow my trail of logic, that I am still a yopicatl but as of late, due to certain circumstances, my peaceful, gregarious, eternally friendly yopicatl nature has fallen away. I can truthfully, and in all sincerity, now say that I am the closest thing to Night Axe this world will ever see."

His eyes like stones, Tzintzuntzan bows his head and whispers, "Revenge."

"Yes," Night Axe says, his voice growing louder with excitement. "Revenge. Exactly. That is what we are about here. Not mourning, not hand wringing, but revenge." Night Axe holds up both hands before him, eight fingers up, two held down; "So it is by your actions, eight nights hence, you gain revenge, and help ensure the future safety of Xochimilco."

"Eight nights," Tzintzuntzan echoes, already thinking ahead to mechanics, methods and procedures, how to gather and prepare an army in secret.

"Check your ritual calendar. Eight nights hence is the second echo of the Fire God's annual feast. There will be a celebration, with music, dance, a few captured soldiers sent on to paradise, or Mictlan, the usual stuff."

Tzintzuntzan, grasping the thread of the idea, tugs it, "They will be expecting visitors."

"Precisely. They will be expecting visitors."

For a few moments both sit in silence, each to their thoughts.

"Power is like water held by a dam," Night Axe offers. "A single breech, a crack, and poof! The power pours out, goes someplace else. Eight nights hence (again holding up eight fingers, let there be no confusion), Q-you-know-who will be on his way to Mictlan, the sacred fire of you-know-who goes out (meaningful nod towards Tzintzuntzan), and…"

Tzintzuntzan takes the thread, "And an army of Xochimilco's finest warriors comes out of the darkness on the lake to fall upon a confused and unsuspecting Azcapotzalco."

"Precisely. Your soldiers are to round up certain names, I'll give you the list, and we'll raise up beloved Cihuacoatl who, -and of this She is most particular, requires certain rites by which She will embrace said prisoners offered in her honor."

Tzintzuntzan smiles enthusiastically, and vigorously nods his head.

◆ ◆ ◆

In the pale light of daybreak Night Axe, leaving Xochimilco for the surrounding forest, is swallowed up in a thunderstorm that engulfs the land pouring down cascades of jungle-thick water.

23

Kulcan Visits Xipilco

———

Those who saw the palaces of King Tezozomoc
  knew,
How powerful was his command.
Watered with ambition and greed he flourished,
  for a time.
Yet nothing is so perfect it does not fall and
  disappear,
Leaving the rivers, springs and streams to flow on.
Let the birds enjoy the wealth of Spring,
And the butterflies sip the nectar of its flowers.

Ueue Zacatzin

In his mind's eye, tricks of electrochemistry that give vision
to imagination, Night Axe sees his hand grip Quinatzin's
neck ever so tightly, and then tighter and tighter still

until pop! Yet for that patience is required for there is a duration, a definable period in between the evanescent now and a future *then* that remains a transitory sequence of events ahead: to wit, the elapsing of so many sunrises and sunsets, or in other words, Time, invisible imperceptible Time who holds us transfixed in its unblinking stare.

Kulcan, trapped between the trudging plod of the universe and the lightning-like flight of the mind, faced with an interval of days between engagements decides, whimsical notion, to visit the town of Xipilco, famous for its oracles. A town within the buttressed flanks of Mount Axochco from whose height flows the great spring of crystal water given the same name. A place of caves and caverns, some of which are said to be without end, or said differently, at least no explorer has ever returned from their depths having found an end.

We see Kulcan winding his way up the forested slopes of Mount Axochco. Were you to ask him he would admit to being skeptical of oracles and their prophecies, though truth be told he would admit to curiosity, for as everyone knows there are oracles and *oracles*. He might also, given the opportunity, reflect upon the madness his life has become, -yet, not madness per se, there are underlying mechanics, it is just that he had imagined doing other things with his life. He finds within him, within his garden of a soul not flowers and butterflies but a burning torch of anger for a number of popoloca, and so too for that matter Tezcatlipoca- perhaps his name first on the list, but so the world is.

Half a morning through birdsong-filled forest takes Kulcan from Xochimilco to the southern edge of

Xipilco, a town of finely crafted stone houses nestled within the shade of the surrounding forest. He passes through a great swath of pecan trees where he pauses to fill a sack with the fallen treats. Kulcan comes to a height that overlooks the wide, well maintained footway which brings to Xipilco any number of popoloca, bound on the one side by a stream of cold water pouring forth from the spring of Axochco, and on the other (his perch) uneven, rough rocky ground. The footway here passes between twin temples of modest height, perhaps but some twenty feet, dedicated to The Lord and Lady of the Duality who live within the 13th heaven, the summit of the world where the air is cool and delicate upon one's brow.

Though it is famously known for its oracles, most journey to Xipilco for the fine-crafted orange-ware pottery made from a curious upwelling of clay on the slopes of Mount Axochco: jugs and pitchers great and small; plates, cups, bowls, pots, censers, trays, platters; *tlachtli* ball rattles. Some of these pieces are thick-walled and some thin; some rest on three-legs and some on four. All visitors seem to leave Xipilco with a piece of orangeware be it large or small, showpiece or trinket. One might find, for example, a bowl of astonishing orange color with a handle shaped as a hummingbird painted in a swirl of rainbow-like colors who perches lightly on the rim as if about to dip its needle-like beak into the contents of the bowl. Popular are the miniature ceramic figures of gods and goddesses, which seem particularly cherished as possession of such a trinket, in truth but fired-clay, seems to bring good luck, repelling the dark forces which roam the world.

The market, the oracles, and the charming nature of the town draws visitors from great distances, the Hot Lands, certainly, and from towns and cities along the coasts of the eastern and western seas. Within the market of Xipilco we now see a group of traders who have come from distant Uaxyacac, they who speak some oddly constructed chattering language where everything is broken down into finer and finer delineations:

ciki = I pick up a round object
ciya = I pick up a long object
cinaki = I pick up a flexible object
cineeki = I pick up a container with liquid contents
cinyaki = I pick up a container with solid contents

In the Xipilco market one finds a variety of incenses, a handy offering to any god or goddess. Cloaks, dresses, blouses, loincloths all woven so as to declaim a thousand different patterns in as many different colors. Sections of the market are devoted to tapestries of feather or cloth, so too small statues of wood or stone. There are sections devoted to that crafted from gold, silver, or copper. In other sections of the market one finds tools, and paper, and diverse inks and paints, and flowers freshly arrived from Xochimilco. Fruits and vegetables in unending varieties, bags of cacao beans, and so on, with the encompassing crowd peacefully milling about the marketplace admiring what they see, exchanging greetings with friends new and old, and entertaining themselves by watching others.

One edge of the market plaza is defined by a number of stalls offering prepared foods for purchase, from stews to tamales to chocolatl to dried strips of deer, boar,[27] dog, or turkey. There is also an arcade of roofed shops where one can find, for example, barbers to trim the hair, and places where one may sit at tables and have food served them to enjoy. There are several shops where diverse herbs, to any purpose, can be purchased, as well as poultices and ointments. And throughout all this well-behaved commotion pass priests swinging their censers from which seep aromatic smoke; visitors will stop these priests, hand them a token or gift, tell the priests what it is they wish for, and so the priest imbibes the smoke with the needed prayer.

A small distance from the market one finds farces played out upon a stage adorned with arches and gateways made of branches and flowers pleasing to the eye. Kulcan watches a young male popoloca secure a love poison to capture the heart of a certain female. The Trickster God is introduced to the audience, a god all popoloca love, sometimes envisioned as a Raven, Fox, or Rabbit of The Many Wiles, who switches the love poison for another and which turns the female into an eternally hand-washing raccoon. The youth runs after his desired female, now raccoon, calling out, "My feather, my heart, my precious jewel," passing his neighbors who see but an indifferent raccoon and that their neighbor has gone crazy. Kulcan laughs and claps with the rest of the audience. The love-struck popoloca undergoes many trials, defending the raccoon, his true love, from a pack of coyotes, murderous popoloca, and so on, until the Trickster God, his heart moved to compassion, changes the raccoon back to her female popoloca form.

---

27 Peccaries.

Such is the town of Xipilco: a pleasant place to visit, to pause for a moment and there rest. A place where one might sit on finely crafted wood benches and observe a gathering of diverse customs and beliefs, and yet for that there reigns a certain politeness and respect. In this place, in this time, one hears the soft musical hum of a town at peace. But more than this, Kulcan notices how the popoloca of this town spend much effort in education of the young who attend schools, male and female to their own, where they are inured to hard work, undertake exercises to gain strength of mind and body and become, in the end, a trait necessary for surviving in this harsh world, stoic. The parents choosing teachers who they feel worthy of trust, capable in their ministrations, for a teacher is the path, the tradition, the way by which the world is revealed.

The girls, overseen by a mistress and under the protection of Xochiquetzal learn the arts of the home: to spin and weave; dye and embroider; to prepare for little popoloca-birth, and by such means become good mothers. The boys, overseen by a master and under the protection of The Warrior, one of Tezcatlipoca's many manifestations, learn fellowship and strength, fortitude and skill, of work and war. A communal existence, with troops of young male-popolocas sent to cut wood for the sacred fires, the infirm, or the unmarried widows, take part in public works, and learn to skillfully wield weapons that puncture and cut. But more than this, perhaps unaccountably, the elders strive to instill a degree of calm, humble bearing, and wise, prudent politeness in their young. For example, one hears the elders impart to the youths:

Do not wait to be called twice, answer at once the
first time.
Do not be too outlandish in your clothes, nor
freakish;
On the other hand do not wear poor, torn garments.

The young popoloca more inclined towards the great
mysteries, parsing out the why and how of the membrane
of existence, are sent to a different school where they
learn that which is written in their holy books, taught the
forces of heaven and earth, the turning of the stars, moon,
and sun; the secrets of time; of omens and the proper
interpretation of dreams.

The novitiate oracles vigorously starve themselves,
by which they more readily gain vision. So too, they
intentionally puncture themselves to drain themselves
of blood, -offering up a bit of their life in honor to that
which is unfathomable. Some immerse themselves, for a
time, within the ice-cold waters of the spring and so gain
vision clear as the crystalline water itself.

◆ ◆ ◆

For all this you might imagine Xipilco is a town held dear
in the heart of The Unfathomable. However there is a
king, either raised up by the popoloca of Xipilco or who,
tricks of power, raised himself up: King Xiconoctzin, the
wise and just, with a hundred spear-wielding popoloca
behind him who ensure each idiotic whim of his is put
into effect. The taxes, the offerings of the pilgrims comes
not to all, share and share alike, but to King Xiconoctzin

who, curious hobby, when not abusing the citizenry devotes himself entirely to his dogs, and of these he keeps tens of hundreds. Taxes and offerings can be paid in dogs, or food for the dogs, or collars of shiny stones for the dogs, and so on. As well, no tying a hind leg to their neck to keep these dogs in place, they are kept in cages adorned with decorations of silver or gold. And within their fine cages they are carried about on palanquins so they might take in the sights and enjoy the air. So it is that at the name *Xiconoctzin* no two popoloca from outside Xipilco can look at each other and not laugh, and no two popoloca from Xipilco can look at each other and not cry.

Kulcan considers Xiconoctzin, a popoloca who has done him no harm. Yet for that Kulcan has had his fill of a certain type. He considers doing the world a mercy by tearing Xiconoctzin into small pieces and feeding him to his dogs. However Kulcan has a greater purpose and so leaves the king, such as he is, and like any other pilgrim goes to visit one of the town's famed oracles.

24

The Oracle

A footway leading out from the northern edge of Xipilco passes between twin temples, one dedicated to The Lord of Mictlan and the other The Lady.[28] Between the paired-temples an Arbitrator stands, one who weighs the heart of each candidate and who turns most of the oracle-seeking pilgrims away no matter what gifts they offer. Of those the Arbitrator lets pass, gratefully accepting what offerings they give him, great or small, he seems to heft their cares, weigh their intent, then point down one of four branches the footpath divides into just beyond the temples, suggestive of the four sacred directions of the world.

For a time, from a convenient bench, Kulcan watches the comings and goings of pilgrims seeking to visit an oracle, that is to say, the sorting of souls. The few the

---

28 Mictlantecuhtli and Mictlantecacihuatl, respectively.

Arbitrator lets past filter down their designated trails that lead, at the end of its twists and turns, to a grotto, small cavern or cave, within which an oracle awaits. And in time these pilgrims return, some walking much slower as if carrying a great weight, some walking faster, allegory of what wily-Tezcatlipoca has in store for them.

Against his first inclination Kulcan decides not to sneak by the Arbitrator, but instead see what this popoloca has to say. Kulcan, just another Xochipilli priest, slow careful pace, approaches the Arbitrator, and as he does detects some odd scent he cannot place, yet for whatever reason reminds him of being but a young yopicatl, no greater in size than his father's knee. Kulcan then hears the song of a bird that, for all his Wanderings, he has never before heard, and that he does not espy among the branches of any tree. To Kulcan the song of the bird seems celestial, as if all the mysteries of the world were woven into its melody. "Curious," he says softly to himself. "How very curious."

The Arbitrator proves unconcerned by the appearance of the large Xochipilli priest, an appearance that, in truth, must be considered unusual. He gazes upon Kulcan for a moment, a sparkle in his eye as if he looked upon a singular marvel, offers Kulcan a warm smile, and says, "The Lord and Lady of Mictlan ask you for a poem, one of your choosing. And, from those you carry with you I request, for I am hungry, a few pecans."

What does one say before penetrating vision that lays bare the world? Kulcan takes a handful of pecans from one of the sacks he carries and places these into the Arbitrator's waiting hands, cupped together to make a small bowl. "Excellent," the Arbitrator says observing their fine quality. "And now the poem."

Kulcan thinks for a moment, his wits having momentarily fled, then suddenly, of an instant, one comes to mind. "Here is," he says, "something from the far reaches of the second world, from which I have not long returned:

'The swift stream disappears into the sea, never to
      return.
See the far tower, within which
A white-haired one sorrows before a mirror, saying
'In the morning these locks were raven-black,
Now in the evening they are like snow.
I sigh, and the light of day passes.'"

The Arbitrator bows his head towards Kulcan; "I am grateful to have heard that. You are welcome to pass. Select whichever trail you feel best suits you. Though, I submit, your choice of path has already been made, for all is fore-ordained in the mind of The Unfathomable." He pauses a moment, and grins. "Or so some say; it is not my nature to argue. Yet, if you can spare a moment, I now ask you an additional favor, a boon, if you will."

"Yes?" Kulcan replies.

"A second poem, but one of your own, so that I can tell my children I once heard the most singular priest of Xochipilli recite his own work."

Kulcan smiles, tips his head; there is something intrinsic to this Arbitrator he inherently likes. "Certainly. But only if you take another handful of pecans."

In silent answer the Arbitrator bows, and holds out his cupped hands that Kulcan, little by little so that none spill, again fills with pecans. Kulcan raises himself to his full height, loosens his shoulders with a shrug as if preparing for an epic task, and declares:

The stars pale, the moon grows dim,
A tzintzcan bird welcomes the pale light with song,
While at the edge of Lake Texcoco hawks circle.
Sunrise.
Over the mountain streams mist hovers for a
    moment,
And then is gone.
There comes a wind blowing from the south,
That brushes the fields of maize.

The Arbitrator puts his pecans down on a temple step, claps his hands and says, "A poem appealing in its restraint, a poem without the need for metaphor, comparison, nor allusion. Which, with but a hint of implication shows the thing itself: in a word, magnificent. Thank-you."

He gives Kulcan a friendly pat on his giant arm. Kulcan, at a loss of what to say, nods, and walks forward in the direction indicated by the Arbitrator, not down one of the four paths but in an orthogonal direction towards ancient forest.

✦ ✦ ✦

In time Kulcan finds himself upon a trail that seems no trail at all, endless forest before him and with the glimmer, the hint of a trail he is following vanishing behind. He traverses up the mountain, though he seems to gain no height. He comes to the edge of a sharp precipice, no doubt some metaphorical message from The Immanent, carefully edges past the danger, finds himself upon a flat expanse of rock that suggests no hint of path, and in time almost despairs that he is lost. Then, from nothing, after a moment Kulcan sees the faintest hint of a mouse trail that, in time, becomes a rabbit trail that, in turn, becomes a deer trail, which is to say all is laid bare before him. There is a fifth path, a fifth oracle, that of The Center, The Here, and this path he follows, in the end coming to a grotto of magnificent sycamore trees. Kulcan sees a scattering of large rocks, a small spring, and within a rock escarpment the entrance to a cave. He sits upon a convenient boulder, looks at that which surrounds him and, strangeness building upon strangeness, has a feeling that all is right with the world. Immersed within some calming aura of 'rightness' Kulcan reflects upon the greater implications of Seers and Oracles. If the future is something that can be revealed ahead of the moment, magically glimpsed over time and space, the logical upshot is that all is predestined and the universe is infinitely larger than we can imagine, -but it already is infinite, so now just infinitely more so. A child's game, infinity-squared, infinity raised to the infinite power, it's all infinity. Yet for that, infinitely deep thought upon infinitely deep thought, there is simply the mechanics of Kulcan traveling to some poorly illuminated smoky cave to pose a question to someone within.

"This is absurd." Kulcan says to himself. He stands up to leave yet curiously cannot, unable to find a route by which he might depart the grotto. He then sees, some few steps away, leaning against a tree a popoloca who by his countenance, his scars, he understands is a warrior.

Believing at first the warrior is staring at him Kulcan twitches, eyes on a nearby tree branch that would well serve as a club. Then he realizes the eyes of the popoloca are unfocused, or focused on nothing, and that what he sees is not here at all.

"Pleasant day to you," Kulcan says, and nods.

Startled into the 'now,' the popoloca looks up at Kulcan and echoes, "Pleasant day."

Kulcan, remembering his clever-disguise that seems proof to all observers, sighs. He picks up his sack of pecans to offer the warrior a few, but before he can do so the warrior stands up, eyes fixed on the cave entrance, and as if called, or suddenly invited (though Kulcan sees no one else, hears no one else, in fact hears nothing save the water of the spring miraculously gurgling forth, the leaves stirring, bird song, and the soft whine of insects), walks into the cave where he is soon lost to the darkness within.

Kulcan sits near the entrance to the chthonic dwelling: on the one side the darkness of encompassing earth, and on the other a forest of light and birdsong. He comes to notice a most fragrant aroma, and after a moment stirs himself to follow it to its source: a hand-sized clay dish in which small balls of incense smolder, and so too sheets of maguey-paper that have been carefully folded into various miniature shapes, -butterflies or birds, creatures of heaven, and upon which prayers have been written.

Kulcan sits near the lambent flame, delights in smelling the threads of scented smoke rising up to

The Unfathomable, and enjoys an idyllic moment in an idyllic corner of the world. He looks down into the folds of his pecan-holding sack of woven cotton, in truth but a modest example of the weavers art, and strangely enough sees within the texture of the cloth a deep, endlessly receding, mysteriously lavish world: a limitless complexity of light shading into darkness; shade and hue subtlety transforming into shade and hue. He sees the evanescent allness of a curve, light shimmering upon light, and within but the humble circle sees Infinity itself. Kulcan sees his humble pecan-carrying sack as something satisfied in and of itself, without pretense, a sufficiency that gives proof to the glory and wonder of pure existence.

There is the uplifting melody of a flute. Soon, -or is it soon? He cannot say with certainty, after a time he realizes the tapestry of colors he sees within the weave are changing in tempo with the music. For a moment Kulcan is on the edge of an abyss where nothing, fundamental essence, matters yet, revelation of mathematical precept, he sees that nothing (No. Thing.), zero, is just as important as everything, as Infinity itself. Kulcan then sees, and for a moment understands with crystalline perfection the Duality eternally hinted at by The Eternal, like the trail of clues left by a good teacher: evening star – morning star; sunrise – sunset; one divided by infinity is zero; one divided by zero is infinity. Kulcan is the very point of inflection, and there balances within the vibration that binds the universe and to that, -wait. Wait. Sequence of events: Kulcan sees the popoloca-warrior leave the cave, quickly journeying off to his purpose. Kulcan finds a young, diminutive female popoloca standing before him. She motions, and he follows her into the earthly darkness, passing from small circle of candlelight to small circle of candlelight, a path winding in and out of stalagmites: Careful! One does not trip before an oracle of Xipilco! His young guide leaves him upon a large, smooth flat stone. He sits, strangely content at what seems the heart of the absolute; The Utmost.

The cave is populated with strange, mesmerizing fumes, odd lights, and sounds that seem to reach up from the furthest of terrestrial depths, as if the ground itself were given voice. Kulcan realizes he does not understand the mysteries, yet part of him thinks he does understand the mysteries, and part of him recognizes he doesn't care if he understands the mysteries or not. Revealed, trick of light, upon a shelf of stone, near distance, a very large female popoloca, very large, who has shrouded herself within a headdress of intricate pattern and solemn robe adorned with symbols that suggest the encompassing presence of time. There is a grin upon her face.

"Funny how time is," begins The Oracle, a serene voice that suggests the speaker is at peace with Actuality. "You eat a large meal, think, 'I'll never be hungry again.' Yet soon enough, succession of moments, the belly empties itself, and you find yourself, once again, hungry. If one so desired, one could mark time by the filling and emptying of bellies. Just as the moon fills and empties. Though I am no philosopher, only one philosophically inclined, it seems there is a great secret hidden at the core of this, of which we are shown just the stray thread. Yet it seems, supposition, if we can keep tugging on it, pulling on it, perhaps we can unravel the whole and find, at the center, Tloque Nahuaque Herself. Or Himself."

"What the Mictlan?" Kulcan wonders. "The Oracle speaks as if she were a yopicatl. Is she mocking me?"

"Which is to suggest, friend," a big oracle illuminating grin upon her face, "that I am hungry, and would ask you to share a few pecans."

Kulcan, though he has already fallen silent, is shocked to silence. Surely a trick lies here, some popoloca due process of law, -yet there is no scent, no sound suggesting ambush. Kulcan hands her the sack of pecans.

"All of them?" She asks, mock serious in her mellifluous voice, "Why thank you. Now tell me, for I wish to know, what question brings you here?"

Kulcan sees existence shift between here and there: a trick of space, a sleight of time. Astounded, he gapes and gawps at the charming oracle seated before him, and remains speechless, wonders: What should I ask the oracle? Now when the answers to all questions can be known, all questions seem of no consequence. His mind races from one trivial, idiotic, pointless question to another.

"The next world?" Kulcan squeaks out, at a loss of what else to ask, the sound just barely passing his lips.

She smiles, "You haven't yet come to your own conclusions?" And here then she laughs, laughter as bright as the sunlit waters of a high mountain stream. She then cracks a pecan, tosses the meat into her mouth. "It is in ourselves, friend," she says, "that we are thus." She winks. She waits; her eyes seeming to scan the dimly lit cave as if searching for something lost, then, of a moment, she fixes them on Kulcan. "No?" She asks. "I have it wrong?"

She puts a finger to her lower lip; "Maybe I'm confusing you with another oracle-seeker?" She sighs loudly. (Alas!) Japes, "The Oracles of Xipilco are not what they used to be." Big smile, intent gaze; a moment passes. "You have another, more deeply seated matter that consumes you?"

Kulcan tries to speak, but his voice catches.

"Fair enough," says The Oracle, "Right. Let me tell you what you want to know." Closing her eyes and emptying her face of expression, a transformation within a moment, she speaks out in rhythmic cadence:

A list of names scattered in space,
That chimerical Kulcan soon hopes to erase.
From a mob of Mexica he soon will inquire,
Of Tlacotzin and Petlatzin who smoke by a fire.
Make haste, Night Axe, the chilies are ripe,
An ephemeral instant soon lost to sight.

Kulcan turns away from the darkness of the cave, back towards sunlight, overwhelming, powerful, life-giving sunlight, and runs; Kulcan Night Axe flees in terror through the forest.

25

Kulcan Ponders A Mystery

———

Kulcan runs down the forested slopes of Mount Axochco, across broken ground no less swiftly than a bear or wolf. Along his spine there burns the cold sensation of fear. If an oracle can know certain unknowable things then the world is much, much stranger than Kulcan had ever imagined. In time, night solidifying about him, Kulcan comes to the edge of cultivated fields just south of Cuilcuilco, and within a ravine, underneath an overhang of stone, exhausted, he lies down to sleep. Yet for that sleep does not easily come, his mind churning over the words of the oracle trying to find the stray thread to unravel the mystery:

(1) 'The chilies are ripe.' So?
(2) 'An ephemeral instant soon lost to sight.' Yes, time is fleeting.

(3) 'Tlacotzin and Petlatzin.' Two names on Kulcan's list of popoloca to remove from this world, and this cannot be a coincidence- yet how could she know?

(4) 'Who smoke by a fire.' What does this mean? There are fires everywhere.

Big sigh! Big question mark! Kulcan recognizes there are knowns he knows, for example he knows what a chili is, unknowns he knows he doesn't know (e.g. where precisely Tlacotzin and Petlatzin are to be found), and the unknowns he realizes he knows he doesn't know. Which is to suggest that underneath his protecting roof of rock Kulcan comes to a moment of despair. By necessity he has become accustomed to many forms of ugliness, yet it now seems that he lives only in the past, within a period of time that held meaning for him, a time of peace with family and friends. Yet he can also see, faintly, a meaningful future, a point in time where outstanding issues will be settled satisfactorily and he can live without the overwhelming need, compulsion, to hunt down certain popoloca and see them off to Mictlan. Which suggests that it is the present that plays havoc with Kulcan, the now in which Kulcan, alone and lonely, lying on a cold shelf of stone looking up at a cold roof of stone, recognizes that his life has been reduced to, to... Best not to say.

(5) 'A mob of Mexica.' An unsavory lot, but hardworking, and to their credit the Mexica have quickly transformed their reed-covered

island of muck into Tenochtitlan, great crowded fair city.

Fact: Azcapotzalco and Tenochtitlan are but a small distance from the other. Which, suggests... And to such thoughts, the riddles remaining riddles, Kulcan falls asleep.

+ + +

Kulcan awakens within a fog-enclosed world. Kulcan wanders the forest-field border sampling from diverse gardens following the yopicatl axiom of granting the four outer rows to the needy hungry with the remainder inviolable, then, hunger sated, enters deeper into the forest, north over rolling hills. Kulcan's intent, certainty of purpose, is to remain unseen. He walks silent of footfall as a mouse, his mind awash in some convolution of profundity, the word 'ephemeral' gnawing on his conscience, suggesting: Make-haste!

From a distance comes the smell of wood smoke. Kulcan then hears curious chatter to which he silently draws near through concealing fog. He soon espies a handful of popoloca about a modest fire. He hears one of the elders imparting wisdom to the youths about him:

Do not eat too quickly or in a careless manner.
Do not stuff your mouth, nor gulp your food like
    a dog.
Eat calmly or you will be mocked.

The elder popoloca pauses, politely burping into his hand, and continues:

> Walk quietly, neither too fast nor too slow.
> Do not walk looking about in every direction like
>   an idiot."[29]

Cloud-silent, Kulcan steps back into the cloaking fog. Walking on, Kulcan thinks of any number of valuable questions he might have asked The Oracle. Funny how one seeks to look beyond the turns of the sundial, learn of things greater than our tawdry existence that, full moon by full moon, dissolves. And the more one Wanders, sees how great the world is, studies the cosmos, that is to say, infinity, one recognizes how incontrovertibly insignificant one is. Yet for that there is the strange essence of Time within which we play out our lives. Kulcan thinks of a popoloca he knew who once, time past, having received a particularly keen blow to the head and yet survived, had no memory and so lived in an eternal now: no anguishing over the past; no worrying about the future. Curiously, he was the happiest popoloca Kulcan ever met.

And with that, of an instant, Kulcan glimpses within a sudden clearing of the fog a grim looking pack of popoloca with spears, bows and arrows, who grin and joke among themselves. "Disturbing," Kulcan thinks, disappearing. "A sorry omen for the planet."

Kulcan continues on and, remarkably, while lost in thought considering the nuances of 'chilies,' soon comes upon yet another band of popoloca. The fog now

---

29   An *ixtotomac cuecuetz.*

thinning, across a small clearing he sees some popoloca youths to their bow and arrows, and an older teacher who has the youths kneel, nock an arrow, draw and aim at a squirrel fatally idling upon the height of a great oak. The teacher asks the first youth, "What do you see?"

"What do you mean?" The boy replies.

The teacher pats the boy on the shoulder, has him relax his bow and go stand a ways off. He then approaches a second youth, and asks: "What do you see?"

"I see a squirrel," the youth answers, "the tree the squirrel rests upon, and the sky beyond."

The teacher pats this youth on the shoulder as well, and asks him to relax his bow and join the first boy. The teacher passes to a third, and asks of him the same question; "I see the squirrel," the youth says, a tone of voice that suggests no correction, "and the bark of the limb upon which the squirrel rests."

This youth too is asked to join the others. And so the teacher then comes to the fourth youth, the last, and asks him the same; "What do you see?"

"I see the eye of the squirrel," says the boy.

"Release your arrow."

The arrow, swift messenger, flies, and the squirrel, journeying to The Distant Forest, a land cloaked in ever-bountiful oaks, chestnuts, and shagbark hickories, falls to the ground dead.

Kulcan retreats ever so silently into the forest, and reflects upon whether there is some specific precise thing or things he needs to do to stay in accord with The Oracle's nuanced events of the future, and if so what? So on and so forth go Kulcan's thoughts, when the world fills with the sound of many horns, long hateful howls coming from over here and over there, but of this Kulcan gives little thought, imagining priests summoning the faithful to pray or bring gifts, yet for that, his thoughts somewhere else, he overlooks that he is in the forest. Momentarily, Kulcan's attention is drawn to a deer running past him, then another, and rabbits, coyotes, a bear, and of an instant Kulcan knows what an idiot he is, knows what lays before them all, yopicatl and furry-brethren within a bowl-shaped stretch of land enclosed by a ring of sharply defined hills, upon which a necklace of popoloca-warriors drive all to the center where all non-popoloca, the implied 'them,' will be slaughtered. Yes, it is a dangerous world, like everyone says, the peaceful idyllic 'now' of but a moment ago, the paradise of a fool, unalterably vanished.

Cognizant of Time's mono-dimensional ever-forward voyage, no going back to undo choices that have led to an unpleasant 'now,' Kulcan finds himself a young tree, just the right width and height, puts his hands about its base, firm grip, says, "My apologies, friend. I must cry your mercy and take you for a better cause." Its grip on the earth eased Kulcan pulls it up, snaps off the cumbersome roots and branches, swings it about a few times to limber up, stretches, takes a few deep breaths, focuses on the task at hand, crouches behind a large rock and soon enough hears the swish-crunch sound of popoloca footsteps drawing ever closer until, of the moment, they are upon him. He leaps out from behind the rock, swings his stout staff (a fine, eight-foot beam), landing it against the chest of an unwary hunter.

A game, though not a game, Kulcan darts this way and that, yopicatl-swift, turning-bingo, leaping-bango, to ease The World's burden of so many popoloca. "Tell Quetzalcoatl I said hello!" Kulcan laughs. How good it feels to give the popoloca a bit of their own, his staff shattering knees, chests, arms, and heads.

"Did the Oracle foresee this?" He asks himself while rolling up the popoloca flank. The arc of the circle broken, his four-legged friends soon discern the opening in the battue and surge past him to freedom, the ground becoming a flurry of brown, gray, black, and red-colored fur. He sees an aged wolf, limping, her right shoulder deeply cut, and his exhilaration at slaying popolocas, a bit of a lark for all its inherent danger, turns to a different emotion. Kulcan scoops her up and tucks her beneath an arm, "Come, old mother," he says to her. "Shame on me if I am not strong enough for the two of us."

He carries her some distance, to the cusp of the surrounding height when of a moment, sudden trick of chemistry, Kulcan finds himself enraged, -infuriated, completely and fully finished with fleeing. Of an instant his yopicatl-pleasant disposition is gone, and it is Night Axe who roars out into the forest, "Tloque Nahuaque I have had enough!"

He puts the old-mother down, gives her a grin that suggests what he is about, says, "This is our world more than it ever will be theirs." And then he howls; a great, deep-throated piercing howl of anger that echoes off the surrounding hills. No time for great thoughts now. Time and space collapsed to but a small section of a small forest, an infinitesimal portion of the earth in which it will be seen just who will or will not first pass out of this existence. "We will settle this now," Night Axe whispers to himself, "Right here."

Night Axe charges down the hillside towards the popoloca who he finds crying over their fallen comrades, -some realm of heartache, trying to pierce the mystery as to why their comrades have been struck down, parsing out the circular logic of Camaxtli[30] this and Tezcatlipoca that, wondering if they have come upon some evanescently thin membrane of rationality, on the one side, 'given X then Y,' and on the other side... Something. Something they cannot even begin to guess. The popoloca do not smell, hear, nor see their death until, arrow swift, it is upon them. Night Axe, vision of a demon set loose upon the world, kills all the popoloca he can kill until, finally, exhaustion overcomes him, or simply a sense that he has done enough, or perhaps that there are no more popoloca to kill.

In pausing, leaning upon his staff for a moment, a shift in reality from that of a death-struggle to simply a calm moment within the forest (the song birds, unaffected by that which has passed upon the ground, continue singing), Kulcan suddenly feels the icy whisper of The Immanent upon his neck suggesting: Make Haste. No matter what scales of perception we experience existence through, one comes to an instant when they sense time is irretrievably rushing off. And of that instant, it had seemed to Kulcan that he had gone from having all the time in the world: 9 sunrises and 9 sunsets, to almost nothing, -with but an ephemeral instant left in which

---

30 God of the Hunt.

accounts might be settled. Kulcan returns to the injured mother-wolf, she who is now transcending this world, kneels down and puts a hand upon her soft fur, says, "You now have many guides for your journey."

Kulcan waits there with the wolf as she leaves this world and then, time and space, sequence of events, through the night he walks north along the gardened fields of Cuilcuilco, Copilco, and Coyoacan. Once again he comes to the stone escarpment of Chapultepec and there enters the waters of Lake Texcoco, swimming to the island of the Mexica that he reaches at sunrise. Upon a mudflat, within an enclosing clump of reeds and low bushes, a drizzle of rain as his blanket, Kulcan sleeps.

✦ ✦ ✦

The Sun is at a modest angle within the sky, suggesting mid-morning, when Kulcan awakens to a sky of unfathomable blue that the wind has swept clean of clouds, and to birdsong no less encompassing as the sunlight. For a moment Kulcan feels overwhelmed by the difficult task put before him: to find two specific names upon an island of murdering popoloca and neatly remove said names from existence. Yet he has not forgotten absent loved ones, -so many echoes of sorrow it makes an overwhelming din.

Fourth Bundle

26

Events Held Bound Within The Past: The Drought

———

From his palace set within the heart of Azcapotzalco, Queen of Nahua cities, King-of-Kings Quinatzin reigns over the valley and realms beyond. Azcapotzalco. A city so magnificent pilgrims journey some 500 miles to see it. Or did, before the rains stopped. Quinatzin, no longer having to contest with men must now parse what passes with Tlaloc. One of the greatest of gods, one that he fears he has taken for granted, but this is perhaps not surprising since for all the years that he or his counselors can remember dry season has been followed by rainy season, season of life following season of death as regularly as the sun rises in the morning. From his palace Quinatzin can look across Lake Texcoco to the majestic forest-covered shoulders of Mount Tlaloc, that since anyone can remember has always been a place of rain and storms and now is but an emptiness of dazzling blue sky. Which is to say Quinatzin finds little happiness for having become King-of-Kings. As his death came upon him his father, Acamapichtli, had said to Quinatzin, "I shall ascend now to *Ipalnemoani*, Lord of the Imminent, to pray for you and Azcapotzalco." At the time Quinatzin had not thought to say anything, but now he does; "Please do, father."

Upon the slopes of Mount Tlaloc one finds no small number of ruins: partially carved, uncompleted statues of immense size that seem filled with a disquieting, ill-defined power, long abandoned quarries and mines, and any number of crumpled pyramids. Ask the yopicatl about these ruins and they'll shrug, and without seeming to change the subject. And though Quinatzin has no idea why this would be so he understands that if the rains do not soon fall that which surrounds him, the glory of Nahua, will join its ancient brethren as so much sand and stone.

It is a puzzle, yet another that existence has laid before him: all agree, or rather all that matter agree the rites have been done properly, so how is it that Tlaloc cannot defeat the dryness? Each day the sinuous smoke of untold censers wind their fragrant way heavenward, yet for that no dark clouds form. In what way are the people not sustaining Tlaloc? Why would the rites that reach back to Distant Time suddenly no longer be sufficient?

Many think an evil spell has been cast upon Nahua, and so it would seem, for certainly the lands near the two coasts do not lack for rain. But there is more afoot than simply Tlaloc. During the past dry season Iztaccihuatl, She Who Wears a White Dress, no longer content within her snowy realm saw fit to have it snow within the valley for six days, encompassed within cold so unimaginable that much of the lake froze, something never seen, something never written of in the ancient books, nor something ever imagined. And with the cold many of Nahua took ill, suffering fits of coughing, their blood turning hot, and then dying. But far worse Iztaccihuatl returned in the spring bringing with her a hard frost just when the young plants were sprouting. Since then, day of limitless blue sky has given way to day of limitless blue sky. The Valley already creeps into disorder, for with the freeze much of the remaining seed corn has been eaten, and the forests little by little cleared of their game, and the shrinking lake gradually emptied of its frogs, fish, and fowl. The royal granaries from which Quinatzin allots each district so much per day slowly empty.

Since Distant Time the ceremony of Huey Tozoztli, the Great Vigil, has been sufficient to enable Tlaloc to defeat the dry season, as the sun must defeat the night for there to be day, and as far as any can tell the last Huey Tozoztli was performed perfectly. Perfectly. The nobility of the Valley and beyond, those of Cholula, Tlaxcala, and Huexotzinco, journeying to Tlaloc's Mountain, arriving in the evening to spend the night in shelters crafted of boughs and thatch near the summit just below the gleaming white-stuccoed merlon-crowned stone walls of Tlaloc's Temple, the greatest, most important of his temples. More than equal to the difficulty of the climb is the view from Mount Tlaloc, an encompassing sweep of the mountain-girded lake-filled valley with the air so clear that all seems but an arms distance away.

With sunrise, gleam of light upon the far eastern horizon, to the sounding of horns and drums, echo of thunder, the nobles had entered Tlaloc's temple walking west down a long narrow corridor, delineation of space by 12 foot high stone walls, and when it seemed the corridor would never end in a transition of but a moment they stepped into a rectangular courtyard, neat wall-defined x-y space with limitless sky above, to see Tlaloc, who had once seemed such a kindly god, gaze upon them from within his flat-roofed shrine that bears a gleaming castellated crown of gold. Seated upon a splendid dais covered with a cloth of green and blue Tlaloc stares down eternity, in his left hand a leather bag filled with copal, in his right a yellow-painted wood-carved thunderbolt crafted so as to twist, curve, and turn like lightning as it pours from the clouds. Tlaloc's green eyes, shaped from gems rarely seen in this world, gaze upon one wherever they stand within the courtyard, and if these wonders are insufficient his face is covered with a powder of light-flickering pyrite so that to look upon his countenance is to be dazzled. Upon Tlaloc's chest, ears, head, arms and legs is the wealth of cities, more jewels, gold, and feathers than can be imagined given to honor and sustain Lord Tlaloc, for without rain there is no life.

With all gathered upon Tlaloc's flagstone courtyard, a subtle mosaic of color that suggests rain, King-of-Kings Quinatzin entered the shrine and placed before Tlaloc that which pleases the God and makes him strong: feather mantles; water-colored jewels of jade, sapphire, emerald, and turquoise; fantastically crafted gold earrings, bracelets, and anklets. Then King Copiltzin of Texcoco did the same, and then King Chicomotzin of the Mexica, then the rest, all to their order and rank, the jewels and gold and feathers and mantles rising up before the God of Rain.

Then food was brought within the temple and laid before Tlaloc, so much of it that it soon overflowed his shrine to lay claim to the courtyard: turkeys, fish, stews of fowl and game, breads, tamales, gourds of chocolatl. When all the food was laid before Tlaloc the throats of the captives were slit and their souls, manifest within their blood, sprinkled upon the food so that it was no longer food for mortals, but gods. The nobles then retired to their shelters, ate their morning meal, and descended the mountain to return home, having ensured by their actions the rains would fall. Guards were set in place, changed each six days, who watched over the temple until all the food, baskets and gourds were rotted, or supposed to be rotted, which is to say consumed by Tlaloc. Or so they have in the past, when there was rain, and now there isn't, so the baskets, gourds, and food largely remain, and so the guards continue to wait, waiting for the time when they can bury the mantles, the gold, the feathers and the jewels within the courtyard, womb of the earth, and leave for home.

Each step of the ceremony has been minutely considered, reconsidered, envisioned and re-envisioned, and all agree that the rites were conducted perfectly, these same rites that have worked since Distant Time, since people have cultivated fields and honored Tlaloc, the god by whom the land blossoms.

Yet for that the rains do not fall. And the rains do not fall.

◆ ◆ ◆

King-of-Kings Quinatzin calls together the most knowledgeable prophets and diviners of Nahua, and to those gathered says, "Something vital has gone wrong with the world. The heat, the parching ground, the diminished flow of the springs, the dying foliage, and the slow yet steady withdrawal of the lake from its shores. It seems we have been left naught but to suffer the heat, and watch the sky. Yet the events of the sky are heavy with portent, that seen and unseen. I charge all of you with the task of determining what must be done to have the rains fall again."

Sent to their purpose some seers and wizards simply sit and think. Some pass to shrines or forgotten ruins deep within the forests, or certain rocks, or caves, and there, each to their nature, eat green mushrooms, drink strange liquids, burn certain types of incense, fast, give voice to certain incantations and make certain offerings, and thus come to vision.

The wizards of Malinalco, those most widely regarded for their skill, say the drought will last a little less than three years and that it will lead to the downfall of Lord Quinatzin. Quinatzin considers this, and then thinking how one must be content with small pleasures, for in the end small pleasures are all that anyone is given, orders the magicians thrown into jail, there to be given food in the smallest of measures so that they ever so slowly starve to death. Later, recovered from his anger, Quinatzin instructs his attendants to bring the wizards before him, to learn more of what they have to say, only to be told that they have disappeared from their prison although the jail is still closed with locks and beams. Quinatzin has the jailers brought before him who, prostrating themselves before the great king, all swear they have attended to their duties, and that the prisoners escaped through their magic. And to this, Quinatzin is perplexed at what action to take though Zacancatl, a quivica who has come to serve him, calms Quinatzin, saying, "This is but naught; it is no matter."

New soothsayers are found who, cheerfully unburdened by facts or doubts, claim some strange absence of vision, and so say nothing. Quinatzin has these prophets immediately put to death, their families sold into slavery, and their houses razed. So it is visions come to the diviners and priests. Some suggest that Tlaloc must be raised above, or equal to the titular god of each city and town, a course of action that seems particularly wise, save for the many hungry who will move the stone and dirt but as to that, well, their voices are not heard. So it is in Tenochtitlan that Huitzilopochtli, the fierce war god of the Mexica, comes to share his temple-height with Tlaloc,[31] and so too other cities that do not already suitably honor Tlaloc, but of Azcapotzalco, the idea of Xihcutli sharing his temple, well, one understands fire and water poorly mix, easier to raise up Tlaloc's temple to an equality.

Other diviners, priests, and magicians suggest, after the deepest and most careful contemplation, that since

---

31 As it was when the Conquistadors arrived.

blood, wherein the soul resides, nourishes the gods, and since it is the heart that sends and receives the blood, that if the heart of the sacrifice was offered up that it would better sustain Tlaloc, better sustain all gods, and so better sustain the balance of the cosmos and prevent the atoms from scattering into the void. And to this idea all concur.

27
All Does Not Fair Well With Tlaloc

Though it required the hard labor of many within Azcapotzalco, Tlaloc's temple has been raised up to a height equal that of the God of Fire. The shrine of Tlaloc is painted blue and white, and decorated with symbols that encourage rain and moisture. Inside the shrine one finds ceramic pots holding consecrated seeds, jade necklaces, seashells, coral of different colors, and mother-of-pearl. So too one finds the skeletons of fish as well as Olmec antiquities known to possess strange powers. And for consecration of this temple Quinatzin has seen fit not to peacefully resolve an argument over how poorly some traders were treated within the marketplace of a certain town. Which is to say during the consecration of Tlaloc's new shrine within the

Queen of Nahua cities many souls, many hearts, are given to sustain the god.

Yet for that no rain falls, and the land parches.

* * *

The inter-locking gears of the world are built upon sunlight and water, and day after day, month after month Tlaloc has withheld the rain. The waters of the lake have fallen away from the chinampas, turning the once proud gardens into but so many neatly defined rectangles of elevated dirt. Many of the mountain streams that once watered irrigated fields have run dry. The forest trees bear no nuts. The earth is swept clean of that which might be eaten, and then swept clean again. Wolves, coyotes, and cougars are driven down from the mountains by thirst.

There is no explanation for the drought save that some sin has been committed. However most priests, bound to their realm of temple and formulas of historical precedent are ill-equipped to address new questions, so that which is at hand must serve for the whole. Thus it is the priests attend to the rites most vigorously. If a mouse or a bat is seen to enter or leave a shrine, or if a cloth belonging to the temple is found gnawed, the priests know a sin has been committed among the believers. The priests then, to their purpose, carefully discover the culprit who has profaned the god and to avenge the insult, no matter as to rank, they are immediately slain.

Slavers come from Couixco and Totonacapan, coastal cities where the rains still fall. Some among the Nahua sell themselves hoping simply to end their hunger, while some sell themselves hoping that the maize gained in exchange might sustain their families through the length of the drought. Some parents sell their children that they might live where there is food, partings which speak to the utmost desperation, or which speaks of distemperate children for rumors have spread that they are to be fattened and eaten. Quinatzin orders a minimum price of 400 ears of maize for a woman, and 500 for a man. Many decide to leave the valley, migrating to lands where the rains still fall, but to leave the mountain-girded valley requires a certain quantity of strength and endurance and so in time the footways become bordered with fat crows.

+ + +

Phantoms begin to lay claim to the night, with many encountering ghosts wandering the dark city streets. One, an old woman who strides out of midnight's cave, dressed in white rags with long flowing ash-colored hair, has flesh so lean she is little more than bone. She is heard across the city, crying out, "Alas, my children, where will we go!"

To rid Azcapotzalco of these specters a special ceremony is held: on a midnight, demarcation of time by sparkling stars, announced by the mournful howl of conch shell trumpets, all men and women of the city light torches and carry these as they walk from temple to temple so that there is a radiant glory of light within the darkness.

After this the weeping woman is no longer seen, but still the rains do not fall.

✦ ✦ ✦

Each day a seemingly endless flock of arguing nits comes before King-of-Kings Quinatzin, or so he has come to think of them. There are seemingly interminable conversations, insights and hypotheses, as to why the gods punish the One World and what might be done to appease them. So too there are many who speak of great deeds done on behalf of the King-of-Kings, details he recognizes as so much political theatre, making requests, excuses, reporting omens, advising as to how soldiers need to be sent here or there, quantifications of how quickly the granaries are emptying if not already empty.

As an illustrative example, after the defeat of Xochimilco and her allies Quinatzin at first saw the wisdom of having the city of Culhuacan ruled by a group of captains who saw to the timely payment of tribute. Then, the rule of Azcapotzalco firmly established, Culhuacan and her suburbs quiescent, the King-of-Kings raised up Zohuatzin, a cousin, to rule the city. Zohuatzin, as King of Culhuacan, denies any number of nobles their rank, and by this swift action confiscates their lands. Many of the newly-dispossessed leave the valley however others, seeing wrong in the decision of Lord Zohuatzin, do not accept it and so journey to Azcapotzalco to appeal their case directly. Most prominent of these petitioners is Chichipon, their spokesman, a well-educated man of ancient nobility, one well acquainted with the sublime splendor of historic Culhuacan.

Chichipon speaks, and Quinatzin listens, and while listening thinks, "Strange to now be giving audience to the complaints of former enemies. Yet, how odd that one speaks of a future, which in its speaking becomes later, though nothing has physically changed, then 'later still' should one speak of it again. Which suggests past and future are not manifest events, but rather ideas."

Lord Quinatzin sighs, considers how one cannot see the end consequences of any action, little things leading to big things and big things more often than not leading to nothing. He shifts his attention; "We are in a wretched condition," he hears Chichipon say, which he follows with some incomprehensible idiom that the King-of-Kings is too tired to bother having clarified. Quinatzin muses on how though Chichipon and he live but twenty miles apart, and speak the same recognizable language still he could make use of an interpreter. Then, rubbing a sore muscle, a smile crosses his face as he realizes doctors are in effect translators, listening to what the body has to say, whether the twitch, the sharp pain, the dull ache are something serious or insignificant.

"With Lord Zohuatzin taking possession of our cultivated fields we are but poor people, tending the fire and sweeping..."

After a moment Quinatzin realizes Chichipon has stopped talking, and with head bowed awaits a decision. The King-of-Kings admires the beauty of the sapphire-gold ring the petitioner wears, considers how the spark of unrest may burn within such a complaint as that which has come before him, so too how executions multiply rebels, and says, not unkindly, "Take back your lands."

Later, hearing of his cousin's decision Lord Zohuatzin grows angry and returns to Azcapotzalco to arrive before the great lord where he says, "Lord Quinatzin, King-of-Kings; you have given back my lands to the Culhuacan. I ask you, what will the Lord of Culhuacan gain by this? Lands are to be apportioned for reward, for otherwise the rule of power is lost. Now these men clamor to be considered nobles, and once they are nobles they will clamor to be the kings they once were. What we have here is the seed of rebellion."

One Quinatzin listens to the complaints of his cousin, Lord Zohuatzin, within the council chamber hall of his palace, and considers the words he hears carefully for he seeks to be a good king, or King-of-Kings. A second Quinatzin is simply a tired man who wishes for some rest. A third Quinatzin considers how much of Azcapotzalco's strength lies in the ability of its many craftsmen to make more high quality weapons than other realms: arrows, shields, swords, spears, none last for long, and they do not grow on trees, or actually they do, or at least parts do, but require transformation. A fourth Quinatzin thinks of a certain charming 2nd wife, she of the long neck, tiny nose, dark brown eyes and wistful expression. Then, funny, he reflects upon the mystery of trying to see in the darkness: why is it easier to see what you do not directly look at? Just like life seems better observed, seen more clearly, at an off-angle: perhaps it is for this reason Tezcatlipoca carries a finely polished mirror. He then turns his mind closer to the conversation at hand, with the word *rebellion* filtering through the depths of his thoughts. Rebellion. They have the right to rebel, he posits to himself, if they succeed.

"I have heard your words," King-of-Kings Quinatzin says, his mind arrow-straight on the topic before him.

"The right to property is the foundation of a state. If property can be randomly taken away then why would anyone wish to live and work here? Thus, my decision: Let those of Culhuacan who wish to be considered nobles, be considered nobles. Who for their past actions you have permission to strangle."

So Chichipon and several of his noble companions journey to the realm of Mictlan, and no more complaints come from Culhuacan.

28

All Does Not Fair Well With Chalchiuhtlicue

———

On a certain day, amid news of hardship following news of hardship, the Headman of Tepetzinco, a small island of rock within the middle of Lake Texcoco, comes before the King-of-Kings. Tepetzinco, home to a few tens of families, fishermen and fowlers, of which the sublucastrine Pantitlan spring lies just to the east. The spring of Pantitlan is a marvel, a surge of water rising up from the depths at times strong enough to turn a passing boat, the waters more often than not flowing fresh and clear but on occasion, more often than not when Mount Popocatepetl furiously sends out smoke, brackish and brown. Quinatzin, slowly working past the man's manifestations of fear: ashen face, trembling hands, stuttering voice; learns that the Pantitlan spring, one of

Chalchiuhtlicue's most sacred sites, is no longer a spring but a consuming whirlpool that draws into it the waters of the lake.

Thinking how the world is much stranger than we can ever know, Quinatzin orders his fastest *acalli* prepared, an arrow-shaped arrow-swift craft of 80 paddlers, and orders those whose counsel he trusts to join him: General Cuauh Petlauh, various high priests of the great gods, and Zacancatl, the quivica. Soon all are to their purpose and the craft speeds east across Lake Texcoco, demarcation of distance by paddle-stroke, beneath a sky of unrelenting sun. At ease beneath the awning that shades the stern, whisper of passing water, no line of complaining petitioners before him, Quinatzin considers the *huitzilin*, a creature of the transparency, a bird clad in sparkling violet-colored feathers with a long narrow black bill. At the onset of the dry season it seeks out a crack in a leafy tree and into this crawls, and for a time sleeps. When the rains return the *huitzilin* awakens, coming back to life.[32] There's your Unfathomable Mystery for you, Quinatzin thinks, why can this bird sleep through times of hardship but not man? Do the *huitzilin* suffer hunger? Do they tire of their belly always demanding its sacrifice? Only the stones are self-sufficient, while everything else exists by consuming something, and as to that, so he met Zacancatl while hunting in the forest. Following a wounded deer blood-drop by blood-drop he suddenly came upon Zacancatl, silent and still as a tree, as if he had just risen up from the earth itself. Strangely

---

32 Perhaps the Common Poorwill, which hibernates for several months during the winter.

enough the deer idled nearby, as if Zacancatl had told it: "You can stop running now. You can stop running."

One creature's destruction is the meal of another: there is the Will of Tezcatlipoca for you. And as for meals the deer, freed from its skin and slowly roasted over a small fire, solitary light within the encompassing darkness beneath the forest canopy, is shared equally between Quinatzin, four friends that he trusts well enough to hunt with, and Zacancatl. Quinatzin and his companions, who he has known since childhood, wear no badges of rank, no jewels nor rare feathers, wear but plain mantles and loincloths, wear and carry but what hunters wear and carry, and use but nicknames between them.

Zacancatl informs Quinatzin that he is traveling to join a powerful wizard who is performing a *conchololtico*, a month-long ceremony used to destroy demons that are known to inhabit, on occasion, certain places. A river, say, or a lake, demons only existing where the flux of certain realms intersect, in this case a particular mountain some twenty miles away.

"I would like to meet this wizard," Quinatzin says.

"Impossible," Zacancatl answers, shaking his head. "He cannot be distracted. No."

Yet Quinatzin is determined to meet this great wizard. So by hand-signs and the faintest of whispers, words no rabbit could hear, Quinatzin tells his companions to keep close watch upon Zacancatl. They will follow him to meet this demon-battling wizard.

At the moment this is agreed upon Zacancatl throws back his head and laughs. "It seems I am now a prisoner of

Lord Quinatzin. I am content to travel in your company, friends, though you may bind me with ropes if you wish. I have already informed the wizard of your coming."

Considering this, Quinatzin thinks, "Great, another lunatic."

Yet for that several miles from where he hopes to find the wizard, crossing broken ground two-dozen sturdy hillmen rise up before Quinatzin's small band. "Lord Quinatzin is asked to return home." The foremost among them says, "His curiosity unsatisfied."

Though the hillmen are armed, rather than nocked arrows they offer small presents. After a moments hesitation Quinatzin removes the ancient Olmec amulet he wears about his neck and gives this to the man before him, asking that he present it to the wizard as a gift. Quinatzin nods to the arrayed hillmen, then turns back the way they have come to discover Zacancatl has chosen to accompany him. Curious as to this turn of events Quinatzin is about to ask what passes, then changes his mind and without comment accepts it.

So roll the cacao beans of life, thinks Quinatzin, everything changing in but a single moment. He thinks of the Xilotepec woodcutter who won Azcapotzalco a war, as did the Lady Xocotzin. He thinks of the poison meant for him accidently taken by his first wife who he had dearly loved. He thinks of the periodic yet unpredictable passions he has struggled with all his life. In the end, thinks Quinatzin, considering the here-not-here nature of the universe, none claim naught but the earth they are laid upon, and even that but for a fleeting moment. So! Enjoy the brilliance of the night's uncountable stars, build temples to the unfathomable mystery of it all, or listen to the hints and suggestions of a quivica, no matter. Everything is but a question of dimensional scale, and being at a certain place at a certain time. The question now, however, this time this space, is what ails Tlaloc, what trick to solve the puzzle? But for that, once Zacancatl and Quinatzin came upon an eremite living near the edge of a river who had, some twenty years before, renounced the world to spend his time in meditation and prayer. Zacancatl, strangely enough, or so it seemed to Quinatzin at the time, did not speak to the hermit, curiously intent on something in the near-middle distance, -a bird, perhaps, or dragonfly.

"What have you come to learn in these twenty years?" Quinatzin asked the man.

"For one, I have learned to walk upon the water," the man answered, "and so may now cross the river when it pleases me."

Later, some distance away from the hermit, Zacancatl exclaimed to Quinatzin, "Twenty years! Poor man! The ferry would take him across the river for a single cacao bean."

Quinatzin steadily eyed Zacancatl for a moment, then in a flat voice asked, "So what powers do you have? Can *you* walk across a river?"

"Can I walk across the river?" Zacancatl answered, a tone of voice that suggested, faint whisper, that he found the question funny. "That is a question more complex than you might imagine, Lord Quinatzin, with an answer that is, in many ways, elusive. Absolute knowledge is a tricky thing, often enough guarded not by things but by the absence of things, by any number of interstitials where this and that is readily lost. Said more simply one's net of understanding has any number of holes within it, if you follow my logic. I submit our friend back there may or may not walk across the water, but he certainly thinks he does, and so will we if we starve ourselves long enough. Perhaps, Lord Quinatzin, more importantly, I can tell you what Tezcatlipoca suggests we see within his obsidian mirror."

"And what is that?" Quinatzin sharply asks.

"For many, their own worst enemy."

♦ ♦ ♦

The *acalli* slows, sinking down lower into the water. In time to the rhythm sounded out by a small drum the paddlers turn the boat about so the stern faces the whirlpool slowly consuming the lake, and all who gaze upon the sight know they look upon the very death of the Valley. After gazing at this harrowing sight for a time, what seems to all a great duration but in truth is but a few moments, Quinatzin orders the return to Azcapotzalco. Those who have seen the whirlpool feel a tickle upon the back of their neck, the breath of death; the paddlers push for their lives making the craft seemingly fly across the water towards the safety of land.

A distance is passed in a silence profound as a grave, each to their thoughts. "Why is it," Quinatzin wonders, "the favor of the gods shift back and forth like the play of shadow and light, here a rainbow, here a bolt of lightning that sets fire to a temple, but there are neither of these now, for the rains have stopped, and now Chalchiuhtlicue has replaced her spring of water with an all-consuming drain."

Quinatzin turns to his trusted companions on the *acalli*, says, "It seems Chalchiuhtlicue has become jealous of Tlaloc, and so now reclaims her own. What might appease such manifest wrath?"

"Her image, I think," a priest suggests after a moment, "would please her, carved in wood, or perhaps even stone. Or paintings. If we offered them to the goddess, dropping them into the whirlpool, perhaps she would be satisfied."

"The whirlpool can only be a punishment," another offers, "and to interfere with the whirlpool is to risk greater punishment."

So on and so forth; a point is reached where Quinatzin is too tired to concern himself with the debate. Rather, he listens to the music of the passing water, the pulsing rhythm of the paddlers, and muses on how within the steps of his life one thing has neatly followed the other as if there had been a plan to it all. His father having built up a certain foundation of power; his sister Miahuitl to serve as the perfect cord to bind the great realms of Azcapotzalco and Texcoco. The idea of a plan, or pattern, leads him to wonder, who made this plan? And is there some purpose to it? And if it is all a pattern, then does the first strike of a *tlachtli* ball determine the outcome of the game? Do the dead, after the fact, see a pattern or plan? No wonder holy men spend twenty years meditating by a riverbank. Then Quinatzin thinks, full circle, there is no plan, rather the mind is but a device for finding pattern within the chaos. Finding the poisonous serpent hiding amongst the scattered sticks and fallen branches. Why is life shrouded in such confusion, save the obvious answer, that life is confusion itself, and yet for that, he thinks...

The craft slows, having reached the muddy lakebed that now serves as Azcapotzalco's wharf. Quinatzin orders all his diviners, magicians, sorcerers and prophets to his chamber hall. Entering his palace he is told the spring at the base of Chapultepec has run dry, and tribute has not arrived from Tizayuca because those of Tizayuca not already dead have simply disappeared. There is more, of course, an unyielding stream of decisions that need be made and petitioners that must be dealt with.

The wizards arrive and prostrate themselves, "Gracious lord," they murmur. "We are here in answer to your call. What is it you wish of us?"

Quinatzin, his voice with an odd hum to it, bids the wizards to rise, saying, "I have called you here to see if you have heard or dreamed of anything of importance regarding the realm, for you study the night sky, you divine in the water, cast your bones in dark caves, and carefully observe the course of the stars. Please, tell me all that you have seen. Is there anything new that should concern us?"

The magicians speak of diverse things: rumblings within the earth, in the north a child born with but one eye in the center of its forehead, to the far south a serpent thirty-five feet in length that was slain while consuming an old woman, strange darting lights in the night sky, and to all of this Quinatzin nods, but does not otherwise respond. As the diviners finish a silence descends upon the council chamber hall that grows increasingly uncomfortable for the wizards and magicians as its duration, demarcation of so many heartbeats, lengthens.

"Lord Quinatzin," one finally says, a younger man well regarded for his insights to the complexities of the gods. "The visions we are given are not ours to control, they are sometimes of the past, sometimes of the future. The mysteries can be difficult to unravel. We spend almost all our time considering the rites, trying to determine what it is that Tlaloc requires for the rains to again fall."

"Yes," says Quinatzin. "Perhaps, you do. Certainly, I give voice to but a fact, you do call yourselves 'children of the night,' and say you know what happens within the earth, underneath the waters, in the caves and clefts of the hills, in the springs and water holes. Yet I say, this is all pretense; I say, this is all a lie."

Quinatzin calls his justices and orders the prophets and their families sold to slavers in exchange for maize, and this is done.

◆ ◆ ◆

Later, Quinatzin calls to his palace chamber austere priests who there argue and dispute over the whirlpool, carefully considering it from the perspective of each god or goddess, and so minute are the discussions, and so endless, each pontificating with a seemingly endless supply of energy and words, that Quinatzin cannot keep track of it all, and with each passing moment the lake further empties itself. Quinatzin fights his panic, reassuring himself that it is a big lake, a big lake that will not disappear in a day, or a month. Yet moment-by-moment it diminishes.

"I think," a priest says, his voice carrying over the others, "that while we have offered much to Tlaloc we have overlooked Chalchiuhtlicue's needs and she is now much diminished. We must give her strength, and to do this we must offer her that which we hold most dear."

◆ ◆ ◆

Sunrise two days later, within the cities of Azcapotzalco, Texcoco, and Tenochtitlan, triumvirate of power within the Valley, and so too within some of the lesser cities, Xochimilco, for example, and Culhuacan, amid music and the smell of fragrant incense the priests of Chalchiuhtlicue, clad in blue or green loincloths and cloaks, their skin covered with blue chalk, lead the lords and nobles of their cities to their *acalli* within which the paddlers, some number between eight and eighty depending upon its size, stand waiting with their long-handled paddles. The *acalli* are decorated with blue-green feather banners that long thin poles raise up above the stern. The awnings have been decorated with paintings of fish and frogs, fountains and cascading rivers, while upon the hulls of the *acalli* have been painted any number of symbols pleasing to the goddess. When all are to their places priests come forth carrying palanquins shrouded in blue-green cloth, and ever so carefully these are laid across the gunnels of some of the larger craft, and then the fleets depart for Pantitlan.

The *acalli*, there are two hundred if there are twenty, gather at a safe distance about the consuming vortex; from the height of a cloud one would see a dark pupil surrounded by a speckled blue-green iris. With all gathered a deep-voiced drum sounds that causes the water to shimmer, so resonant a voice it must awaken Chalchiuhtlicue herself, if not all the gods and goddesses. Then there are many prayers, for there is a hierarchy of priests and each is allowed their say, with each to their purpose throwing flowers and incense upon the surface of the water, which are slowly pulled into the orbit of the whirlpool, quick spiral, descent into the consuming void. The prayers finished we discover a young child rides within each palanquin, that which is most precious to the realm. At the proper moment a certain priest reaches into each litter, past the curtains, and with a small knife deftly slits the child's throat, tenderly bending their necks so that their blood flows into the water. Then, after a few moments, their blood flowing less profusely, their bodies are eased into the liquid to enter Tlalocan, a paradise of peaceful happiness where there is no hunger.

The souls of the children given to Chalchiuhtlicue, the lords and ladies give her their most exquisite feathers, gems, and fish, tadpoles, frogs, eels and water snakes shaped in gold. Into the water Lord Quinatzin throws the most singular gems of the realm, to never again be seen by Man. Then, demarcation of time by revolutions of flotsam about the void, in grave silence all return to their cities. Yet for that still the rains do not fall, and still the lake empties itself.

29
The Air Burns

———

Within the sky there is not the faintest suggestion of rain. The air scorches. The earth has become so dry that deep cracks have opened up by which one can peer far into the earthen depths. Many rivers and streams have ceased to flow, and springs run dry. The trees have shed their leaves; no juice flows within the veins of the maguey, and the leaves of the prickly-pear cactus are limp. Many, the poor to be sure, have become little more than thinly wrapped hunger. Whatever sprouts and lives does so only because it is painstakingly watered by hand, bucket after bucket taken from a well, or the ever-receding lake, and as for that the Pantitlan whirlpool, each moment, subtracts from that which is left.

✦ ✦ ✦

Amid land that burns like fire,
What matter if you hold jade or dust?
A hungry mouth curses both.

• ✦ ✦

Quinatzin decides he must talk with Aztacoatl.
Teotihuacan is not far from Azcapotzalco, quantification
of distance in paddle-strokes and footsteps, yet the yopicatl
landscape is so overwhelming Quinatzin feels strangely
uncomfortable there, as if he was transcendent, as if he
was already dead and at rest upon Quetzalcoatl's Golden
Shores. Though knowing it impossible, nevertheless the
yopicatl have built Teotihuacan to withstand eternity:
fire-colored monuments of stone that rest within a sky of
such deep blue that it seems hallucinatory. Laden with a
basket of Azcapotzalco avocados, the trees painstakingly
watered through the drought, Quinatzin winds his way
along the path that ranges from Texcoco to Teotihuacan
listening to the sweet-voiced coyols who carry a thin
copper-colored ring of feathers about their neck, and
who consider the world theirs: each branch, each leaf. So
too he hears the hammer-echo of a distant woodpecker.
He pauses to watch a kite glide in effortless circles in the
cloudless sky: so light, so finely balanced it need rarely
flap its blade-like wings, but merely tilt them, gliding
upon the crystalline sky. Quinatzin blinks his eyes, and
in that instant the kite has plucked a dragonfly from the
air, one easily the size of a song bird, which it carries to
the open branch of an ancient tree and there, beak full by
beak full, consumes.

As he walks Quinatzin considers the odds and ends of his life, and comes to a realization of keen importance, penetrating insight. However before he can permanently lodge this in his mind he is startled by a yopicatl that guards their border who, having seen and heard Quinatzin from a considerable distance, his ears no less sensitive than those of a wolf, has squatted down near the path to await the visitor with a finger idly drawing a spiral of increasing radius in the earth near his foot, and the idea, point of clarity Quinatzin momentarily had is forever lost to him.

◆ ◆ ◆

"Drought and famine are tragic," Aztacoatl says to Quinatzin, "but nevertheless a reoccurring reality of existence. Build the greatest civilization that you can possibly imagine, or the meanest village, take away water and you have nothing, or at least certainly not life, as we are familiar with it. But maybe rocks talk to rocks, though I doubt it."

"Is there anything that can be done?" Quinatzin asks.

"The choices are limited. Eke out an existence, however harsh. Or migrate, and migrations raise questions of scale, since the people of other lands can only accept so many additional people before *they* starve, -a plate of tamales, however much you wish otherwise, will not feed a thousand, so soon enough it comes to war, which has a neat way of reducing the population to match the available food and water. You get the idea, I'm sure."

Quinatzin, a distracted look to his eyes, "The priests endlessly talk of appeasing the gods."

"Your friend Tlaloc? Well, I suggest the idea of Tlaloc implies a certain rigidity of mind that ill serves you. Each to their own perspective, of course, and what drives one's set of beliefs is usually what fills one's belly. But, I don't think this is so much about Tlaloc as about the fact that weather patterns, which are generally predictable over a certain time scale, are unpredictable over others. That is to say there is a hit-or-miss element within their predictably unpredictable nature. So my advice, friend Quinatzin, if you follow my logical thread, is to deepen your wells, and instead of burying your feathers, gold, and jewels, that which is so valued among you, take them to the coast and trade them for as much maize and beans as you can carry."

"I must speak with you about Pantitlan."

"The spring?"

"It has become a whirlpool that drains the lake."

Aztacoatl peers intently at Quinatzin, raises his eyebrows, "A whirlpool that drains the lake? A whirlpool? You are talking about the Pantitlan spring?"

"Yes."

"Once a spring and now a whirlpool, and this is real, not metaphor? 'Whirlpool of power,' and so on?"

"Yes. Real. We have made offerings to Chalchiuhtlicue, but still the vortex drains the lake."

As if trying to pierce the puzzle, Aztacoatl looks carefully at Quinatzin, asks, "You've seen this? For a fact?"

"Yes," he answers. "I've seen it. Draining the lake moment by moment. At this instant."

Aztacoatl considers this a time, whispers, "I see." He then considers the premise for a longer period of time, in which he comes to an idea, says, "Basic plumbing, more than likely, some sort of a two-way valve. There are streams, passageways in the earth beneath us, caverns and tunnels and so on. When rain falls upon the mountains the water pressure, think of it as a great weight pressing down, is such that water streams into Lake Texcoco; but no rain, no water pressure, the valve switches the other way and these underground paths, apparently, can act as drains taking the water someplace else. Water seeks the lowest level, a trite adage, I admit, but for that true." Aztacoatl pauses, again considers for a time. "This is not good. Did your offerings to the whirlpool, to Chalchiuhtlicue, include an *acalli*-load or five of rocks? Stones?" He sighs, looks up into the cloudless sky. "What did you offer the fair goddess, a troublesome grandmother? Perhaps an infertile second wife?"

"We offered Chalchiuhtlicue feathers…"

Aztacoatl lifts up an open-palmed hand, hisses, "Stop, please. No need to answer, thank-you. A rhetorical question." Aztacoatl sighs deeply, and collects himself over a moment. "Forgive my speaking to ill purpose. There are many perspectives by which we can admit to the tragic nature of existence, yet for that 'tragic' is not an absolute quantity. A healthy, life-sustaining snack for one is the misfortunate doom of another, and this duality is scale-invariant, whether we talk of birds, rabbits, or cities. However, more to the point, it is my strong suggestion that you offer several *acalli* filled with rocks, broken pottery perhaps, clay and gravel to Chalchiuhtlicue's whirlpool."

Quinatzin, who has long since lost the logical thread of what Aztacoatl has been saying, fixes on the last, asks,

"You suggest we give rocks and broken pottery to the goddess? Did I hear you correctly? Are you joking?"

"There you have it, King-of-Kings, and not joking in the slightest. Something that plugs the hole, as you would plug a hole in a leaky water bottle, or your roof. The gods guide us, and the gods don't exist. The gods give us meaning, and there is no meaning."

A look, some odd transience of anger flashes across Quinatzin's face.

Aztacoatl beams a big yopicatl smile. "We miscommunicate. You think of gods and goddesses while I speak of plumbing. Consider, as an example, a leaky roof. To fix this leaky roof do you offer up your blood while invoking prayers to sustain the God of Roofs? Do you throw gold and jewels up upon the rooftop? No, you don't, or at least I hope you don't. You get some tar, or mortar, and seal up the crack. It's that simple."

"I…" Quinatzin begins. "They are not the same."

"They *are* the same. However one is a mystery to you, tricks of un-seen subterranean plumbing, and the other is not. Your roof is well known to you, the bottom of the lake is not. But wait, I understand your dilemma and can suggest a compromise. Fill ten of your *acalli* with stones, large stones and small stones, shaped, carved, or painted in Chalchiuhtlicue's image, and fired-clay masks upon which her image is impressed, and send these into the vortex. Poof! I imagine she'll be so pleased she'll stop emptying the lake."

Aztacoatl waits for Quinatzin to say something. Quinatzin, considering what Aztacoatl has said, says nothing. Although yopicatl patient, ultimately Aztacoatl tires of waiting for Quinatzin to parse out the mystery, says, "The whirlpool is serious business you should take seriously. Though we would like to think everything is as simple as moving from Point A to Point B, some logical chain of sequence as impartial and just as gravity, I can assure you it is not. Whirlpools have the ability to draw things to them, like gravity, like power, each of which are extensive properties, the whole much greater than the sum of the parts. That is to say, what is important for the whirlpool is that it keeps feeding, keeps consuming, and so continues to exist. Like a king, or a state: everything will go into the maw so that the maw is sustained. Would you rather throw rocks into the vortex, or yourself?"

Quinatzin slowly, carefully nods his head. "I had not considered that perspective."

"Plug the hole or not, either way the world will plod on without you, or me. Ultimately everything blends into some neutral gray. However, no matter what your prophets and seers say, King-of-Kings, you carry the stars of your fate perched upon your shoulder like an owl. Twenty large *acalli*, filled with rocks, a mixture of large, medium, and small. That's what will most please the goddess, not the blood of your stoutest warrior, not feathers. My word of honor."

30

The Pantitlan Whirlpool

Returning to Azcapotzalco, Lord Quinatzin immediately orders the artists of the valley to their craft, shaping a great many images of Chalchiuhtlicue in diverse forms: statuettes, statues, bas-relief carvings in stone. So too, her countenance impressed upon any number of clay masks baked to an unyielding hardness.

◆ ◆ ◆

Quinatzin gives audience to priests who come before the King-of-Kings suggesting a number of young maidens be offered to sustain the goddess, dressed and adorned as Chalchiuhtlicue to do the goddess honor. The question is, of course, how many young maidens? This is a question of considerable importance considering the dire prospect facing the Valley. Quinatzin listens to the priests, and though he has never been one to joke and jape like others, thinks, "What is the right number for the rite?" Then, his voice oddly brittle like an obsidian blade drawn across granite, Quinatzin states, "No maidens, no blood, no hearts, no souls. For now, we will offer Chalchiuhtlicue her image, and no more."

The priests, surprised by this, politely suggest the wisdom of including at least a few souls to help sustain the goddess, the maidens being allowed to enter the paradise of Tlalocan, where there are warm gentle rains, no hunger, and eternal peace.

Not inclined to argue, nor repeat his order, Quinatzin waits out the priests in silence with a distant stare and one by one the priests, who understand the hierarchies of power, fall mute, and into this silence he then speaks.

"Do you wish to explore the whirlpool yourselves?" The King-of-Kings asks his priests. "Swim your way to Tlalocan? You are welcome to, and have my permission to do so. It can easily be arranged. In fact, perhaps an *acalli* or two of Chalchiuhtlicue priests would best sustain the goddess. What say you to this?"

Quinatzin looks out over the gathered priests who hold their gaze fixed upon the floor, heads bowed, and remain silent. "I should put them all into the whirlpool," Quinatzin thinks. "That would solve the problem." After a time he notices several of the priests are sweating, though the air is cool. His point made, the King of Kings relents.

"Not wishing to explore the whirlpool myself," I speak like a yopicatl, he thinks, "I am left to imagine what the whirlpool is. Perhaps the whirlpool is the entrance to Tlalocan, or perhaps it is a mirror that reflects time. Perhaps Chalchiuhtlicue speaks to us in a riddle, but if so I am not sage enough to discern the inner meaning. Nor apparently are any of you. Nevertheless, I believe the images we have made of her she will find pleasing. We will give her the gifts I have ordered made and, at least for now, no others."

+ + +

Sunrise two days later a number of *acalli* set out from the larger cities of the valley, Azcapotzalco, Texcoco, Tenochtitlan, Xochimilco, and Culhuacan, and make their way across the lake to Pantitlan. In listening to the music of passing water, there is still water, Quinatzin considers the absence of his brothers, how he has, at times, missed them and how, his younger brother lost for his tendency to drink, and a fit of anger, that there should be checks and balances to power. Quinatzin silently recites to himself a poem Ueue Zacatzin composed what now seems several lifetimes ago.

+ + +

From among the gathered flotilla that collects outside what was once the spring of Pantitlan, after prayers, after the casting onto the water of incense, a few green-blue quetzal feathers, and pieces of paper upon which prayers have been written, twenty offering-laden *acalli* are pushed forward into the relentless grip of the whirlpool and slowly drawn towards the center. The *acalli* spiral inwards, increasing in speed, bump against each other, tilt, fill with water, and release their contents at the very center, the dark eyed vortex of the whirlpool. Some moments pass in uncertainty as the water shifts, seethes, surges and churns about, then of an instant all see Chalchiuhtlicue has accepted her gifts and has put an end to the life-draining whirlpool. Those who witness this clap, shout with joy, and give thanks to the goddess, and so too Lord Quinatzin. Curiously, though she has accepted the gifts the goddess returns the *acalli*, presumably since the prows of the craft have not been painted in her image, an oversight, but no matter.

Yet for that there is still no rain.

✦ ✦ ✦

The lake glitters beneath the revolving sky.
The air is ablaze; the air is so much fierceness.
Again and again the green harvests wither, the
    waste and ruin of earth.
What crime has been committed,
That Tlaloc sends such destruction and death?

31

Zacancatl

———

Zacancatl has become a different man than the one Lord Quinatzin thought, however tenuously, he knew. Zacancatl has taken to covering broad expanses of the palace walls in murals of the most intricate detail; great sweeping creations equal to any that one will find anywhere, even upon the walls of Teotihuacan. Moreover, one finds in talking with Zacancatl that his gaze, once sharp as an osprey's, has become lost in an elusive middle distance.

Quinatzin has taken to visiting Zacancatl, busy at his paintings, putting aside for a moment cares of the realm. Or so some might think, but as for that who is to say that Zacancatl might not reveal what will end the drought? The man is, after all, a quivica.

The drought weighs heavily on Quinatzin and now, as he watches Zacancatl paint flawless brush-stroke following flawless brush-stroke he asks, not for the first time, if Zacancatl knows how the wrath of the drought, the wrath of Tlaloc, might be turned aside.

"You would better understand the drought," Zacancatl says by way of answer, "if you can comprehend the idea that there is a Mayan stele in Quiriga that refers to 7 *Ahau*, 3 *Pop*, that is, 400,000,000 years ago. Four. Hundred. Million."

Not insincerely, Quinatzin says, "That's difficult to imagine."

"Yes, it is. And by 'understand the drought' I mean, more correctly, be able to place it in better perspective. Now one might reasonably ask who could grasp such a length of time, and to what purpose. The Mayan attitude towards numbers is so mystical they use not only lines and dots to represent them, but portraits of deities whose attributes are key to the very numbers. How they love to spy on the universe, the Maya, divine its secrets, always ready to discover the supreme order of things! Now, of course, while the stele refers to 400,000,000 years you might logically ask if this was but an allusion to some children's tale, or if it was a mushroom-addled priest who wielded hammer and chisel. One answer is that large heavy rocks are not moved about and intricately carved on a whim. Of course the wild imagination of a young king or queen might have dictated the carving, difficult for us to say with any certainty. The Maya language is a dense weave of allegory, mythics, allusives, metaphors, and epic similes so that if you are not fluent with the language, truly fluent, well, good luck, and I mean it: Good luck.

"Consider how your Mayan might use five different metaphors, or for that matter six or seven, to identify a single city: The Moon in the Water; The White Heron; Eagle and Cactus; The Obsidian-feathered Eagle; The Place Where Spears are Made. If you are not familiar with an expression, well… you will lose much if not all of what is conveyed, or not conveyed. Certainly when I first came to learn Mayan I thought it all nonsense, but then, a task of years, I parsed out the riddles, and find that like almost all languages it is concise, in its way, and well able to describe existence and our passage through it. And there is a refreshing honesty to it; consider, as an example, that their word for 'war' translates as 'I have a desire for more.'"

Quinatzin, not unreasonably, asks, "Do any of these Maya stelae speak to how a drought might be ended? Perhaps some manner to placate the gods we have overlooked? To somehow draw the clouds?"

"Unfortunately no," Zacancatl says. "And not to go on about the Maya. Let me step back a moment, so to speak, so as to not look at the brushstroke, but the painting as a whole. All languages have their quirks, their strengths and weaknesses. While I could talk at length on the subject, let me give you but a simple example, what you might consider the most fundamental tenet of existence: numbers. One thing. Two things. Three things. In Uaxyacac, how one counts is based upon the subjective evaluation of what is being counted: there is a proper way to count round things, ellipsoidal things, a proper way to count long things, square things, or living things, or non-living things, and so on. While Uaxyacac children can pick it up quickly, to learn the language as an adult, well (shrug), it's not easy, and since the whole point of speech is to be understood the numbers who speak this language seem to be dwindling. Then, some languages have gone completely in the opposite direction, where instead of parsing out existence into finer and finer detail they lump more and more into a given word, and say that word ever more softly until you don't hear anything at all. That is to say, by saying nothing, everything is conveyed."

Brush halfway to the wall Zacancatl pauses, catches Quinatzin's eye, winks, and returns to his painting. "At least I think so, sometimes I inadvertently make things up."

"And of the drought?" Quinatzin asks.

"Yes, the drought. A harsh mystery. And mysteries are rarely understood except by those who know not to reveal the underlying secret. *Q'iiiiing!* '*Q'iing*' is the Mayan word for time, and can you think of a more perfect way to describe it? *Q'iiiiing*, like a gong singing out at the heart of the universe. The ancient Maya texts suggest, and I'm not saying I agree with them, but for that I'm not saying I disagree with them either, that the universe is perpetually evolving and dissolving, cycle after cycle, and that the destruction of the universe is as certain as the death of a butterfly, and no more important."

Quinatzin remains silent, listening to the rapid succession of brush strokes that makes a sound like the surresh of water.

"But," Zacancatl sighs, "though I speak of the stele that piques one's curiosity almost all Maya events are dated from a specific day about 4,000 years ago, or 4,400,

if I do the math correctly,[33] as the Maya like to count
the passage of time in days, noon to noon, *Chumuk k'in*,
the middle of the day or, if you prefer, *u lamay ka'an*,
at the center of heaven, some 1.6 million of them, give
or take, at which time in the past something important
happened. The shaping of the first man and woman
from mud, fall from paradise or what have you. How
the Maya love precision and so parsing out the secrets of
time, assuring us, for example, that 365.2420 days equals
a year. Instead of the somewhat vague '3 years,' as we are
apt to observe, the Maya make note that 1,461 days have
passed. I believe you would agree with me that even if not
always necessary such numerical precision is admirable.
So many *baktuns* of 144,000 days, *katuns* of 7,200 days,
tuns of 360, *uinals* of 20, and *kins* of one.

"Our historians think of the Maya as so many
fragmented city-states, amuse themselves by mapping
out their rise and fall, parable of everything, but in truth
the Maya see the need to abandon their cities every
94,963 days, picking up that which is convenient to pick
up, and walk out of their homes never to return. Now,
no doubt you wonder, or at least I wonder, what is so
magical about 94,963 days? The answer to that question
is difficult to parse out, for there is no universal time.
Some argue that a single day of *their* Creator is equal
to 4 billion years, as we know them, and a single night
equal to the same, and such a day and night equal to but a
twinkling of the eye of The Immutable, who some claim,
fact, is simply the impartial redistribution of atoms."

---

33 With reference to the Gregorian calendar, the Maya date their history
    from August 11, 3114 B.C.

He turns from his work to glance at Quinatzin, asks, "You understand, I'm sure, the Universe being a closed system that existence is but temporary aggregations of this and that? So, all of us can truthfully say we were there at the birth of the universe, and likewise we'll be there at the end. Just not in our current form." Zacancatl laughs softly, and after a moment continues: "Our Universe, and an infinite duration of time, has yielded philosophers who study the Universe." He pauses, takes a deep breath then clucks his tongue; "But be that as it may, there remains a lack of rain, I grant you, and I really have nothing to suggest beyond what we are already doing. Dig our wells deeper, and wait."

Quinatzin remains silent. For a time all that can be heard in the council chamber room is brush-stroke following brush-stroke. "Too bad you didn't know Calli, one of your great grandfathers," Zacancatl continues. "Now there was a man who understood the present time, *k'ij yu'nac*."

"You knew him?" Quinatzin asks, voice flat, too tired to disbelieve.

Zacancatl nods, no interruptions to his brush-strokes, says, "I knew him, not a man easily forgotten. One who saw the geometry the universe is built upon. He knew what Tezcatlipoca had in store for him, yes he did. As the Maya would say, he saw *ah cuy manab*, the harbinger owl, omen of his death, yet for that he never flinched when they put the rope about his neck."

"He was strangled? What was his crime?"

Zacancatl smiles broadly, for coming from the King-of-Kings he considers the question amusing, if not absurd. "His crime? Why, not being in power."

✦ ✦ ✦

Zacancatl paints faster than one imagines possible, translation of vision to paint but a matter of mere mechanics, yet for that no brush-stroke is out of place with fine detail seeming to appear within the drying paint. One painting, some twenty feet in length, twelve in height, completed in but a few days shows a man of indeterminate age, wings on his back, beating a drum the reverberations of which create the six directions of which the sea, there is a sea, is at the very center. Yet, the sea is not of water, but of time, and it is upon this existence floats, pulled one way or the other, and there is a shore, thin sliver of the present, upon which waves break. There is a sequence within the painting, a duration, a sense of loss and yet too a shining though improbable future. Upon the beach are dancers who carry a strange expression upon their faces, as if they were real and looked out upon an imaginary world.

✦ ✦ ✦

"Many," Zacancatl tells Quinatzin on another day, "notably the experts, think the basis of language to be the noun, which furnishes the relation, the substance if you will, of the verb. Their thinking is that the verb is just so much abstraction of thought while the noun, great sturdy noun, describes that which one knows from their senses: a stick, a bowl, a cloak. However the experts, my opinion, have it backwards. Language is not so many things: plate, dog, knife; language is the conception within the mind by which the relationships within the world are described: I breathe, you run, you ran, while the nouns fill in around the edges."

Zacancatl pauses for a moment, quantification of time by brush-stroke, says; "It's a bit amusing, don't you think, that the collective noun for a group of apes is 'a shrewdness'?"

✦ ✦ ✦

In time Lord Quinatzin insists doctors inspect Zacancatl, which he agrees to, though seemingly amused at the idea. The healers pore over him, and seeing them look carefully at the thin white scar which runs across his chest Zacancatl informs them, "Before my first battle, and last, Teteoinnan[34] gave me a drink that would make me invincible, but only after repeating a few magic words which at the onset of the battle I found I could not recall. Something like, '*Philama yelo mayak*,' or perhaps, '*Phila'- ma yelo' ma'-yak*.' And so, at least on that day, I was not invincible. You must admit that for as tough a species as we are, we are remarkably soft as well."

---

34 Mother of Deities.

32

The Departure Of Zacancatl

———

Some suggest the drought has come to raven Zacancatl as it has the land. Certainly, Zacancatl's distance between this world and some other, although the imagination falters at what that other might be, has become so great as to seem irrecoverable. While working on what is to his be his last painting, at least in this realm, he tells Lord Quinatzin, "I find no language more elastic and rich in words, so delicate to the ear and yet so dignified in sound as Nahuatl: a language that flows smoothly and easily but yet is so concise that there is no end to its subtlety. However you will note that in Nahuatl we can hardly make a sentence without using the concept of time. With Uaxyacac the relationship to time is not the important distinction, but rather the relationship to space: near me, near you, near them, far away, and so forth, and what it is that is near you, round thing, square thing, or long thing.

"Oh?" Quinatzin thinks to say.

"Yes, now in Nahuatl we might say 'The man smelled a bear,' an action of the past being spoken of at an indefinite location: *the* definite thing, *man* singular person who does the action, *smelled* action in the past, *a* indefinite singular, *bear* thing that was smelled."

At a loss of what else to do, Quinatzin raises his eyebrows and slowly nods in agreement.

"It is not time that is important for the Uaxyacac, but rather space. In Uaxyacac the comparable statement is built with the following pieces: *the* definite thing, *man* with a suffix added to indicate where this man currently is; for example: far from me yet visible, far from me but not visible, near me and visible, near you and visible, and so on; *smelled* action in the past with a suffix added to indicate where this smelling took place in relation to the speaker, for example far from me and not visible, near you and visible, and so on. Then within the sentence will be an indication of where this information comes from, for example whether by the speaker's own experience or by hearsay. Then, finally, there will be an indicator as to whether this smelling has been the subject of a previous conversation."

Quinatzin, distracted by the shattering metal-on-metal whine of a cicada outside the window, says merely, "Oh."

Without interrupting his brushwork Zacancatl continues, "All of us live within, and generally recognize the same world, rocks are hard, trees are immobile and provide shade, fire burns things, and within this physical world we must survive. Survive by sensation, feeling, deliberation and intuition, so no matter how we speak we must, in the end, describe the same fundamental processes of existence."

"Okay," Quinatzin answers.

"Almost all languages possess beautifully logical discriminations about the directness of experience, causation, matters of functional thinking: dynamic qualities, and so they have consistently through all five worlds."

"Only five?" Asks Quinatzin.

"Five, and I know what you're thinking: rise and fall, rise and fall: Why bother? Yet for that, you'd be surprised at how the world lays itself out in neat compartments, here a world consuming flood, there a war to end all wars."

He pauses, looks to Quinatzin, asks, "I'm not telling you something you already know?"

"No, no," answers the King-of-Kings. "Please, continue."

"Well, of the first world our wily friend Tezcatlipoca grew unhappy with the people and so set upon them countless jaguars. Quetzalcoatl found man lacking in the second world, and so turned everyone into howling monkeys. Tlaloc, third creation, deluge of lightning and fire, turned all the people into birds. The fourth world was destroyed by a flood that lasted 52 years, with all people turned to fish save but one man and one woman, who sheltered in Omeyocan, the immense ceiba tree than binds the 13 heavens and 9 underworlds. And so we come to the cosmology you are familiar with, over which the Lord and Lady of Duality reign."

Quinatzin slowly nods.

"Now, what you might not know is that no one wished to rule Mictlan, all being content to reside within paradise, so the Lord and Lady tested the gods, decreeing a particular tree of fragrant flowers and sweet fruit could not be touched, save by the birds of heaven who were allowed to alight within its branches, there to sing their songs and enjoy their fruit, as birds are inclined to do, forbidden or not. But to that, captivated by the tree's beauty and scent, one goddess picked a garland of flowers for her hair, and one god a fruit to taste, and so the two became Lord and Lady of Mictlan, realm of dry plains, howling winds and, of course, serpents.

"Now, let me tell you as an expert, this fifth world is doomed to disappear in a tremendous earthquake that will release the *tizitzimime*, skeleton-like monsters, who will take it upon themselves to clear the earth of all people."

Quinatzin considers this within a silence broken only by brush-stroke. After some moments, he offers, "You suggest the gods are indifferent?"

Zacancatl, after making sure he has heard Quinatzin correctly, laughs; "Surely you know about that? It's all a question of scale. Do you, Lord Quinatzin, or anyone really care if a soul or two is lost to the stray puma? A rhetorical question to which we all know the answer: No. It's just so much market-day gossip unless it's you being gobbled up, or one of your dear family members or friends. Now, keeping that principle in mind, it simply becomes a matter of scale. At some point there is the great wall of indifference, a metaphor that lies closer at hand than you might begin to imagine."

Quinatzin, who does not feel completely well, bids Zacancatl goodnight and retires.

◆ ◆ ◆

Gazing upon Zacancatl's final painting one sees a magnificent sweep of forests, rivers, and distant mountains upon which waterfalls cascade feeding swift-flowing streams. There are orchards, lakes, and low rolling hills. And curiously, the harder one looks into the painting the more detail one sees, vista giving way to vista as if one can follow the very paths. Strangely enough, the school of fish one sees within the lake appear in a different position when one looks again, and so too the deer or wolves one finds within the forests and fields. To look upon the painting is to be lost within The Unfathomable.

Quinatzin, after looking at the painting for a time, smiles, and says to Zacancatl, "No drought there. It looks enchanting, an idyll."

That evening there is a small gathering of friends within the palace at which Zacancatl parses out gifts Quinatzin recognizes as the most treasured possessions of the quivica: small round disks of an unknown dull-yellow metal at the very center of which there is a square hole, the metal itself encompassed with engraved symbols none claim to recognize; oddly shaped stones that, when held, bring relief from any type of pain; a superb flute of the-most exquisite tone; a necklace made of the spear-like upper canines of the boars[35] that he has slain in the deep forests; small Olmec statues that, at night, absorb any incident light and so leave one who carries the statues surrounded by a pocket of absolute darkness.

For his part Zacancatl recognizes that a certain path that has always been before him in some vague, poorly defined future is now at hand, sharply defined within the moment. He sees the divergence with utmost clarity, the here not-here aspect of existence. Gone is gone, as eternity is always hinting. Gone.

The evening's meal finished, the night grown late, Zacancatl turns to Quinatzin, says, "The Maya give homage to *Ah Beeob*, They of the Road, gods who clear the path for travelers. Busy gods, for there are as many paths as there are glittering stars in the night sky, and once a path is chosen it must be followed to the end, however one defines it. Now that the time we have shared the same path comes to an end, our destinies uncross, I bid the *Ah Beeob*, The Unfathomable, to guide your steps."

Zacancatl reaches across to Quinatzin, takes his hand and squeezes it. Then Zacancatl rises, bows to his companions, his friends, and starts to leave the room; Quinatzin stops him, asks, "And where does your path now take you?"

Zacancatl pauses, turns, looks directly at Quinatzin and smiles, "The council chamber hall, King-of-Kings." He then bows deeply, and leaves the room.

---

35 Family, Tayassuidae; Order, Artiodactyla.

Quinatzin and the other guests look between themselves, and after a moment stand, and together cross the distance to the council chamber hall where they expect to see Zacancatl gazing upon his recently finished painting, or perhaps adding a final brush-stroke. Yet the room is empty and the guards, to their purpose, have seen Zacancatl enter but not leave.

+ + +

To trace the history of how one came to a certain point is to arrive where one is. The palace is carefully searched, Azcapotzalco is searched, and yet for that Zacancatl is never seen again. Or perhaps is never seen again. One day an attendant within the council chamber hall, to his task of sweeping and mopping, casts his eyes for a moment upon the painting and cries out in surprise. Lords and ladies, captains and generals gather; the attendant points to where he has seen Zacancatl, or thinks he has seen Zacancatl, a clearing in the forest where a butterfly seems to linger, but for the moment is otherwise empty.

33

The Bright Heavens

The palace is thoroughly cleaned each day, the floors of mortared-stone carefully swept, the statues dusted, the mats and blankets of the beds aired, so it is surprising that Quinatzin, within the darkness of the night, between bed and bathroom steps upon a *teoayocoatl*,[36] a serpent quite rare to Nahua, being almost exclusively found in coastal rainforests, and is bitten. Though the bite of such a serpent is almost always fatal doctors are nearby and so Quinatzin is quickly treated. He is made to drink water into which finely powdered bark of the movivipana tree, ash, charcoal, and goose fat are mixed, and a thick paste of chilies is laid upon his skin.

His heart pounds, he burns like fire, he profusely sweats and he feels a thousand ants crawl upon him. Quinatzin laughs unceasingly, then weeps, then laughs,

---

36 Hognosed viper, the venom of which is hemotoxic.

then falls into a coma. There is no Quinatzin now, within his mind all sense of self is lost; he simply is, watching and experiencing, untethered from all existence. He first sees dazzling folds of light, ever-changing combinations of colors, now turbulent, now quiescent, shifts of form, pattern, and texture: grids, lines, zigzags, bizarre filigrees of color interspersed with a thousand glittering jewels. Blood surges into his head, then ebbs away, and then surges back, and then ebbs away, and with this ebb and flow he sees within the surrounding colors faces that grow ever more precisely detailed, and yet contorted.

Quinatzin is again a boy, standing in the shallows of life, accompanying his father, King Acamapichtli, who is thrice checking sums and totals of tribute paid the city of Azcapotzalco. Coyotzin, Quinatzin's older brother, carefully attends his father, if need be to check the totals once more than thrice, while as to his nature Ueue Zacatzin, his younger brother, waits outside the storehouse idling away the moment by composing a song. Miahuitl roams the storehouse examining the quality of the many shields, darts, swords, bows and arrows, and spears. Within the storehouse Quinatzin gazes within a deep-rimmed earthen dish filled with dazzling emerald, beryl, jade, and turquoise stones, which are but a small portion due the city every eighty days. Quinatzin gazes ever more intently into the small dish holding these stones of fire which, after a time, seem to contain spectral lights of all imaginable colors. The voice of his shouting father receding into the far corners of the storehouse, Quinatzin realizes the ethereal light of the stones is not simply within, but rises up above their unyielding hardness to form a film, a particulate sheen of diverse colors that swirl about as wind-blown fog, with whirlpools and eddies of light shifting like warm honey. He sees chroma and tint given life: he understands it is the thrum, the pulse, the heartbeat of Tezcatlipoca. Quinatzin now ascends up over his palace grounds, above Azcapotzalco, sees as if from an inconceivable height, vision of an osprey, the center of the world, the One World, realm of the Nahua people. He gazes down upon Lake Texcoco, great lake of glittering shallow water that brightly reflects the sky. Looks east to the mountain of Lord Tlaloc, and then beyond, the land falling away from the escarpment to the Hot Lands, realm of iridescent butterflies and birds, cacao trees, fields of pineapple and maguey, papayas and guavas. Then past the Hot Lands to a realm of palms; feather palms, coconut palms, wax palms, and so on, and then a strip of sand or rock, and then the *Atlatic*[37] sea. Strange vision.

Quinatzin sees near the peak of Mount Tlaloc the ruins of buildings where once poet-priests came to be inspired and pay Lord Tlaloc homage that are now but blocks of stone, their order and symmetry lost in the night of time. Descending now from the uppermost height within the sylvan coolness of the mountain forests Quinatzin sees ruins of a more recent age, yet for that long since abandoned by man to be claimed by tree, vine, and bird. He sees piles of rubble that had once been crenellated walls and towers, and knows that the names of all those who once lived there have long been forgotten.

---

37 Atl = water; Atic = unending.

Coming nearer to the lake, as if the past is somehow multiplied and projected upon the flat surface of the present, Quinatzin sees ruins more recently abandoned that have not yet lost their war to grass and bush, while at the edge of the water is today, realm of now, realm of man. Quinatzin realizes, a truth that need not be said to be apparent, that to descend the mountain is to ascend the stream of time, and that Tezcatlipoca is revealing not that Quinatzin will rule, or does rule, but that he has, for a time, ruled all of Nahua as *Chichimeca Teuctli*, King-of-Kings, but that is now just one more iota of the past sealed within an irretrievable forever. Quinatzin is on the cusp of a more profound revelation when his vision shifts, a change of perspective, and he now sees that Lake Texcoco is in a constant flux as if stirred back and forth by a giant paddle, -it is not clear if the basin holds water or liquid light, but he understands, looking at the frothing surface, that it is as it should be. The priests often suggest prayer or meditation to calm the soul, remove from it the petty, daily distractions of life to see The Unfathomable. Well, he realizes the truth is just the opposite; it is in the chaotic whirl and turmoil that one sees The Unfathomable, the chaos of chance that one finds at the heart of existence.

The sun, freed from its harsh prison of geometry flies about the sky and, joyous at its freedom, sings, lilting voice of endless space, and then disappears, receding into some immeasurable distance, becoming but another star, one of an uncountable dazzling number that decorate the void. Using a rope that has been let down for him, gift of Tezcatlipoca, amid a swirl of wind that suggests rain he climbs up into the heavens and there rides across the darkness in a small *acalli*, using his paddle to brush aside the stars that lay within his path. Now he floats across the void towards the sparkling object that lies at its heart.

◆ ◆ ◆

Quinatzin finds himself within a stone chamber, the axis about which the universe indifferently turns. Before him on a wooden table are two baskets, both with their lids closed. The one basket holds the paradise of Tlalocan, and to open this basket is to release the rains upon Nahua and put an end to hunger. To open the other basket is to finish the transformation of Nahua into a desert realm of eternal night. Curiously, a yopicatl stands beside each of the two baskets, one of whom says; "To help you choose the basket most to your liking, you may ask us any question, but keep in mind one of us always speaks the truth," he points to himself, then pointing to his companion says, "and the other always lies."

The other yopicatl now speaks; "All concepts and processes of logic can be reduced to mathematical form. Look, I'll show you." Of an instant the yopicatl has a stylus in his hand, a pot of ink, a sheet of paper laid out before him on a table of convenient height.

Given x as a variable we have: $6x - 18 = 4x - 12$
Factoring, we have: $3(2x - 6) = 2(2x - 6)$
Divide both sides by: $(2x - 6)$
We are left with: $3 = 2$

"Any questions?"

Quinatzin feels his anger rise, how typical of a yopicatl he thinks, to spout fountains of useless information, metaphor piled atop analogy.

Now the first yopicatl is speaking; "Given b and c, two positive numbers:

So that b > -c and c > -b
And c > -c and b > -b
Multiplying bc > c^2 and bc > b^2
Therefore b > c and c > b

Quinatzin realizes there is a hole in the stone floor, not necessarily up or down, for he is at the center, but a passageway that leads, simply enough, to someplace else. He picks up the two baskets, the one Mictlan, the other Paradise, and throws these into the emptiness.

"That was the wrong thing to do," says one of the yopicatl.

"Bravo," says the other, "well done."

✦ ✦ ✦

With unmistakable clarity Quinatzin comes to understand that existence is not some mindless cascade of cause and effect, piecewise linear progression of causality from arbitrary beginning to capricious end, rather one's existence is but a note of the music of the universe, each note reaching out through the silence that defines it, to the next, and in this way binding the translucent ether into a cohesive whole.

✦ ✦ ✦

Quinatzin drifts in and out of the present now, though there are many intangible points to the idea of *now*. But for that, fine thread of reality he remembers he is the King-of-Kings, and that the land burns, and the people suffer:

> I gaze upwards at the wide, bright sky.
> The Demon of Drought consumes everything.
> Sorrow rises from my heart, as smoke from a fire.
> There is no god to whom I have not given homage.
> No sacrifice have I withheld for love.
> Why have I not been heard?

Epiphany. With a shock as startling as a lightning bolt Quinatzin realizes the drought is a yopicatl trick to claim the Valley, ridding the land of the Nahua: a fact of undisputable certainty. The yopicatl encouragements of peace have served no purpose but to weaken the gods, for if no rain, -clever, then the people will go elsewhere. As for draining the lake, 'tricks of plumbing,' the blood of warriors nourishes the earth just as it sustains the gods, and without it the duality that sustains existence is shattered. But surely the yopicatl could not have done all this without help? And to say the question is to know the answer, a truth so obvious as to be transparent: the high priest of Tlaloc has committed an intentional sin, has intentionally made mistakes within the rites and rituals and so offended the god, and who better to release a poisonous serpent within the palace? We have been tricked, he thinks, tricked: a foul stench lies within the very heart of Azcapotzalco. Quinatzin, still ill but very much alive orders justices to bring the high priest of Tlaloc before him, -all the high priests of Tlaloc.

◆ ◆ ◆

Within Azcapotzalco there is a legalist system of 80 standardized laws, and for that not written there is the standard of reasonable behavior, so that one does not have to unravel knots of law by making more knots of law. The empire is ordered by defining proper behavior and responsibilities, allowing suitable appeals, then meting out punishment with the impartiality of gravity. Of this legalist system, and the Nahua tend to a litigious nature, there are a variety of courts each with their diverse officials, and each case has its files and record of testimonies. In contrast with much of the world, past present future, no one is tortured, threatened, or coerced into confession. Further, those of power are not only held accountable, but held to more exacting standards with the penalty for wrongdoing increasing with position. For a noble to rob his father the sentence is death, while the penalty for the same crime by a common worker is to be sold into slavery. The public drunkenness of a common worker results in their hair being shorn, while that of a noble or priest is death. Being a carpenter or mason of mean quality is no great crime, while dishonest or incompetent judges are strangled, as are over-accommodating civil servants and lecherous priests.

Since the actions of the Tlaloc high priests are considered treason Quinatzin himself serves as judge, and as for his decision, though nuances of cause and effect are complex it is easier to make accusations than disprove them. After careful consideration, a prudent weighing of evidence, for the lesser of the high priests, eighteen in number, Quinatzin orders them stoned and their bodies dragged to the marketplace where those who suffer hunger might dine upon them.

♦ ♦ ♦

As for the high priest of Tlaloc, Atipac is his name, a man Quinatzin had always thought earnest and humble, scrupulous in his morals, considering the overwhelming harm that has been done to all Nahua, and the attempt on his life, Quinatzin believes a less merciful death is in order, and so the King-of-Kings commands. Atipac is stripped and laid upon his back within the bottom of a small *acalli*; both arms are stretched wide and secured, so too his legs. An *acalli* of equal size is then laid upon him. Hungry insects soon find Atipac and begin feeding, and as they are insatiable, continue. Eggs are laid that soon hatch, and these creatures too are eternally hungry. Nibble by excruciating nibble Atipac is slowly removed from this existence.

♦ ♦ ♦

And yet for that, no rain falls.

Fifth Bundle

34
The Present, Which Finds Kulcan In Tenochtitlan

Kulcan, his life reduced to skulking, skulks about Tenochtitlan, realm of the Mexica. On this particular day he espies priests of Huitzilopochtli, yet another sun-god war-god, ranging from house to house, and there swinging their censers back and forth, back and forth, sending out aromatic billows of smoke over all aspects and things of the household. Kulcan sees the priests energetically cense, and so divide and demarcate by so many pendulum swings, the hearth, the grinding stone, the tortilla-cooking grill, pots and jugs, plates and bowls, baskets, tools, blankets, what have you, and for each item censed those of the household give the priests an ear of maize. The priests wear a ground-reaching black robe, a large black hat, and upon their skin the black pitch. The priests are encompassed within a mephitic fog, stinking of sulfur, of carrion. Their hair, never cut since joining the priesthood, reaches to their waist or knees. Their hair is matted with what in time Kulcan realizes is dried blood, strange ethos of personal hygiene. Yet for all this it is said that these priests lead pious lives, governing the schools, the rites, and the purposeful heart of the Mexica.

When surrounded by Huitzilopochtli priests one must *be* a Huitzilopochtli priest, thus it is at nightfall Kulcan, yopicatl-silent, visits a house of Huitzilopochtli priests there collecting three robes, two hats, a bundle of lovely quetzal feathers and, an afterthought, a handful of brilliant, smooth-polished green stones. He notices a number of popoloca decorating the city with boughs, arches of fragrant wood, and flowers. He passes a number of popoloca kept within a wooden cage and thinks how astronomically improbable it is that their lives will end happily, but for that who is he to say?

Kulcan considers how the Mexica are allies of Azcapotzalco, and reflects upon the idea that if, -provided with the condition that, enemies should attack Azcapotzalco would the Mexica, alerted to the commotion and but a mile or two away, take to their *acalli* to give aid? Would they climb upon a height and watch the show, or fall upon Azcapotzalco to gather up whatever loot they could? Might Kulcan, supposition, set fire to a small collection of Mexica temples and thus channel their energies to internal purposes? Or would a burning shrine infuriate them as bees provoked? Kulcan ponders these questions and sees no path forward, and so for a time puts the matter aside.

✦ ✦ ✦

Sunrise. Clad in the worn remnants of his Xochipilli garb, Huitzilopochtli robes and hats in hand with his once small tree now trusty staff, Kulcan passes to the house of a skilled seamstress he has earlier made note of, seeing along the way a small cluster of popoloca gathered upon a modest courtyard. Curious, he pauses to watch events unfold. Among them he sees a small popoloca infant, and he cringes, not wanting to watch but yet having to watch, some deep-seated compulsion, for he knows in his heart of hearts, some sort of sacred ritual, they are going to roast and eat that popoloca baby.

The sun just-peaking over a height near Mount Popocatepetl a female holds the baby in one arm and in the other takes hold of a little ceramic vessel that is handed her, -some sort of flavorful grilling sauce Kulcan imagines. Then holding the child she faces west, sunlight racing down the mountain into the valley, and sprinkles not sauce upon the child but water, and as she does so she calls out, "My child! Take and receive the water of Tlaloc and Chalchiuhtlicue, which is our life, and given for the increase and renewal of our bodies. I pray these heavenly drops of water may enter into your body to wash and purify it, removing from you all the evil and sin which was given to you before the beginning of the world."

"All to the good," Kulcan thinks. "Death now would save the popoloca a good bit of heartache and, inevitably, a more painful death later on."

While continuing on with her speech the woman gently washes the baby with water; "You that are hurtful to this child, depart, for the child lives anew, having been born anew, and is purified and cleansed. Lord Tlaloc, see here your creature that you have sent into this world, this place of sorrow, suffering, and penitence. Grant this child your gifts and inspiration for you are the Great God, and with you is the Great Goddess Chalchiuhtlicue."

Then come murmurs of acclaim, approval, and strangely enough sounds that suggest implied happiness by those gathered. Kulcan is most touched. "Best of luck, little popoloca," he whispers, and continues on.

✦ ✦ ✦

The husband of the seamstress departed to his purposes of the day, Kulcan stands to the side of the doorway, a humble thick-walled house of clay-covered reeds that stays cool in the summer and is easily heated in the winter, and knocks, to which he is bid pass in. Kulcan ducks his head, enters, and in a voice ever so polite and yet authoritative, or so he imagines his voice, says, "Tezcatlipoca has sent me to you, both in a literal and metaphorical sense as we, the two of us, request your aid."

The seamstress prostrates herself upon the floor.

"Tezcatlipoca sent me to check on how things fare with the Mexica, and Huitzilopochtli of course, but things being what they typically are (look of exasperation), neither my robe nor hat fit. I ask you, on behalf of Tezcatlipoca, to adjust these so they do." Kulcan places the bundle of quetzal feathers before the seamstress. "And in exchange, I will give you these."

Her face still held to the floor, she answers, "I live but to serve the gods."

Kulcan, yopicatl-patient, waits her out, and after a time she lifts up her head to see the feathers piled before her, and to that her eyes grow large. She slowly reaches out a hand and touches one of the feathers, then quickly resumes her manifestations of grace softly tapping her forehead upon the floor.

"Come now," Kulcan says. "The day does not wait for us. Let us begin." He puts the robes down before her. "So, I would imagine that I am larger than most of your customers."

Her head remains pressed down upon the earth.

"I have three robes, all of which are too small for me, of which I need you to make one that fits; likewise, the hats. Now, would be a good time to begin. Now this very moment."

For a period of time, demarcation by gazes, she is content to alternately look between the pile of robes and caps laid before her, Kulcan, and the feathers, yet for that she still lays upon the ground which suggests, deductive chain of logic, that no sewing is being done.

"All to the good then," Kulcan says, giving her his biggest, warm-hearted yopicatl smile. "*Now!*" (The walls tremble.)

Swept into motion the woman leaps up, fetches her tools, her kit, and with a marked roll of twine first measures width, then with his help (he towers over her) height, arm length, and circumference of his head. She then measures the scope of the robes and hats, and with a piece of chalk marks out her plan of attack. She then takes to cutting, all the while murmuring to herself, "Teohuatzin,"[38] a word he is unfamiliar with, and when Kulcan asks, "What is a Teohuatzin?" She says in return but "Teohuatzin," sustaining a thread of consistent logic.

"Teohuatzin." He echoes. "Teohuatzin."

There is a knock at her doorway, to which the seamstress tells the potential customer to please return another time, explaining that she is doing work for Teohuatzin. Soon, he hears outside the house "Teohuatzin," the one voice repeated by another, and then another. Hearing many Teohuatzins echoing about outside, Kulcan sighs.

And as for the 'now,' revelation, Kulcan remembers her starting to work and then, snap of her nimble fingers, her finishing. He puts on the long, flowing, voluminous, concealing robe to find it fits perfectly, so too the hat, as if her fingers had been divinely guided. Bows and expressions of gratitude flow back and forth between seamstress and customer. When, finally, very priest-like in appearance he steps outside her house Kulcan finds some number, a 'shrewdness' he believes it is called, or a 'congress' of popoloca awaiting him who, seeing him, all bow and murmur "Teohuatzin!" So many are the "Teohuatzins" that the word seems to ripple out to the far edges of the world.

Of the popoloca gathered about the house there are any number of black-robed, black-capped, black-haired, black-sooted priests, and it seems they confuse Kulcan for some official, or simulacrum, whatever or whoever Teohuatzin is, precisely. But, and here the key fact: Poof!

---

38 High priest concerned with details of ritual.

Just like that Kulcan is someone! Yet having suddenly become someone, an Arbitrator of sacred observances, questions fall upon him like darts.

"Most honored Teohuatzin, are you here to see the festival?"

"I wouldn't miss it."

"Most honored Teohuatzin, will you help offer those captured in the *Xochiyaoyotl*?"[39]

Having seen the offerings of Tezcatlipoca, Kulcan knows better than to ignorantly play along. He looks over the priests gathered about him, selects the largest of the bunch, a keen-eyed one he thinks most likely to give an intelligent answer, and asks him to walk beside him as the group, collective we, amble their way towards the center of Tenochtitlan.

"Your name?" Kulcan asks him.

"Epcoatl, most honored Teohuatzin."

He pauses for a moment, collecting his thoughts. "I am concerned, friend Epcoatl, that the young priests are not learning what they properly should be learning. So that I might better judge the quality of instruction I wish to ask you some questions that, to the best of your ability, I would like you to answer. Let us begin with the *Xochiyaoyotl*. Please, share with me your views on the subject."

Kulcan speaks with the utmost authority for no one will believe he is Teohuatzin unless he believes he is Teohuatzin, and not for Kulcan to play a poorly defined role among many tens of thousands of lethal popolocas.

"My views?" The young priest asks.

---

39 Literally, 'The Flower War,' or 'War of the Flowers.'

"Yes, *your* take on the mechanics, purpose or purposes, and outcomes. Pretend I don't know anything about it and make me an expert on the underlying significance and merit."

"Our interpretation of The Flower War?"

"Not *our*," he says slowly, carefully. "*Your*. I want to know what it is *you*, a typical young priest, knows about The Flower War. Or think you know about it."

"Well," Epcoatl begins, warming to his task. "The highest virtue for a man is to go bravely to the battlefield, for it is by the *teoatl*[40] effused in battle, whether it is spilled upon the battlefield itself or, more commonly, the warrior captured, spilled upon the god's altar, that the gods are nourished and existence sustained. So the Sun has strength to rise up each morning defeating darkness, and strength to pass across the heavens. A tournament that serves two purposes..."

Kulcan is no longer listening, his attention on the many shops selling food they walk pass.

"It is surprising how often peace used to inflict its wounds among us, the gods faltering from hunger. So it was our King-of-Kings, and wise councilors, agreed upon the Flower Wars, by which the gods are nourished and strengthened, and since the Flower Wars began rain has been plentiful."

"I see," Kulcan offers. "Very interesting. And say, I am looking for Tlacotzin and Petlatzin. You know them?"

"Yes, of course."

"Excellent! I'd like to find them."

"Certainly. We should see them up ahead. So as

---

40 *Teo* = sacred, *atl* = water; sacred water, or blood.

maize gives its magical essence, its life, to sustain us, we give our essence to sustain the gods."

"Hmmph!" Kulcan, offers. "Of course, the kernel(!) of the question is what is meant by *sustain*. Words are but symbols, and though we hope we are 'understood,' whatever that means, by the very fact that symbols are intrinsically limited they reduce our awareness of the world, and the ability to communicate to others our experiences thereof. That is to say, and let me speak here as precisely as I can, a fraction of the whole is forever, unavoidably lost to the nuances of meaning just as, for example, we must forever work with an imprecise value of π. You don't see Tlacotzin and Petlatzin, do you?"

"No, but I'm sure we will. A bit further ahead."

"Good. Good. So… You like being a priest? Many think it a demanding profession."

"It's the only life I've known. I was orphaned as an infant, and ended up in Huitzilopochtli's care. He sustained me then, and now I help sustain Huitzilopochtli."

"I see." Big yawn! "Very interesting! And so this festival today, celebration of some great Flower War massacre?" Kulcan smiles his pleasantest of smiles and looks carefully at Epcoatl while raising his eyebrows, to suggest that if there is a flaw in the logic to please correct the Teohuatzin, which Epcoatl does.

"No massacres honored Teohuatzin. (A tone of voice that suggests the question is amusing.) The numbers are modest. The *Xochiyaoyotl* is an honorable battle with the objective, of course, not to kill on the battlefield, though of course that happens, and is good, or acceptable, but to capture enemy soldiers so that their soul, their essence, their *teoatl* can be offered to the god or goddess at the proper time upon their altars."

"Hmmpf." Kulcan suggests. "Yes, it's all of a piece, an integrated whole as you say. I have reflected upon the idea at great length finally deciding that, in the end, each mind is alone. Our thoughts, feelings, and ideas are islands unto themselves. So, our existence is but a universe of reduced awareness."

"That's the hard stone" Epcoatl muses. "My supposition is that we would be better off talking less, and painting more. Momentous signatures surround us: a rock, a sprouting seed, or an iridescent butterfly. A brilliant swirl of vision is what the idea of existence is, or for that matter eternity."

"Strange," Kulcan thinks. "Epcoatl speaks as if he has come to a wisdom as profound as that of a yopicatl. Though a young yopicatl, to be sure."

✦ ✦ ✦

Kulcan-Teohuatzin nears the center of Tenochtitlan, where he is overwhelmed by the shear numbers of popoloca all to their purpose of coming or going. Bands of porters pass, each to their loads, with some carrying baskets upon their backs, others large earthen jugs full of small fruits, honey, this that and the other. There are great wide streets bordered by canals and gardens, or canals bordered by streets and gardens, or magnificent gardens bordered by streets and canals. From a nearby mountain, across the lake an aqueduct of mortared stone brings water into the heart of the city giving life to a cascade of fountains and baths. The city appears to Kulcan an ant-pile of orderly activity, each to their purpose, each to their comings and goings.

"So tell me this, Epcoatl. With all your wars, it seems to me that in a few generations the fighters will get bred out of existence. Then the next thing you know, you're sustaining someone else's god with your essence."

"Not possible."

"Plenty possible."

"Within our schools the teachers determine the inclinations of their young students, and send those so suited to the priesthood, or suggest others become artisans, or perhaps scribes. However, many are filled with courage and, as soon as they are old enough, and there is occasion, they join the soldiers serving as porters, carrying supplies to the battlefield, so they may come to understand the nature of battle. If a youth shows bravery, perhaps bringing food or water to the front in the thick of battle, he is soon admitted to the company of warriors and, depending upon his inclination, sees action."

"And soon killed off. 'We are the superior killers.' Blah. Blah. Blah. I've heard it all before."

Kulcan turns his attention to the shining white buildings, fine craftsmanship of stone and wood: temples and oratories, towers and bastions, -and any number of pleasant, clean plazas. And throughout, the eye falls upon statues, monuments, bas-relief panels extending the length of a building, wall, or *tlachtli* court. Everywhere dazzling and curious art, and above all this, above the city, rising up from houses, public buildings, *tlachtli* courts and temples he sees sky-piercing flagpoles which carry upon them banners of woven feathers, streams of lavish brilliance against the sky showing, emblem of the city, an eagle perched upon a cactus holding in its bill what first appears, at a distance, a serpent but, closer inspection, one realizes is a ribbon; red, yellow, black, upon which are drawn symbols that inform the reader this place, this very island, is the center of the world. And in this Center of The World a great number of vendors sell foods of all types. Kulcan stops at a stall, picks up a sack of fruit, then a second, and in exchange hands the seller the glittering-shining stones he earlier borrowed from the priests. There is a look of horror, or something akin to horror upon the vendors face.

"Not enough?" Kulcan asks.

Epcoatl, laughing, speaks on behalf of the fruit-seller, "That should be sufficient." He then continues on with his unstoppable, unceasing discourse that Kulcan thinks has been going on since time began. "Thus a youth may go to a Flower War serving as a porter, and return having earned the insignia of a valiant warrior."

"Or return in small pieces, sure to impress either way. You're keeping an eye out for Tlacotzin and Petlatzin?"

"Soon," Epcoatl says, nodding towards a cluster of good-sized temples.

"Excellent."

"Most of the youths inclined to this sort of life are the sons of knights, lords, or warriors, eager to gain honor, cover themselves with glory."

"Covering oneself with glory," Kulcan observes. "An interesting metaphor. Now, will you look at, oh good grief." Kulcan-Teohuatzin, abruptly halting, and so too the accompanying crowd about him, points at what lays directly before them: nine timbers, set upright within the stone plaza, each some thirty feet in height, and aligned in a precise row some eight or nine feet apart. Arrayed across each adjacent pair are sturdy poles, one atop the other to define a ladder-like structure, an array of ladders, and carefully threaded upon these poles, temple-to-temple, looking out upon forever: skulls.

"Explain for me," requests the Teohuatzin, jab of a forefinger for emphasis, "the symbolism and logic of this."

"The *Tzompantli?*"[41] Epcoatl observes. "Does it please you?"

"Does it please me?" Kulcan repeats. "Well, I suppose it's… commendable. Or at least, all things considered, a good start. And I have not seen its like. Certainly a momentous signature, allowing one to vividly see the solemn consequence of defying authority! And the height, how do they get the skulls up there?"

He forces his gaze away from the Skull Rack, turns to Epcoatl and gives him a warm friendly smile. Kulcan recalls having seen, on his Wanderings, popoloca skulls piled up in rounded mounds or carefully crafted pyramids, skulls mounted on the end of staffs or mounted over doorways or on the prows of canoes, hung from trees, used as candle holders, planters, drinking cups, percussive instruments, so on and so forth, all of a decorative piece. "It does have its artistic merit, while the quality of the woodwork suggests an excellent work ethic and meticulous attention to detail. And it certainly is tall."

---

41 Skull Rack.

Epcoatl, a look of shock on his face, "Small? You think it too small?"

"Have your teachers taught you the underlying purpose and meaning of the skull rack?" Kulcan continues. "It's significance?"

Epcoatl, unhappy at the suggestion the Skull Rack is too small, frowns. "The Skull Rack honors those who gave their lives to sustain…" he lifts up his arms, turns gracefully back and forth in a half-circle: "This." Epcoatl, though not asked to recite a poem, takes a deep breath, looks into the distance and recites a poem:

> You there, we here, rich in heroic offspring,
> Wield our spears to vanquish every foe,
> So that our realm encompasses the earth.

Those of the surrounding crowd clap in appreciation, and after a moments hesitation, in affirmation, the Teohuatzin nods his head.

"So, you are pleased with the *Tzompantli?*" Epcoatl asks.

"Pleased?" The Teohuatzin responds. "Well. There is a clear 'resonance' of spirit to it, a 'life-motion' if you will. And, certainly, it concisely teaches the idea, and consequences, of 'us versus them.' Like good art it provides an opportunity to recognize both beauty as well as pain, making an aesthetic statement on both a representational and non-representational level. And, it is decorative, certainly, with the skillfully sanded, oiled, and orthogonally joined pieces of wood supporting the skulls providing a strong geometric element, and the different surfaces, -hair, bone, teeth, and wood providing the sculpture with a strongly expressive character. And as for the 'test of time' that the more temperamental artists are always whining about, the fact that this is no mere piece of carved rock but a plastic art, something that changes with time, the spare piece of bone or tuft of hair occasionally falling away, provides the observer a dynamic experience. Said more strongly, it gives the observer a kinetic sense of the essence of Time."

Epcoatl bows to the Teohuatzin, says, "So one comes to the idea of artistic vision, and its ultimate limitation. An artist may begin with so many paints and canvasses, proceeding through different types of paintings, such as landscapes, portraits, abstracts, and so on. However in time the artist, intrinsically unsatisfied- the very nature of the artist, coming to understand the limited nature of existence mixes more colors, and experiments with tricks of shading and hue, building upon the three dimensions to suggest a fourth, time, and a fifth, the meaning that underlies all meaning. Then, full circle: the artist decides to simply leave the paint before the empty canvas and let the viewer imagine the art they find most pleasing."

"You suggest the same effect could be captured by heaping up the skulls in a pile?" Kulcan asks. "Now, as to that I remember-"

Epcoatl darts out his right arm pointing towards the top of a temple that the crowd, like the push of a river, has drawn them to. "There! Tlacotzin and Petlatzin. You see them? They are Eagle Knight captains."

Upon the height of the temple Kulcan sees a glittering array of ornately dressed popolocas, their hands and feet hidden behind talon-like devices, suits with feathers sewed upon them, or suits of shimmering feathers, either way, uncomfortably hot, with a helmet that suggests a great-gaping beak girding their face. Kulcan shifts his gaze, looking out over the swirl of popoloca surrounding the temple, sees upon the plaza soldiers arrayed in blocks, each troop identified by their own sky-reaching feather banner. In one place a block of jaguar warriors in their black-spotted yellow suits peering out from, strange illusion, face-encompassing fanged helmets carved of wood. Another block, front and center before the temple, is defined by the Ocelot warriors who wear quilted-cotton armor suits decorated with elongated black-edged spots patterned in chain-like bands, while further back one finds the less distinguished killers. From a distance it appears a dazzling garden.

A trumpet sounds, and with its sustained resonant voice brings all to silence. Popoloca are brought forth who begin to climb the stairs to the utmost height of the temple.

"I thank-you for our conversation, Epcoatl." Pointing to a smaller, nearby temple that seems strangely empty, Kulcan says, "I am going to observe the festival from over there, out of the way of everyone."

"The Temple of Chilico,"[42] Epcoatl observes.

"Yes, the Temple of Chilico, how about that. Now I must give you a vitally important task, -important for a number of reasons I will not tire you by itemizing. Find Tlacotzin and Petlatzin, and tell them I must speak with them tonight, when midnight is sounded, upon the

---

42 The God of Chilies.

height of Chilico's temple. Tell them, simply, that the Teohuatzin requires it, and bids them to come alone so that secrets may be kept."

Epcoatl nods in agreement, yet for that his expression suggests a loose thread.

"Tell them they have no reason to be afraid, for Huitzilopochtli sees to the safety of his Eagle Knights, and will protect them from Chilico."

Epcoatl bursts out with a deep-seated all-consuming laugh, and with that Kulcan knows his friend eagle-knights will be there.

Amid the surrounding crowd of popoloca Kulcan gives Epcoatl a friendly pat on the shoulder and turns away, yet as he does so, unexpected, Epcoatl speaks to him in Uaxyacac, a chittering-chattering language one can hear upon the market plazas of the valley but in truth few, very few, Nahua understand, and that he has no way of knowing the Teohuatzin knows, "*Hunanwat-li-tkis.*"[43]

---

43 Have care or caution, imperative command.

35
Chilico's Temple

Eyes fixed on the intricate festival-ceremony before them, dazzling display of convoluted symbolism, most popoloca little notice the Teohuatzin crossing the small distance to Chilico's temple. Kulcan climbs the temple steps and finds, upon its modest height, a convenient place to sit amid many sacks and baskets of chilies. Slow on the uptake, it is only then that Kulcan understands Epcoatl's caution is not referring to his climbing the temple-steps.

Surprise. Kulcan, his sense of smell overwhelmed by the incense, smoke, and many baskets and sacks of chilies that surround him, his hearing overwhelmed by various trumpets and flutes and drums, his eyes gazing upon the priests and soldiers, this that and the other, suddenly realizes a popoloca has approached near enough for a swift spear-thrust. Yopicatl-quick he slides off his perch, slips away a distance then leaps, staff cocked for a good solid swing, to find, so he thinks, yet another priest. Kulcan thinks 'yet another priest,' but of course if one visits a temple one logically expects to find priests.

Kulcan, large presence dressed in black robes and hat holding a staff the size of a small tree (so it was, so its size), says to the popoloca priest of chilies, "You startled me."

In turn, the Chilico priest answers, "And you startled me!"

For a moment Kulcan and the priest loudly guffaw. The priest gestures to the baskets of chilies that surround them, says, "Well, can I offer you some chilies?"

"No, thank you. In fact I just ate. I am Kulcan-Teohuatzin (he bows). I hope you don't mind my sitting here, to watch this, umm… Festival."

"Oh it's a festival alright, and I am Axaycatl. I saw you approaching the temple. You draw a crowd."

"Well, I am Teohuatzin, and everyone wants to get their rites right. Right?"

"You're, not from around here?" Axaycatl asks.

"In fact I am from around here. But I have been gone awhile. So (glancing around the shrine), why doesn't Chilico have a sacrificial altar? Seems unusual, in these modern times."

"No, no sacrifices here," Axaycatl sighs. "As I would not wish to be sacrificed, so I do not sacrifice. That to me seems the starting point for religion." Axaycatl points to the popoloca upon the height of the opposite temple dressed as one god or another who have joined the chalk-clad prisoners. Seeing Kulcan's glazed expression he helpfully suggests, "It's all rather complex, and seems to get more complex each year, what with each priest defining their own little bit of expertise, their own little niche. Job security, I suppose. Not like Chilico, who is simply Chilico. No doubt you know the temple across the way is that of Xipe Totec, god of the sprouting seed, renewal of the earth and so on. But that in itself is too simple, so the one is also three, if that makes sense, a trinity of Tota, Topiltzin, and Yolometl."[44]

Kulcan, at a loss of what to say, offers: "Hmmph."

"And just as there is a trinity of 'good,' that is to say warm, heart-felt gods, so too, in accordance with duality, there is a second trinity of the not so good, that of Totec, Xipe, and Tlatlauhquitezcatl."[45]

"Really?" Kulcan suggests. "A balanced duality, so many on one side, an equal number to the other, and each with their own festivals, offerings, and presiding officials. A most clever, or should I say *meaningful*, theology."

The two are silent for a time, Kulcan and Axayacatl seemingly intent upon the ceremony. After a moment, Kulcan suggests, "So many gods, they're going to need more space."

"You think?" Axayacatl answers. "But (sigh), be that as it may watch closely, the ceremony begins. I think you'll find this instructive, Teohuatzin (Axayacatl winks), of how things have changed over the past few years."

Kulcan watches a prisoner led down from the temple

---

44 Our Father, The Son, and The heart, or soul, of both.
45 Terrible Lord Who Fills One With Dread, Man Who Has Been Flayed, and Mirror of Fiery Brightness.

height to the plaza, then onto an immense, disk-shaped slab of stone raised up some four or five feet above the plaza, its rim intricately carved into a sequence of panels showing Mexica conquests. From the very center of the disk, through a small hole, passes a securely fixed rope, and to this rope the left ankle of the prisoner is bound. The prisoner is given a shield, and given a sword-no-sword, the razor-sharp obsidian teeth replaced by small red feathers. Kulcan sees the captive popoloca inspect the edge of his sword-no-sword and, upon his face, a look that suggests some mixture of resignation and determination. A priest, in truth there seems no end to them, walks twice about the stone swishing a censer back and forth, back and forth, delineating time by the swing of a pendulum. A jaguar knight then comes upon the stone: sword-real-sword; shield; helmet; light flexible armor of dense quilted-cotton.

"A contest of equals," Kulcan observes. "And so we watch the absurd resolve the absolute, although in truth they seem much the same."

Axaycatl shrugs. A trumpet sounds, and the jaguar knight advances dancing out small mincing steps, two steps left, one back, two steps right, one step forward. It is but a lark! The prisoner, no weakling, defends himself, featly parrying strikes and swings for several turns while landing more than one blow upon his well armored opponent to little effect. The jaguar knight, quick turn, a feint, cuts the prisoners thigh and there is a sudden splash of blood.

Unexpectedly, the small spill of blood suggests the contest has ended. Four priests rush onto the stone and grab the prisoner, each to a limb, and lay the popoloca down flat upon his back whereupon a fifth priest, more regally decorated and thus, supposition, more highly esteemed, joins his four colleagues, and this fifth priest, in but a heartbeat's worth of time, removes the prisoner's heart. The priest holds the vital organ up high for a moment, the steam from the heart rising up to the gods above, then tosses it into some sort of sacred receptacle.[46] Though Kulcan doesn't fully understand the symbolism inherent to the process, he understands that such actions help sustain the universe by reducing the number of popolocas.

Kulcan laughs. "Nice. Do that another ten million times and we'll be getting somewhere. (Big chuckle!) What a difference in cosmologies between here, and right... over... there. You should be careful, friend Axaycatl, that you don't end up on yonder stone holding a feathered-sword."

The slain prisoner is carried into a small house off to the side of the stone slab. After a moment, seemingly but an instant, a popoloca emerges wearing the skin that so recently belonged to the prisoner; hands and feet, too complicated to suitably remove and don, dangle from wrists and ankles. Carrying a bowl and staff the popoloca, adorned with an extra layer of skin, passes through the crowd begging for alms, and in exchange granting prayers to those in need.

"You've got to be kidding me," Kulcan says.

"Nope," says Axaycatl, "and you'd be surprised how long they wear those skins."

"Let me guess," Kulcan answers. "A day? Eleven days?

---

46 Cuauhxicalli, or Eagle Vessel

One day for each level of Mictlan? Or is that nine? Wait, thirteen, right?"

Axaycatl frowns; "A month, if you can believe it. *Twenty* days. Each day a new beggar borrows the 'cloak' and goes out into the city blessing supplicants, collecting alms, and returning at night to hang the skin upon a sacred hanger. At the end of twenty days the skin is buried, the collected alms split between the temple, he who captured the prisoner, and the different beggars."

"Wow," Kulcan observes. "Something new every day. Yet, here we have a philosophy that motivates the soldier, helps the indigent, and helps Xipe Totec himself."

"It's not so extreme if you really believe that 'putting on the golden cloak' will in fact ensure that seeds sprout," Axaycatl philosophizing, " so that everyone has food. But otherwise, yes, it's pretty extreme. Yet on the other hand, potential enemies of the state require an example of what happens to enemies of the state."

The next prisoner fights so tenaciously he knocks his opponent, an Eagle Knight, senseless, but, some sort of gamesmanship, this knight is simply replaced by a fresh one. A minor scratch and the prisoner is set upon by priests and laid upon the stone, de-hearted, and flayed. The next prisoner simply lies down upon the stone and has done with it. One after the other the skin-clad beggars scurry off into the city.

"You must admit," observes Kulcan, "this festival is a downer."

"Yes," opines Axaycatl. "It is at that. Up north we spice it up with more females and fewer clothes. Fewer bodies as well. You don't have to kill everyone you capture to set an example, maybe just one or two. The rest of the prisoners can work in the fields, haul timber or stone, do something useful."

"You're from the north?" Kulcan asks. "I've heard rumors of yopicatl up there."

"Yes, I'm from the north. And yes, I've heard the rumors. But no, I've never seen one, up north anyway."

"What brings you here to Tenochtitlan?"

"The desire to kill someone. What brings you here?"

"Ah, well. There you go. You know Axaycatl sometimes, funny coincidence, I hope you don't mind, but I've asked a couple of eagle knights to meet me here at the hour of *icama*, thinking the temple would be empty. Which is to say, if you are following my logical thread, I plan to send the two off on a journey."

Axaycatl's face breaks into a wide smile. "It appears Chilico has finally heard my prayers. Please, if I could show you someone."

Axaycatl and Kulcan walk back into the shrine where they find a popoloca grown, perhaps some twenty-five years of age playing with toys, two opposing armies of wood-carved warriors that he is alternately knocking down with small stones.

Axaycatl nods toward the young man. "My son. A certain captain within a certain army wished to earn the glory of capturing a certain town. Rather than await the rest of the army he raced his troops-ahead, those he was responsible for, and had them, alone, assail the town walls. In effect the soldiers were sacrificed to the God of Ego, who of all the gods strangely enough doesn't have a temple. So many died at the walls that when the rest of the army arrived they had no need to make ladders, they simply climbed up the bodies of our fallen, which included my son. He did survive though, but with the mind of a child."

"He seems happy," Kulcan offers.

"Yes, and he is alive. Yet a life has been taken."

"The captain?" Kulcan asks.

"As daring and ambitious as he was conceited and incapable, yet for that removed from our army to its rare credit. Though one might think other treatment more appropriate. As I'm sure you know, the purpose of power is to protect those in power."

"Yep," Kulcan acknowledges. "For a fact."

"Should I repeat that?"

"No need."

"The purpose of power is to protect those in power. Only rarely, when it is expedient, is there ever any accountability. I have followed him, our ex-captain who the Mexica saw fit to again make captain, waiting for an opportunity to alter his life as he has altered my son's."

Kulcan and Axaycatl leave the shrine, returning to the steps to watch the end of the festival. A priest, specially designated and trained to his purpose, brings out to the stone slab a sinuous serpent made of feathers, paper, rubber, and hot-burning incense that he sets afire and throws onto the blood-sotted stone. As the serpent burns, the metaphor-symbolism lost to Kulcan, the priest throws into the fire handfuls of incense and metal filings that blaze up in different colors all the while walking about the stone censing, censing, giving forth the pendulum swing of eternity. Then the priest puts down his censer and unfurls a thick sheet of paper that covers the stone which, for a moment, smolders, then bursts into searing flame, and soon all that was on the stone, -paper, feathers, incense, blood, is turned to ash.

Upon the plaza a group of young popoloca start to dance, and as they dance they sing:

It may be, that I go to destruction;
I, the tender maize plant.
I, whose seeds are the gold of sunlight.
I, whose heart is jade.

"So," Axaycatl begins, clearing his throat. "One hears tales about the yopicatl."

"Oh?" says Kulcan.

Axaycatl, looking away from Kulcan, in his hands a chili that he turns about, "If such a character from such a tale were to come to my temple, some odd, inexorable convolution of fate, seeking to settle an account, so to speak, though I know such things can't be truly settled, why I would be delighted to help him, and in turn hope that he might help me, as you now understand, send someone on his way to the lowest-rung of Mictlan."

"An alliance." Kulcan suggests.

Axaycatl nods. "An alliance. I know an excellent way to send someone off to the next world."

"I like what I hear. Although, if a few bodies were found atop a certain temple a certain priest and son might be held to account, just to, you know, keep up appearances."

"Of course," says Axaycatl, a gleam in his eye, "which is why recent events at Teotihuacan come so quickly to mind. Nothing like a good fire! A shrine burns, remains are discovered, but who-is-who and why-is-why remains forever a mystery."

"It would make quite a blaze, all these chilies. You'd be short one temple, but the Mexica would cough themselves to Mictlan."

◆ ◆ ◆

Axaycatl collects his son and the two leave the temple. Axaycatl returns after a time, having made a certain invitation based on a rumor of spies, suggestions of rewards and so on, bringing with him coiled ropes, a jug filled with flammable oil, and a small blue-tinted ceramic pot filled with hot-burning black tar. He departs the temple again to return with bundles of dried pine that he carefully stacks within the high-peaked shrine, and then fusses with ropes, and then fusses a bit more. After a time Axaycatl joins Kulcan upon the edge of the temple height, where Kulcan is looking up into the night sky gazing at the island-like flat-bottomed clouds floating by, and in between these clouds momentarily revealed and then hidden, revealed and then hidden, an endless sweep of scintillating stars. The night grows cold, and we come to the hour of *icama*, a demarcation of time that within Tenochtitlan is sounded out by trumpets from atop the Temple of Huitzilopochtli.

36

Tlacotzin and Petlatzin

At the hour of *icama*, demarcation of time by the rise and fall of stars, Tlacotzin and Petlatzin, who consider it a matter of honor to arrive promptly at the agreed upon moment, climb the steps leading to Chilico's shrine, a modest height of some thirty feet, which seems far too little considering the importance of chilies to the Mexica diet. Tlacotzin and Petlatzin do not need fear for their safety within the heart of Tenochtitlan, yet are armed; perhaps simply a habit of caution, or perhaps a premonition.

Priestly Axaycatl and Kulcan-Teohuatzin stand before the two eagle knight captains. Kulcan looks at the curious necklace Tlacotzin wears and recognizes that he sees, threaded upon gold wire, dried hearts, the size of which, suggest? Kulcan, for a moment confused, looks into the sharp eyes of Tlacotzin and, of the instant, realizes the necklace is made of dried yopicatl hearts. Night Axe swings his staff about, and down, and unfortunately swift smashes Tlacotzin's head. Yopicatl-quick Night Axe grabs Petlatzin 'just-so' about the throat. His spear knocked aside, as useful to Petlatzin now as if it were on the far edges of space and time, Petlatzin grabs for his knife. Night Axe squeezes his neck with that much greater force and part carries, part guides Petlatzin towards the waiting shrine where Axaycatl deftly, swiftly, winds a rope across Petlatzin's mouth, trundles his arms to his sides, and lashes his feet together. Night Axe pulls that which was once Tlacotzin into the shrine and, anticipating another guest, cleans up as he can about the temple height.

The ex-captain now-captain who possesses the courage to order many popoloca of less authority to their deaths arrives with two guards. Each guard wears quilted armor, a helmet, and carries a shield; each carries a bow and quiver of arrows; one carries a spear, the other a sword. The three look suspiciously about. Axaycatl leads the captain towards the shrine for the whispering of secrets, while Night Axe tries to put the guards at ease by reciting a poem:

> By many paths one can reach the height of the
>   temple.
> But all who climb there see the same quality of
>   moonlight.

Night Axe smiles warmly at the two guards who shift nervously, and for good reason: Night Axe is no small, gentle, easily slain creature of the glens. As Axaycatl enters the shrine with his guest Night Axe makes further use of his trusty staff. With the moment for revenge at hand Axaycatl sets upon the captain, yet for that realizing his death is upon him the captain fights back with a grim determination. Night Axe quickly crosses the intervening distance to step behind the ex-captain now-captain and pinch his neck 'just so.' Axaycatl, after a moment to catch his breath, sets to his ropes, several of which dangle from high up within the shrine. One of these dangling ropes Axaycatl ties to the lashings that bind together the ex-captain's now-captain's ankles. Satisfied with his knot-work, Axaycatl motions for Night Axe to pull the other end of the rope and so he does, raising the ex-captain now-captain a height into the sky. After securing the rope on a convenient beam, Axaycatl has Night Axe push the modest sacred fire of Chilico, held within a shield-sized dish-like basin, beneath the captain. Axaycatl empties a basket of chilies onto the fire and then gives the captain a push so that he swings back and forth, back and forth, through the smoldering chili-smoke that sears the lungs like fire. Night Axe retrieves the bodies of the two guards, placing them within the shrine.

Night Axe, Axaycatl, and Petlatzin watch the carefully trussed captain, who now defines the end of a pendulum swinging back and forth, back and forth, in and out of the chili smoke, and listen to him relentlessly cough. Over time, the receding of so many moments, the amplitude of the pendulum's oscillations decrease bringing the captain more directly into the smoke until there is nothing left to breath but searing fumes. Axaycatl then gives the pendulum another push, imparting motion to it, the force F of the push equal to the mass m of the captain times the imparted acceleration a, allowing a momentary breath of not fresh air, but something certainly fresher. Night Axe, Axaycatl, and yopicatl-murdering Petlatzin watch the pendulum swing back and forth, back and forth, back and forth.

Night Axe, to break the tedium, says, "You're aware the force of gravity can be determined from a simple pendulum?"

"What?" Axaycatl asks

"Gravity," says Night Axe. "The force that ensures things always fall, or return, to earth. Rocks, darts, arrows, what have you."

Axaycatl gives the pendulum another push then, after several oscillations demarcated by choking coughs, says, "That's great. I'm really glad to know that."

The ex ex-captain is dead. Night Axe gives the pendulum a big push, and then cuts the rope at the apex of the swing so the ex ex-captain falls into the back of the shrine. Axaycatl looks to Night Axe, who nods in answer. Axaycatl grabs the end of another rope that dangles from the height of the shrine and ties it to the lashings holding Petlatzin's ankles. Night Axe hauls him up above the smoldering chilies, secures the end of the rope on a convenient post, and imparts force to the pendulum.

As Petlatzin swings back and forth (coughing, gasping) delineating space in heartbeats, Night Axe, as if discussing the moonlight upon the waters of Lake Texcoco, says to Axaycatl, "It seems a shame to lose such a valiant warrior." Then, as if suddenly remembering the pendulum, no harm done, Night Axe stops the motion of the suspended body, considerately holding it away from the smoke, patiently waits for Petlatzin to stop coughing, or almost stop coughing, says; "If you give us the names of those in charge of the yopicatl-murdering, I would be willing to let you down."

Petlatzin, dry rasp, flecks of blood coming to his lips, shakes his head to suggest "no." Night Axe sets the oscillator back in motion; back and forth, back and forth through the chili smoke. But suddenly, of a moment, Petlatzin is nodding, suggesting he has changed his mind.

Night Axe gently holds the Petlatzin-pendulum out of the smoke; Axaycatl cuts the rope that binds Petlatzin's mouth and slowly, slowly, through a good bit of coughing Petlatzin speaks names, of which one is new to Night Axe and that he adds to his list. Night Axe makes sure Petlatzin has given him all the names that his memory serves him to recall and then, ever so gently, swings him back down over the chilies.

Petlatzin looks wildly to Night Axe, who smiles warmly, says, "I said I would let you down, but neither how nor when. What we have here is a linguistic hoax, a sleight of lexicology, a trick worthy of prosecutors and judges. What we have here is your death."

Axaycatl busily sets fire to the bundles of pinewood that he has placed within the shrine and wet with oil, and then disappears down the temple steps. Night Axe, in a solemn, ringing voice, though no one is listening, and of this fact he does not care, says, "*Ca ye ompolihuiz in moteyo* Tlacotzin, *ti* Petlatzin *aca ca ye in mocuica?*"[47]

---

47 For your name shall perish, Tlacotzin, and you, Petlatzin, where are your songs?

Of a moment, Night Axe decides the more Mexica temple-shrines he can set fire to the better. Night Axe snatches a bow, a quiver of arrows, and the small blue-tinted ceramic pot of black tar away from the hungry fire. He carefully dips the business end of an arrow into the pot of tar, then momentarily holds this in a nearby flame; afire, he sends the burning arrow, swift flight of purpose marked out by rules of gravity and trigonometry, sine and cosine, onto the thatched roof of Xipe Totec's temple, a perfect end to the days sublime ceremony. He then sends out another fire arrow to its purpose, and another, and so on, setting fire to the surrounding shrines and temple houses.

The inner city comes alive with flame, accompanied by cries, shouts, commotion, and soon enough Night Axe finds he has but a single arrow left. Night Axe, illuminated by a number of burning temples, looks across the considerable distance to the shrines of Huitzilopochtli and Tlaloc, the two neatly placed together upon the height of Tenochtitlan's greatest temple, a distance possibly broached by a strong bow and archer. Night Axe nocks, pulls and aims his last fire arrow, says to himself, or perhaps the god, "Let's light up the night, friend Huitzilopochtli!" Yet just before releasing said arrow, ouch, the bow snaps.

Night Axe throws the broken bow into the blazing torch that was once the shrine of Chilico. He considers standing out upon the edge of Chilico's temple and letting out a roar that will shake the very foundation of Tenochtitlan, cause the water to rise up and reclaim its lost mud. However, he then considers how unwise it would be to stand upon the temple height illuminated from behind with so many armed Mexica scurrying about. So instead Night Axe looks quietly out upon the burning shrines, the center of Tenochtitlan illuminated as if in the light of day, and smiles the smile of an artist who looks upon a finished work and is content.

37

An All Consuming Fire

Kulcan leaves Tenochtitlan with a smaller number of shrines, yet for that many remain. No one gives up the gods and goddesses of their childhood willingly, and if an empire is to grow by peaceful assimilation of alien cultures, well, soon enough you have a lot of gods and goddesses, and thus a lot of shrines. Coming to the western shore of the island Kulcan turns back to gaze at the fire-lit sky and curiously enough envisions the oracle with him, and he begins to laugh at the give and take of an imagined conversation.

"Religion is but a perspective of illumination," Kulcan says to the oracle, with a sweep of the hand to draw attention to the flaming, sky-reaching shrines burning upon their pyramidal heights; "a nuanced play of luminous energy."

"Oh really?" She says, bright moonlit smile. "You

suggest that one's understanding of The Unfathomable is due to a certain, um, incandescence? Or perhaps a particular radiant intensity that allows one a certain, -perception?"

"Spark of discernment," Kulcan suggests.

"Ah, just so," agrees the oracle in her mellifluous voice. "One's understanding shines out. Or should I say, 'shrines out'?"

Kulcan and the oracle snort with laughter.

Kulcan begins to wonder if he is delirious. He shakes his head as if to clear it, looks about and finds himself alone at the edge of the lake upon an egregious mudflat where rest a good many *acalli*. Kulcan, who had at first thought to swim to the western shore of Lake Texcoco thinks upon the legally-sanctifying nature of war, and considers how his staff, and those nearby sacks of fruit resting just so against a nearby doorway would fit ever so neatly within a small *acalli*. Considering the nature of 'the greater good,' he collects a few sacks of conveniently placed fruit (thank-you), sweeps clean some racks of drying fish (again, many thanks), and sets off from the shore in a yopicatl-sized *acalli* slowly passing into darkness.

In time, -always in time, and space, -always in space, Kulcan comes to the western shore of Lake Texcoco, south of Tlacopan. Kulcan sets the *acalli* adrift, then heads inland for a distance before turning north. With daybreak approaching he climbs an immense ahuehuetl tree, and well above the ground snuggles himself within a clutch of enclosing branches. Kulcan sleeps, and as he sleeps he dreams of Time who he sees as a brume, a nebula of encompassing light. And of this light, not a blending, folding of colors to make white, but rather a weave, a binding fabric of complexity with all colors distinct yet inseparable from the other. Kulcan realizes he is dreaming, and wonders: Why is it our dreams in sleep seem so real, and that which we come to while awake seem so much a dream? Kulcan puts his hand into a particular patch of light, or rather Time, and sees it swirl about his arm which is to suggest that being within Time disturbs it. "Curious," Kulcan observes: "how very curious."

Time then, manifestation thereof, speaks to Kulcan, saying, "A *tlachtli* ball can be stopped (brought to a halt, its energy absorbed), reflected (energy sent off in another direction), and if struck just so amplified, its speed (energy) increased. So too, light can be absorbed and reflected, and with the use of clever mirrors and crystals, amplified. So what of time? Time is certainly absorbed, but can Time be reflected or amplified? You know, more over there and less over here? (Pause.) My question is rhetorical, in a sense; I don't think you can answer it. I'd be surprised if you could. Yet keep it in mind. You never know how a piece of a puzzle will suddenly fit. And as for pieces, there is a dance tonight upon the great plaza of Azcapotzalco which I suggest, quite sincerely, that you attend as you may find it, in many ways, illuminating."

✦ ✦ ✦

Bird song. Kulcan awakens to a bright gleam of late afternoon sunlight so sparkling, so clear, it seems as if there might never have been a moment of sorrow within the world.

+ + +

Twilight. Kulcan returns to Azcapotzalco and prowls the city carefully observing where guards stand or rest amid a landscape of great buildings interspersed with courtyards of interlocked flat stones, all overshadowed by a scattering of magnificent trees. Kulcan looks for his friend Totomotzin and does not find him. Moving as if but a shadow, a *naolli*,[48] a *tetzauitl*,[49] Kulcan comes to the edge of a great plaza upon which there is a dance, and makes himself comfortable within the wondrous height of a nearby oak tree.

The musicians hold the center of the plaza, with the dancers slowly circling about them. The drums, trumpets, and flutes sound out a phrase to which the singers respond, back and forth, back and forth, an acoustical pendulum, all the while the dancers, both male and female, in time with the cadence ever so carefully step this way or the other. The young popoloca glide and whirl, shuffle there, skip and leap here, swaying and swirling just so. In truth, most impressive: the measured, synchronous footsteps, the rhythmic tempo of the music seeming to shake the foundations of the city. As the dance goes on there begins to seem an inexhaustible quality to it, as if the dancers strive towards something elusive, some intangible evanescence, some sort of here-not-here transcendence.

---

48 A wizard.
49 An apparition.

In time, Kulcan assertion, on that plaza of smooth white stone beneath the moon and a glittering cascade of stars, through their endless repetitive dance and song those among the plaza release themselves to The Immanent with their energy, somehow multiplied, transformed into a glow of serene radiance that shines out into the night like a burning shrine. High up within the sturdy branches of friend oak, within the very heart of Azcapotzalco, a city ruled by King-of-Kings Quinatzin who commands well more than 200,000 spears, and to each spear a popoloca, Kulcan gazes down upon the plaza filled with dancers, musicians, and is overwhelmed with an irresistible urge to join the dance becoming a part of the collective energy he observes. In truth, the action is not as outlandish as it might seem for the young popoloca dancers have been joined by diverse types, old and young, some simply dressed, some dressed ornately, some clad in long robes, some dressed as birds, and some clad as butterflies. Kulcan joins them, wearing his loose-fitting Teohuatzin robe, and dances. And as he dances his perspective changes, curious trick of gravity-refracted light, to where it seems he looks down upon the dancer-filled plaza. Kulcan casts his vision further to see the city, the mountain-clad escarpment of Nahua, the surrounding Hot Lands to the south, the eastern and western salt-water seas, and beyond to the sweeping curve of the earth.

Curiously, the encompassing, soul-filling music then fades away to a faint whisper and time ceases to matter; Kulcan sees existence as no more than a *tlachtli* metaphor: here is the court of smooth planar limestone, here is the spherical elastic ball; what more need be said? Everything is but a matter of moving just so at the proper moment. Kulcan is the ether; Kulcan is a beam of light; Kulcan is the choking smoke of smoldering chilies. Then, of an instant, comes a transformation in which Kulcan's essence, -those too of all the dancers, are drawn out and melded into a collective whole, a transformation that all seem conscious of at the same moment, with the *we* becoming something greater than mere mechanics, base determinism. Kulcan looks upon the faces of his fellow dancers, -for the moment his brethren, realizes that no longer is anyone concerned with objects in space, events in time, but rather as part of a unitary energy they have become functions of hope, purpose, and meaning. Now this: If death is the diffusion, redistribution of one's atoms within a bounded whole, then what Kulcan experiences dancing upon the plaza that night suggests that death is a joyful thing, for it is with death that one comes to be part of something ever so much greater. Which suggests that the whole point of life is death, to finally arrive in Tlalocan, a paradise of peaceful happiness where there is no hunger.

"Time is an all consuming fire," he thinks, "and we are the fire."

Yet for that, of an instant, stop: Kulcan realizes however great and encompassing the whole he was momentarily a part of that pain, the absence of those close to his heart, is his pain alone, and he will now, ahead of schedule, nodding goodbyes to fellow dancers, make his way to Quinatzin's palace. Time, Night Axe understands, is an avenging yopicatl, and he is that yopicatl.

38

Night Axe Attends A Dinner

———

Night Axe, Teohuatzin, finds Quinatzin entertaining guests of high repute within a great hall, beneath a high-beamed roof of polished wood. He enters the hall amid a flurry of attendants, priests, various nobles, warriors and messengers. In between some decorative potted fruit trees, near a trellis upon which perch three parrots of eye-dazzling colors, Night Axe, Teohuatzin, sits and rests, and is delighted to discover that young popoloca attendants bring him all the food and chocolatl he desires. Night Axe watches three popoloca walk and dance about as a tower, with two balanced upon one, one balanced upon two, each dancing with outstretched arms and their hands filled with flowers. At times the uppermost dancer, call him a juggler, puts all his flowers into one hand, reaches into a large bag hung across his chest, and tosses out puffed kernels of maize that fall upon the guests as if so much snow.

Night Axe watches jugglers toss back and forth bowls and plates, knives and spoons, so many the air seems more filled than not: nothing is missed, nothing is dropped. Then the jugglers leave off with their earthenware and take to juggling torches that burn fiercely from both ends, catching and tossing the torches so fast it seems the air has become flame. "Remarkable," Night Axe thinks. "Difficult to believe." Night Axe watches the skilled entertainers, and listens to the conversations of those who rule.

✦ ✦ ✦

"…Yes, I know the talk, I hear it. But I will be open with you, for here we may speak freely. Although King Oconitzin is without merit, as vile in his ways as he is to look upon, this is the man I arranged for my only daughter to marry, for which most believe me heartless. Yet she marries him as Queen, and his wealth is considerable. Further, as soon as she has her first child I expect the king to, well, let's just say he never struck me as a healthy person. Not one who would have a long span of years."

✦ ✦ ✦

A jokester upon stilts appears through a doorway who, seemingly distracted by a fly buzzing about his head walks through the passing torches of the jugglers, oblivious to the fires flashing by just before and just behind him. Suddenly taking notice of the torches he snatches them from mid-air and throws them back from whence they came, so fast he does this that torch seems to blend into torch, and all the while he dances slowly about upon his stilts. "Fantastic." Night Axe thinks. "A marvel."

＊ ＊ ＊

"All states are police states," says one. "That you can tend your fields, your chinampas in peace is because soldiers defend the borders."

"I recognize that." His companion replies. "The trouble comes inside the borders when the soldiers, or their counterparts the police, or any government official, start abusing the citizens they are supposed to be protecting. A system of checks and balances is needed, for all of us. Law and justice shouldn't just be an exercise in power. Though I admit power is a mirror that both reflects and enlarges much."

"Well, people are people, particularly when they have power. (He sighs.) Yes, I admit things can get out of hand. 'Who will watch the watchers' is an age-old question. And more often than not the answer is no one."

＊ ＊ ＊

The jugglers vanish, replaced by a singer accompanied by a single flutist:

A large flake of snow floats over the lake. No
    harbinger of winter,
But a white owl who stands motionless upon the
    shore.
It gives a mournful cry,
As if it had remembered something it wanted to
    forget.

✦ ✦ ✦

"There was not an equal division of trophies, if you
recall. Copiltzin had his men immediately collect yopicatl
heads, bagged them up and had them on their way to
Texcoco before any of us knew what he was about."

"I can see having a skull or two, but why so many?"

"I haven't seen it myself, but it's said he uses the skulls
to border the pathways of his private gardens."

"That seems strange, in my opinion. With due
respect, that seems not only out of character but, well, he
can do what he wants. Yet why he would do that I don't
understand."

✦ ✦ ✦

Two jugglers enter who, while tossing back and forth
ceramic pots between themselves, appear to slip and fall
upon their backs, yet with no missed beat start to juggle
the pots using only their feet. "Bravo!" thinks Night Axe.
"Nicely done!"

✦ ✦ ✦

"You had your own soldiers destroy a party of your own traders? (A raise of the eyebrows, a small frown.) Why?"

"My soldiers?" his dinner companion answers with an incredulous look upon his face. "Witnesses swore they were soldiers from Maqualco. And while there is never a shortage of traders, we could never let such an insult go un-revenged."

"I'm astonished, and impressed. Clearly I need to raise my game."

"Well, think about it. If we were to suddenly start attacking other cities and towns without provocation our neighbors might soon see the wisdom in forming alliances that would prove inconvenient, if not difficult."

"What if the soldiers talk?"

"No danger of that. None. What. So. Ever."

✦ ✦ ✦

The jokester upon his stilts reappears, dashing into the room as if Darkness Itself pursued him. The jokester staggers about always just on the cusp of falling, -leaning this way and that only to, somehow, unimaginably, impossibly, recover and totter on, circling in and out between attendants set to their task of bringing or taking away.

✦ ✦ ✦

"He was a skilled soldier, General Acicotzin, one with a keen eye for the nuances of battle. But for that he was a little too taken with the honors he earned."

"Soldiers live for honor, fight and die for honor."

"Alright, let me put it this way. My supposition, if you will, or rather as our scholars would say, my *postulate*, is that Acicotzin might have been a little too engrossed not with honor in and of itself, but with its display. He was ever striving to stand out upon a battlefield, always wearing a more noticeable uniform, tiered helmets adorned with height upon height of feathers and so-forth. A presence, as he was keen to suggest, that Azcapotzalco troops could rally to. In a battle against Ecatepec, in addition to his usual ornaments Acicotzin adorned himself with a rich surcoat of brilliant feather-work and a tiered panache of beautiful feathers rising high up above his head, the green and red feathers interwoven with cascading ribbons of hammered gold foil. And if this were not enough, rising up from his back was a tall staff bearing a flag of gold foil, his singular symbol of authority."

"One not easily overlooked upon the battlefield," a companion observes.

"By anyone, on either side. At a specific command the Ecatepec soldiers carved a channel directly to Acicotzin, -an action those who saw it describe in metaphors of thunderbolts. Acicotzin was so encumbered by his uniform he could hardly move. They cut him down, and that quickly our troops had no direction. It was not a good day for our army, and all in the work of a moment."

"Still, he died with honor."

"Let me be more precise since I don't think I am clearly making my point. We lost a battle due to his excessive indulgence in display that but satisfied his ego.

If the gods were sustained by egos, rather than blood, just one or two among us could power the universe."

✦ ✦ ✦

Night Axe makes to leave, but feels held in place as if the hands of The Immanent were pushing down upon his shoulders. And so he sits and watches the dinner party progress to its end with the sacred gleaning of future visions.

To each exalted guest, which does not include Night Axe, who seems there but not there, the odd priest no one wishes to insult by asking to leave but yet no one wishes to talk to, upon a conveniently sized tray of polished luminous wood an attendant brings a gold goblet filled with chocolatl, accompanied by a beautiful spoon of finely-wrought tortoise shell, and a small turquoise colored bowl of minced *teonanacatl*.[50] The subject of *teonanacatl* is not a simple one, with certain types desired for long vigils at altars, others desired for endurance and speed, while some are desired so that the eyes, made large and clear, are able to find evil sorcerers. To wit, each of the guests mixes into their vanilla-flavored chocolatl just the right amount of *teonanacatl*, each to their own adventure, takes a swallow, and allows this to dissolve in their mouth. Conversation ends, with all awaiting their visions: and as to this some rest quietly, some toss about, some are overcome with laughter, and some weep. The attendants stand motionless against the wall next to the guards.

---

50 Mushrooms.

After a time the guests awaken, and discuss among themselves what they have seen. Curiously, all speak as though everyone has shared in their dream: "The trembling we felt was the anger of Xihcutli." Or, "It was the green feather you saw in my left hand by which I controlled the wind." One speaks of the trading excursions he will make to the southern lands, returning home with priceless feathers, dyes, and jewels. Another speaks of his going off to war and performing great deeds of valor, while others see their death in war. One guest says he will commit adultery, and so have his head crushed by a huge rock for the offense. Quinatzin speaks not of having his head squeezed off, but rather speaks of forthcoming victories, the defeat of enemies, and the receiving of tribute.

Curiously, one speaks of seeing pale-skinned men such as those Kulcan has met in the 2nd world, wearing inpenetratable armor made of a metal the color of sorrow. Some of these pale-skinned popoloca come armed with weapons that hurl small metal stakes through Nahua shields, and some ride large hornless deer. Then, stranger still, one speaks of metal beetles the size of large houses that chase each other across a desert landscape striving to consume one another, the air little more than black greasy smoke through which great metal insects fly, the creatures launching particles of light so powerful nothing stands before them.

Their visions told, the night giving way to a luminous blue, Lord Quinatzin leaves the hall and the guests disperse.

◆ ◆ ◆

Night Axe leaves the great Quinatzinian building, coming to a courtyard of modest size enclosed by raised beds of flowers the scent of which is ethereal. The private courtyard is a small island of peace about which Azcapotzalco swirls, with the floor made of large smooth stones the edges of which are neatly jointed and many of which are decorated with carved pictographs. Night Axe looks about and realizes that the tall, narrow pillar of stone rising up from the courtyard is a gnomon. The year turns about itself, each day the sun tracing out a path subtlety different than that of the day before, so in turn different is the shadow swept-out by the gnomon. Each day the sun reaches an apex in the sky and the finely tapered gnomon casts a shadow that just touches a particular bas-relief of stone. Night Axe realizes he is looking at a memorial calendar of astonishing artistry, the shadow cast by the sun, year after year, forever honoring certain events on the calendric day of their occurrence. "Magnificent," he thinks. "Such meticulous observations of the heavens. Bravo!"

Priestly-clad Night Axe rests a moment on a finely polished smooth stone bench. He thinks, first, of Prester John, a wise popoloca king of the 2nd world's middle continent that he met on his last Wandering, an event that now seems unimaginably long ago. He then tries to parse out yet another riddle put forth by The Immanent:

$$55: 5^3 + 5^3 = 250$$
$$250: 2^3 + 5^3 + 0^3 = 133$$
$$133: 1^3 + 3^3 + 3^3 = 55$$

After a time Night Axe shifts his attention to the courtyard itself, looking carefully at the many stones ornamented with bas-relief carvings. Seeking to interpret the artist's vision, he first sees what he thinks are depictions of dancers, yet with an odd wildness to their limbs, in defiance of gravity flung this way and that to suggest something beyond the conventional norms of dance. Then he sees one sitting with his hands across his stomach holding in his entrails. "Curious," Kulcan thinks.

Another stone shows a wild-eyed warrior grasping with his right hand his severed left; "I see," says Kulcan. Another depicts a king-like figure missing a small but vital fraction of him lying within what must be, yes, a puddle of his own blood. Kulcan realizes the courtyard is part monument, part historical archive to Quinatzin's toppling of enemies that he can visit, when taken by the notion, to relive fond memories, or use to impress certain ideas upon reluctant individuals. After some moments Kulcan finds another stone, and what is carved there upon its surface tears at his heart.

39
The Heart of Existence

Kulcan awakens in the early morning to the sound of trumpets and, for a moment, does not remember where he is, and if memory is imprecise then, logical consequence, our identities are equally imprecise, a here not here trick of electrochemistry. Yet Kulcan knows there are certain plants, one in particular comes to mind of which a tea is made, and with this tea[51] one can scan up and down the continuity of their lives to recall, with startling clarity, the encompassing detail of any moment. Kulcan has seen popoloca give their lives over to this tea, the unhappy *now* sacrificed to the happy *then*, and he understands the nuanced pull of such an idea.

Kulcan finds that the trumpets are part of yet another sacred procession comprised of any number of censer-swinging priests, dancers, and so on, who fritter about

---

51 Presumably *Datura stramonium*.

those who carry a tree-trunk of some length, modest diameter, stripped of all bark and sanded smooth. Flowers are thrown upon the road before the sacred pole, while trailing behind come popoloca who whip themselves with knotted ropes, or pierce their flesh with sharp-tipped thorns. Kulcan thinks, simply enough, that the whole species is insane: a simple observation that explains so much. Amid many prayers, speeches, the tossing of this and that into the sacred fire of Xihcutli so the smoke turns from gray-blue to colors of startling intensity: now red, now green, now blue, the tree trunk is raised up in the courtyard before the great temple of the Fire God. Its end is sunk within an embracing hole, its height secured by flower-decorated ropes.

"How enthralling," Kulcan sighs. "Simply magical!"

Atop this pole, perhaps two feet in diameter, a height of some forty feet, within a crowning nest of flowers and twigs the popoloca place a bird shaped from dough made of amaranth and honey. The pole itself is decorated with long streamers of coruscating colors, dappled hues and tints that shift and play with but the slightest breeze. Throughout the morning any number of freshly washed popoloca, wearing their sacred-festival best, place about the pole vast quantities of food, flowers, and diverse gifts. And for this festival Kulcan observes that a second sacred fire has been lit, set within a basin upon a raised platform some ten feet in height above the plaza, an elevation that helps those upon the courtyard to observe the sacred activities. From his perch Kulcan looks down upon this secondary fire, sees the fiery coals, sees the shimmering of the air above, and looks across to the bird crafted out of amaranth-honey dough quietly resting within its nest atop the pole, and tries to puzzle out the intrinsic relationship of the two, and in this fails.

Kulcan watches the offerings placed about the sacred pole carried into the temple-compound, which takes what seems a considerable amount of time even though there are a good number of helpers for there is, truly, much to take away. The task finally finished, the great priests of the great god of the great city of Azcapotzalco, wearing wide tunics and robes of cotton, tiaras of feathers, gold and gems that scatter the light, gather about this hot, -truly very hot, fire. These priests are joined by four males and a female, dressed and adorned like gods and a goddess and who have been, according to the loud-mouthed popoloca picnicking with his family beneath the tree within which Kulcan rests, pampered and catered to for the past month. The four gods-not-really-gods, and the one goddess-not-really-a-goddess, are given something to drink after which they feel compelled to dance, so expressing to the gathered crowd, perhaps, the idea of joy. Kulcan, yopicatl-patient, endures more prayers, chants, songs, censing, a casting into the sacred fire of a dust-like something that causes the smoke to reflect the light as if it were so many millions of tiny mirrors, and the area about the sacred fire swept ever so carefully to ensure no ash nor ember is misplaced, and then watches several helpful priests take hold of *Yacatecutli*, He Who Goes First, one each to a foot, one each to an arm and, as if he were no more than and a sack of water, salt, fat and minerals, swing him back and forth, back and forth, and release their grip launching him into the fire.

"Hmmpf." Kulcan grunts.

After a few moments *Yacatecutli* is removed from the fire, carried over and placed supine upon, curiously enough, a *teponaztli*, the two-toned drum made from a hollow log the popoloca so love to play. Kulcan wonders if the two tones of the drum suggest a duality, and if so then what better place to send one from life to life's counterpart? The small party is soon joined by an officiator, or judge, someone of title who neatly, if such a thing can be done neatly, removes *Yacatecutli's* heart, which the official raises up to the sky, way up, as one might raise their chalice of ale skyward then, after a moment, casts it into the fire. *Yacatecutli*, now freed from mortal cares and worries, is rolled down the temple steps.

"Big yawn!" Snorts Kulcan. "Big, big yawn!" Beyond a subsequent interval of time Kulcan spends daydreaming a singular, deep-throated horn sounds and he braces himself for the next excruciating, blood-soaked stunt the popoloca are going to pull. All gathered about the temple turn their gaze to its utmost height where the Fire God's High Priest stands amid considerable quantities of pomp and glitter and calls out to gathered:

You will fear, honor, and love the gods.
You will not use the names of the gods in your talk, at any time.
You will honor the feast days.
You will honor your father and mother, your kinsmen, priests, and elders.
You shall not kill.

You shall not commit adultery.
You shall not steal.
You shall not bear false witness.

Horns demarcate the end of the somber moment; smiles reappear upon the gathered faces. Kulcan grabs a handful of leaves and wipes his nose, thinks; "Funny. Funny. Funny." Some ten, perhaps a dozen captured soldiers, scurf of Azcapotzalco's last conquest, are sent on to Xihcutli's Ash Pit. Finally the festival progresses to that which is part impulse, part skillful expression, which is to say, a dance. The courtyard fills with young male and female popolocas wearing net-like cloaks of red and black adorned with white feathers. Some females wear red feathers on their arms and legs to signify they have not yet but are ready to begin breeding, while the males wear jewelry imitative of that which they will earn when they have captured an enemy soldier upon the battlefield-and whose essence will then be given, within the context of proper ceremony, to Xihcutli. Among these dancers passes a trickster god, disguised as a black-feathered bird, or perhaps a bat, twisting and turning about completely out of order and rhythm to the others, and who from time to time speaks loudly saying words that few, if any, understand, which suggests he is symbolic of the chaos that lies at the heart of existence.

◆ ◆ ◆

Kulcan naps, awakens, and finds the popoloca still dancing. Then, revelation, Kulcan sees any number of jugs, of something, some sort of liquid, most likely wine, but what have you, being carried up the side of the Fire God's Temple by hard-working priests, and he smiles a deep, satisfied smile at this gift of Tezcatlipoca. "Excellent," he says to himself. "The pieces of the plan fall into place."

✦ ✦ ✦

An hour or so before sunset drums sound and the plaza clears. The males, those who have participated in the dance, cast off their adornments and align themselves at the edge of the courtyard. A trumpet sounds; a sprint for the pole; a tussle as each youth strives (and here words such as spirit, fury, and speed come to mind) to be the first to reach the apex: many youths fall from the lower part, some from the middle, and one falls from the height itself which is, truly, a considerable distance to fall.

Kulcan has difficulty imagining what the popoloca youths believe awaits them atop the pole, but certainly more than a few mouthfuls of amaranth mixed with honey. Kulcan ponders the mystery, and finds no answer. There is a winner, a 1st to the height, one who tears the head off the bird and then, the small piece of dough held gently between his lips, descends by one of the support ropes that help hold the pole in place. To the 2nd and 3rd go the two wings, while the 4th takes the tail, and so the contest ends. These four victors are secreted away by priests into a nearby apartment. Kulcan can guess what is coming next, and shudders, however the four soon reappear freshly washed and adorned in new clothes to great acclaim, the chosen ones of the god. Kulcan shakes his head in wonder. And with the reappearance of these four youths axmen set to work and chop the pole down, and such is the multitude that fall upon it, -all struggling to claim something, be it a sacred crumb of dough or hallowed splinter of wood, that in less than an hour there is nothing left.

40
A Second Dinner
With Quinatzin

Nightfall. The momentary 'now' for revenge is near, but has not yet arrived. A handful of hours before the planned arrival of his Xochimilco allies Night Axe, cloaked in the flowing black robes of the Teohuatzin, high official of the sacred realm, a large sweeping hat, a staff in one hand and a censer in the other, filled with nervous energy, decides to leave friend tree and again visit the torch-lit palace to see how the King-of-Kings occupies himself during these last few hours of his life. Night Axe discovers that on this night Lord Quinatzin shares food and drink with those of a harder type, as suggested by the fact that former enemies, drained of blood and then dried, are used as torches that emit a yellow-green light as they burn. Seeing this Night Axe feels very much alone.

One can encounter an event so far outside one's realm of experience that it cannot be integrated into a conceptual whole. Nevertheless these torches burn so hot there seems a fitting completeness to it all, like changing a 'c' to an 'o'. Night Axe recognizes the truth that all our actions come, in time, to nothing, even books, even sculpture. Sculpture. Night Axe thinks of the courtyard laid in sculpted stones, and thinks of how limestone burns to a powder. He stops a passing attendant, asks, "There are more of these torches?"

The youth nods.

"Show me."

The youth leads Night Axe past several sharp-angled corners to a storage room. There is an unusually suspicious guard there who Night Axe quickly claims. Seeing this the attendant turns to flee, although one might ask: To where? Night Axe, a few quick steps, pinches the youth about his neck and slowly, calmly, says, "Your plans to escape Azcapotzalco tonight will be for naught, and your life end, save but these torches, wood, and all the hot-burning oil you can find are piled upon the memorial courtyard ready to kindle. We must signal our allies when the time comes, and besides, the night air has a chill." He winks.

Night Axe sees a dim comprehension replace the fear in the face of the youth. Perhaps, sees even the conceptual idea of freedom. The youth slowly nods.

"Good. You have the responsibility for the task, but I will send help." And to the youth's credit, stout heart, he sets to work. Kulcan hauls the body of the transcended guard to the rear of the storage room, and there leaves what was once him.

+ + +

Night Axe, torchlight silent, enters the palace through the realm of kitchens, home of cooks and stores. He comes upon a youth bent to his task polishing the gleaming wood floor who, faint whisper, recites to himself a poem, -though perhaps it is a prayer:

> A book of annals, written and painted in colors,
> Said I was once a prince, son of a king and queen,
> And brother to five princesses.
> So it must be that my realm was once greater than
> a kitchen.
> Hear my voice Quetzalcoatl!
> May a time soon come when the distained and the
> slaves
> See their oppressors amid fire and ash,
> Listening to the howl of pursuing wolves.

Night Axe bends down to this youthful polisher and softly whispers, "There is one upon the courtyard who requires your help. Go now."

The youth bows his head, and without looking up rises to his feet and vanishes.

Night Axe enters the dining hall behind a flock of servants carrying platters and trays, and amid this bustle, this flurry of comings and goings he sits precisely in the same spot he sat the night before. Night Axe is but a few arm-lengths from Quinatzin's neck, a neck that tilts and shifts this way and that through the evening, now listening to that speaker, now reaching for this cup. "Big squeeze!" Thinks Night Axe, "And pop!"

The dinner is similar to that of the night before, save tonight the guests are more concerned with the mechanics of power and less the underlying motivation. They talk, and Night Axe listens.

◆ ◆ ◆

"Their army is not to be taken lightly, and they are cautious, preferring to have a foot in each camp."

"Yes, well," a dinner companion interjects. "Matters can be settled in different ways. When King Teconal sent his army against Texcoco he awoke from slumber to find a stack of tortillas laid delicately upon his chest, and his guards, who had left this world for the next, neatly stacked atop the other. The message was not lost upon the good king, who recalled his army and made peace."

"Hmmpf" his friend grunts, and nods in admiration.

◆ ◆ ◆

There is a farce for entertainment. Amid a sweep of decorations against the far wall, a setting to suggest the interior of a common popoloca home, the occasion a day dedicated to yet another religious festival, a male and female, bound to each other by the rite of marriage, rest. On this solemn occasion the wife, as required by the gods, serves her husband a plate of plain-water[52] tortillas.

---

52 *Atamalli*, plain-water tortillas prepared without the use of lime or ash
    to soften the maize.

Accepting the plate his face is brightly lit with a smile that suggests he is delighted with the sacred repast, yet for that his smile disappears when she turns her back suggesting, in truth, he is unenthusiastic about the meal.

✦ ✦ ✦

Attendants bring into the dining hall a number of stewpots, and with utmost care set these amidst the guests, partitioned out so there are no more than four to a pot, and from these pots comes a pleasant scent that Night Axe cannot place. From each pot, into which squash flowers are mixed, a single popoloca portions out the meat to his companions, which they eat slowly, carefully, as if to absorb the full essence of the food.

"A ritual," Night Axe infers, "a ceremony of warriors."

Night Axe watches and listens, puzzles out the mystery, realizes captured Tlachquiauhco soldiers are being apportioned, with warrior consuming fellow warrior, the living honoring the slain. Night Axe smiles with approval. "Good. Better they eat each other than everything else."

✦ ✦ ✦

The wife leaves the room for a moment, in which the husband takes the opportunity to bring forth some hidden tamales.

✦ ✦ ✦

"No, listen carefully to what I am saying. Three soldiers emerge from a battle, a smudge of blood on the forehead of each. While they are laughing at each other, and before they can look in a mirror, their captain says to the three that although none know whether he himself is smudged, there is a way of finding out without using a mirror. The captain suggests: 'Each of the three of you look at the other two; if you see at least one whose forehead is smudged with blood, raise your spear.' At once, each raises his spear. 'Now,' says the captain, as soon as one of you knows for sure whether his own forehead is smudged or not, he should lower his spear, but not before.' After a moment or two one of the soldiers lowers his spear with a smile of satisfaction, saying, 'I know.' My question to you is: How did that soldier know?"

"Clever!" Muses Night Axe, puzzling out the logic while enjoying some avocados and a large mug of chocolatl.

+ + +

"His army might have held the pass against us," an Azcapotzalco General says, "or ambushed us on the uneven terrain, however King Yatzin chose to send against us his conjurers, telling them, 'Destroy those of Azcapotzalco with your enchantments.' Some wizards made spirit figures of us and threw these into sacred fires, while others sent against us magic arrows of sickness. Yet flames did not consume us, and we did not sicken. Some conjurers sent serpents, scorpions, and spiders against us, but while a portion of our army slept others always moved about, keeping watch, so these creatures could not creep upon us. And as for the visions they sent against us, those of defeat and death, we ignored them, for our hearts are strong. In the end their wizards and conjurers admitted defeat, suggesting we were of a different disposition and manner than they had ever before encountered, that our flesh was so tough magic could not harm it."

✦ ✦ ✦

The wife suddenly returns to the room and the husband, having no time in which to hide the tamales anywhere else, hides them under his loincloth. The wife, seeing the bulge beneath her husband's loincloth insists he continue eating the plain-water tortillas.

✦ ✦ ✦

"And so when the conjurors failed?"

"They fought us with noise," the General continues. "Whistles, conch-shell horns, drums, all of which seemed to pierce the very air. In truth they made a great din, a presence you could feel." (He pauses for dramatic effect.)

"And?" One asks.

"And we had three soldiers for each one of theirs. Their conjurers, their noise, and their walls could not stop us. In the end we left not a stone upon the other."

Satisfied grunts come from his companions.

"I have heard said," another observes, "that King Yatzin was a mighty wizard. That visiting ambassadors would enter his council room to find him in the form of a jaguar. Or at times simply flame."

This idea is considered for a moment. "Well, he may have been a mighty wizard," one suggests, "just not mighty enough."

◆ ◆ ◆

Within another conversation, one says to his three companions, "King Malatzin was intent on war, and from that purpose could not be dissuaded. He cast about, finally deciding the Chiahuac were the enemy."

"The Chiahuac?"

"The Chiahuac."

"It was the Iguala that made off with all your stores, killing a good number of your traders in the process. Chiahuac? I don't follow the logic."

"Yes, and you are not alone in that. We would ask King Malatzin why, exactly, he felt it necessary to war against Chiahuac and he'd give some vague answer: 'There are tangible and intangible reasons.' As for Iguala, it was if they were invisible to King Malatzin, or didn't exist, certainly they were never mentioned, save as valuable allies. Then when the Chiahuac ambassadors arrived Malatzin had them locked in a room, a fire of chilies set against an outside wall and the smoke directed inside. Then he had their bodies thrown out along the lake road where traders would find them, and so convey a message."

"What message? A city attacks you, does you harm, and in response you attack an entirely different city famous for minding their own business."

"Yes. Exactly. Which part of the logic don't you follow?"

✦ ✦ ✦

"Nine shrines burn. Nine. Of these, all except that of Xipe Totec is interpreted to mean the temples should be abandoned and their land given to Huitzilopochtli."

Already aware of the temple fires, and their consequence, his companions but nod. One, as his contribution to the conversation, offers, "The theology of Huitzilopochtli suggests the Mexica are to rule the world. Which I assume includes Azcapotzalco."

"The Mexica are our allies," his friend answers.

"If we do not trust the Mexica then we would be wise to prepare for an attack," another says, a man of barely contained energy who seems but tenuously bound to his cushion, "and I know of no better way to prepare for an attack than by attacking."

"The Mexica are skilled fighters who more often than not serve in the vanguard of our armies."

"Yes, so they serve today. My question is, what of tomorrow? What if they become too powerful?"

There is a pause in the conversation, an emptiness of time that passes in silence. Finally, it is King-of-Kings Quinatzin who takes up the conversational thread; "The Mexica are fierce, courageous, and hard-working, the last of the Seven Tribes to arrive from the Seven Caves. For now, they serve in our armies. This seems sufficient, though I admit they are otherwise unruly and a nuisance."

+ + +

After several glances between the guests, a captain-general clears his throat, raises his voice and says, "We have all heard stories of the Seven Caves, Lord Quinatzin. Or scattered pieces of the story, but we have never heard the whole, nor heard it from an authority. *The* authority."

By quiet nods, the request is seconded by the others. Quinatzin glances at those about him, the men who command his armies, considers, and decides to tell what he knows of the founding of Nahua, that like all histories he recognizes as a curious mix of fact and legend. He takes a sip of chocolatl to wet his throat, savors it, rubs the scar upon his calf made by the bite of that vile serpent, what seems but yesterday, and begins:

41
Quinatzin's Tale

"First of the 7 Tribes to leave the 7 Caves, our ancestral home, were those of Xochimilco. After many years wandering the desert they arrived here, perhaps some 500 years ago, settling on the southwestern edge of the lake. Founding the city of their name, and so too founding Culhuacan, Cuilcuilco, and Copilco. Then those of Chalco arrived, who came to live as neighbors of Xochimilco, the two realms peacefully adjusting their boundaries to fill the southern portion of the valley.

"Our people were next to arrive settling on the western shore of the lake, founding Azcapotzalco and towns and villages along the entire range of the western mountains. Then those of Texcoco arrived. When the Tlalhuica came they found the lake encircled by the four tribes, and so settled to the southwest of the mountains making Cuauhtla their capitol, from which they dispersed to build great cities and towns throughout the region.

"The Tlaxcala were the sixth to arrive, and settled upon the fertile plains to the southeast of the valley beyond Mount Popocatepetl, founding their great cities of Tlaxcala, Huexotzinco, and Cholula. And then the seventh of the tribes arrived, the Mexica, who have built a city upon a mudflat that no one wanted, that no one hardly knew existed, recruiting to their banner the outcasts and refuges of the valley.

"When I became King-of-Kings I recognized that I had, uniquely, the power to find the 7 Caves. The place written of in books and that many speak of, but none know. A paradise watched over by the sister of Xihcutli, the goddess Tocuital, She of Smoke. A paradise that our ancestors chose to leave having grown bored of contentment.

"As to its location, that which is written says the 7 Caves are somewhere to the northwest. So it was there I first sent warriors to search. In time they returned, or some did, to report that they had, for all their searching, found nothing. So I gathered wizards and sorcerers, those wise in the arts of magic. 'Discover the land that gave birth to us,' I tasked them, 'and see if Tocuital still rules within her realm.'

"These sorcerers departed, some forty of them, laden with gifts for the goddess, and in time came to the hill of Coatepec, within the province of Tula, a place where, for their purposes, magicians travel. There they invoked their powers each turning into their *nagual*,[53] and in this way travelled to the land of our forbearers.

---

53 Their animal reflection or soul.

"The wizards resumed their shape upon the shore of a large sweeping bay protected by an enclosing reef. Beyond this bay they found a margin of land decorated with cave-filled hills, separating the sea from inland fresh-water lakes. A sublime, temperate land of trees and orchards watered with many springs. They saw people attending their plots of tomatoes, amaranth, beans, chilies; saw fields in which maize was ripe, other fields where it was nearly ripe, and still others where the maize was just sprouting. It was a paradise where none thirsted, none hungered, and none grew old. They came to the foot of the hill called Omoma, realm of Tocuital, where they met her high priestess who called out to them: 'Welcome, my children! Who are you? What is it that brings you here? How may I help you?'

" 'Fair Lady,' the wizards answered; 'we have been sent by Lord Quinatzin, King-of-Kings, to seek this place, home of our ancestors. We have brought gifts.'

" 'Who is Quinatzin?' The priestess asked. "He was not of those who departed here."

"She recited several names, those she knew, to which the wizards answered, 'Those who you mention are gone from this earth. We know their names only because they are written in our books.'

"The high priestess smiled, paused a moment as if she expected the wizards to say more, which they didn't. Couldn't. 'Then pick up what you have brought,' she said, 'and follow me.'

"The wizards put the gifts on their backs and followed the priestess climbing up Omoma, but though she climbed the hill with ease the wizards did so only with great difficulty, their feet sinking into sand. She, who walked with such lightness that her feet seemed not to touch the ground, looked back to see that the sand almost reached the knees of the wizards, making it impossible for them to go on.

"Seeing this the priestess shook her head. 'The wealth you possess,' she suggested, 'weighs upon you. Give me that which you carry and wait; I shall call the mistress of this land so that you may see her.'

"She then picked up the many bundles that so burdened the wizards and carried these over a crest of the hill, and as she did so the goddess Tocuital appeared before them, shoulder-length black hair bound back by a single white ribbon, clad in a gray dress that continually shifted in shading and light. 'Welcome,' she said, 'I am grateful to my children for returning.'

"The wizards and sorcerers found themselves freed of the sand. They bowed before her, said: 'Exalted Goddess, we have travelled here on behalf of Lord Quinatzin, King-of-Kings, who sends you gifts, -precious gems, works in gold, and the finest cotton garments that you might be pleased and find honor in them.'

"Tocuital took the offered gifts, smiled as if she thought they were amusing, or dangerous. 'You have grown old,' she said, 'weakened by what you eat and drink, and spoiled by the riches that draw upon you hungry scavengers. There is a structure, one that binds you that even I cannot change: One seeks to reign, for a time reigns, and then one has reigned. But your people will, in their fashion, continue, and so they remember what they might live upon I give you humble gifts of plants and fish, and clothes spun from coarse fiber.'

"The magicians and wizards accepted her gifts, bid their farewells and descended the hill, the sand holding firm beneath their feet. They passed to a place deemed suitable to their purposes and there again transformed into their *nagual* selves, and so traveled to Coatepec Hill where they regained their natural form. However over half were missing, by which it was understood that there was a price demanded by the powers with which they dealt.

"Returning to Azcapotzalco, the sorcerers and magicians told me that which I have told you. So too they told of Tocuital's final prophecy. Or not a prophecy as we understand them, but rather a declamation of something already transpired in an unalterable future. That in time the greatness of Azcapotzalco will dwindle to a point, and then be forgotten. Let me repeat this: A time will soon come that none will remember our power, our greatness, our strength, our being. On this I struggled for a time, wondering how I might make Azcapotzalco immune to the turn of sequence. However I came to realize that this is the unalterable duality given to us, and intrinsic to our being. Such is my story, -make of it what you will."

After a duration in which all are silent, the guests shifting uneasily upon their cushions, Quinatzin motions to a man standing nearby, and a *cuicani*,[54] accompanied by several musicians, enter the hall and begin to fill it with music.

The caverns of the earth are filled with dust
that was once the bones of great rulers,

---

54 A singer. To sing is *cuica*; a song is *cuicatl*. A composer of a song is *cuicapicqui*, with *picqui* being a derivative of *piqui*, to make, to create.

who sat upon thrones commanding cities.
The caverns of the earth are filled with dust
that once governed armies and conquered realms.
The fires of Popocatepetl send skyward plumes of
    incense
upon which, for a moment, the light reflects, then
    all is as before.

Listening to this song, Night Axe gazes upon a vase filled with opalescent flowers and sees transient shifts of color as if the flowers breathed. He shakes his head to clear it of the vision. The dinner is at an end and the guests, followed by Night Axe, make their way from the dining hall. Night Axe inspects the memorial courtyard, confirming that it is now heaped with oil-wet wood and dried-popoloca torches. He pauses to look up at the gems of the night sky, the uncountable brilliance within which, gazing for a time, are seen ever fainter stars in the infinite vastness, and so too stars fainter still that seem to rise up out of the darkness towards him, and so a sensation of falling into the consuming infinity of night. With a start Night Axe realizes two dinner guests have come upon the courtyard to continue a discussion, and who take alarm at that which awaits but the smallest of sparks. Quickly, deftly, Night Axe claims them both, and for a fleeting moment notices how their blood seeps into the cuts and grooves that define the sculpted patio stones. Seeing this Night Axe repeats to himself a rhyme learned in his youth, one he has not thought of for a great many years:

Green, brown: The cypress by the riverbank.
Hard, soft: The boulder within the stream.
Thick, thin: The grass on the river's edge.

It is now time, he thinks, to find King-of-Kings Quinatzin.

42

The Departure of Night Axe

―――――

Night Axe silently passes down palace hallways in search of Lord Quinatzin. Turning a sharp corner he finds, strangely enough, neatly laid out upon a yopicatl chest-high table, a large bowl of *ahuacamolli*,[55] a yopicatl favorite, within which rest diced tomatoes, chilies, and onions, while nearby is a basket of warm corn tortillas. Night Axe could eat *ahuacamolli* and tortillas for days on end, and he is on the cusp, the edge, the thin margin of starting to eat said *ahuacamolli* when he stops, for he knows should he start he will not be able to stop until the bowl is empty and here, on the verge of squeezing Quinatzin's head off and overthrowing the city of Azcapotzalco, is no time for a hearty meal. Night Axe sighs; and though it pains him, small particle of emptiness in his soul, without eating a single tortilla, a single scoop of *ahuacamolli*, he

―――――

55 Guacamole.

continues on down the hallway. He notes the singular absence of attendants within the palace; perhaps, their prayers answered, all are now safely on their way home.

Night Axe nears the royal sleeping chamber, -there is no confusing it for anything else: great sweep of space adorned with art of astonishing beauty that will, surely, be treasured for all time, including feather weavings that capture the very essence of life in such exquisite colors they seem to defy one's ability to comprehend, and intricate sculptures of diverse metals that appear more real than that which is living. Night Axe passes another waiting bowl of *ahuacamolli*, thinks, "It is as if someone knew I was coming and prepared my favorite meal, but perhaps a snack for patrolling guards."

Night Axe enters Quinatzin's bedchamber and, surprise, finds him on his knees, hard at prayer. Nearby, within a bed, a female popoloca sleeps: sleep, that luxurious, restful form of prayer to the goddess of peaceful slumber. Night Axe is just about to clear his throat and say something witty, or profoundly meaningful, when he finally, at this last moment realizes that he has been too clever by half, knows that the *ahuacamolli* he has passed is poisoned, having been arranged for his enjoyment, and knows that he has walked into a trap, set and sprung.

An imposter, Quinatzin-not-Quinatzin, slashes at Night Axe with a long obsidian blade, sharp as a new idea, curved like a nightmare, and slices his chest to the bone. Surprise. There is another bite of pain, for the sleeping female is in fact another warrior armed with a sharp-tipped spear. With one hand Night Axe grabs hold of the spear and, despite the best efforts of the popoloca, stops it from going any further into his flesh, steps backward putting this warrior between him and the warriors who now fill the doorway, drops his staff, and with his free hand grabs the warrior's nearest arm and with a sharp, hard, downward jerk pulls the arm off. Blood spray. Night Axe shoves this warrior, wet slippery cascade of blood, towards the cluster of attacking warriors; they fall back, and one slips and falls to the floor comically tripping others. For all their number there is confusion. A big howling confusion of red-faced furless apes attacking poor Night Axe, who experiences a shift in the essential character of time, reality blurring to a series of painstakingly drawn sketches with each increment of 'now' requiring completion of a rough sketch of 'the moment' before moving on, step-wise in discrete increments, to the next.

Yopicatl-quick, Night Axe picks up his staff and so defines a radius of momentary safety. He sees a finely crafted shield upon the wall and, in mock terror (though he feels, to some extent, terror), retreats towards it. To Quinatzin-not-Quinatzin's credit he bravely rallies the soldiers to attack the profusely bleeding, retroceding yopicatl. Then, trick of wily Tezcatlipoca, Quinatzin-not-Quinatzin turns away from Night Axe, just a mere handful of heartbeats in which he does not expect the retreating, profusely bleeding yopicatl to step forward and swing his staff 'just so' to remove the top portion of his head. The ambushing warriors who have advanced from the doorway are coated with Quinatzin-not-Quinatzin spray. Bleeding from two wounds, Night Axe leaps through the window into the darkness. He strikes the ground, rolls, comes to his feet and no less swift than a wolf leaves the palace behind. "A near-run thing," he thinks. "Near run."

Night Axe soon comes to the margin of the city and climbs atop a lesser temple; from the edge of its modest sacred fire he scoops up handfuls of hot ash and puts this into his wounds, stemming the flow of blood. After some moments Night Axe regains his composure, looks at the stars and knows it is too early for his Xochimilco allies to arrive; he has been impatient, yopicatl-impatient, and started the festivities too soon. He tears strips off the bottom of his robe and wraps these about him to bind the wounds. Night Axe realizes that unless he immediately flees into the forest he will, astronomically high probability, be killed. But of course should he flee into the forest, and Azcapotzalco remain atop the ant pile, he will be hunted down and, astronomically high probability, be killed. He hears a cacophony of chirruping, howling, grunting and screeching; it is the soldiers hunting for him, no doubt following the trail of blood-drops he has left behind. He takes a deep breath and collects himself. He looks up into the starlit heavens for a final moment of calm and, omen or coincidence, sees a star lose its grip upon the heavens and fall into the darkness, a sign that leads itself to diverse interpretations. He pauses for a moment, says, "I had best begin."

Night Axe silently winds his way back towards the center of the city, sending the occasional Azcapotzalco warrior on to the Next World. He comes to the window he so recently leapt out of and climbs in. From the wall of the room he takes down the shield he had noticed earlier, made of stout fire-hardened wooden rods closely bound together, covered with detailed feather work of many colors, and the whole outlined in gold foil. Armed with shield and staff Night Axe passes down the halls of the now empty palace, walks swiftly to the memorial courtyard, flicks a torch upon the pile of tenuously bound energy and sees the bonfire roar to life. "How nice," he thinks, "If my Xochimilco allies see this fire and decide to arrive early."

Of course, this is what he says knowing the world being what the world is they will arrive late, or not at all, or opt to make alliance with Azcapotzalco in trying to rid the world of the last yopicatl. There are shouts of alarm, whistles, and the periodic tapping of drums, the warriors of Azcapotzalco filtering through the city. Night Axe carefully makes his way to the temple of Xihcutli to there extinguish the gods eternally burning sacred fire, an omen that would strike dread into the hearts of the Azcapotzalco warriors, yet he realizes there is no surprising anyone now, and that in all probability he has but a few moments left on this earth. Coming to the base of Xihcutli's temple he finds there a number of well-armed warriors, thinks: "A fleet of Xochimilco *acalli*, filled to their rims with warriors, would be most convenient." Meaningful pause. "Most convenient." He thinks of how handy one of the large steel swords that the pale-skinned popoloca warriors of the 2nd world use would be. How Night Axe could use such a sword to cut his way through this sorry lot! He is bleeding, not thinking clearly, and finds in each direction more warriors, and he realizes there is a high probability that he will not reach the steps of the temple, nor climb them, nor extinguish Xihcutli's sacred fire. There are too many warriors, too many spears and swords. Night Axe recognizes that for all the popoloca warriors he sends to Mictlan that his own sacred water is slowly leaking away, his very essence seeping out upon the plaza. The task before him is too much for a single yopicatl, simply too much.

+ + +

Unexpectedly, in fact inexplicable, there is a cry of fear among the warriors; a shudder of dismay echoing out like the waves of sound from a golden cymbal, and with it a momentary loss of death-dealing purpose. Night Axe seizes the moment, smashes his way through to the temple steps, now it is just a matter of climbing said steps, pouring out a few tens of jugs of wine, or whatever, but, funny, looking up upon the height he sees Xihcutli's inextinguishable sacred fire has been extinguished, and he doesn't understand it, perhaps Totomotzin? It is all confusing, but this: an ember of fear has sparked to life within the hearts of the Azcapotzalco warriors. "If they are afraid," says Night Axe, "then let them be afraid." And there on the temple steps, raised up a convenient distance from the carnage on the plaza, puddles of blood, dead and injured, the last of the yopicatl lets out a primordial howl of rage, the consummating sound of darkness turned upon itself, and for a moment the battle stops, the warriors frozen. Easier for them if Night Axe had fed on the poisoned *ahuacamolli*, but he didn't. Across the courtyard he sees a general rally his warriors to the attack with the intent of sending Night Axe across The Far Waters.

Night Axe realizes his Xochimilco allies are, more than likely, at home eating vision-inducing mushrooms while guzzling down cups of chocolatl. Existence for Night Axe is reduced to mere mechanics: so many strikes and blocks with his staff and shield, strikes and blocks. His movements can be seen as a dance, or a form of prayer, -instead of kneeling he steps nimbly this way or that; instead of folding his hands across his chest he swings his faithful cylinder of hard wood. Night Axe kills one warrior to have two replace the one, kills two to have four replace the two, and so on, mathematical progression. "One stick cannot make a fire," he whispers. "Give me two or three, then there will be a blaze!"

Night Axe is bleeding, and the world seems to rapidly shrink about him. A large rock flies through the air, someone's bad aim, passing well over his head to strike the warrior-rallying general. "A bit of luck!" Night Axe says to himself. He flinches as another rock sails by, just missing him, but fortuitously striking a particularly fierce warrior who had stood, just a moment ago, *right there*. One of the stone statues that decorate the temple arcs by, twirling end over end as it travels like the samara of a maple tree striking not one, but three warriors, punching them backwards as if toys.

"No doubt I am being unfair to my Xochimilco allies," thinks Night Axe, yopicatl-bitter; "I'm sure they had the best of intentions: 'We would have been there (imitative high-pitched whine), but got lost, what with all the darkness! Sorry!' "

Another rock just misses Night Axe, striking a warrior squarely in the chest who cascades back into another. Leaking blood, thinking poorly, Night Axe suddenly realizes a popoloca could not throw such stones, and he is surprised to realize the Nahua have come to the invention of catapults, those great hurlers of stones and burning oil, yet he does not hear the familiar 'twang,' or 'thumphhh,' that he knows catapults make, -they seem to have invented a silent catapult. Which seems odd, or in fact remarkable. He sees another warrior share time and space with a fast moving large stone. "Comical," he thinks; "They hit everyone *but* me!" He grows ever more tired: Overhand, underhand; step, block, strike. Strike. He is so tired that he begins to imagine he sees Xihcutli's shrine on fire, glorious blaze reaching up to the gods, and realizes he should have done that at the beginning, that that would have been the thing to do, putting joy and courage into the hearts of his absent Xochimilco allies. One makes mistakes in life, try as you may; it is difficult, truly it is difficult to do everything right, everything just so with the one try. Another rock sails through the air, sending yet another Azcapotzalco warrior onto Mictlan. Night Axe is now staggering, his prodigious yopicatl strength almost spent. He feels the sharp prick of another blade, but for that continues removing what warriors he can from this world, and then a stone finds his shield, pushes the shield back into him, knocks him down and sends him rolling across the warm blood-wet stones of the courtyard. "Finally!" He laughs, "Was I that hard to hit?"

Night Axe, who thought he would live forever, a life of great meaning, is surprised to find the end is nigh, his life meaningless and comical but, philosophically inclined as he is, thinks life is change and so be it, at least face the change bravely. He once heard a philosophy espoused that beyond death all is possible; perhaps he will join his family and friends in some post-existence eternal yopicatl-paradise. Teetering on the edge, dreaming, he sees the shrine of Xihcutli is now but a sharply defined tower of flame, the dream so vivid the brilliant light hurts his eyes, *et lux in tenebris lucet*. Set against this brilliant light he sees a shower, a veritable cascade of rocks rain down upon nearby warriors, the popoloca catapults gone insane.

He is at the border, the boundary between this world and another place, somewhere else, not here. He sees the night air glitter, some overwhelming luster of light, comes to understand, here at the very end how we are like the fish who live in the dark waters of the deep who know nothing of the overarching sky above. Illuminated by the burning shrine, the all-clarifying Torch of the World, which is to say, the Light Within Us, he sees The Immanent close at hand, ready to guide him into, on to, and here there is some confusion, The Next World, or nothing, but call it what you will, in his new abode he sees many hallways and rooms which he understands are no more than the hearts of others, which is to say love, and the windows of these rooms are from where one gains the encompassing sweep of Eternity. He has had a good life, he thinks; much left unfinished, true, but name a life for which that isn't so.

Night Axe, light-dazzled eyes, suffers tricks of the subconscious that starts showing the consciousness, the mind's upper floors, what it wants to see, which seems to be an enchanting female yopicatl coming down the steps of the temple. He is certain now that death is close at hand; she is, must be, as the popoloca of the northern middle continent would say, a Valkyrie, tasked with guiding him to the next world. Though she is certainly fetching, a certain charm and grace about her, she seems an unusual celestial spirit, tricks of the mind as it slips into the distance; she seems, in point of fact, a basket of stones under one arm, the goddess of catapults, hurling out stone missiles with unfailing yopicatl-aim.

He is going now, a peaceful darkness embracing him, narrow tunnel of vision, it is but a single step to where The Unfathomable, great shining beacon, awaits to greet him. But, funny, or momentous, he sees a small yopicatl female and knows her to be his daughter, and within a small glade she is chasing about a slightly older, slightly larger male yopicatl who he knows to be her brother, his son, and the two are laughing, as happy together as the moon and stars. And he sees this as a future of what can be should he turn back, and that he must turn back, and so he turns back to the pain and embraces it. Pain. Pain. Pain. Unending relentless pain. He rises up out of the depths to hear orders being shouted, surprisingly enough by the stone-struck general who is still alive enough to recognize that with the burning of Xihcutli's shrine Cihuacoatl has triumphed, the battle over, but who is injured such that he does not speak clearly, slurring his words and, curiously, Night Axe hears him heap abuse upon Xihcutli, ex-patron god of Azcapotzalco. Night Axe turns to the fetching yopicatl kneeling at his side, says to her: "I can't stand profanity with a lisp; if I hear 'Oh Xiuhwecutwee' again I'm going to scream."

She laughs, which sounds enchanting to his ears and there, at the edge of the void, he realizes it is the oracle herself, and though perhaps he is dreaming, perhaps he isn't, and she, the courtyard, the inner city is illuminated by that which was once Xihcutli's shrine, now torch, and the echoing in his ears is the mournful, soul-searching cry of conch-shell trumpets which suggests the soldiers of Xochimilco now range across the city. So too, he realizes, he is still alive, and the wind carries the muted cries of a battle that has passed beyond him.

"That went well," he says to the yopicatl-oracle angel Valkyrie.

So much for reality, or what he considers reality. His brain shuts down despite his efforts to hold on; there is dying, a process; and death, a state. He looks into her eyes, would like to say something clever, endearing perhaps, but realizes he no longer has the strength, or motivation, to do so. He wants only to sleep. "Hmmphf," he thinks, which is the best he can do, everything winding up just so. Deprived of blood the brain runs out of oxygen; the tissue starts to necrotize, and with this our passage to the next world is gentled: The Immanent's great gift to us. Night Axe hears a song carried on the wind, song or dream, difficult to say:

> We don our thick-quilted armor; we grasp our
> swords and spears.
> The drums sound advance, we press forward.
> We have come a great distance, but the way home
> is longer.

And still, as far as he can tell, he is not dead. The fetching yopicatl, still by his side though he blinks and blinks again, has been joined by popoloca who are attending his wounds. And though he is lost to the cares and woes of the world, still he's not dead. Still. Of a moment, how suddenly the mind can work, he realizes he knows the name of this wondrous yopicatl: she is Teya, the younger sister of a friend, what seems millions of years ago. The world spins, overwhelming odors of ash, fire, and blood.

The popoloca doctors press something very painful into his wounds. He smiles at Teya, thinks, the descent into Mictlan would be so easy, but she is holding his hand, quite fiercely it seems, not to guide him to The Distant Land, but to hold him here to this world. Somehow, her holding his hand gives him strength he did not know he had; he tells her, as clearly as he can manage to speak, which is not very clear, about the poisoned *ahuacamolli* in the palace that, perhaps, some hungry Xochimilco soldiers are already enjoying. There is a look of confusion on her face; his eyes lose focus, he can't hold on, he no longer sees her face, nor the burning shrine that illuminates the world. His soul rises up from his body so that he looks down from a height, and so he sees his self, or just his body, a body, sees the popoloca trying to keep him in the One World, sees Teya, sees Xochimilco warriors swarming over the city; sees the surrender of the Azcapotzalco soldiers who, Cihuacoatl having proved herself greater, no longer have a purpose to fight, the will of the gods set forth in gleaming clarity. He now sees a distant mountain, and to this he is swiftly traveling while blackness collapses about him. He sings softly to himself:

Ahuehuetl and cypress flank the broad paths.
Beneath them lie those who died long ago.
Black is the cold night that holds them.

So he mumbles, and then the abyss.

Sixth Bundle

"The other people there [the One World] were said to have been giants [*quiname*, in Nahuatl]. I should like to tell of the treason and deceit by which the people annihilated that nation. They pretended to want peace with the giants, and after having assured them of their goodwill invited them to dine and made a great banquet, for which an ambush was prepared. During the feast some men slyly robbed the guests of their shields, clubs, staffs, and many other kinds of weapons they used. Then, having feigned peace, having fed the guests, and having stolen their weapons... suddenly came out of hiding and attacked. The giants tried valiantly to defend themselves, and as they could not find their weapons tore branches from the trees and so fought. But finally all were killed."

Fray Diego Duran,
The History of The Indies of New Spain
Published circa 1581

43
More Unchangeable Events Within The Past

———

The Nahua realm teeters on the edge of collapse. At a
loss of what else to do Quinatzin has word sent to
the Speakers of all cities and towns, Headmen of even
the smallest villages, to pass among their people who are
known to dream to see if any have had extraordinary
visions regarding that which affects the realm, and if so
to bring these people before the King-of-Kings.

The hour of meeting set with the geometry of the stars,
Quinatzin, a few moments to himself, leaves the palace to
sit within a garden kept alive through the drought only
by painstaking labor. The late-night darkness is alive with
more stars than his mind can take hold of, "No drought
there," he thinks. Then, curiously, Quinatzin recalls one of
Aztacoatl's little whimsical riddles, or message of profound

importance; Aztacoatl acted like it was the descriptor of the geometry by which the universe holds itself together. So it is with the yopicatl, their keenest insights spoken in the same fashion as their most undecipherable idiocies: 1 through 9, in order, can be combined in various ways to arrive at 100. After some moments he realizes:

$$100 = 123 - 45 - 67 + 89$$

And for that, he feels somewhat closer to The Unfathomable having parsed out a trick of the universe, translucent fire of a logical AND/OR.

Of those who come before Lord Quinatzin, there are some who look upon a basin of smooth water and see reflections of the future. There are some who cast kernels of maize or strings upon water and by their movements, so many floating or sinking or turning this way or that, understand how events of today will manifest themselves in the future. There are some who ask questions of small cubes carved from bone each side of which are marked in a certain way, and with a casting of these cubes, this or that symbol landing up or down, find their answers. There are some who eat or drink specific mushrooms or herbs, or set aflame particular plants to breathe their fumes, and considering this Quinatzin begins to understand why so much of modern Nahua art he finds disturbing.

Of his audience, an old man first speaks who humbles himself before the King-of-Kings and says, "Lord Quinatzin, as you command I shall describe my divinations, in which I believe there is meaning, though I do not wish to offend your ears, or concern your heart."

"My concern is the realm," Quinatzin answers. "Describe your visions."

"The Lords of Sleep have shown me the shrine of Xihcutli shining out like a beacon over the entire valley, His brilliance, His Majesty, for a time rivaling that of The Sun itself in defeating the darkness of the Night Lord."

"And of rain?" Quinatzin asks. "Do the rains return?"

"Yes, all Nahua is once again green, the dreams are most clear upon this. Rain. Food. All is again in abundance."

"When do the rains return?"

"I am sorry my lord, but I am not given that knowledge. All I know is that they do return, and the realm thrives."

Another man speaks, says, "From Xihcutli's temple, below His shining beacon, manifestation of His glory, I saw rocks rain down."

"Rocks?" Quinatzin asks, startled by the odd divination. "Perhaps," he asks the man, "what you saw were simply large water-stones from the sky?"

"Perhaps, Lord Quinatzin." He bows still lower. "Perhaps."

One man speaks most curiously, precisely detailing what the future holds for Quinatzin, Azcapotzalco, the Nahua Valley, and Mankind itself, for the gods allow him to see everything of the future with unblemished clarity, space-time revealed before him like an eagle upon the highest aerie. Yet too, for punishment of some transgression, a trifling detail now lost to time, while he sees all, swift flight of a heart-piercing arrow, anything he reveals, any wisdom he imparts, is immediately forgotten by those who hear it. So too the gods, who appear to have forgotten him, do not allow him the gift of death, and so he lives on, quantity of time followed by quantity of time, knowing the beginning and knowing the end and being helpless to change a single thread of that which unravels before him.

$$100 = 1 + 23 - 4 + 56 + 7 + 8 + 9$$

Quinatzin, who has never felt entirely himself since being bitten by the serpent, yet for that presses on with his duties, considers the words of the presagers, those his memory has retained, and has some strange inclination to make a joke, -and why this urge should be upon him he has no idea; save but to himself the King-of-Kings does not make jokes. The average person is easily offended and readily provoked to violence. Since there is no universal agreement on humor, being specific to perspective, setting, and intelligence, any joke he makes is bound to offend someone. He recalls King so and so, the name momentarily slipping his mind, he was a great joker that one, who was found dead of a mild rash and four stab wounds. In effect, Quinatzin realizes with a yopicatl-like lucidity, he talks with a cluster of easily angered furless monkeys, and so he says nothing.

$$100 = 1 + 2 \times 3 + 4 + 5 + 67 + 8 + 9$$

One old woman lifts up her chin and begins to open her mouth as if to speak, but then seemingly changes her mind, drops her head and remains silent. Seeing this

Quinatzin, in a most kindly voice, asks, "What is it you have seen that concerns the realm?"

"My son," the woman answers, after a moment's hesitation, "What I have seen has frightened me greatly, though I ask that you not be troubled in your heart. In my dream, I your mother saw a mighty river enter the doors of this royal palace, in its fury smash the walls, and carry away the beams and stones until nothing was left. The waters surged over the temple of Xihcutli, extinguishing His sacred fire. So too washed away was that which we know as Teotihuacan, realm of the yopicatl. It seemed, in many ways, all was plunged into darkness."

Quinatzin considers her words and can make no sense of it. He asks, "In your visions, has the rain returned? Do the springs give forth? Do the rivers and streams flow? "

"Yes, Lord Quinatzin. The rain, rivers, streams, and springs of the Valley once again are as we would have them, and the land is fertile."

At a loss to understand what he has heard Quinatzin, sweating profusely for reasons he cannot understand, thanks the men and women, gives them gifts, and sends them off to their homes.

◆ ◆ ◆

Quinatzin long considers the words of the seers, recognizing that the truth one puts into words, whether describing a vision or a midday meal, does not define a direct path. There are nuances, inflections, verbal sleights of hand, the misunderstood trope or allegory, and the utmost certainty of uncertainty. Lord Quinatzin finally comes to understand what is needed for the rains to fall. The people of Nahua can offer Tlaloc and Chalchiuhtlicue a proper sacrifice that will sustain them, make them strong, and when the rains return, and the springs and rivers flow, when there is water and food, then it will be possible to raise up Chalchiuhtlicue's temples equal to those of Xihcutli and Tlaloc, and this is the right thing to do, and this is what the gods demand. Step by logical step, Quinatzin thinks, he will do what is necessary to help Tlaloc, He Who Is the Embodiment of Earth, and Chalchiuhtlicue, She of the Jade Skirt, so that the world will be set right, everything bathed within an immortal light like transparent emerald.

$$100 = 1 \times 2 - 3 + 4 - 5 + 6 + 7 + 89$$

He discusses his idea with Senior General Cuauh Petlauh, who receives it poorly. Normally of keen mind and sharp discernment, General Petlauh cannot grasp the insight Lord Quinatzin puts forth. At some point in the discussion between the two men Quinatzin realizes Cuauh Petlauh does not, and will not, accept Quinatzin's vision of what is necessary for the rains to fall, and with this, logical consequence, Quinatzin realizes that Cuauh Petlauh is no longer his most trusted general and counselor but a potential enemy who, with but a single word, can bring all of Quinatzin's plans to ruin and so ensure the destruction of Nahua.

Understanding this, the clarity of a moment, Quinatzin smiles, and admits the wisdom of the general's words. "Power is a funny thing," he tells

General Petlauh, patting him warmly on the back. "Laborious to come by, but quickly lost. I thank-you for your sage counsel."

* * *

Later that night Quinatzin, reflecting on his conversation with Senior General Cuauh Petlauh, considers the fall of Cuaro, vast walled city that once spanned the Chapala River and, for a time, held sway over the land from the western edge of Nahua to the ocean. Cuaro, that came in the end to be ruled by the zacotic King Maloyan who, having no enemies to contest with, amused himself by abusing those who served him, and eating. Endlessly, endlessly eating. King Maloyan who, displeased with Huemac, his chief counter of inventory, had served the man the roasted body of his oldest son and called upon him to sample it. But for that Huemac sampled the meat, declared it delicious, helped himself to more and by so doing lived. Sequence of events played out in time, there came a certain morning, and of mornings King Maloyan would break his night-long fasts by consuming many bowls of blue-maize soup, the kernels finely ground and cooked with chicory milk, flavored with honey, vanilla, bears fat, and a certain type of chili, when Huemac, passing through the kitchens while checking on quantities and qualities for King Maloyan, added to the pot within which cooked the king's blue-maize soup a spice curious in its effect, which is to quickly dissolve the flesh of those who eat it. Said to be a sight no one ever forgets.

However Huemac had not limited himself to obtaining a rare spice, for outside the walls of Cuaro there soon arrived a great army collected from her many enemies and, curiously, presumed allies.

Since King Maloyan, who had long out-stayed his welcome on earth, could not abide to designate a successor, someone whose light might one day outshine his, and so too had removed all the strong men of Cuaro, those who might in some way pose a threat, it was the timid and the weak who peered over the walls, calling out to the gathered host, "We are Cuaro. Our warriors are innumerable and invincible. All towns and cities of the land pay us tribute."

To this General Totochtzin, who commanded the surrounding army, smiled, but said nothing. After a time those behind the walls asked, "What is it you want?"

Calling out in a loud voice so all upon the walls could hear, General Totochtzin answered, "What we want is your land, your food, your goods, your slaves, and the women and children who appeal to us."

Those behind the walls, after some moments, asked, "What will you leave us?"

"Your lives," the general offered.

And so that the realm of Cuaro would never again rise to power General Totochtzin had the walls dismantled and the stones thrown into the swift flowing waters of the Chapala River.

◆ ◆ ◆

Two nights later a shadow enters Quinatzin's sleeping chamber that, in a moment, proves to be a man. Spider silent, Quinatzin hands the man a scrap of paper upon which is written a single name. The man reads the name, and then swallows the paper. The task will be accomplished in utmost secrecy, and the body will vanish never to be a found. Without a sound the man bows his head and, suddenly as a serpent, disappears. It is not enough to love the power of Azcapotzalco, Quinatzin muses, the power of Azcapotzalco must love you. Yet for that Quinatzin cannot help but feel something has been overlooked, and so too there is a feeling of being watched. Yet Lord Quinatzin turns about, looks in all directions, and sees no one save his ever-present guards.

44

Texcoco

It is from Texcoco that royal messengers leave for
Teotihuacan to invite the yopicatl to a feast celebrating
Chalchiuhtlicue sealing the life-draining whirlpool,
following suitable offerings as suggested by Aztacoatl, for
which all Nahua is grateful. So too great nobles and high
priests have been invited from across The One World since
all honor Tlaloc and Chalchiuhtlicue, and all live by the grace
of water. As to such celebratory feasts one might think harsh
droughts are not the logical time for such events, for the rains
still do not fall and that which still grows and blossoms, the
avocado orchards of Azcapotzalco, for example, do so only
for their being watered bucket by bucket from the receding
lake, a pitiless task, but there is logic which suggests that
such generosity within times of hardship, symbolic of
endurance and fortitude, might please the gods. The sages
counsel that when all fails, try something else.

Although the city of Texcoco need not be described for the purposes of our story, since it is one of the most beautiful cities that man will offer up to the shores of Time and Space and will, some years hence, disappear in a proverbial heartbeat, we will pause for a moment to consider it not here within the throes of a pitiless drought but rather some time beyond when water is once again plentiful and the land green.

The city ranges from the edge of the lake that bears the same name to the high slopes of Mount Tlaloc, where cultivated fields give way to immense forests of ancient trees, and within which lie ruins forgotten people built for forgotten gods in some shadow-world of the distant past, a protohistory of which none now can speak, but perhaps can sing, as about the ruins one finds a great number of red-collared *zacuan* birds fluttering within their sylvan grottos.

> The city reigns within jade circles:
> To the east rich fields and green mountains,
> To the west the Queen of Lakes, she with her
>   mirror face,
> About all, there is a flowery mist.

The flat-roofed houses of Texcoco, of which there is a clean simplicity to the furnishings, are of pale-colored polished wood and white-stuccoed stone. The pride of the people is in their children, their work, and their gardens, -the gardens that one finds atop the houses, hanging down from the roofs of the houses, about the houses, and within the central courtyards of the houses. As to be expected of such a devout people within Texcoco there are a large number of temples. The temple of Tlaloc, built beneath the very shadow of Mount Tlaloc, is the greatest of the many, a tiered-pyramid of stone from the height of which the city is revealed. With temples come sacred fires, and thus at night the city glows like a shining mist of jewels.

A curious temple within the city is worthy of description, built by order of Queen Miahuitl. Atop a truncated pyramid common to the land a shrine of nine stories rises up representing the nine levels of heaven, for so they believe in Texcoco, and then a tenth story painted black on the outside and studded with large jewels symbolic of the glittering stars, while on the inside it is adorned with gold, silver, and feathers of the most brilliant colors. Within this temple there is no idol, no statue, for this god is known only through actions, unseen but felt.

You are everywhere, but I worship you here.

The heart of Texcoco is a mile square realm neatly defined by stone walls fifteen feet high and nine thick, with four openings where the walls are contrived to overlap for some 40 yards, the passageway between commanded by guards who stand upon both heights. Within the walls are two great stone-paved plazas one of which, surrounded by an arcade of shops, is the public marketplace, orderly kingdom of buying and selling. The other plaza is surrounded by buildings such as council chambers, public archives, armories, and houses for the storage of tribute. To speak of maize alone, each year Texcoco receives some 250,000 tons, brought by boats that pass upon canals intimately linking city and lake, and by the lake all cities of the realm.

A city of airy halls, bright arcades, houses of books and paintings, schools, hospitals, and houses where aid is provided to widows and orphans. Less in extent only to the palace is the *Cuicacalli*, the Houses of Dance, great buildings splendidly built and handsomely decorated where young popoloca are taught singing, dancing, and the playing of musical instruments.

Not far from the palace is the *Calpixque*, where one finds those in charge of public works by which roads, walls, plazas, and aqueducts, to name but a few of their purposes, are built and maintained, who within their house hear the decisions and commands of the royal council, the laws and edicts that are to be enforced, and then see that they are enforced, the orders of the *Calpixque* passing on from one set of officials to the other. It is a marvelous sight to see the Speakers and their Captains account for the people who are to go forth to some business or task, with guides for the old, guides for the youths, and guides for the married people. So the whole city is controlled with the work divided among them, and all is counted then accounted, and the officials of the republic seem innumerable. With such discipline do they join in public works, and so methodically, with he who has attended this week not attending the next, that no one feels weighed down. Such is the order, rigor, and concert with which they govern themselves that not a man is lost nor a thing mislaid. And if it is decided to attack a certain city or town on a certain date, those of the *Calpixque* notify the intervening towns and villages to ensure the army is received with provisions and the roads empty for their swift passage.

Within the palace itself there are rooms for diverse officials, rooms in which counselors and sages meet to consider matters of good government, rooms for poets and musicians, rooms for visiting kings and queens, and rooms for visiting ambassadors, scientists and diviners. There are houses for wives of the king, of which there are many, for it is by marriage that the empire is knitted, and there are classrooms where those of the royal family, not given to idleness, can learn the artistry of metal, or that of poetry and discourse. Of the palace grounds there are some dozen ponds in which tame fish and fowl make their home. There are fine-crafted stone paths upon which one might wander through groves of cypress and cedar, giants from the world's first age. It is a realm of porticos, statues, friezes, fruit trees, fragrant flowers and shrubs, fountains of diamond-clear water, and clouds of butterflies who contest to see who can clad themselves in the most glorious of colors.

The day is demarcated by sounding the drum of Quetzalcoatl, kept within the god's circular temple of smooth mortared stone, there being no rough edges to offend the wind. At sunrise the drum, called *Ehecatl*, Wind, so big its voice it is heard throughout the city, is sounded denoting the moment farmers, fishermen, traders and merchants leave to their purposes. At sunset the drum is again sounded, and with its echo the city falls into silence: the markets are dismantled, and all leave for home. "Let us retire," one hears, "*Ehecatl* has sounded."

A prosperous, peaceful city: a magnificent dream.

As for the disappearance of Texcoco, that as we know it here, it will not disappear due to drought or storm, nor earthquake nor fire. The people will disappear largely due to a variety of imported diseases, and the buildings will disappear for this: the Nahua cast small jewels into the mortar that binds the stones of their buildings, -but a harmless trick to bring luck. However there are other men in this world who the Nahua are fated to meet who greatly value such shiny stones, and for them will eagerly grind down not just buildings, but the universe.

45
Tetzcotzingo

———

The feast, celebratory dinner, is to be held at
Tetzcotzingo, the foremost of King Copiltzin's
idyllic retreats, built upon a sharply defined rise some four
miles east of Texcoco, at the edge of the foothills beneath
Mount Tlaloc. From the base of the hill to its height there
are 520 neatly defined steps cut from the living stone and
polished bright. A colossal aqueduct, towering edifice of
mortared stone that spans several miles in length, fed
by springs mid-height on Mount Tlaloc that still, even
at the height of the drought, mercifully flow albeit more
slowly, brings diamond-clear water to the very apex of
Tetzcotzingo filling a reservoir within which, rising up
from the water like a blade, is a large stele on which the
principal achievements of Copiltzin are recorded in stone.
From this reservoir flows two streams, and these wind
their way through the terraced gardens upon the hillside,

realm of trees, fragrant shrubs and untold scented flowers brought from all lands and here carefully cultivated. The two streams fill four smaller reservoirs, all crafted of finely joined stone, in three of which stand statues of the Empress Miahuitl that Copiltzin ordered carved in honor of his first wife, the queen by whose vision and care the gardens have reached their current glory. Within the fourth reservoir there is a statue of a winged jaguar. The streams divide, divide again, and again, and amid the maze of streams, flumes, channels, and rivulets, the reservoirs and pools there are basins carved from the natural porphyry, one of which is dedicated to the sacred purposes of Chalchiuhtlicue, and two others reserved for bathing which can also be considered a sacred purpose. The waters drain away from Tetzcotzingo to pass through a maze of orchards, with the water bit by bit subtracted from the remaining whole until soon the water is no more, and there is but parched sere earth where it has scarcely rained for over two years.

At the base of Tetzcotzingo, facing south, amid a grove of gigantic cedars one finds the royal villa, so great in size the yopicatl might call it their own, as there are polished cypress beams some 120 feet long and 8 feet in diameter, stone blocks neatly joined the size of which seem to defy the power of men. A place of airy halls, polished jasper floors, patios covered with cotton awnings, arcades, and well-lit rooms where one might rest and enjoy the sweet perfumes of the gardens and watch the flame-colored pheasants roam the hill.

✦ ✦ ✦

The festival begins at twilight tomorrow, day 12 *quiauitl,*[56] a most auspicious day for honoring the gods of water. But of the night before the celebratory feast, duration of sleep demarcated by turning of the night's stars, some do not sleep well having unusually odd dreams.

+ + +

Lord Quinatzin dreams of a time when, as a young man, he was forced to rest at home for several days having been struck by an errant *tlachtli* ball. Now, there is confusion within the dream. He is unsure if he is Lord Quinatzin dreaming of a forgotten past, or a youth dreaming of an as yet unrealized future, for dream seems nested within dream, but either way he awakens to find that he lies upon a soft bed of dust with his mother, gone now for so many years, wiping his forehead with a cool cloth.

"Mother," he says. He tries to get up, fails. "Mom."[57]

"Rest," his mother says. "General Petlauh says to be at ease with yourself. Everyone makes mistakes, one only hopes that they are little ones, of a recoverable distance."

A bright light flashes across the distant horizon and rapidly surges closer. Quinatzin does not know if this is his mind shutting down or if it is man's crowning achievement, the final war. Quinatzin realizes something has gone wrong, terribly wrong, but he is unsure of what. Too late to seek shelter, and there is no shelter, the burning light sweeps over them and Quinatzin awakens with a start, his bedding wet with sweat.

---

56 Rain.
57 *Nana.*

✦ ✦ ✦

King Copiltzin dreams that he sits upon the height of Teotihuacan's greatest temple, or monument, call it what you will, that now serves as his royal cushion, symbol of authority, encompassed within a hall so immense it embraces mountains, blue-green forests and lakes, and untold numbers of well tended fields. All within the hall, bound by walls an immeasurable yet finite distance away, call him King-of-Kings and pay him tribute. Lord Quinatzin is there with him, or rather, curious accident, just the head of Lord Quinatzin, comfortably resting upon a nearby cushion, and from his unusual vantage point Lord Quinatzin serenely gazes out upon the world. A quechol bird rests upon the shoulder of Lord Copiltzin, gold-bright fiery bird of heaven, and with a knife-edged voice whispers, "Lord Quinatzin has had an accident."

✦ ✦ ✦

Queen Miahuitl dreams she alone now rules Texcoco, her husband-king absent, off to someplace else. Perhaps, she thinks, he is in another room, though after a moment's consideration she believes this to be incorrect, no matter, and puts the idea out of her head. Within an alcove of lavender flowers she sits upon a stone bench, soon realizing it is a garden in which she used to play as a child and the nearby voices she hears are those of childhood friends. She looks down a path enclosed on each side by flowers and tall grass, and sees a small man of indeterminate age, perhaps forty, possibly fifty, who from a near distance is walking towards her. He wears a red loincloth with white trim, and a vest of the same design. Although she does not believe the man means her harm she becomes increasingly afraid as he draws near, and awakens.

♦ ♦ ♦

Aztacoatl dreams of a day unalterably bound by the past, where he plays in a river at the base of Mount Popocatepetl with his son Kulcan and daughter Koxocuitl. It is a river he knows he knows the name of, a familiar all his life, but yet for that cannot bring to mind. His children have found a flat-shelled golden-colored turtle the size of a large plate. Holding the shell of the turtle flat to the water, curling their wrists in towards their chests, with a flick of the wrist to set it spinning they send the turtle back and forth between them skipping it across the surface of the water. After several successful passes Kulcan, laughing so hard he gasps for breath, misses the spinning-turtle Koxocuitl has sent his way; the turtle sinks, escaping into the cool depths. There is bright sunlight upon the water, a soft breeze, and the sky is filled with great cotton-like tufts that are white above and dark below. The moment is one Aztacoatl wishes to hold forever, yet for that the idea of the river, the going beyond, pulls strongly at his mind: an irresistible urge to float and let the current carry him onward about the next bend, an urge that becomes so overpowering he must yield to it. First, however, heavy step by heavy step as if a great weight were upon him he splashes through the shallows to his children, takes them both into his arms, says, "May The Unfathomable watch over you." He sees his wife, dear wife, standing upon the shore, and is overwhelmed with an urge to hug her as well, but he knows this is impossible, that it is impossible, even, to speak, so instead he simply smiles and waves good-bye for that is all left to him. Then the current takes him, pulling him out to the middle of the river where it is strongest, swift onrushing force, and he is carried away-yet, still, before he disappears about the bend of the river for a moment he struggles against the unyielding current, his head held high, and over the singing of the water yells back to his family, "I love you!" Then is gone.

Strangely enough Aztacoatl forgets this dream until he is at the edge of death, when he remembers it with startling clarity: it is the last thing his mind will hold in this incarnation.

46

The Feast Of Tetzcotzingo: I

For centuries the yopicatl have debated how best to deal with the popoloca, and all that can be agreed upon is that it is best to deal with them from a position of strength. Though there are popoloca generous and kind to a fault, most are violent and treacherous. Each species has its fetters of chemistry, and whether it is a lack of magnesium in their blood or too low a pH the popoloca are not long content. Their bellies sated, soon enough they desire not only all that they see, but so too all that they imagine, with the perceived instant only a point along the continuum of becoming. Which is to say there are windows of time: three drumbeats we know as three, six drumbeats we know by counting from memory, and in-between a matter of ambiguity. Despite their endless wars, and however much one might wish a plague would rid the land of these creatures the popoloca numbers continue to grow. So it is necessary for the yopicatl to think in terms of peaceful co-existence while keeping close guard of Teotihuacan's borders. Yet while it is recognized that danger lies at the borders, some insist more danger lies at the interstitials, and some argue both, for the strand of the spider web is dangerous, and the open space between strands is dangerous for that is what tricks you into thinking no binding-strand is there, and it is within this setting an invitation to a royal event is received, celebration of Chalchiuhtlicue's beneficence, to which all yopicatl are bid welcome. It is the chance for a good meal, certainly, if the food is not laced with poison. The yopicatl are a gregarious species, companionable to a fault, and so too do not wish to offend the popoloca by spurning what appears, upon its surface, a generous invitation. So, yes, the majority of the yopicatl agree to accept the invitation of King-of-Kings Quinatzin and King Copiltzin and attend the gala fest.

Dusty footstep by dusty footstep the yopicatl leave Teotihuacan for Tetzcotzingo, though of course not all the yopicatl for some are too feeble to cross the distance, some remain as guards, and some simply detest popoloca. So too a great number of Nahua Lords and Ladies arrive for the gala event for all Nahua suffers in the drought, and all give honor to Tlaloc and Chalchiuhtlicue. Skilled musicians have spent many days rehearsing new songs for which the dancers have made new costumes and ornaments, wigs and masks. Then too there are cooks, servers and attendants. Which is to say, the event is great in scale, and not easily arranged.

Twilight blends into evening; the food prepared, lanterns are lit and the celebration begins. The poison-wary yopicatl soon realize the Nahua lords and ladies are quick to devour anything laid before them, and so join in the companionable feasting. There are dishes made from cherries prepared in several different ways, so too plums and guavas, avocados and sapotas, and from the Hot Lands pineapples, all procured at great expense. There is turkey and dog, rabbit and deer, pheasants and ducks, and grilled peccary upon which salt has been generously sprinkled.

Near a shallow pond where a tame roseate spoonbill rests, beneath a jacaranda tree, Quinatzin tells Aztacoatl of Zacancatl's odd disappearance, so too his talk of world following world.

"Interesting," says Aztacoatl. "I'm sorry I missed it. But as to Zacancatl's cosmology, the idea of world following world is a common one. Creatures are products of their local environments, and if these environments are similar, -water, earth, trees, and so on, it is not too surprising that they arrive at similar patterns of behavior by which success, that is to say survival, is achieved. You'll find pots, blankets, and spears all over the world."

"What do you mean 'a common one'?" Quinatzin asks.

Aztacoatl, after swallowing several amaranth-cherry-honey tamales, answers: "Well, common. As you know, to the far south, beyond the Maya, you run into nasty jungle, and head north you run into desert. But if you press on, and know the trails, the land opens up in either direction, by which I mean north or south.

East and west too, for that matter, although everything is, ultimately, bound by an ocean, except the ocean, which binds itself. But, if you travel far enough to the northeast, where I *think* my daughter is, 'my brother gets to go on a Wandering so why can't I?' you come to popoloca who share a kindred view of cosmology as you do, how the universe is structured, and so on. However these popoloca, while similar to you, upright, about the same size, hands and feet, and so on, have skin the color of old-bones and blue-colored eyes, and many of them have yellow hair, though some have black hair such as yourselves, and the men, most of the men, have very heavy beards, presumably to keep their faces warm during the winters. By which I should explain, deep snow and a corresponding deep cold cover their land for almost half the year. But they are clever, adaptable, and have come to eke out an existence from a land not nearly as rich as this."

"Oh," is all Quinatzin can think to say.

"Umpteen heavens, gods similar to yours, Thor-Tlaloc, Tlaloc-Thor. Funny-bunch, the Thor worshippers, or not so funny, everyone waving their swords about all the time. Like you, they seem happiest when they are miserable; *Wie viel ist aufzuleiden!*[58] you can hear them cry. I would think you'd get along great with these distant relatives of yours, after you were done chopping each other into small pieces. But pretty country, to be sure, well worth seeing."

Aztacoatl pauses, asks, "Have I answered your question?"

---

58 How much suffering there is to get through!

Some moments pass before Quinatzin, trying to grasp all that Aztacoatl has said, realizes he has been asked a question that requires an answer. "Yes," he says hastily. "Thank-you."

"These pale-skinned popoloca," Aztacoatl continues, "I think, if I recall correctly, which I admit at times is 'iffy,' believe those they slay in battle serve them in the afterlife." Aztacoatl laughs, "Now there's a motivator for you!" Then, horrified at a thought that has come to him, he looks intently at Quinatzin, asks, "You don't believe that, do you?"

Shocked at the idea, Quinatzin shakes his head back and forth, "No. No. No. What an absurd idea."

"Good. Or at least in my opinion, good. But who knows, maybe they have the truth of it."

A stream of attendants surge forth from the kitchens, carrying upon large wooden trays a river of food apportioned between bowls, platters and pots: orangeware, Cholula blackware, pots on four legs and pots on three. Shallow-rimmed bowls, deep-rimmed bowls, and bowls of polished crystal. Round platters and rectangular platters. Some pots and dishes are so finely painted they equal the feather-weavings that adorn the walls of the royal chambers. Quinatzin sees a certain dish, a peccary stew, and has this ladled onto Aztacoatl's plate and then his own.

Ropes have been woven between the immense cedar trees, and upon these ropes small men and women dressed as birds or monkeys gambol about, sometimes swinging down to steal a tasty morsel from a plate or dish, gently pull upon a braid of hair, or tap one upon the shoulder.

"But, as to your bone-colored kindred," Aztacoatl continues, "a curious contrast is that your metal-crafters spend their time trying to make metals softer, more easily shaped and crafted into fantastical art, birds with wings that flap with the breeze and so on, while their metal-crafters spend their time trying to make metal harder, and turning that hard metal into weapons, which is their art."

A golden-feathered tzintzcan wanders nearby searching for the stray insect. Aztacoatl swallows a handful of ahuacamolli tamales. From a nearby bush comes a trill of 'chewee, chewee;' it is from a bird who enjoys imitating the songs of all birds it has ever heard, so much so no one knows the sound of its own true song, or if it has one.

◆ ◆ ◆

Miahuitl, corpse pale, through sheer strength of will joins her brother and Aztacoatl at their table; she has been quite ill since her morning meal and cannot stand the smell of food. Though she wears several heavy capes over her blouse and dress she shakes with cold.

"We were speaking of traveling," Aztacoatl says to her. "Of all the lands I have traveled I think this the most beautiful. The forest-clad mountains, the great lake of many individual portions, and of course our snow-capped volcano. Whatever temperature suits your pleasure you can find it at a certain height upon the mountain side; so inclined you can walk up to winter, and then when you tire of winter walk back down to summer."

Though so ill she can barely sit upright Miahuitl smiles, suggests, "Perhaps where one is born and raised is the land most beautiful?"

Quinatzin and Aztacoatl nod in agreement.

A dancer dressed as a trickster god, or perhaps a hunter, there is a question of interpretation, slowly dances about the courtyard occasionally shooting into the canopy heights with a blowgun. From up above dancers dressed as birds swing down on thin ropes, the air suddenly filled with a mesmerizing swirl of color: emerald and indigo, malachite and sapphire, crimson and gold, scarlet and sand; the birds-not-birds land softly upon the earth and begin to dance upon the courtyard.

"You don't look well, Miahuitl." Aztacoatl says. "Not well at all."

She nods. "I'll leave soon."

"You should leave now, get a good nights sleep."

Quinatzin orders a litter to take her back to Texcoco, with the doctors there to attend her.

✦ ✦ ✦

Inside one of the chamber halls a yopicatl and a popoloca sage from Cuilcuilco converse while leaning over a table upon which paper, inks, paints, and a variety of quills and fine-brushes are laid out. The yopicatl instructs on some of the nuances of Mayan writing (white paper, logo-syllabic swirl of red, crescent of blue); "Here is their symbol for time," he says, "as you can see a road that goes in five directions."

The sage, mesmerized by what his companion has drawn, murmurs, "Astounding."

"Yes," the yopicatl echoes. "Astounding. Much like a mirror, with that which is reflected strangely there but not-there."

The yopicatl pauses to scoop up a large mouthful of an exceedingly delicious treat, crushed pecans mixed with honey, powdered cacao, a bit of salt, then baked within an amaranth-honey crust, which he then follows with a chili. "But what would you expect," he continues, "from a people whose name for ants is *zompopos. Zompopos!*"

+ + +

Musicians stand at the center of a courtyard, and about them dancers swirl. Accompanied by horns and flutes the skilled musicians sound out strangely compelling atavistic rhythms on drums that seem to magically induce the bodies of the listeners to move in tempo. "Ah," the bodies of the dancers seem to say as they surge back and forth upon the courtyard, "Ah-ha."

Twilight: the many sharp colors fade into a dull whole.

+ + +

A small group rests upon low benches, wondrous creations of wood and reeds, and savor small chunks of fish that have been soaked in a salty-brine of chilies.

"To the west," says a Tenayuca lord, "there is a lake not of water but small smooth stones that together act as water, with waves and tides. No boat may pass upon it without destruction, yet for that fish are found upon its shores, and are said to be delicious."

Hearing this the popoloca among his audience glance between themselves, sharing the odd smile. However a yopicatl among them speaks up, adding, "They are delicious, for a fact. The fish one finds there. But the stones you speak of are no mere gravel, but rather that which you so treasure, rubies and the like. However before you think to start searching for this lake, know it is not easy to find. In fact, most difficult."

◆ ◆ ◆

Fireflies blink their here not-here existence, bats turn and twist overhead.

◆ ◆ ◆

Off to themselves, in low voices two captain-generals talk. "…Yes, the attack on Zolan was successful, but it was less successful than you've heard."

"Oh? How was it not successful?"

"Well for one our army, under the command of you know who, began by attacking the wrong town. Apparently there was some confusion."

His friend takes a deep breath, shakes his head; "By The Immanent! Does he not know how to read a map?"

"Funny how nothing is said about that. With Cuauh Petlauh gone command has fallen to generals unable to attack the right town."

His companion shakes his head, back and forth, back and forth. "This is bad. Bad. The penalty for murder is death, yet wipe out a few towns and no one misses a beat."

"Yep, mistakes made by those in power are not mistakes. It's that simple."

◆ ◆ ◆

Attendants pour forth carrying what seems an endless stream of trays loaded with stews and baskets of fresh tortillas. Like the murmur of waves coming to shore one hears music and conversations punctuated by sudden laughter.

"On a scale of tribes or villages," Aztacoatl tells Quinatzin, "usually everyone can have their say, so you might end up with a democracy, but democracies have within them the seeds of their own destruction that, if you will, ripen upon a certain dimensional scale. Now, here is the issue. Though everyone has an opinion, there is a tendency among you popoloca to sort yourselves out: those who want to rule others, and those who want to be left alone. Soon enough power concentrates, and those who want to be left alone soon find they are not left alone. So instead of a multitude of small ponds you have one great big lake, and on big lakes, when a storm comes it's 'hold onto your loincloth.' "

Aztacoatl bursts out laughing at his own joke; Quinatzin, despite himself, laughs too.

◆ ◆ ◆

Music echoes out into the surrounding forest. One sees a blue coatinga, hand-raised from the egg, eating crumbs from a woman's hand.

✦ ✦ ✦

King Copiltzin, face as imperturbable as a worn out drum, speaks with Iniollo, one of the oldest yopicatl. "In the past," Copiltzin says, "to speak metaphorically, the Xiuhquechol[59] always brought rain. Now the rains are locked away in Tlaloc's jade box, so to speak. I've always found literal truth or metaphor equally correct when discussing cosmology. However, as a fact I'll tell you this: The people perish, and the land suffers."

"It's difficult." Iniollo says. "Very difficult."

"It seems the Lord and Lady of Mictlan," Copiltzin continues, "thirst for us. Some priests have taken to offering children to Tlaloc that have tufts of hair growing in different directions,[60] as if stirred by gusts of wind. The priests believe these children will be particularly pleasing to Tlaloc, considering how the winds gust about before a storm."

Realizing that Copiltzin has finished speaking, yet another moment locked irretrievably in the past, Iniollo asks, "What do the children think of it?"

"I can't say for sure. However based on appearances they appear exhilarated, as they go to Tlalocan. Paradise. And who can argue that? I certainly can't, and if I did I'd have all the priestly hierarchy screaming for blood- my blood specifically. As you know there are many interwoven structures inherent to power, and to deny one is often to deny the entire structure."

"Well, there you are," says Iniollo. "Keep doing what

59 The fiery Bird of God.
60 Presumably 'cowlicks.'

you're doing long enough and I'm sure it will rain. And if not, most likely neither you nor I will be here to care."

✦ ✦ ✦

The turning of the stars, brilliant dewdrops cast upon the dark cloak of heaven, the declination of the moon, suggest it is late and time to sleep. Sleep, Death's little brother. There are far too many guests for all to sleep within King Copiltzin's halls and houses, so any number of pleasant shelters in which one can rest have been crafted throughout the groves, artistry of boughs, mats, and feathers. Going to sleep that night Aztacoatl hears a woman singing, a voice sensuous as melted amber:

We shall go on to leave our flowers, our songs.
We shall go on to leave the earth, everlasting.

47
The Feast Of Tetzcotzingo: II

Let us imagine Quinatzin and Copiltzin suffer from an allergy to a certain spice that will be used within an as yet undetermined fraction of dishes served at this celebratory fete, and wish to unmistakably, 100% certainty, avoid it. The spice, commonly called Tlaloc's spice, is used on occasion by certain priests and diviners: by rubbing the leaves on ones skin, particularly after a steam bath, one is given visions of the future, or what the future may be. The spice is found, or was found when the rains still fell, atop Mount Tlaloc, what was once the realm of relentless rain. Save themselves, and Miahuitl who we will discuss separately, King-of-Kings Quinatzin and King Copiltzin wish each and every one of their guests to enjoy Tlaloc's spice while they scrupulously avoid it, but do not wish to ostentatiously draw attention to themselves by suggesting to their august visitors, 'You eat this, we'll eat that.'

If precisely one-sixth of the dishes have the spice in them, and the guests randomly eat *j* different dishes, the probability that they *will not* eat a spice-containing dish is:

$$\text{Probability (\%)} = \left[1 - \frac{1}{6} \right]^j \times 100$$

Which suggests that with two courses some 69% of the guests will not have had a Tlaloc-spiced dish, and after six courses some 33%. It seems unfortunate to Quinatzin and Copiltzin to allow so many yopicatl to not enjoy the spice, which suggests that it should be added to a greater fraction of the dishes.

Different fractions are considered, and in the end it is decided to settle upon one-third. One-third of the dishes prepared within the kitchens will have Tlaloc's spice added to them. After six courses only 9% will not have sampled the spice, and after ten courses, what one might readily expect for the average yopicatl, only 1.8% will not have sampled the spice, and considering how they eat, they'll probably have 12 courses, or 15. So all is to the square then, the up and up: Tlaloc's spice will be added to one-third of the dishes.

But then a new question arises. What if an esteemed guest, perhaps Aztacoatl himself, were to insist Quinatzin or Copiltzin try one of the exquisite delicacies that he had just sampled? If one were to refuse dishes offered with the best of intentions might this lead to unwanted suspicions? What is the likelihood of this event happening?

After the most profound consideration, since in

truth they require an absolute, flawless 'this or that' division of the food, the 1/3 with Tlaloc's spice and the 2/3 without, Quinatzin and Copiltzin take to memorizing the ornamental dish patterns that will define the 1/3 or 2/3 realms. Though at first the task seems daunting it is easier than one might imagine for the serving ware is determined by a finite number of themes: Cholula blackware; for example, the well-known glazed earthenware from Culhuacan featuring bowls and platters painted pale blue with yellow trim, the Xipilco orange-ware, and so on. Certain dishes, with a certain spice, will be served in bowls or upon platters of certain design. And as for keeping such important details straight, the work of kitchens can at times be chaotic, each kitchen is ordered to prepare only certain dishes that are then served within a particular motif of serving ware. So too strict orders are given to the attendants not to mix the serving ware, and not to re-use serving ware, as that would offend the gods. Failure to follow these simple orders carries the penalty of death and the erasure of one's family.

Of course as one looks deeper one always finds more details over which to worry. There are questions of concentration, efficacy, and portion size. Does the active ingredient of Tlaloc's spice react differently, say, with acidic food as compared to basic? If so, how does this affect, if at all, its potency? Perhaps it is impossible to be sure of all details. Ultimately, the universe is more than mere facts: sometimes one must simply feel their way along, step away from the tendency to over-quantitate and go with a best guess.

Tlaloc's spice is not a commonly used ingredient, in fact it is relatively rare, and putting this into every dish from the apportioned kitchens requires the absolute and complete cooperation of knowledgeable priests. However for governments in general, and more specifically men or women of power, such cooperation is not difficult to obtain. So too the absolute cooperation of the cooks is required, but this too is not difficult to obtain for cooks tend to have families, loved ones. And to implement various details, for with almost any project there are always more details than you first imagine, the absolute and complete cooperation of certain captains and generals is obtained which, again, is not too difficult. After all such complexities are necessary to divert the anger of Tlaloc and so ensure the rains again fall ending what has become a desperate drought, offer an opportunity for rewards, -land, jewels, promotions in rank, honor and esteem, and so too will prevent the extermination of themselves and their families.

Then there is Miahuitl, who would not think of missing the festival, but uniquely of all the guests that will attend neither King-of-Kings Quinatzin nor King Copiltzin wish to trouble her with issues of statistical sampling. Conveniently, on the morning of the great celebration with her morning meal she becomes quite ill. So ill that eating is the last, the very last thing on her mind.

So it is that Tezcatlipoca impartially hands out lessons in applied probability. But more to the point, there are little crimes made to look big, and there are prodigious, immeasurable crimes that seem oddly invisible. So too there are blessed offerings to Tlaloc by which one transcends to the paradise of Tlalocan. To clarify, Tlaloc's spice will later be known as tetrodotoxin, $C_{11}H_{17}O_8N_3$, which is odorless and tasteless, and nine hours after consumption of but a small amount one starts to convulse, quickly lose their coordination; tongue, arms, and legs go numb; their heart begins to beat wildly, uncontrollably, and then abruptly stops.

✦ ✦ ✦

A student of probability will understand that at the end of the night there will be a number of yopicatl alive: distraught, angry yopicatl. It is for this reason King-of-Kings Quinatzin has marshaled Tenayuca soldiers in the nearby town of Chapingo. The troublesome, arrogant, meddlesome Tenayuca, the 'We are descended from Toltecs!' Tenayuca. The Tenayuca who ceaselessly argue over fishing rights, hunting rights, land rights, -something rights. The Tenayuca always ready to encourage a revolt, always ready to betroth a princess who is already betrothed. That Tenayuca.

The early hours of night giving way, Copiltzin and Quinatzin safely departed from Tetzcotzingo, the Tenayuca soldiers, adorned in their finery of war, are ordered to encircle Tetzcotzingo. With the set of the stars 'just so,' a time of night that suggests most of the guests will be asleep, or thinking of going to sleep, dead or near dead, or alarmed, armed, and enraged, the soldiers, who have been given certain magical amulets, magical not in that they will preserve the wearer from danger but rather the fear of danger and so allow them to be braver, are told that yopicatl, aided by certain Nahua lords and ladies, have attacked Tetzcotzingo. The soldiers are spoken to in terms of honor, fame, rank, and told that to defeat those upon the Hill of Tetzcotzingo is to restore Tenayuca to her former glory, and for all time free the city from having to pay tribute. The soldiers, to their purpose, set out on their mission: their orders are to kill everyone and everything they find in Tetzcotzingo, except of course the tame birds.

There is a second body of troops who have been marshaled in Texcoco, equally apportioned between the Jaguar Knights of Azcapotzalco, the Ocelot Knights of Texcoco, and the Eagle Knights of Tenochtitlan. These Knights do not wear their usual garb of brilliant colors but simply white; white loincloths, white armor, and white shields that bear no emblems save but the blankness of death. Late night, these Knights are arrayed about Tetzcotzingo and informed a Tenayuca-yopicatl force has attacked Tetzcotzingo. To inspire the Knights in their task of slaughter Tlacotzin, the commander of the combined force, speaks of ephemeral ideas such as honor, duty, fame, and orders the Knights to slay everyone found there upon the hill, save for the tame birds. Darkness giving way to light, the sun just touching the heavens above Mount Popocatepetl, the Knights surge forward.

✦ ✦ ✦

There is a book written and painted in colors;
It glows like the maize-silk bird[61] and gleams like
    a rainbow.
Within its pages are the stories of daring eagles,
    ocelots, and Jaguars,
Who frightened the world.
Whose deeds won them everlasting renown.

✦ ✦ ✦

As for Teotihuacan, realm of squash, maize, beans, chilies, and orchards, where one finds unparalleled art the likes of which the world will never again see, a city so vast in scale its ruins will survive well beyond the last age of man, it is surrounded by the *Cuachictin*, The Shaved Heads, those of Azcapotzalco, Texcoco, and Tenochtitlan, a murderous army of viper-eyed warriors who carry titles such as Land Breaker, and Cougars Paw. The *Cuachictin* are perhaps best described as men intoxicated by death, who have come to find purpose in their lives by shedding the red liquor. For this battle the *Cuachictin* have been given *ixquich* to snort, a fine powder made in equal parts of seeds from the tree of the same name and fire-roasted lake-snail shells, which takes away all reason and fear so that they fight like demons.

    Gathered on the outskirts of Teotihuacan the Cuachictin are addressed by Petlatzin, a Mexica who, like Tlacotzin, King-of-Kings Quinatzin has come to trust and honor with great responsibility. Petlatzin informs the Cuachictin that a combined Tenayuca-yopicatl force

---

61 *Miahuatototl.*

has attacked Tetzcotzingo, in an attempt to slay King-of-Kings Quinatzin and King Copiltzin and take control of all Nahua. For the safety of their cities, their homes, their families, for the sake of their honor and fame they are to empty Teotihuacan of all yopicatl, and when all are slain they are to destroy all statues, all friezes, all paintings or weavings, tapestries or mosaics that depict yopicatl so that all memory of them will be erased from the earth.

And this is done.

Let your soul be roused, awaken your heart,
So that it turns toward the field of battle.
Let us defeat our enemies, and may Xihcutli
    reward us
With the bright flowers of wealth, fame, and
    power.

✦ ✦ ✦

That same night Koxocuitl, far to the north of Nahua within a realm of pine, spruce, and fir forests, trees of immense size many hundreds of years old, dreams of the land she now passes through, realm of fragrant scent, finding herself upon the sunlit shore of a large river within which rest smoothly-polished green granite boulders, and in which swim delicious red-fleshed fish that are pursued by eagles and ospreys, and so too pursued by bears greater in size than even the largest yopicatl. She sits upon a convenient rock and gazes out over the diamond-clear flowing water, upon which sunlight sparkles, bright mirror of the gods, and which seems in a hurry to reach the sea. Her attention is drawn to the middle of the river where she sees... something dear to her swept along in the current, for a moment, a bear, no not a bear... yet when she looks again, clarity of purposeful focus, she sees but water.

Near the edge of the river to her left a quetzal bird hops along, which is curious as this is a bird of the Hot Lands and unknown in this realm. It perches upon a nearby rock, and Koxocuitl expects to hear a clear song of wavering melody, a lilting voice like the trill of the swiftly moving water that frames it, but the bird remains strangely silent.

"Walla Walla," she says to herself, a tear forming in her eye. "Walla Walla."

✦ ✦ ✦

That same night Kulcan has no dreams, nor insights into the unknowable, for though fatigued he does not sleep, consequence of some ill-defined malaise. His ears sharply gather the night's mysteries, including the water-smooth hoot of a distant owl: 'Who looks for you? Who looks for you?' Perhaps, speculation, he is kept awake by the spirits (energy unbound from tedious matter) of his mother and father saying good-bye. Spirits who now perceive their son not as so much flesh but kernel of energy, perturbation of the ether. However Kulcan cannot discern them; that sense, save for the few so gifted or cursed, -a question of perspective, was lost generations ago, just as yopicatl cannot detect light or sound above or below a certain wavelength. Which is to say a great deal of existence that surrounds one is unperceived. Yet Kulcan has a strange supposition that something is wrong, which suggests that perhaps he retains a faint vestige of what was once another sense. Or perhaps that night Kulcan is not kept awake by a churning of the ether, but by the ceaseless scrape of wind against rock and the faint smell of a hunting tiger.

48
The Drought

—————

The spilled blood nourishes Tlaloc and She of the Jade Skirt, and so sustained dark clouds form over Mount Tlaloc and briefly, for a short span of time, call it a moment, the clouds give forth and water, life-giving life-sustaining water falls down from the sky. However the clouds soon scatter, and vanish.

◆ ◆ ◆

Of those slain in Tetzcotzingo the priests suggest that those departed have left this world to enter the paradise of Tlalocan, suppositions that cannot be proven by any known mathematical operator, nor weighed upon a scale. Yet the idea of a life after death suggests this life (sunlight upon one's leg, laughter, holding your child within your arms: sensation) is not the central reality. Rather that which is truly important is someplace else. There are hypotheses, diverse interpretations, and then there are the lines and points the geomancers trace out upon the ground that suggest a truth, a proof, and so the scope of one's world recedes to something ever smaller until it disappears completely: Poof.

◆ ◆ ◆

Trying to make sense of the hard fist of reality King-of-Kings Quinatzin holds talks and councils, councils and talks. As for the duplicity of the Tenayuca and yopicatl, there are a great many ifs and whens, but it is not the Tenayuca nor yopicatl who will write the histories, and for sure the world, sequence of events, grinds on without them. Gone is gone, as the wise ones tell us. Should there be a truth as to the events of Tetzcotzingo, a truth beyond that all states or nations ultimately become ends in and of themselves, it seems no more forthcoming than rain.

Councils, talks; councils, talks; and day by day the people of Nahua vanish. Of those with energy left to parse out the riddle inherent to the drought some have come even to dispute the very idea of gods, suggesting chaos is all that lies at the heart of existence. Drought, flood, drought, flood: mindless hardship following mindless hardship, all of it meaningless, or so some hypothesize, while others postulate pattern, but if there is a pattern who made this pattern and to what purpose? Ultimately, sequence of logical deduction, the idea of pattern suggests there are gods, though perhaps our actions are of no consequence to these gods. However, be that as it may, almost all agree that whatever is to be done to have the rains fall again should be great in scale, as a big display is better than a little one.

✦ ✦ ✦

A time comes when, in one of these many council meetings, a Tenochtitlan-Mexica speaks, Tlacal his name, one who carries no title greater than advisor yet who seems strangely king-like in his manner. Tlacal, advisor, speaks, and we listen:

"King-of-Kings Quinatzin, -Azcapotzalco and her allies have conquered much of this world, so much so that her enemies are now distant: the Mechoacan, the Huaxtecs, cities and towns along either coast. Not an easy task, of course, to send our armies across such distances. Since most of the land has been conquered and no city, town, nor village dare rebel, if the gods are to wait for a war by which sacrificial victims are gathered, why... they might starve! And I submit that it is for this very reason the rains have stopped. Yet, more than this, not only are our enemies now quite distant, a journey of weeks, I submit the gods do not like the flesh of those barbarous peoples, savages who speak strange languages. I suggest that to our gods their souls are like hard, tasteless bread that does not satisfy.

"It takes strength to hunt the deer, and it takes strength to plant, tend, and harvest maize; that is to say, it takes energy in the form of food: I state but an undeniable fact. Now most of us, though of course I acknowledge the few sunbaked prophets who think otherwise, agree the gods require nourishment for strength, and it is by their strength the world is sustained. Thus if we wish to sustain the gods so that the earth flourishes they should not be forced to wait for the occasional war to obtain nourishment. So too peace has brought yet more unfortunate consequences. The sons of lords grow idle and soft with no way to distinguish themselves, thus like a slow poison boredom seeps into their souls corrupting them.

Consequently, I suggest a tournament, a contest with rules and structure, that the gods might view as a marketplace where they can choose the warriors most pleasing to them, fresh, just as we enjoy fresh tortillas hot from the griddle. Further, since the gods prefer souls/ blood of the highest quality, which is to say those of the Nahuatl-speaking peoples, I suggest this tournament, call it a fair if you will, be near at hand, accessible, a place where our armies can readily travel. Upon the plain of Tepepulco I suggest the armies of the Valley battle those of the surrounding plateau, Tlaxcala, Huexotzinco, Cholula, Atlixco, and Tecoac.

"Now, let me make sure you understand this is not a real war, we seek to destroy no people, burn no temples, overthrow no gods nor goddesses, capture no towns nor cities. Rather, when our gods go hungry, as clearly now Tlaloc and Chalchiuhtlicue are hungry, more accurately weak with hunger, we can have a Flower War,[62] as I suggest we call it. This will be a way of relaxation for our soldiers, as if they were going hunting, a way young men can learn the skills of combat, and a way skilled warriors

---

62 *Xochiyaoyotl.*

can show their valor, earning merit through the capture of prisoners. No sooner will our soldiers have gone than they will be returning with captives, -fresh, warm souls delicious to the gods, and when the gods again grow hungry, as we know the stomach stays full only for a moment, another tournament can be arranged. It would be but an excursion, an outing to which the soldiers would happily go, and for the gods but a trip to the market to obtain desired foodstuffs. With our skill and courage we will purchase from the marketplace the captives that will sustain the gods, and so sustain the world. But as this will not be a real war, but a tourney, a contest, there must be an agreement between all parties with rules, and referees, and a defined field of play just as there is in *tlachtli*.

"I suggest we call together all the Speakers, the major lords, and the honored generals throughout Nahua to ask their opinion at this time. Then once we have agreed, we can begin."

King-of-Kings Quinatzin, King Copiltzin, those of the council look carefully between themselves, pondering the idea Tlacal has presented. Although some are concerned by certain points, for example the odd verbal inaccuracy, confusion of past and present tenses, all agree to the logic, the need to sustain the gods and through them existence. There is no clear path through to the future and though coincidental, perhaps, it does seem that the drought came with peace, or if not peace certainly the lack of wars. Surely trying something is better than doing nothing? And this much is fact: If the rains don't soon fall there will be no Nahua to quibble over.

Thus it is decided to present the plan to the leaders of Nahua, and so these men and women, time and space, come to Azcapotzalco, and there meet within the great hall of the city, and within this great hall they speak, and we listen.

◆ ◆ ◆

Quinatzin: "It seems we have discovered that there is a price to be paid for peace. The gods starve and weaken, and so the earth turns to dust just as man, without food or water, turns to dust. So too, with peace our sons grow soft and idle. I now suggest that we have tournaments, set within well-defined rules, where warriors might prove their valor earning honor and glory. Yet for that, the main purpose behind the tournament, the Flower War, as it will be called, is to provide the gods with suitable sustenance. As the gods become hungry they may select the warriors whose souls they wish to dine upon, that offer them the most nourishment. So too, just as we select our foods within a convenient nearby marketplace, the location of these tournaments will be the plain of Tepepulco.

"I want all present to express their opinion on this plan, so that we can quickly come to an agreement and, as the earth parches more each day, soon put this into practice."

◆ ◆ ◆

Those gathered within the chamber hall are silent for a moment, and then a 1st speaker stands, a man in his middle years who is well known for his ability to track the turnings of the stars with the utmost precision, predict the appearance of certain bright stars that slowly pass across the night sky, and so too predict times when the sun is consumed and then reborn. He raises his voice, speaks, and we listen: "I believe it is good, healthy you might say, albeit often painful, as change can be painful, to periodically re-examine the tenets one builds their life upon. Though we acquire bodies of knowledge there is always a question of our missing something along the way. There is cause, and there is effect, and we should not confuse the two. That is to say, are we utterly certain the fundamental principles that underlie our acquired body of knowledge are correct? Consider how there is a predictable objectiveness to things: sunrise, sunset; birth, death; things fall down rather than up. That which we understand, we find predictable and ultimately tedious. That which we do not understand we lump into the category of 'and then a miracle occurred.' Let me raise a question some of us have come to ask: Are there gods? A question to which many answer: One must have faith in the gods. Which admits to a circular logic.

"Perhaps before rushing forward we should pause, look within the many books in our libraries, and consider just how and when the link between offering up souls/ blood/hearts to sustain the gods, and hence our world, was first established. Was it heuristic analyses? A mathematical proof? Or was it based upon the spittle-flecked ravings of a mushroom-addled lunatic? While rest assured I am the first to offer thanks to the gods, still I ask: Are we utterly convinced of the logical basis of our actions? There seems, after all, a predictable non-predictability to weather patterns that may or may not suit our pleasure. Perhaps, mere conjecture, we do not need to start pretend wars to sustain pretend gods while providing a pretend purpose to the lives of the nobles."

Finished, he bows to the audience. The audience claps; he again bows, and sits down.

◆ ◆ ◆

A 2nd speaker then stands, the Lady Xocotzin, now Queen of Tetelpan. She clears her throat, waits until the hall is silent, says, "Might the drought be punishment for, or an occurrence of, something beyond our possibility to imagine? For example, perhaps the ants have given offense to the gods and we could please the gods, sustain them, by stepping on as many ants as we can find to step on. (The crowd laughs.) Or, perhaps a certain type of tree has given offense to the gods, and by chopping down these trees we might put an end to this drought? (She again pauses, waiting until the laughter has died out.)

"I do not suggest we set fire to the forests, nor that we dedicate our lives to squashing ants. I merely propose the possibility that our train of logic, as a society, seems ever more absurd and senselessly violent. Though it is hard to imagine, in truth the world seems unmoved by what we do or not do. You must admit the chance, and if so then what we do with human souls/blood/hearts are of no consequence to anyone save the warriors asked to give up their souls/blood/hearts, and of course their families, their loved ones, and as go families so goes society. Think of how, as history teaches us, often the most brilliant, life-sustaining ideas of today turn into the laughable jocularity of tomorrow. I submit, as politely as I can, and I mean no offense to anyone, that most of what people think at any given moment is boar shit."

The meeting hall echoes with laughter that she waits to slowly fade into silence; "I will not wear out your ears with a long speech. I simply put forth the possibility that instead of this proposed 'Clown War,' -excuse me, a slip of the tongue. Instead of this proposed 'Flower War' the gods might be better satisfied by friendly contests between our peoples, such as running races, or wrestling matches, or seeing who can throw a rock the furthest. I believe there are a large, perhaps infinite variety of things the nobles can do to engage themselves which would both please and sustain the gods. Such contests would divert our energetic sons while keeping them fit, out of trouble, and alive."

Finished, she bows to the audience. The audience claps; she again bows, and sits down.

✦ ✦ ✦

A 3rd speaker then stands to address the assembly; he bows to those gathered in the hall, clears his throat with an *ahem*, and begins: "In my youth I traveled a great deal, swept up with the exhilarating energy of youth and the pull of the horizon. South to impenetrable jungles, and northeast to the realm of bison, creatures like deer and just as swift, only ten times larger. Rivers so large they seem a flowing sea, one so unimaginably large it is called by those who live along its shores 'The Father of All Waters,' and to see the river is to accept this as truth. I have met any number of different peoples, and from these experiences I have come to understand that religion is a *perspective*, no more. That is, a certain view of the landscape of reality that surrounds us. Not that I suggest any of us truly understand 'reality,' but we can leave that discussion for another time. Nevertheless, as a point of certainty, the hostile indifference of nature seems so overwhelming it is almost necessary to believe in a God, singular or plural.

"Now, there are over 200 temples in Azcapotzalco, great or small, to as many or more gods, a fact which in my opinion gives rise to any number of legitimate questions such as, for example: Why is the universe overseen by so many gods? Or conversely, why is the universe overseen by so few?"

He increases the volume of his voice, and slowly turning back and forth to address all members of the crowd asks, "Can anyone in the room suggest how we might have come to 200, give or take, and I offer a conservative estimate, gods and goddesses here in the city?"

Those within the council hall look among themselves; no one suggests an answer.

"Let me tell you then. We, meaning those of us whose task it is to make sure Azcapotzalco functions properly, the streets are swept, the marketplace not looted, the city walls not carried away to build the house of a distinguished noble and his relatives (he winks; several within the audience shift their weight and suddenly feel the need to scratch), can encourage the people to do right, as we define it, set good examples and so on, or pass laws for the people to obey on pain of death or destruction. However in the end it is easiest if we let the great gods themselves lead the way to proper behavior. Now, since no one gives up the gods they worship in childhood willingly, and as we assimilate vassal towns and cities, provinces, to facilitate the transition between 'them' to 'us' *their* gods are included in *our* pantheon. Which is all to the good, promotion of community spirit and so on, but my point is that there is, in truth, no underlying rhyme nor reason to our collection of gods other than town so-and-so was worshipping who-and-who when we conquered them. This makes life no less mysterious; the mystery of life is indisputable. I raise this point simply to emphasize that the underlying logic of our beliefs regarding cause and effect, and the associated rites, is not particularly sound.

"So this then. If we can give the gods nothing greater than our life, and we can only give it once, we should do so only with the utmost wisdom, after the most careful consideration. To me, the idea that my son's life might be frittered away to 'sustain the gods' seems a horrific nightmare: an absurd, sick idea that can come from only the most mushroom-laden minds."

Finished, he bows to the audience. The audience claps; he again bows, and sits down.

◆ ◆ ◆

A short break is called so that the members of the council might refresh themselves.

49
The Flower War

────────

A 4th speaker rises to his feet. An old man of thin white beard, a few odd tufts of hair of the same color upon his head; a face of wrinkles, one eye covered with a white film; he addresses the audience in a trembling, labored voice, and he must periodically pause to collect his breath.

"I am, I believe, the oldest among you. (He turns slowly about looking at all within the hall.) Yes, the oldest it appears, and perhaps in that time I have accumulated some wisdom worth considering. As I reflect upon my life, I remember a childhood of great simplicity, with my life continuously changing into something ever more complicated, a knot of emotions, desires, and expectations, both mine as well as others. For a time I thought to find meaning within this... (He raises up his arms so they are outstretched from the waist, shrugs, then drops his arms.) -existence. Yet in time I came to understand there is no sense in trying to understand the senseless. Of this... perspective, some have suggested to me that at the very moment of death there is a moment of revelation that makes sense of the whole. However, I have strong doubts; the evidence is, I believe, at best contradictory.

"Yet there is a profound mystery to life, no doubt of that, the how, the why. From start to stop we are a walking sack of liquid-mystery. Should we seek to understand this mystery, and many of us do, how best to proceed? Some dedicate their energies to prayer. However while it is easy to imagine, in fact pleasant to imagine that someone, perhaps The Unfathomable Himself, or Herself, shares your concerns, anxiously waits to hear from you, in seeing someone else pray I think: 'there is a mind whispering to the self-same mind.'

"Instead of prayer some grasp upon the predictable mechanics of the world and there try to find meaning: the mysterious ratios of a circle; numbers that cannot be evenly divided save by the very same numbers; why it is that rocks fall to earth with unfailing regularity. However in my opinion trying to find meaning in such patterns, and the mystical regulations they imply, seems equally pointless. As pointless as if one was tasked with trying to understand the echoing silence within the history of random chance.

"So that there is no confusion over what I am saying, let me put this bluntly, borrowing an expression from Lady Xocotzin, the much respected Queen of Tetelpan. We but stumble our way from the first boar shit government to the last boar shit religion. When it comes to understanding existence, cosmology of the why, real is what happens in your head. Rather than sacrifice our sons and grandsons in an absurd 'Flower War' I believe we should all decide that polishing rocks, or jumping up and down while shouting 'Quetzalcoatl!' sustains the universe. Anything is better than this idiotic idea and, my opinion, just as effective."

Finished, he bows to the audience. The audience claps; he again bows, and sits down.

◆ ◆ ◆

A 5th speaker rises to his feet. Based upon his appearance it is safe to assume that he is among the youngest within the council hall, perhaps 28 years of age, at most 32: luminous smile, hair cut short. "I am Nocuicatl," he says, with an easy confidence surprising in such a youth.

He pauses, knowing a few among the audience might have heard his name, that of some wild-man sage who lives upon the middle slopes of Mount Popocatepetl. An ancient wizard, surely, if not just some legend or myth, so how strange this youth of the same name stands before them to speak.

"I am, I believe, the oldest among you. (He turns slowly about looking at all within the hall; many in the audience laugh at what they consider a fine joke. He waits for the laughter to die away and then continues.) Perhaps the oldest, but each of you, based only on your casual observation, think not. By which I hope to make a point, that things are not always as they appear." He bows his head as if to apologize. "Now I will be as brief as I can in what I must say, and of what I must say I must necessarily partition it, make generalizations all the while realizing there are, of course, exceptions to all generalizations. With that in mind I ask you to try and learn from my generalizations, rather than seek for the small pebble of exception. Free your mind to think of trends, likelihoods, high degrees of certainty, how one thing will probably lead to another and what that 'another' might be.

"Let me begin with the subject of water. As we are all aware, water defines, or rather sets limits to our existence. Though in the recent past we have had to struggle with flood, our plants rotting in the fields, our concern now is drought. Quite simply, without water there is nothing- although one can argue there *is* sand and rock, but with no one to observe this sand and rock one wonders: Is it really there? And though there are different answers to this question, I believe the most revealing answer comes in posing it to one of the Olmec statues scattered about. They'll tell you if they are 'really there' or not, relics of a nation once so prosperous and mighty it seemed they would last forever, but in this they are certainly not alone. Each realm, each empire, each great city thinks it will last forever. This is an important fact to keep in mind, a measure by which the actions of sage leaders can be quantified. Scattered about us, I can assure you, are a great, great many relics from nations who once thought they would last forever.

"So, with that in mind, let us turn our attention to Lord Tlaloc. Now as for Tlaloc, and whether or not he is happy, tummy full and so forth, I wish to make a few points. First, consider water within an open pot: as is commonly recognized the water slowly disappears- if one does not periodically add water to the pot it soon runs dry. Now, where does this water go? Placing a lid over the pot readily solves the answer to this mystery. You'll find moisture collects upon the underside of said lid above said pot, drops form, and these drops, miracle of gravity, fall back down into the pot. You have made rain. All of us have seen wet things dry: clothes, stones, wood, our skin, puddles, -water evaporates and goes into the sky. When there is enough moisture in the sky, a function of temperature and wind, it rains. It is that simple, but yet it is that complicated in the sense we cannot control it."

Nocuicatl then reaches down and picks up a *tlachtli* ball. Deftly, he sets the sphere spinning balanced upon the skyward pointed index finger of his right hand. "One revolution. Two revolutions. Three." He counts out. "Four." He gives the ball a gentle upwards push, then catches it in his opened palm. "That the ball, our spherical orb here rotating about an axis, is wider at the middle means that a given point on said middle is moving faster than any other point, since for each revolution it must travel a greater distance in the same amount of time. A remarkable idea, if one thinks about it. Now the surface of this ball is not smooth, there are lines and ridges that catch the air as it spins about, and so the air that surrounds the ball will move at different speeds at different places. Which is to say, about the spinning ball there is turbulence, a mixing of the air between the different regions. Does everyone understand this?"

Whether they understand it or not, and certainly some don't, everyone nods.

"Good. The surface of the spinning ball is rough, on a certain scale, different regions moving at different speeds, the surrounding air mixed. Now let's go one step further. The earth is a very large sphere that spins about an axis. This is, of course, manifest in the fact that however far you travel you always see a distant horizon that step-by-step comes into view, or step-by-step disappears. A fact the yopicatl certainly knew, though little good it did them. (He bows his head and for a moment remains silent, then raises it up and continues.) As the earth turns the air is mixed, this way and that, now dry air from over a sunny desert, now moist air from over a storm-tossed sea. Moisture. Evaporation. The mixture of air as modulated by local temperature and topology, cloudy and cool in one region while sunny and hot in another. So goes the weather. Drought and flood have plagued civilization as long as there has been civilization. Mohenjo-daro is an example that comes readily to mind, but they weren't the first to come and go. The idea that we might make it rain by offering up the blood of our sons, or someone else's sons, saving the gods and thereby us from the ravages of peace, seems as baffling to me as the dreams of serpents. Where the annulate logic of this Flower War came from I can't begin to imagine."

Pause.

"Or perhaps I can. To the south of here, in the jungles of the Maya, there is a serpent whose bite brings upon one a thirst that all the water in the world cannot assuage. It seems Nahua has been bitten by such a serpent only we crave not water but blood, logic as empty as a freshly dug grave.

"But putting aside the issue of rain (he motions), in contemplating the past and future our species is able to mentally grasp a duration of time equal to three generations; after that it's all ephemeral, too vague to contemplate. Nevertheless, I am asking you to look ahead more than three generations, understanding that there are Real People scattered all across this very large world who, like you, also enjoy a good war, but who have fundamentally different concepts as to what war actually is. More specifically, there is a second world from which we are divided, far to the northwest by but a narrow thread of cold water. To a trader intent on profit this barrier is not at all formidable, and as we all know where traders lead armies soon follow.

"In this second world one finds warriors who ride creatures you might consider as large tame deer, hornless, incredibly swift, and with such great endurance they are able to run down wolves. Let me repeat that: Run down wolves. While riding these large deer the warriors, at full speed, from a considerable distance, can readily put a hard-metal-tipped arrow through someone's unsuspecting forehead. So too, for enemies close at hand they have very sharp and very hard swords. You have absolutely no idea how sharp and how hard.

"Imagine swords as sharp as obsidian and, remarkably, able to hold their edge; as unlikely to shatter as gold, but yet are not much heavier then dense wood. Further, their idea of war is profoundly different than yours: No fighting until a shrine catches fire then calling it quits.

The people vigorously compete to see who can slaughter the most, with the more the merrier. A mind-set of, and I quote, though I will spare you the details, 'Kill them all, God knows his own.'

"Now keeping these potential, or more accurately future enemies in mind, let us consider the logical consequences of the proposed Flower War. To sustain the gods, ensure rains fall, seeds sprout and so on, it is now suggested that the very *flower* (he winks) of Nahua youth, sorry, battle each other hand-to-hand with clubs so that one can take the other captive. Fair enough. But once this Flower War is started, proposed as an ongoing institution to compensate for the ravages of peace, rest assured it will not end until Nahua ends.

"Queens and kings come and go but bureaucracies are all-powerful, immortal, generally amoral, and largely operate with no oversight. Ultimately, the bureaucracy becomes the government. Once the institution of this Flower War is established, jealously guarded and advanced by its clerks and minions who benefit from it, it will continue into Distant Time, a perpetual motion device, a spinning-top that never falls unless, or more correctly until, The Unfathomable sees fit to reach out and stop it.

"So. A question. How long does an empire exist?" Nocuicatl looks about the room; "Anyone? No? The answer is so long as it has the superior capability to kill. Were the yopicatl the superior killers they would still be here, but they are not. You can hide the truth beneath all the flowers in the world, but the fact remains that the army is the source and means of government. Now year after year, generation after generation you propose to cull the strong and brave from among you leaving the cautious and meek to reproduce. A dysgenic process that will, in time, ultimately have its effect. It is not for their weaknesses that wolf packs exist. You suggest year after year, battle after battle, to advance the skill of clubbing and capturing, not killing.

"I ask you, very specifically, to think of what will happen to Nahua if our selectively culled, club-bearing descendants meet modern armies from this second world? (Pause.) Anyone, anyone have an idea? (Pause.) No one? (Pause.) I submit, and please take this for a fact, our soldiers will be slaughtered, and our cities razed to the ground. The future of Nahua is being decided today, in this hall, and how *you* choose will directly affect the future of *your* descendants, with the consequences rippling out through Time and Space."

Nocuicatl pauses, slowly turns his gaze upon those who surround him within the council hall. "I hope you will heed my words that there are men in this world well more dangerous than you, or us, the armies of the One World, and soon or late our paths will cross. These things my conscience, that is to say Tloque Nahuaque, requires me to say, but sadly you are not required to listen."

He stands for a moment in silence, and then bows to the audience. The audience claps; he again bows, and sits down.

✦ ✦ ✦

The discussion finished, almost the entirety of the hall, the lords, the nobles, the captains and generals, agree that the Flower War is essential. They kiss the earth before Lord Quinatzin, his vassals unto death, and wherever death awaits them, soon or late, here or there, ultimately it is, after all, the same death. So it is all Speakers, lords and nobles, rulers, return to their towns and cities and provinces to make public this ruling, and prepare for the *Xochiyaoyotl.*

◆ ◆ ◆

A date for the first Flower War is soon set, the earliest that logistics allow. To the sound of conch-shell trumpets the marshaled soldiers of the Valley set out for the plains of Tepepulco. The towns that pay tribute provide, as they can, toasted maize, of which there is little, pumpkin seeds, pinolli, and salt. First, the vanguard passes, then warrior-priests who carry the sacred effigies of Tlaloc and Chalchiuhtlicue, then priests carrying relics and incense-burning censers, then rank after rank of knights, those of Azcapotzalco, Texcoco, Tenochtitlan, Xochimilco, Culhuacan, and so the rest. They camp upon the plains of Tepepulco, with the gods carefully arranged within their tents upon a convenient promontory so that they might, on the morrow, pick and choose among the warriors that they see before them. The boundaries of the battlefield are carefully defined, referees agreed upon who will ensure equal number is arrayed against equal number, and who will conclude the tournament when sufficient captives are taken, or one side unequally weakened. Since the objective is to capture, not kill, only clubs shaped as swords are allowed upon the battlefield.

In the morning the soldiers gather upon the plain arrayed in their uniforms of dazzling color, the more dazzling the better so that the judges and gods may more easily see their deeds. One sees suits of padded armor dyed green or red, blue or yellow, feather adorned helmets through which thin ribbons of gold are wound. One sees Jaguar-knights wearing their black-spotted armor gazing out from their fanged helmets, and Eagle-knights in their feather-fringed armor staring out from beaked helmets. The shields carry every design and coloration imaginable: flowers, animals, geometric designs that seems to encompass all structures of the earth. Each cohort of twenty men are identified by their standards: raised high on thin poles one sees long thin evanescently fleeting creations of woven feathers that seem to hang upon the very air.

Those of Nahua face those of Nahua and clash amid dust and confusion. One by one men are captured, their hands bound by ropes, and led away from the field. Amidst the battle judges walk making note of acts of valor, confirming how many captives are taken and by whom. At a certain point a sufficiency of captives is declared, whistles sound to signal the tournaments end, and each side slowly lead home their captives whose deaths, like all deaths, are assured but for the moment postponed. Yet for that, consider: though there are pleasures in life, some of which might be difficult to willingly leave behind, the warrior who dies in battle or upon the altar stone helps save the lives of those he leaves behind, and so too dies to go to an eternal paradise. To live within a paradise for not some but all of eternity, which is to say: Infinity, one divided by nothing.

＊ ＊ ＊

The armies returned to their homes, amid great ceremony the captives are offered to Tlaloc and Chalchiuhtlicue, bright scarlet blood cascading down the temple steps, and when this is done a night passes, and then a day in which the earth bakes, and then a night, and then at dawn of the second day rain pours down as if the sky had turned to water.

Seventh Bundle

50

The Present,
And We Meet Teya

Kulcan floats within the depths of the sea: no bottom, no borders, no surface: just weight, and diffuse light that suggests the palest hint of color. "Another strange dream," Kulcan thinks as he nears the glimmer of light that defines the surface. Then, of a moment, as if he had gone to sleep some months earlier in some far distant country he awakens within a great immobility of things: fixed walls; immovable window; inalterable bed; deep-rooted covers. Upon an irrevocable table there is an unyielding pitcher of water, several inelastic cups, and a rectangular basin carved from exquisitely hard white-green stone that is filled with plums and guavas.

The view from the window, sweeping panorama of Azcapotzalco, the bordering lake, and distant green

417

mountains suggests that he is in a small room of the palace. A statue, floor-to-ceiling sized allegory of a wind-dragon shaped from dark-blue marble stands in the corner nearest the window upon the ledge of which a war wages, or small battle, question of scale: the luxurious vine that has conquered the outside wall has laid claim to the ledge of the window, carrying with it cluster upon cluster of small, star-like purple flowers, and has sent the vanguard of its forces, long tendrils, to vanquish the statue itself. There is a tap upon the window ledge as if a small dart has struck, quickly followed by a few more, and then a flurry of them which becomes a cascade, loud drumming rhythm that is overwhelming, encompassing: Rain. The world is sustained; the world is made wet.

Listening to the rain Kulcan falls back asleep and dreams that he is within an *acalli* out upon Lake Texcoco on a bright, sunlit day, just the right amount of clouds, the temperature just so. He lies back within the *acalli* and lets it drift, gazing up into the encompassing bowl of sky, hums a line or two of a song he is working on, *cuicatl inic Kulcan*,[63] sees a flock of white herons pass overhead, both hears and feels waves nudging against the wood that defines the interface between wet and dry. His attention then shifts, leaving the *acalli* to return to the room, which is to say he awakens: between window and doorway is a couch, cleverly crafted of various shaped and smoothed pieces of wood in between which, and across which, span tightly-woven reed mats, and upon these are any number of cushions made of goose-down enclosed by the softest cotton. Next to this couch, leaning against the wall is his

---

63 The Song of Kulcan.

staff: hard wood, yet for that supple and resilient; the staff is dented and stained from use.

Upon the couch, clad in pale-blue quilted-cotton armor of popoloca design, vision of a dream when the world was no more than a playground, rests Teya. The color of her eyes shifting with the play of light, -now amber, now gold, now yellow. Eyes that take in the whole, take in the fine detail, all the while demarcating time by the soft tap of a fingernail against a wooden armrest that comprises, in part, the couch she rests upon. Seeing Kulcan awake Teya shines out a smile no less luminous than sunlight reflected off the high mountain slopes of snow-clad Iztaccihuatl, and how that smile lifts his heart!

"So what was the plan?" Teya asks in her soft pleasant voice. "You against Azcapotzalco? Audacious, though it might have gone better had Quinatzin not got wind of it." Teya stands up, crosses the distance to Kulcan and softly pats him on the arm.

"Hmmphf," he says, glad to still exist and, by inference, be in the now. "I'd tell you more but, as an oracle, well, I'd just be telling you what you already know."

"There are oracles," she says, handing Kulcan the large pitcher of water from the table, "and there are oracles. I'll bet you're thirsty."

Kulcan, desperately thirsty, empties the pitcher, hands it back to her, nods, "Delicious."

A silence falls between them. It seems everything is too overwhelming to speak of, or too trivial, though perhaps it is of no importance what is next said for there is time enough for all discourse.

"It's not a bad life, being an oracle," she begins. "Being brought piles of food in exchange for revealing to popolocas the basics of popoloca nature."

Kulcan smiles, thinks of the herb burning in the censer outside her oracle-cave, is about to ask her if 'we won,' realizes the transparency of the question and so does not.

"Oh we won," she says, handing Kulcan a guava. "The sun rises, turns about: a new king is in and the old one is out. Our Xochimilco buddies are as happy as well-fed wolves. So too your friend Totomotzin who, apparently, is to rule Azcapotzalco, or not so much rule as just make sure the city functions and tribute is collected and sent on to Xochimilco. You know the routine. The priests of Xihcutli aren't too happy. And of course there's the fact that Quinatzin escaped to Texcoco, where he is supposed to be plotting one thing or another."

"Texcoco?" Asks Kulcan.

"Quinatzin's sister, you may remember her, Miahuitl, married Copiltzin, King Copiltzin, a few years ago. Ruling family intermarries with ruling family. If things go bad in one place you slip off to the next."

"Right."

"Anyway, good thing you don't have a morbid fear of death."

"Right. (Pause.) I remember you were always good at throwing stones," he smiles. "Lucky for me."

"Yes," she says. "Lucky."

Gazing at Teya, Kulcan considers the subtle-nuances of life that has brought him into her company, or rather once again brought him into her company, only before, footfalls of life, events were not momentous, or so they did not seem at the time, as if their existences were misaligned, each offset from that of the other by some few arbitrary divisions. He examines the earliest appearances of Teya in his life and carefully examines these moments to see if within them there was some indication, presage or omen that, retrospectively, he can now understand was suggesting that which now is, and in this is unsuccessful.

"So, if the Oracle recognized me, why didn't she introduce herself?"

"With you dressed up as a Xochipilli priest?"

"A convincing disguise, you must admit."

She raises her eyebrows by way of answer. He asks, after a moment, "So, how many of us are left, and where were you that you missed the fun?"

"Two that I know of, though there are rumors. Some were on Wanderings, including your sister who left four years after you. As for me, I was in Tula."

"And Teotihuacan?"

"After hauling off what they could, and burning the rest, they tried to settle on our land. However, it turns out Teotihuacan is haunted by a particularly nasty ghost. A ghost who thinks revenge is better than mourning. So it is mostly left alone now. Save for the priests of course, and soldiers."

"You've stayed busy."

A silence settles in with an irresistible gravitation. Teya hands Kulcan any number of guavas, a plate of majestic bean and avocado tamales, a platter of venison tacos, some tomatoes, and a pineapple. It seems to Kulcan that every movement of Teya is sublime: the way she grasps a basket of tortillas, the way she scratches her leg. From outside comes the smell of cooking-fires, sunlight, bird-song, and the murmur and hum of popoloca at work.

A healer enters the room, complexion like a ripe plum, carrying a basket within which are the tools of his trade; seeing Kulcan awake he gives out a wide grin.

Affable Kulcan smiles warmly at the doctor, says, "Welcome!"

"My large yopicatl-friend," answers the healer. "Glad to see you awake. You have suffered a good bit of blood-loss due to puncturing, which is always to be avoided, if it can be, my opinion. Your wounds have been cleaned and sewn up, and to speed healing and prevent festering covered with plasters made of ground-obsidian powder."

"Thank-you," Kulcan says most earnestly.

"My pleasure."

The doctor carefully inspects Kulcan, poking and prodding in a few places, and carefully massages a particularly large bruise on Kulcan's left thigh.

"Do you have many yopicatl patients?" Kulcan asks.

"No, you are the first. But flesh is flesh. There are of course nuances to healing, but at the same time guiding principles. Setting and splintering broken bones, well, that's done easily enough, so too treating most cuts, though the deeper they are the more problematic. And, we know our medicines well enough: *toloatzin*[64] to relieve pain; *iztacpatli* to reduce fever, *nixtamalaxochitl* to reduce inflammation, and so on."

"And tobacco?" Kulcan suggests.

---

64 Datura.

"Yes, many think tobacco can cure anything, and so it can for a time, particularly if you throw in a few special herbs. Of course some healers, and I use the term loosely, prefer to have their patients breathe in a powder of dried tobacco leaves, while some steep the leaves in water for a week or two and then trickle a bit of this into their patients noses, if not their own, while upside down. (He whistles softly.) So one crosses the bridge that leads to other worlds, and if tobacco doesn't take you there then there is always peyotl." He raises up a finger to emphasize what he next has to say. "Yet for all our skill, as I said, there are nuances to healing. Some portion of healing is simply letting the body do what it knows to do, helping it along if we can, encourage the mind to help the body, so to speak." The doctor smiles at Teya. "And so, with that, I will leave you to spend a little time with this charming lady, and I will tell Totomotzin you are nearly well so that we may schedule the dedication of Cihuacoatl's new temple which, I understand, you had a thing or two to do with. In the meantime eat, drink plenty of water, and rest."

The doctor bows to the two yopicatl and then leaves the room. From outside comes the crystal-like resounding shimmer of a gong: KONG-AI! KONG-AI!

"He's to be trusted?" Asks Kulcan.

"As much as anyone," says Teya. "But of course it's a dangerous world." She smiles, and pats the pale-blue quilted-cotton armor she is wearing.

"Hmmphf," Kulcan suggests, and falls back asleep.

51

A Far Place

———

After a demarcation of so many sequential events, or said differently, time, Kulcan awakens. He eats prodigious quantities of food, drinks a large fraction of his weight in water, and then hobbles about the room to use the various tubes and chutes that carry wastes away to where wastes go.

"So tomorrow," says Teya, who now wears a most pleasing golden-colored red-highlighted suit of quilted armor, "is the temple dedication. From what Tzintzuntzan, now highest of the high priests, tells me it's your special day, with no less than Night Axe himself having suggested the dedicatory rites."

Kulcan smiles, "I hope you enjoy them."

While eating, the usual tedium of chewing and swallowing, Kulcan thinks of the yopicatl tales of male-yopicatl finding female-yopicatl, losing said female, and then, after various challenging yet ultimately predictable courses and discourses finding said female again. "How formulaic!" Kulcan reflects, "How tiresome!" He thinks to himself that since it appears Teya is the last female yopicatl alive, and quite attractive, so too a pleasant personality, and hard working, responsible, handy with a rock, and so forth, maybe he best get along with her, and how maybe, after popping Quinatzin's head off, an event in time Kulcan keeps slowly progressing towards, he will marry Teya, if she is keen on the idea, and raise a yeti[65] of yopicatl.

There is a momentary silence as Kulcan, having finished eating, looks at Teya, and she looks back. Unable to think of anything else to say Kulcan asks, "So, what have you been up to all this time I've been napping?"

"Oh, I've been thinking about Quinatzin and his friends, and I've been watching them build Cihuacoatl's needle, as they are calling it. Tomorrow we'll have our special ceremony, per your instructions, to ring in the new, which I trust will be entertaining. I can't stand tedious social events."

Kulcan raises his eyebrows and gives his head a small shake. "Neither can I. However I'm sure there will be a few speeches to suffer through. Most likely a set of logical postulates written to encompass the rise of Cihuacoatl, that Cihuacoatl is the *acalli* and all else the lake. A speech or two that suggest the purpose of power is to keep those of power in power, and then a dance. (He shrugs.) What can you do?"

+ + +

---

65   Yopicatl collective noun.

The next day Kulcan awakens feeling resilient. So it is, he thinks, the body knows just what to do in order to mend itself, inexplicable miracle. Liquid blood, exposed to air, turns solid and so seals the leak, and beneath this temporary seal the underlying flesh reknits itself.

Kulcan realizes that Teya has come from her adjoining room, stands leaning against the frame that defines his room from hers, and seeing he is awake, says, "All our wisdom, knowledge, and skills crumpled before the audacity of a few organized killers. The popoloca grow like algae, expanding to consume everything and then complain they are hungry. It's unbelievable; truly, unimaginable."

"I can't argue with you," he says. "It's astonishing as it is heartbreaking."

Oddly fragmented music enters through the window. Here in the heart of Azcapotzalco the many great buildings play tricks with sound and perhaps, Kulcan realizes, they were built precisely where they are just to do so: here a reverberation, there a dead space. Teya, yopicatl-calm, continues to lean against the wall. There is a look upon her face which, if you knew her well, you might interpret as suggestive that she had expected a life very different from the one she is now living, one that did not entail the violent murder of those she loved and her wearing, as a matter of course, protective armor. Yet for that she understands she has no choice but to endure and this, firm resolution, she will.

"The morning glory climbs above my head," she begins, "Pale flowers of white and purple, blue and red."

It is a couplet known to every yopicatl, and that Kulcan thinks to finish but of an instant the words vanish from his mind, so he says nothing, and after a few moments suddenly falls back asleep.

✦ ✦ ✦

Kulcan stands atop a pyramidal monument in Teotihuacan decorated in a cacophony of vibrant colors, but though he knows the city he does not recognize the height. All surfaces of the temple are carved in symbolic forms, layers of detail striving with layers of detail, and there are many *ilhuicatzitzquique*, statues with uplifted arms whose purpose is to hold up the sky. No, this is not Teotihuacan; it is a city he does not recognize. Kulcan shifts his gaze outward to encompass the further distances of the valley and sees a polychromatic mosaic of untold farms. Although what is perceived in the dream is familiar to Kulcan there is some essential otherness to it, and he realizes he is unclear as to where in the three times the moment rests. Nearby, upon the temple height but a few steps away, a popoloca father speaks to his son imparting words of advice, sage wisdom by which those of Nahua live; "Our Lord God Tezcatlipoca sees what is in the heart and knows all secret things; be humble, wise, and prudent, peaceable and calm. Let not your humility be feigned, or otherwise you will be called a hypocrite.[66] So too never complain, for it is but a sign of weakness."

Kulcan looks down the steep temple steps and sees, slowly drawing near, step by right angled step, a popoloca priest wearing a robe of coruscating color who, of an instant, Kulcan finds standing before him.

---

66 *Titoloxochton.*

"Who are you?" Kulcan asks.

"I can't imagine."	A voice.
"You don't."	Like the wheel.
"Recognize me."	Of the universe.
"Kulcan."	Slowly turning.
"But no matter."	About its unoiled hub.

Kulcan, internal dialog within an internal dream, thinks, "This is just a dream. Some random trick of the mind like when I'm very, very hungry."

"Random, Kulcan? Don't think the world is unpredictable simply because you're unaware of that which underlies its complexity."

"Who are you?" Kulcan again asks.

"Tezcatlipoca, maybe. Or Chaos. Do names matter? However, not to change the subject, but changing the subject, you might be interested in this. Look behind you."

Kulcan turns and sees Teya, shimmering flame-colored eyes, clad in a blouse and skirt of the most luminous blue and greens. One leg and one arm suggest the anticipation of movement, yet she is motionless as stone with her gaze fixed upon a distance. Kulcan blinks, and in that instant Teya, Teya-not-Teya, has crouched down and holds a handful of loose ash in one hand that she slowly allows to seep out, catching this in her other hand, palm outstretched below the first. She is surrounded by any number of reliquaries that she has laid out about her: a hat worn by Tlaloc, a once favorite cloak of Quetzalcoatl, a curious bone that emits soft green light when the air holds rain, a bracelet that Cihuacoatl wore for many years. Teya has brought forth these sacred relics from a polished wooden chest that glows with an internal light. Teya-not-Teya stands and begins to dance, step-by-step taking on an azure fluidity of wind. Her seashell anklets echo out a sea-like shimmer of wave following wave; music defined, measured, and built within a sequence of Time. A melding of drums, flutes, and low-voiced horns join her, so too she is joined by the rain-like sound of gourds filled with the smoothest of small pebbles. Strange dream. Kulcan realizes now that Teya is a goddess... A goddess of something... Some gallivant of Time and Space. And now to the tempo of a resounding drum, the all-encompassing reverberations sounding out to the edge of the universe, Teya-not-Teya begins to sing:

> Though lightning flashes about us, let us be happy.
> Flowers and song are only lent to us,
> One does not take them to Mictlan.

So she sings, and so she dances; of an instant Kulcan realizes she is the Goddess of Love.

Kulcan turns to Chaos-Tezcatlipoca, says, "Strange dream."

"A dream without rules," he answers. "Yet you hope for some underlying meaning."

"Yes," Kulcan admits, "I do."

"Yes," Chaos-Tezcatlipoca echoes, "but meaning is a bit tricky what with each mind subject to their own set of influences which affect how one interprets the world. That I can communicate with you at all is baffling. While I have no proof I suspect that I say one thing but what you hear, or think you hear, verbal clues, within your mind belies a fundamental difference. Be that as it may, we are forced to assume an equivalence between us in understanding, or at least that the differences are so little as to make no difference. But as to the question I know you're going to ask, don't bother. The duality so many dismiss as casual coincidence is the most fundamental truth I can think of."

Kulcan considers this, says; "I don't follow. What point are you trying to make?"

"My point, not so much a point as a factoid, factoids plural, is this: Quinatzin, wily Quinatzin, lays an ambush for Night Axe and almost succeeds in sending him off to The Distant Land. That's one fact. Quinatzin escapes to Texcoco where he is already up to his Quinatzinian tricks. Stirring the pot, so to speak, at this very moment. Second fact. And here is a third fact: Texcoco has a great many soldiers, fighters so relentless they give the Mexica pause for thought."

The music ceases. Kulcan turns away from Chaos-Tezcatlipoca to see Teya who, her dance finished, has crouched down and now waits, patiently, for something. There is now a heaviness to her presence, strange attractor, as if she had been formed in a world of heavier gravity. Gone is her dress of vibrant colors. She is clad now in black robes, her skin coated with black soot and upon this layer are drawn spirals, whirls, lines that suggest waves and wind, symbols from the earliest age of yopicatl. Scattered upon her is the chaos of unpredictable splatter, blowback: the dried blood and gore from countless sacrifices. Kulcan turns sharply towards Chaos-Tezcatlipoca, asks, "Why is the goddess of love dressed like death?"

Laughter, or perhaps thunder from the far edge of the universe. "Death? Dear me no. Does duality mean nothing to you? Haven't you ever reflected on the two-sided nature of existence? Surely you have pondered why the moon endlessly fills and empties itself?"

Kulcan shrugs.

A look of disappointment crosses Chaos-Tezcatlipoca's face. "Flowers bud, blossom, wilt, brown, then return to earth to become, in time, flowers. To wit, there are two sides of the gods and goddesses, with much given and much asked."

"The goddess of love is matted with sacrificial blood," he reminds Chaos-Tezcatlipoca. "Forgive me, but that seems, umm, unexpected."

Chaos-Tezcatlipoca smiles, ever so briefly. "You have never been in love, Kulcan. You'll find there is another side to it, a darkness in which it is easy enough to lose your heart. Mark my words, you'll discover in time certain sacrifices are required."

Music begins again, a cadence oddly familiar to Kulcan. Teya-not-Teya dances among filaments of heaven-rising prayer-carrying smoke, footstep by footstep measuring out the song's tempo. Kulcan sees within Teya an illumination, a radiance, a love within her that is too great to be contained, a blessing, if you will, of the glory of life, and yet for that the light casts a multitude of shadows.

"What is this place?" Kulcan demands.

"If I told you," Chaos-Tezcatlipoca answers in a voice cold as a tomb, "you would not remember, and if you did remember, you would not believe."

52

Cihuacoatl's Needle

───────

The popoloca world is one defined by the conditional AND/OR of alliances; there are allies and there are enemies, and all can shift in a moment. As an illustrative example, although Azcapotzalco has fallen sway to Cihuacoatl her sister cities to the south have not. The nearby realm of Tenayuca, to the north of Azcapotzalco, is never to be trusted. Then what the Mexica, sharp knife poised within the Nahua heart, might or might-not do is anyone's guess. Which is to say a number of diverse nobles who desire to see the events of the day but who, in turn, do not wish to be seen arrive in Azcapotzalco within concealing night and now discretely watch from flower-screened chambers upon the uppermost story of the palace. And so Kulcan and Teya watch from the flat, garden-filled roof of their temporary domicile, a house separate from the palace itself, hidden from the popoloca multitude by a carefully constructed screen woven of dahlias, orchids, water lilies, morning-glories, cotton flowers, purple cosmos, red poinsettia, sunflowers, tiger lilies, and so too the humble blossoms of the bean plant, the pumpkin, the squash, the amaranth, and the maguey: an astonishing, inspiring art that is evanescently fleeting. Carefully chosen attendants ensure the yopicatl guests are content, bringing them *ahuacamolli*, fish with red peppers and tomatoes, sweet potatoes, frog stew with yellow peppers in pimento sauce, and a seemingly endless stream of honey-sweetened chocolatl.

The road that runs from Cihuacoatl's new temple to Lake Texcoco, ending at the jetty where Quauhcoatzin, King of Xochimilco, and his host step foot to land from their *acalli*, is lined with black-cloaked priests all armed with smoke-emitting censers and who wear gourds hanging down upon their backs although the significance, symbolic meaning, of the gourds has long since been forgotten. The priests all wear a coating of the black soot upon their skin, and all wear their hair in a braid that falls down the middle of their back to which so many white feathers, those of the Lesser White Egret, are tied. Each feather signifies a priestly accomplishment such as so many days of fasting, or praying, or the offering of so much world-sustaining blood.

Preceding the emperor is a large but finite number of handsomely dressed warriors who, like Night Axe, carry as their only weapon a staff. Bound to their shoulder-length hair by red cords are two or three blue coatinga feathers, insignia of the emperor's guards.

Here is Quauhcoatzin himself, wearing the royal turquoise cloak, and a magnificent crown of gold, feathers, and gems of polished jade. Ear pendants, labret, nose plugs, all of lustrous metal, anklets and bracelets made of small bells crafted of gold. It seems he is clad in but scintillations of color. Walking from jetty to temple King Quauhcoatzin comes abreast of one priest after another, who with his approach add incense to their censers resulting in a great cloud of fragrant smoke. Back and forth their censers swing demarcating Quauhcoatzin's steps.

"They sure love to dress up," Teya observes. "The anklets of gold have their appeal, and I can understand wearing an armband of gold. (She swings her arm as if clobbering an enemy.) But the labrets, and the bones or feathers they wear stuck through their noses? Really?"

"Not to your taste?" Kulcan offers helpfully.

"No, not my taste. And I try not to be judgmental, but I look at popoloca with such decorations and think what idiots."

"That which is admired has no absolute value in itself," Kulcan philosophically suggests; "it's just a matter of fashion."

"Maybe so," Teya answers. "But I just don't get it."

Following King Quauhcoatzin are his attendants, some two-dozen dwarfs. Reaching the temple courtyard, the newly laid stones gleaming sunlight-bright, Quauhcoatzin is greeted with the music of drums, flutes, and horns. Into the sacred fire priests throw handfuls of finely powdered maize that burst into clouds of flame. No time is lost in pleasantries: the king climbs the temple stairs where he is handed an intricate censer made from thin sheets of hammered gold that issues red smoke, and with this he censes the image of Cihuacoatl, passing about her statue once, twice, thrice.

Kulcan, overwhelmed by the scent of so many flowers, or perhaps simply bored, yawns. Mysteriously enough, though but just a moment before she had felt no need of such, Teya then yawns. Pattern underlies pattern, and so the world builds upon itself.

Quauhcoatzin deftly beheads any number of quail and sprinkles their blood about Cihuacoatl's image; the blood is symbolic of the blood necessary to sustain the goddess, and the state, or perhaps is not symbolic at all but simply inherent to the fact that priests need to eat and quail are a favorite meal. Finished with the birds, King Quauhcoatzin begins to offer his own blood, with a sharp blade puncturing his arms, shins, and ears.

✦ ✦ ✦

Already tired of the ceremony, Teya stares at the needle-like wooden tower rising up from Cihuacoatl's courtyard.

"In the northern middle continent of the 2nd world," begins Kulcan, "many of the popoloca bleed themselves, or have healers bleed them, cutting a vein or two to drain out some blood to help maintain their health."

Teya snorts. "Drain out some blood to maintain their health?"

"Yep. And here they do it to sustain the universe."

Teya considers this a moment, offers, "All that bleeding you were doing didn't seem to much maintain your health, but as for sustaining the universe, well, maybe so."

"I'm just sharing with you some cultural observations."

"Maybe," she says in a flat tone, "we should not talk about popoloca for a bit."

Kulcan and Teya look upon the heart of the city filled with ceremonious officials, dancers, musicians, and soldiers in their most colorful finery. Teya, her mouth full with a turkey red-pepper tomato tamale, motions to the crowd, says, "Therpf mush beh ah phillion off themfph."

"A million," says Kulcan, carefully annunciating. "With a M, as in monkeys. Soon enough billions with a B, as in baboons."

Having finished some rite or another, Quauhcoatzin stands upon the edge of the temple height and in a sonorous voice cries out, "All powerful Lady of the Earth: Goddess whose strength keeps us alive! I offer thanks for the victory you have granted us, by which you have shown your power and your will. All has been won to give you honor and praise! Lady of the Earth, we ask you to please accept our gifts that you may know our esteem."

His speech finished a company of dwarves parade up the temple steps carrying that which only so recently, a moment of but a few days, had been in the treasury of Xihcutli, and these are laid before the idol. The emperor, to his purpose, drapes fresh mantles upon Cihuacoatl, and then adorns her with gold and fiercely gleaming sparkling stones. Ceremony follows ceremony, demarcated by the sun sliding across the sky, while within the shade of their alcove the yopicatl nap. After a large yet finite period of time drums sound, their echo reverberating throughout the city. Kulcan pushes aside a few flowers within the screen to gain a clearer view, says, "Now. Finally."

A select group of popoloca are brought forth, those of certain names who once had certain responsibilities, assembled per the carefully crafted plan of Night Axe, Totomotzin, and Tzintzuntzan, who had been intently sought out and meticulously collected by Xochimilco warriors, a challenging task as these popolocas, possessing the power of locomotion were harder to find than, for example, a tree or street. The select group is arranged near a remarkable edifice worthy of description. Imagine four poles each made from the trunk of an ahuehuetl tree that sprouted some two, perhaps three hundred years ago; the four poles are arranged in a square some three yopicatl-paces aside, securely sunk within Cihuacoatl's new courtyard to rise up above the ground 212 feet, a height Night Axe suggested is particularly sacred. The four-poles comprising the tower are bound by a scaffolding of crossbeams and rungs so that howler monkeys, or their cousins can, with their nimble agility, for a time leave the all-providing earth. At the utmost height of the tower there is a platform that encompasses the small cross-sectional area between the four poles. The whole is arranged so one might think of the structure as a wooden needle of merciless height. At the very cloud-piercing, pitiless apex of the needle awaits a number of neatly coiled ropes. One end of each rope is securely bound to the top of a steadfast pole; all are of a length to almost reach the ground.

"That's quite a structure," Teya suggests.

Kulcan, big yopicatl grin, "What we have here is the utmost *pinnacle* of performance art. Something to liven up their sacred rites." He pauses; "I hope you like it."

Four agile priests wearing white miter-like caps decorated with bright scarlet feathers climb to the platform atop the pinnacle of the sacred needle. Trumpets sound, to which these uppermost priests toss down handfuls of dyed pumpkin and sunflower seeds that have been blessed by Cihuacoatl. For these the crowd scrambles, darting this way and that: one hears the sound of laughter and merriment. The seeds collected, more trumpets sound and the courtyard is cleared. Those who will momentarily leave this earth (-ah, but what is time?), leave it to return to it and in so returning depart for Mictlan, who strangely enough have sacks upon their heads, one at a time, that is to say sequentially, carefully bordered on each side and behind by a boundary-defining, warding, herding, sharply-prodding, stubbornly task-minded priest, climb slowly, methodically, to the very top of the needle.

"Some monkeys of the 2nd world have sky-blue behinds," Kulcan informs Teya.

She considers this, says, "That's difficult to imagine."

"Yes. It's quite a sight."

The first of the yopicatl-slayers reaches the summit of the tower, no doubt glad to have made it for it is, truly, a considerable climb. And having made it to the top the four waiting priests quickly, deftly, remove the vision-obscuring hood of the yopicatl-murderer, tie the unbound end of a rope about his neck and then, timed to the mournful cry of a conch-shell horn, promptly push Cihuacoatl's offering off the tower.

On the one hand is unrelenting gravity, and on the other hand, interactive performance art, a stout rope, and in between a popoloca who only now, supposition, at the very end of his life, understands how powerful a force gravity can be. The first yopicatl-slayer falls some 7/8th the height of the tower at which point the stout, unyielding obstinate rope tied about his neck goes no further. The head of the popoloca, who a moment before was traveling very fast and has now stopped, pops off. Pop! There is a fractal spray of *teoatl* upon the courtyard. The torso lands with a 'thud' sound, or 'thud-scrunch,' while the head makes more of a 'thunk,' or 'thwunk' sound as it lands, and it rattles and bounces about before coming to a rest. Teya, laughing so hard she can hardly breathe, squeaks, "Harsh!" Kulcan, swept by convulsions of laughter so furious he begins to cry, finds some of the chocolatl he has just swallowed leaking out his nose.

Their ward sent safely on to Mictlan, the first group of guiding priestly chaperones start their descent. After a few moments in which Teya and Kulcan just, by the narrowest of margins, regain their composure another party arrives atop the height: Whew! Not an easy climb! The escorts stand to the side while the nimble priests remove the hood covering the head of their charge, tie a sturdy rope about his neck, and ever so artfully give the Mictlan-bound a push. There are more peals of yopicatl laughter.

The tower is soon a flurry of activity: some climbing up, some climbing down; popoloca-attached ropes descending, unfettered ropes pulled back to the uppermost height. The afternoon is demarcated by the periodic release of a popoloca to the embrace of gravity, with the courtyard decorated by abstract patterns within a contradistinction of hues: bright red, dull red, dark purple, reddish-brown, black, visionary abstract-art that will slowly disappear within the auspices of sunlight, rain, and time.

Teya, exhausted, in too much pain to laugh anymore, says, "If only all their cities had one of these."

"That's the beauty of it," answers Kulcan, "they probably will! How they love to share their best ideas."

Another falls. Another. Another. But for that, one is given a finite number with which to please Cihuacoatl. The last head, abruptly separated from the last torso, falls to earth; the pieces are collected and taken away. The crowd seems strangely satisfied. Now drums sound, resounding heartbeat of a colossus that carries throughout the city, and a great cloud of red-colored smoke rises up from Cihuacoatl's sacred fire. One's gaze turns from the heaven-rising smoke to see upon the temple height King Quauhcoatzin, and behind him Totomotzin, now regent of Azcapotzalco.

Quauhcoatzin calls out to the gathered thousands, and what he says is thus: "Although tranquility now pervades Azcapotzalco under the watchful eye of Cihuacoatl, so that there be no disturbances nor difficulties it is necessary that there be laws, so that all might live in harmony, that the realm, in accordance with the old customs, might be ordered in the best manner possible. I rule in Cihuacoatl's stead, serving Her purpose, and so Totomotzin rules, serving Her purpose, and it is She who chose us to do so, and in so doing honor Her, and so it is necessary for you to honor those whose task it is to rule.

"Cihuacoatl has enjoined me to come before you and let all know the laws by which you of Azcapotzalco must live. Consider these laws as sparks from a divine fire. Consider these laws as medicine that, given properly, profits the body and helps it to thrive. (Dramatic pause.)

"On pain of death only I, the King, may wear the royal insignia of a golden diadem in the city, though Totomotzin may wear a golden diadem if I am not in Azcapotzalco. In war, and on no other occasion, great lords and brave captains may wear a golden diadem for these lords and warriors represent Cihuacoatl when at war.

"On pain of death only I, the King, or Totomotzin, my regent, may wear fine cloaks and loincloths of cotton brocaded and embroidered with the royal insignia. I, the King, or my regent, will decide which type of cloak is to be used by the royal person so that he may be distinguished from the rest: no one else may wear the same. The twelve great lords of the city may wear special cloaks and loincloths, and so too the minor lords, each according to their accomplishments. On pain of death, no others shall wear such mantles."

"Funny how everyone gets the government they deserve," Teya observes.

"Yeah," Kulcan drawls, "or not so funny."

"On pain of death commoners will not be allowed to wear cotton clothing, but only garments of maguey fiber.[67]

Teya rolls her eyes and snorts, says, "It's hard to laugh, after a point. And if you think about it, -well, it just eats at you."

"On pain of death, at dances only the king, regent,

_____

67 A coarser fabric.

sovereigns of the provinces, and other great lords may wear gold armbands, anklets, and golden rattles on their feet. They may wear garlands and gold headbands with feathers in them, and no one else may use them. They may wear chains of gold about their necks, and so too jewelry of this metal set with precious stones, and no one else may use them.

"Adulterers are to be stoned and thrown into the rivers, or be given to the buzzards. Thieves are to be sold for the price of their theft, save that the theft be of grave magnitude then they are to be punished by death."

Teya, softly, says, "We've become relics in what was once our own world. Creatures that but walk along the edge. And sadly enough, having won Azcapotzalco for your friends, if we stay around here too long someone will put a spear into us, -or worse."

The two yopicatl share a look, then, after a number of heartbeats pass in which neither speak, Quauhcoatzin droning on like a cicada, Teya recites from the Teotihuacan Sagas:

A stranger brought me a sheet of carefully folded paper.
It held but two lines: 'Do not forget.'
And written below: 'Good-bye forever.'

Kulcan reflects upon these words, says, "Why don't we head east tomorrow? Maybe visit Texcoco. It's said to be pretty this time of year."

"Sure," Teya answers. "The fresh air will do us good."

53

A Shifting of Political Alliances

———

Kulcan, rising up from the depths of sleep can only imagine that Time, wily trickster Time, has overflowed its banks, as rivers are apt to do, suggesting an indefiniteness of form, flooding the landscape and carrying away all proof of line and color before it. Kulcan shifts his focus to the evanescent moment, the now of wakefulness, and soon comes to a precognition of danger due, perhaps, to a shift in the noises common to the night. He rises, looks out the nearest window and sees a large number of soldiers ringed about the house. Where once he and Teya had guards there are now captors, though perhaps all along this was but a question of definition.

Teya, joining him at the window, looks out, says, "So. This is unexpected. Or, -maybe not."

Kulcan points out the window, "No, but this is."

Approaching the house friend Totomotzin slowly emerges from the line of surrounding soldiers, in his one hand the stick by which he taps out the world through which he passes, while cradled in the other arm is a finely polished wooden box.

Totomotzin comes to the doorstep, taps out its width and height and then steps inside.

"When..." Kulcan begins.

"No time for informative discourse, friend," Totomotzin interrupts, "unless you're up for some impartial dispensation of justice."

Totomotzin points to the incense censer he smells but does not see, says, "Quickly, we need a blaze, -mats, furniture, what have you, all to the good. Honor to Xihcutli and so on."

Teya sets herself to this task; Kulcan stares intently at the soldiers arrayed against them, both carefully listen to what Totomotzin has to say.

"My nephew Quinatzin, who never could abide a 'wait and see' philosophy, has been busy, offering King Quauhcoatzin, who by the by is one of his 2nd cousins, or something to that effect, any number of reasons for your capture or, more simply, your two heads. The tribute of a great many towns, fishing rights to certain areas of the lake, an obsidian mine, all and all quite a compliment to you, really, to be considered so 'valuable.' Which is to say, as you can surmise, there has been a shifting of alliances."

"What..." Kulcan begins.

"No time, friend. Truth. After a bit they'll assume

me dead and attack, -actually they will attack one way or the other. The hope here is that I can lure you two out into the open, as I suggested to them myself, minimize mayhem, save the city and so on."

Totomotzin feels his way along an interior wall in which there are several shelves adorned with various small statues, feather-holding vases and the like, but so too there are niches within which rest more substantial pieces of art, rare archeological finds, and strange bits of bright white metal fallen from the sky.

"Of course, I was born and raised in the palace, and know a few secrets that are, well, secret." Totomotzin fusses with a certain shelf, flicking the ancient ornament that rests there off to the side. "Push here, firmly," he says knocking against the back of the niche.

Kulcan pushes. A portion of the wall gives way, and a wooden door hidden by a thin stucco layer swings into absolute darkness. There is a smell of stale earth.

"OK then. No doubt the tunnel was not built with yopicatl in mind. Still, it's large enough, and it will bring you out near a jetty. The tunnel ends at a wood panel concealed on the outside by a layer of stucco, part of some mural or another, easily popped from its frame, just give it a push."

"Why..." Kulcan begins.

"I am going to scream loudly, and when I do you are going to *gently* toss me out the window into a convenient garden, *not* onto the stone, thank-you. As you are doing that fair Teya is going to empty the contents of this box which, clever me, is supposed to contain an herb the smoke of which will put you two to sleep, onto the fire.

Then you will ever so quickly enter the tunnel, close the panel behind you, and depart Azcapotzalco."

"The box?" Asks Teya.

"Ground dried chilies mixed with an herb the smoke of which brings upon one overpowering memories of childhood, as if once again you are playing at your father's knee. The soldiers will cough themselves back to childhood. So then, best of luck, and farewell."

Totomotzin screams very loudly, and Kulcan tosses him out the window.

◆ ◆ ◆

The darkness of the tunnel is at first absolute, but soon fire-light beaming through a crack, separation of space between door and wall, provides a faint illumination, though not sufficient to prevent Kulcan from inadvertently kicking a sack of jewels that lays upon the floor, secreted away by somebody sometime ago in case of an emergency. As they might come in handy, and this is an emergency, Kulcan picks these up and carries them along.

There is a slow curve to the tunnel, and so with distance it slips back into what the yopicatl, at least, consider absolute darkness. The tunnel ends at a wood panel set within a square frame of mortared stone. Kulcan pushes; the panel flexes. He pushes harder, and it pops free. The shift from absolute darkness into the intensity of moonlight, starlight, and that of scattered fires and torches at first seems overwhelming to the yopicatl. The noise of the collapsing wall quite near the jetty sets the guards to their alarm. Teya collects the stray loose rocks at hand and quickly sends them off on precise trajectories. Kulcan deftly sprints here and there, winding his staff in and out among the guards not yet struck senseless by a swiftly moving rock. The two yopicatl jump into a convenient (size, location) *acalli* and paddle out into the lake. However the lake is not empty; upon its surface float any number of *acalli* filled with soldiers. Quinatzin and King Copiltzin, to their purpose, have offered not just King Quauhcoatzin a large reward for the two yopicatl, but anyone, and the prospect of loot seems to have filled the Nahua imagination. Kulcan and Teya are chased back to shore, a reed-filled thicket of mud just north of the city, slink through a marsh filled with nesting birds, then race across farmland into concealing forest, but yet for that the matter is by no means settled.

Quinatzin and Copiltzin cast their soldiers out as one casts an entrapping net. Like a stone thrown into a pond sends out rings, periodic fluctuations in amplitude, that travel outward, so day by day the land fills with soldiers clustered in companies of twenty, with company of twenty linking with company of twenty like a fine weave, and they sweep across the land as an immense yopicatl battue. The many soldiers force the yopicatl to the northwest, toward the Sacred Lands. The existence of Kulcan and Teya, they who once called the world their own, is again reduced to skulking and hiding.

◆ ◆ ◆

To the west of Ecatepec they spend a night hidden within a seemingly impenetratable copse of mesquite. Sunrise, color seeping back into the world, no sign of soldiers, the yopicatl leave their hiding place, following a path shaped and defined by rabbits, boar, and deer, yet for that more effervescence than trail, which they have followed for some distance when Kulcan stops abruptly, claps his hands to his sides, and cries, "Uggh!"

"What is it?" Teya asks.

"Nothing. Except I left our food behind."

Each recognizes that there is little to eat in the prickly wilderness they now pass through.

"No point in the two of us fussing through these thorns," Kulcan says. "I'll be right back."

Kulcan reverses direction and sets off on the trail, within a few footsteps disappearing into the brush. Teya finds a vantage point to rest where, concealed, she can observe the path. There is bird song, and there is warm sunlight. In time she falls asleep, and in time she is awakened by the noise of soldiers passing down the same rabbit-path upon which Kulcan can soon be expected to return.

Teya has seen popoloca hunting before, quietly sneaking about, and from that perspective the behavior of these soldiers seems unusual. It is as if they wanted to scare the yopicatl away, for walking along they whistle, tear leaves off trees, swat at bushes with their swords, and banter among themselves: "My wife ... Blah. Blah. Blah."

"Yeah? My wife... Blah. Blah. Blah."

Staff in one hand, a conveniently sized throwing stone in the other, rabbit-silent Teya follows the soldiers. In time, demarcated by footsteps, the warriors, unknowingly trailed by a yopicatl, pass the copse within which Kulcan and Teya had so recently hidden. There is no sign of Kulcan. Teya pauses, considers, reverses direction and, unexpected, soon comes face to face with Kulcan.

"We keep walking up and down this trail," he says, "and by our footprints they'll think there are hundreds of yopicatl."

"That's possible," she replies, "unless our tracks keep getting covered by those of the soldiers following us. Where did you go?"

"I was following our bag of food that was about to disappear down a brush-shrouded hole, and came back a different way." He pauses, gives her a heart-warming smile; "This is some adventure."

"Oh, it's an adventure," she replies.

The two yopicatl slowly wind their way northward, either to circle the lake or, should the opportunity present itself, cross the lake in a convenient *acalli*. However little by little the number of yopicatl-searching soldiers becomes so great Kulcan and Teya are forced to sleep by day and travel by night, and at that cover little distance for there are soldiers everywhere.

One day, hiding within a well-concealed cave, Teya asks, "What's the strangest thing you've seen on your Wanderings, -single most."

"Well (thoughtful pause) maybe not the strangest, but the most eye-popping thing, which is to say the most memorable, and strange things are memorable you must admit, is in the rivers to the northeast of here. These are big, muddy rivers, some being miles across, with big things in them. One of these rivers, which the local popoloca call 'The Father of All Waters,' -and to see it is to believe it, is some five or six miles across when it nears the sea. The alligators lay claim to the southern reaches of these rivers, and I mean they rule them, growing to some thirty feet in length. Thirty. Feet. They'll float along, almost entirely below the water and, since the water is muddy, unseen, save the very top of their head, their eyes, which they keep just above the surface of the water, and for that matter their skin and eyes are mud colored, or wet log colored, and poof! (He snaps his fingers.) They'll snatch a popoloca off an *acalli*, and I mean snatch, in an instant. There. (He snaps his fingers again.) Not there."

"Hmmphf," she says, "sounds fun."

Kulcan muses for a moment, considers whether to expand on the subject of alligators, decides not to, asks, "How about you?"

"Well, once I met a popoloca wizard, or in their tongue a *shaman*, 'I am *shaman!*' on some vision-quest or something to combat a great wizard-enemy, or so he said. I joined him for dinner, which I soon came to regret as he went on and on about what he'd done to whom, how he was a friend of this spirit, god, king or whoever, -he seemed intent on impressing me. Finally, I was less patient then, I said to him, 'I hear a lot of talk, yak-yak-yak and so forth, is that your special power? Talking your enemies to death?'

"That sure annoyed him! So anyway, this was far to the northwest of here, unending forests of pine trees with a great many pinecones scattered about. He says: 'You desire to eat a pinecone, don't you?' And though I didn't want to, my right hand, no longer my right hand, slowly picked up a nearby pinecone and began to bring it towards my mouth, which opened quite unwillingly, having some strange life of its own. I could move my left arm, but it seemed much weaker than my pinecone-holding right. Mouth open. (Dramatic pause.) Here comes the pinecone."

"So?" Kulcan asks.

"So, I put my left hand about his neck, and started squeezing. Said, 'I know a good trick too.'"

"Pop!"

"No. He waved a hand before me as if swatting at a fly, and of an instant my right arm was my right arm."

"Interesting," Kulcan says. "They are a funny bunch. One moment they offer their undying friendship, the next they offer you a pinecone or poison."

54

The Net Closes

———

Neither fishermen nor fowlers now pass upon the waters of Lake Texcoco, for soldiers have claimed all boats. New popoloca alliances reign within The Valley, and Quinatzin and Copiltzin offer a considerable fortune for what seems a modest task, the death or capture of but two yopicatl. Kulcan and Teya find, water or land, there are always pursuing soldiers. Yet many of the popoloca seem unconcerned with the desires of kings, the prospect of unimaginable wealth. Consider: Once retreating from a press of soldiers, basin and range topology, Kulcan and Teya climb a small ridge and then descend the other side, seeing before them a stretch of flat fertile land given over to maize, beans growing up the stalks, being harvested by several families. Then they see soldiers on the other side of the valley coming towards them. Everywhere a soldier, and these grim men seem intent to their purpose of collecting reward. Kulcan and Teya slip into the maize stalks and start gathering up handy rocks, however the yopicatl have been seen by the harvesters who instead of sounding the alarm send their children into the stalks to fetch them. The children cluster about the yopicatl and insist they follow them to safety, and so they do, coming to a great pile of harvested stalks. The harvesters motion to the pile, pointing with the one hand while swinging the other back and forth to suggest speed. Teya and Kulcan lay down, the stalks are pushed over them, and then all return to their purpose, which is but another day of harvest. The yopicatl hear mock exclamations of surprise and the soldiers depart for somewhere else, while in the sky above Tezcatlipoca laughs.

Then, gifts of The Unfathomable, two events take place. First, passing a small village Teya and Kulcan discover, lost amid a cluster of tall grass, an *acalli* large enough for two yopicatl. Then, gift of Tlaloc and Quetzalcoatl, a strong storm comes from the west: pouring wind, howling rain. The lake is swept clean of soldiers. Teya and Kulcan carry the acalli to the shore of Lake Texcoco, and though the light fades, sunset, moon and stars obscured by roiling torrents of clouds, they paddle east. Waves collapse about them with water and air mixed to an airy froth. They soon fall into a rhythm, paddling as hard as they can to ride upon the back of a wave, then easing off as it sweeps before them to await the next wave, for which they paddle hard to ride its back. Tame lake has turned into raging sea, with wave-slop coming in over the gunnels that they bail with a laughably small wooden bowl. Behind the boat there are but looming waves dark with the last of night. But for that they come to the eastern shore of the lake, too wet and miserable to think properly and so leave the *acalli* along the shore, haul themselves into a forest copse and there sleep.

The next morning soldiers, not those who seem to get in the way of the other soldiers all the while singing and talking, who carelessly leave areas unsearched and drop sacks of food or jugs of water, but rather the grimly intent soldiers find the abandoned *acalli* and after a careful search find what have to be, judging by their size, yopicatl footprints. The land soon fills with soldiers who company by company seek to weave a yopicatl-trapping net, and so great is the press of their numbers that they drive Kulcan and Teya out of the fields and forests into towns and villages, like wolves driven by the press of hunters to hide themselves in the town park. Kulcan and Teya sleep in granaries, beneath bridges, upon roofs.

Then, as if a farce played out upon a stage, parents take to arming their children with bags full of dried turkey or venison, baskets of tortillas, fruit, and tamales, and send their children out upon a game of hide and seek: find the yopicatl, give them the food, return for a reward. How curious the young popoloca can so readily find the yopicatl that the older ones cannot! In a village north of Chiconauhtla, realm of swift-flowing deep streams, rivers, rough low-ridged hills crowned with immense stones that remind one of the teeth of giants, Teya and Kulcan find the villagers leaving food and drink upon the windowsills of their houses. In their first encounter with such unexpected bounty they carefully inspect the food, and sniff it knowing full well not all poisons carry a detectable scent, and as they do so an old white-haired female creeps forward from the depths of her house, says, "Well, well, visitors! I was hoping I might have company. Please, help yourself! "

Slack-jawed, Teya and Kulcan stare at the woman without moving. The woman looks back and forth between the two, says, "*I* am certainly hungry, perhaps you might hand *me* something to eat."

Teya hands her a bean and avocado tamale. The woman eats it, smiles, says, "I'd be happy to eat another."

Teya and Kulcan nod to the old woman, take the food and vanish.

✦ ✦ ✦

On another occasion, another village within which Teya and Kulcan live, ghost-like, for three days, long enough to observe the villagers, adopt them into their usual norm, Kulcan, yopicatl-hungry, approaches a house, sits below a window off to one side behind a *calatl* bush in full bloom, and pitching his voice to those within the house says, "Soldiers now search for the last of the yopicatl. Perhaps, you have seen one?"

From inside, a woman's voice, "No."

"What," he asks, "would you give for a sight of one?"

"When I was a child," she says, "they were common, like seeing the occasional deer. Now, to your question, I would consider the sight of one a rare and fine thing indeed. I would be delighted to give a large meal for the sight of one, and a moment of safety by a warm fire."

"Well then," says Kulcan, "I have brought two here that I will commit to your charge."

The woman, ever so silently, comes to her window and leans out gazing at the *calatl* bush Kulcan hides behind. "I am glad to hear it," she says.

Set to their meal, the woman calls a friend to join them, then another who remembers a fourth they should invite, and so it becomes in time that the house is full of friends thrilled to meet and help, as they can, the large visitors.

◆ ◆ ◆

Each night the yopicatl climb up into the heights of tall trees to judge, campfire by campfire, necklace of sparkling jewels, what passes with the soldiers. This much is certain, each night the encompassing ring of fires comes nearer, drawn tight as a snare. So too the soldiers who seemed strangely unobservant, wandering this way or that, singing, talking, swatting at weeds with their spears, trying to draw birds to them with their whistles, are gone now, replaced by a grim sort who have defined their lives by taking those of others. The search reduced to an ever smaller piece of ground detection becomes more probable, and with each of the many hundreds of campfires, glittering sentinels, signaling at least twenty soldiers, and with soldiers walking back and forth, back and forth, and patrols passing about seeing that all are to their purpose, it seems unlikely the yopicatl can sneak nor fight their way through. It comes then to a certain night, the moon like a sharp sickle, the ring of campfires less than a mile across, windswept open ground, low rolling hills: no choice then but for the yopicatl to try to punch their way to freedom.

But for that there are other creatures within the net, including an old wolf. Perhaps a wolf, or perhaps an emissary of Xolotl herself, wolf-like goddess of the *tlachtli* court, goddess of the dark underworld through which each night she guides the sun. The wolf, emissary, sits calmly looking at the creatures that fate has brought together and thinks how handy the yopicatl would be in a fight.

To speak of this wolf a moment: since a cub she has hunted mice, rabbit and deer across these fields, and has purposely retreated from the soldiers all the while with a particular trick in mind, an opportunity that may well present itself: Space and Time; here, now. She nods her head to suggest the yopicatl follow, and after a moments consideration they do. The old wolf leads the way towards the popoloca sentries over what appears no more than grass, but then becomes a narrow declivity overgrown with grass, which becomes a small gully, which becomes a narrow defile painstakingly carved out of the earth rainstorm by rainstorm over untold centuries.

It is now the last deepening of the night, and the three creep towards the sliver of darkness between two bright fires, their existence hanging upon the careless knock of a loose rock: but for that, no loose rock is knocked. They slowly approach the line of sentinels, the popoloca soldiers coming to within a few feet of the culvert in which they crawl but who then turn and walk back to their eye-dazzling fires. The three move on, and are now ten feet, twenty, thirty feet past the line of soldiers. The wolf leads them on to where the defile joins a stream, and the three of them walk down its ever widening course until it reaches Quimotoctia, the river that drains the western edge of the Teotihuacan valley. Sunrise. The yopicatl part ways with the wolf, emissary, swim part way across Quimotoctia to a small island covered with a scrub of pine trees and there, upon a bed of clean sand, sleep.

+ + +

Night. Teya and Kulcan quickly pass to the road that borders the eastern shore of Lake Texcoco. They visit a temple to borrow some long priestly robes and feather-laced hats, giving them an acceptable if not fashionable appearance, and travel south. The road crosses the hill of Macaltin, and from its height they see, glittering like a star, the city of Texcoco. It is past midnight when they come to the walls of the city. They stop a solitary tradesman, hold out a handful of jewels before him, and suggest the need to bring Queen Miahuitl a message, and should this message be delivered well then some, perhaps all of these shiny stones, some the size of turkey-eggs, are his.

The message, which Kulcan gives him, is memorized; the tradesman now messenger is about to set off to his purpose when the smaller of the two unusually large priests stops him, says, "It may not be easy for a tradesman to gain an audience with a queen." She plucks out a particularly keen ruby from the sack and hands it to him. "This is for your courage."

The tradesman, now messenger, departs to his purpose.

55

King Copiltzin

———

Looking back on how I came to be King of Texcoco, the most beautiful, enchanting city on earth, I can only say it seems inconceivable that I became who I am. But for that, the best I can offer is that I became King Copiltzin step-by-step, what with life being but a continuum of instants branching off into another. Yes, I know, the answer is unhelpful. Yet even if I could recall each step the context, so vital to understanding, would be missing, or take years to explain. So we are left with but introspection as to how event pulled event out of the then current moment, by which I journeyed into the future to arrive at the impossible now. Simplistic as it is, all of us begin in one place and end up in another, and there we are.

My mother and father, both Chichimecas, were born and raised in Tarimichundiro, a small town to the west of Nahua no one has ever heard of and for good reason. One war or another drove my parents here to The Valley, to Texcoco, where I was born. As a child I was never particularly good at lessons, but I was clever, able to link one idea to another. As a youth I discovered what, in so many days, mindless sunrise following mindless sunset, will become widely known as iron. Or so an Outlier told me, I won't dispute what she said. Not that difficult, really, to make iron: a certain type of red-colored earth, a tall chimney of mortared stone about which rises a scaffolding so that one can feed needed ingredients in from the top. A hot charcoal fire, in goes the earth, and charcoal, and a stream of air, fed by a bellows, and out the bottom, beneath the fire, trickles liquid iron. I'm not explaining it well, but the upshot is a very hard metal the uses of which are so obvious as to be transparent. However, back then in time I was told by the priests, or more correctly the priests who then mattered, they are all dead now, that it upset duality. Upset their beliefs, more correctly. Or rather, closer to the truth, upset their architecture of power.

I grew so tired of their hierarchy of who bows to whom, back then in the sequence of events that defines time, that I became a priest just to tell other priests what to do. Then by chance a powerful priest, and next thing I knew I was King of Texcoco with time enough for everything except making iron. If that makes sense, and it doesn't, save but the demands on my time are endless, this that and the other, so much so I scarcely have time to think, and I would have to spend considerable energy ordering and encouraging and brow-beating the idiots into making iron, again. Of course I could do it myself, or could have done it myself, and sent the whole divinely inspired nation into a panic. Not my concern anymore.

I realize that my time is limited, or said more precisely limited to a greater degree than it otherwise would be. Or has been. Thus I quickly jot these notes down, for whomever. Whoever. Though I doubt few will understand, I have to say that I did my best, and that which is recorded of me generally I find untrue, or one shade of gray when the other is just as apt. However, I admit I could have done better, but like everyone else I was, am, easily distracted. Mindless idiotic event follows mindless idiot event, there's existence for you: no more. We are all allotted our number of heartbeats, Tezcatlipoca's will, and no more. *Ixquicha moztla.* I'll see you all on Quetzalcoatl's Golden Shore.

56

Queen Miahuitl

———

Queen Miahuitl receives the message, a quatrain composed by her younger brother, Ueue Zacatzin, what seems several lifetimes ago:

> They call it Teotihuacan,
> For here are the guardians of the land,
> Giants who build temples the size of mountains
> Honoring the vastness of life.

She knows there are few now alive who could know this poem. After a moment of careful reflection she orders to her presence a number of soldiers. They are men who owe her their absolute allegiance, and since government is the nationalization of force this suggests that within the realm there are pockets and ponds of power that, in turn, suggests a variety of purposes, a variety of different ends.

Her soldiers gathered, Queen Miahuitl leads them to a certain section of the wall that surrounds Texcoco there relieving the guards on duty. Unusual, certainly, but it is not the task of guards to argue with the Queen. After she is certain the portion of the wall she now stands upon is populated only with soldiers she calls her own, Miahuitl whistles the song of a tzintzcan bird into the firefly-punctuated darkness, and waits. After a time, so many heartbeats, she again whistles sounding out the tzintzcan's call. In a moment, brief flurry of sound, Kulcan, notable for his size, clad in a priestly robe, stands upon the wall. Then from below, in duration but half a heartbeat, his staff is thrown up to him, and then another, both of which he deftly snatches from the air.

Kulcan shifts his attention to Miahuitl; it has been some years since he has last seen her. He bows his head, says, "Miahuitl."

"Kulcan." She answers in turn, and is about to say more when interrupted by a faint flutter of sound, that of Teya clambering up the wall to stand beside Kulcan. Atop the wall Teya adjusts her robe, nods to the queen, nods to the guards who form a semi-circle behind the queen, takes her staff from Kulcan, and then hands the man who had brought Miahuitl their message, the tradesman for a moment turned messenger, the bag of gems.

"I have heard tales King Copiltzin keeps a certain walkway that might be of interest to us," Kulcan says to Miahuitl. "And," he pretends to smile, "you understand, what with the heart yearning to gaze upon the unknown."

"I wish to speak of Tetcotzingo…" Miahuitl begins.

Kulcan waves a hand, interrupts, "No need. Steal a plate of tamales and it's death; steal a kingdom and receive acclaim. Teya here... Ah, forgive me, but I have not made introductions. Teya (he motions), Miahuitl (he motions; the two nod to each other). Teya and I are all about putting the past behind us, moving forward. It is important to repay evil with kindness (he pauses, smiles warmly), otherwise the world just spirals into some sort of Mictlan-like descent. Which is to say we'd like to see this walkway we've heard so much about, if you would be kind enough to show us the way."

Queen Miahuitl returns his smile. "I'm glad to hear you're all about forgiveness. It seems a rare quality."

Miahuitl leads the two robe-clad yopicatl, the tradesmen turned messenger, and a certain number of soldiers down walkways of smooth stone, through gardens of fragrant scent, past rooms that, during the day, are the empire of accountants. She leads them past libraries and the workshops of artists. She leads them past rooms where judges meet, including one where the bench is made from the skin of a judge found to be dishonest, this carefully peeled off him while still alive, -which suggests that at least certain laws, sometimes, can be taken seriously. The queen leads them past rooms for visiting dignitaries, and past rooms that hold within them small shrines. They pass a room that overlooks a large terraced patio-courtyard where ambassadors are received. They pass administrative chambers, and a small council meeting hall within which, unexpected, Quinatzin, once King-of-Kings, sits conversing with wizards and diviners. Quinatzin wears a dazzling mantle depicting a lesser god, one whose name has been lost to time, sitting at work on an imperishable thunderbolt for Tlaloc, one ray yet lacking to complete its splendor, and this ray spurting flame while shaped with a copper hammer. From the shadow of the hallway Kulcan, Teya, and Miahuitl look into the brightly lit chamber, and observe.

+ + +

"I have asked you," Quinatzin says, his voice like the roll of distant thunder, "to tell me that which you have seen of my future, and though you are all skilled in divination, you claim the fire and wind tell you nothing. I am curious, how it is your sciences can so fail you? (Teya sees an owl perched upon a high rafter in the great hall, a sure sign of death.) I am surprised that when you cast strings upon the water, or kernels of maize, they tell you nothing: how can this be so? Your visions, your knowledge, these tell you nothing of the future? Please, do not fear to tell me bad news, -I seek only the truth of that which is to come."

All but one of the presagers, priests, and diviners stare at Quinatzin in confusion, like the small monkeys trained from birth to pick fruit or nuts from the trees, casting these down to their masters, when there is no more fruit or nuts to pick. And of this one, he steps forward, says, "I have come here not to my purpose, but some strange urging, that of a god perhaps, leaving my home which though humble is a place of comfort to me. My house, here a point of interest, rests upon a hill that was once,

Distant Time, one of the great pyramids of Tulum, overlooking the turquoise waters of the *Atlatic* sea. But to my purpose, Lord Quinatzin, I have had dreams that, strange compulsion, I felt the need to leave my home and tell you of. More than dreams, really, rather a Revelation of Truth: There is a demon called Night Axe, a wanderer who, at night, may approach travelers at a crossroad, for good or ill, and it seems, perhaps, you are at such a crossroad now, one that lies beneath the sharp sliver of a moon and the star of Quetzalcoatl."[68]

The man lapses into silence; high above the room the owl preens itself for a moment, shifts its weight, and with what appears to be keen interest watches that which proceeds below. Quinatzin, in silence, gazes upon the others in the room, waiting for another to speak, but no one else speaks, and so he speaks.

"An ascetic of the wilderness who camps among the ruins of Tulum comes to warn me of Night Axe, the demon whispered of to misbehaving children who won't go to sleep. The rest of you, -students of the night sky, have nothing you can tell me?" He pauses, looks carefully at each before him. "Nothing at all?"

One, a tall woman with a thin narrow face and gray hair, says, "Lord Quinatzin, you seek to know the future as if it were a mystery, but for that, it is no mystery. Only Time wakes us, only Time breaks the dream. Soon or late all of Earth come to their own individual death: no one receives less, and none more. Therefore, it is a puzzle to me why the future should concern you so." Lifting up her chin, she softly clears her throat and chants:

---

68   Venus, seen as the Morning Star.

If I were to bring you into the bowels of the
    temples, and ask you
Which are the bones of brave Nexemitl, mightiest
    of the Olmec kings,
Or his generous and luckless brother Quantema,
    devout worshipper of the gods,
You would answer, 'I know not.' The same as I.

If I were to ask you which are the bones of Kan Ik,
    Empress of Tikal,
Or Zac Kuk, Empress of Uxmal,
Each of unmatched cunning and uncommon beauty,
You would answer, 'I know not.' The same as I.

Though it seemed as if they should last forever,
First and last are confounded in the common clay,
And what was their fate, shall be ours.

The two yopicatl, Miahuitl, her guards, and the
tradesman-messenger turn away from the doorway
and walk on, leaving for a moment the once King-of-
Kings Quinatzin, ascending a staircase that takes them
to a second story, and enter an inner garden courtyard
surrounded by the private rooms of King Copiltzin. At
the center of this courtyard is a fountain, and about this
fountain is a winding pathway delineated on each side by
yopicatl skulls, many of which have been put to use as
flowerpots. Kulcan and Teya stand silent, as if trying to
parse a keen riddle.

After a moment, Miahuitl asks, "What would you
have me do with these?"

"Put them in the sacred fire of The Unfathomable," answers Kulcan. "See that they are reduced to ash."

Miahuitl nods, pipes out a long note from a whistle she wears about her neck, to which many palace attendants quickly respond, and orders this done. Then, after a moment, as if giving voice to an internal dialog she has had many times, says, "The older I get the more it seems we live in a world of drifting shadows, and that our lives are not a series of sequential events but an ephemeral dream: no order, no logic. The common adage is that truth never leaves the palace. In fact, it cannot be found in the palace to begin with, except to say that truth is what those in power say it is. It was a marriage to link realms, no more. And Quinatzin, my brother, who I once so loved, he was ill, bitten by a serpent, and never afterwards the same, and it's ever so rare people tell you all they know, or a small fraction of what they know, and if you do not know you cannot act, and soon enough events spin on to their own mindless conclusions. And here we are."

"Yes," Kulcan echoes, after a moment, tapping the ground lightly with his staff, "here we are, Center of The Universe. We all have a certain number of days allotted us on this Earth, great or small, and no more. Then we make our way to someplace else, a destination ordained by Tezcatlipoca. Or so some say. Not for me to argue. Now, of the moment, King Copiltzin is, I believe, close at hand? Perhaps best we talk with him first, and then chat with Lord Quinatzin."

57
Departures

A smile upon his face, King Copiltzin is sound asleep: deep, untroubled sleep. Kulcan, as politely as he can, awakens the king and says to the bestirring monarch, "How strange to awake from a dream into another dream! Now in your dream (Kulcan bugs his eyes out in mock terror), all of your guards are gone and you find some, plural, more than one, of those you have sorely wronged paying you a visit. Which is to say, if you follow my conversational thread, it's just you, her (Kulcan points to Teya), and me."

Kulcan looks about Copiltzin's room for a moment, admiring the art, then returns his gaze to the King; "So! There is a rumor, and I grant you there are a good many, one can almost take their pick, rumors pile atop rumors until truth turns to an indeterminate shade of gray (so it is the wise man seeks to live as far away as possible from both philosophers and kings), but specifically the rumor

I have in mind is that the yopicatl attacked a little get-together at Tetzcotzingo, to overthrow Nahua and so on, and did a horrible job of it. Bungled, you might say. Which seems strange, considering, it does seem out of character for us. And, you would have thought we could have made a better job of it." (He sighs.)

Kulcan pauses for a moment as if expecting Copiltzin to speak, which he doesn't. Kulcan then takes a deep breath, and with the bright enthusiasm of a young teacher says, "Suppose you and I are running a race, King Copiltzin. You have a mile head start, but I run twice as fast as you."

Copiltzin reflects upon the problem statement, nods, and says, "OK."

"OK. After I have run a mile, you will be half a mile ahead of me. Now when I have covered that ½ mile, you will have, in that same amount of time, run another ¼ mile. And when I run that ¼ mile, you'll be ⅛th of a mile ahead of me, and so on."

King Copiltzin raises his eyebrows, nods. "It seems you would never catch me."

"So it would seem. (Teya hands Kulcan paper, ink, and a quill from a nearby desk.) Let us formalize this to better understand it. For any number of segments I run, denoted by n, you will have run $n + 1$ segments. The distance I cover in my n segments is equal to:

$$1 + \frac{1}{2} + \frac{1}{4} + \frac{1}{8} + \frac{1}{16} + ... + \frac{1}{2^n}$$

But while I was busy running my n segments, you have run $n + 1$ of them, a distance equal to:

$$1 + \frac{1}{2} + \frac{1}{4} + \frac{1}{8} + \frac{1}{16} + \dots + \frac{1}{2^n} + \frac{1}{2^{n+1}}$$

"An interesting formalism." King Copiltzin observes. "If we allow ourselves a finite number of segments, you never catch me."

"Exactly. Although sometimes mathematicians, like governments, have their tricks, by which you expect one thing and get another. Which is to say, I *could* catch you."

"How?"

"Like this." Yopicatl-quick Night Axe reaches out a hand, wraps it about Copiltzin's neck and squeezes hard, very hard, as hard as he possibly can; Copiltzin's head swells, turns bright red, then purple, and then after a moment pops off his shoulders. There is blood spray, quite a bit of which rains down upon Night Axe.

Teya laughs, "Now you look like a real priest."

◆ ◆ ◆

Kulcan and Teya rejoin Miahuitl, the tradesman-messenger, and her guards in Copiltzin's private garden; the yopicatl skulls are gone.

"Burned?" Kulcan asks Miahuitl.

"Yes. Burned or burning."

"Good. And now a last task."

The small party walks back to the council meeting hall. Although the lamps are ablaze as if for a festive celebration they find the hall empty save for an attendant who carefully sweeps the floor. Kulcan, Teya, Miahuitl, the guards and the tradesman-messenger quickly look about to see that they are not victims of a trap, then seeing they are alone, their safety for a time assured, look between each other in astonishment.

Momentarily pausing her sweeping, the young attendant bows her head to Queen Miahuitl and her guests. "I am of the opinion," she says, "that you search for Lord Quinatzin, he who was once the King-of-Kings. Though of course other purposes may have brought you here."

"Yes," Teya answers. "In fact we are looking for Lord Quinatzin, who was here just a moment ago and my hypothesis, which is to say my guess, is that you can tell us where he is."

The young woman looks towards Teya, bows her head and says, "I cannot tell you where he is, for that I do not know. However, I can advise you as to the direction he was travelling when I saw him last. Information that might help you, in your search." She turns about to face south, carefully aligning herself with the cardinal directions. Holding her hand like a blade, shoulder-high she sticks her right arm straight out, then bends her elbow to bring her blade-like hand back next to her ear, then again sticks her arm straight out: South. The path of Lord Quinatzin, once King-of-Kings, leads south.

And at that moment the lamps illuminating the council hall dim; or rather, are overwhelmed by the light of the sun that has risen up beyond the eastern mountains. And it is here we leave them: An attendant tasked with sweeping the council meeting hall, Queen Miahuitl, a tradesman turned messenger, a handful of guards, Teya, and Kulcan Night Axe.

Pronunciation of Nahuatl words

The reader will encounter some Nahuatl words in this book, the majority of which are names: places, people, types of birds and the like. The traditional orthography is based upon the following principles:

All vowels are pronounced as they are in Spanish: e is always pronounced, even when it is at the end of a word, and its sound is roughly that of the French é. The stress is usually upon the penultimate syllable.

The consonants are pronounced as they are in English, except for:

x   which is pronounced sh. For example, Xochipilli is pronounced Shochipilli.

u   is pronounced like the w in **well**, and y like the y in **yet.**

z   which is pronounced s, thus Azcapotzalco is pronounced Ascapotsalco.

qu   which is pronounced k before e and i, but kw before a. Thus Quetzalcoatl would be pronounced: Ketsalcoatl. And quatl would be kwatl.

Major Gods and Goddesses

———

Tezcatlipoca. A multifaceted god, to include The God of Fate, also God of the Night Sky, and protector of slaves; one of the four gods who created the world. Also known as The Warrior.

Xihcutli. The God of Fire.

Tlaloc. The God of Rain, Lightning, and Thunder; He Who Makes Things Sprout.

Quetzalcoatl. One of the four gods who created the world, Tezcatlipoca's brother, God of Wind, and God of Knowledge.

Camaxtli. God of the Hunt.

Chalchiuhtlicue. The Goddess of Springs, Streams, Rivers and Lakes.

Cihuacoatl. Goddess of Childbirth; women who died in childbirth were honored as fallen warriors. Goddess of the Earth to which all comes in time.

Tloque Nahuaque. Master or Mistress of the Universe; The Eternal.

Huitzilopochtli. The Mexica God of War, so too a Sun God.

Xochiquetzal. Protector of young mothers; patroness of pregnancy and childbirth.

Bibliography

Jacques Soustelle, *Daily Life of The Aztecs*, Patrick O'Brian Translator. Stanford University Press, Stanford, CA, 1961.

Burr Cartwright Brundage, *A Rain of Darts*, The University of Texas Press, Austin, TX, 1972.

Fray Diego Duran, *Book of the Gods and Rites and The Ancient Calendar*, translated by Fernando Horcasitas and Doris Heyden, University of Oklahoma Press, Norman, OK, 1977. Originally written circa 1550?

Fray Diego Duran, *The History of The Indies of New Spain*, translated by Doris Heyden. University of Oklahoma Press, Norman, OK, 1964. Originally written 1540?

E. Michael Whittington, Ed. *The Sport of Life and Death: The Mesoamerican Ballgame*. The Mint Museum of Art, Charlotte, NC, 2001.

Kathleen Berrin, Ester Pasztory, Eds. *Teotihuacan: Art from the City of the Gods.* The Fine Arts Museums of San Francisco, San Francisco, CA, 1993.

Miguel Leon-Portilla, *Time and Reality in the Thought of the Maya*, 2ⁿᵈ Ed. The University of Oklahoma Press, Norman, OK, 1988.

Fray Bernardino de Sahagun, *Florentine Codex: General History of the Things of New Spain*, Arthur J. O. Anderson and Charles E. Dibble, translators. The University of Utah Press, Salt Lake City, UT, 1953. Originally published 1577.

James Lockhart, *We People Here: Nahuatl Accounts of the Conquest of Mexico.* Wipf & Stock Publishers, Eugene, OR, 1993.

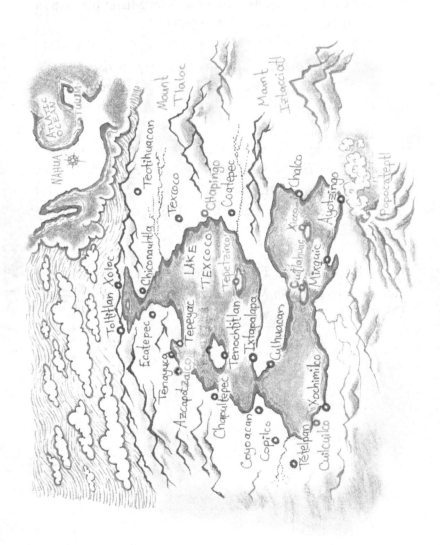

CPSIA information can be obtained
at www.ICGtesting.com
Printed in the USA
BVHW040017270721
612871BV00007B/61